W9-CUL-607

PRAISE FOR

GENELL DELLIN's

"MONTANA" SERIES

"Dellin makes rodeo athletes come alive in this modern-day western romance."
—*Booklist* on *Montana Gold*

"Sure to please her innumerable fans."
—*Romantic Times BOOKreviews* on *Montana Blue*

"Dellin gives her readers a real taste of the west."
—*Booklist* on *Montana Blue*

"A fine contemporary tale.... Fans of Big Sky romances driven by the characters will want to read *Montana Blue*."
—*The Best Reviews*

Also available from Genell Dellin and HQN Books

Montana Gold

Montana Blue

Also by Genell Dellin

Cherokee Dawn

Cherokee Nights

Cherokee Sundown

Comanche Wind

Comanche Flame

Comanche Rain

Red Sky Warrior

Silver Moon Song

After the Thunder

The Renegades: Cole

The Renegades: Nick

The Renegades: Rafe

The Loner

The Lover

Written as Gena Dalton

Sorrel Sunset

Wild Passions

April Encounter

Cherokee Fire

Stranger at the Crossroads

Midnight Faith

Long Way Home

MONTANA *Red*

GENELL DELLIN

ISBN-13: 978-0-7394-8100-4

MONTANA RED

This edition published by arrangement with Harlequin Books S.A.

Printed in U.S.A.

For my sisters, Linda and Bonnie, who share my loving memories of the two funniest and best grandpas any girls ever knew.

Homer Grady Gill and Newton Theodore Smith

ACKNOWLEDGMENTS

Thank you to all the activists, writers, photographers, scientists, filmmakers, organizations and individuals who have contributed to our awareness, understanding and preservation of America's wild horses.

Dear Reader,

The most emotional environmental issue in America is wild horses. Since the late 1800s the question has been whether to love or hate them, slaughter or protect them, and that's still true today. When, in researching this book, I found that two of my acquaintances, both lifelong horsemen and ranchers, consider them useless, it shouldn't have shocked me. The prevailing attitude since the late 1800s has been that letting wild horses graze is a waste of grass that should be used for cattle who feed people.

But wild horses feed our *spirits*. The sight of a band of wild horses running against a sunset sky with manes and tails flying, or a lone stallion standing on top of a mountain cliff with head up to smell the wind, wary, proud and self-sufficient, stirs the blood. Knowing they survive by growing hard, hard hooves and eating snow for water and instinctively spreading their grazing pressure over what rough terrain they are permitted to keep and by huddling together for warmth and watching for danger together, lifts the human heart. Connecting with their primal selves, shaped by the land itself, warms our souls.

The Plains Indians, when they first saw horses, called them "medicine dogs." This is even more true of wild horses because their very wildness makes them our healers. I hope you find medicine in *Montana Red.*

All best,
Genell Dellin

IN WILDNESS IS THE PRESERVATION
OF THE WORLD.
—Henry David Thoreau

MONTANA *Red*

CHAPTER ONE

STEALING A HORSE scared her wildly, much more than she'd imagined it would—which must've been at least a hundred times just today.

Nothing was happening as she'd expected. Ariel didn't nicker a greeting and the security lights weren't shining much farther inside than the doorway and, even if they were, sweat was running into her eyes, stinging them so badly she couldn't see. Clea squinted into the narrow cone of light emanating from the tiny flashlight she wore around her neck and then took another step.

She couldn't breathe. And not just because the humidity was niney-nine percent. It was a bold, hard job, this horse-thieving business.

What had Brock been thinking, building a barn with no air-conditioning? She couldn't imagine that, either. People would be saying he was cutting corners, in financial trouble. Brock's image was what drove him.

Clea wiped her eyes with her bare fingertips and moved deeper into the black of the aisle, straining to see the horses, flashing the torch from side to side to check each one as she passed. If only Ariel were a white! Or a palomino or a gray. Pray God she was still here.

If she wasn't, Clea'd probably just break down and cry, after going through all this. She missed Ari like crazy.

More than that, she *had* to have her back. Somehow, being partners with Ariel was what had given her the guts to finally get the divorce she should've gotten three years ago.

Scared gave way to mad again, in the endless back-and-forth game of emotions playing with her. Suddenly, she wished Brock *would* catch her. *Come on, Brockie. Look out the window and see my little light. Come on down here and tell me I can't take my own horse. Let me practice my new self-defense skills. Hey, Brock!*

Something metal fell, clanging like the bells of hell, to the concrete floor.

Clea hit the off switch on her light and slammed her back against a stall wall. She couldn't breathe, couldn't think, couldn't even pray. She just wished to go right through the wall behind her to hide inside with whatever horse was in there. The one kicking the side of the stall. Twice, and then he quit, thank goodness, or he might have lamed himself and it'd have been her fault.

Not to mention that he might draw somebody's attention.

Or they all would. The whole population of the barn was stirred up now.

Time—who knew how long?—passed until she heard only a few mutterings and rustlings and a couple of thumping buckets from horses hoping that the excitement meant breakfast. The ringing noise must've come from the narrow feed room she'd passed on the way in. Maybe a scoop or a lid. Maybe a rat or a mouse. Or a cat.

Her breathing slowed and she used every intuition she had but she didn't sense another person's presence. Evidently, neither did the horses.

Oddly enough, the scare sort of calmed her down. In a weird, insane way it was as if the worst were over now.

She flashed her little light from stall to stall, found the crooked white star in the black face. *Finally.*

"Thank God." Clea barely breathed the words but the mare heard and nickered to her. Quietly, as if she knew this had to be a clandestine operation. Clea crossed the aisle in three long steps, reached for the halter hanging from the wire mesh wall with one hand and slipped the door latch free with the other. Inside, quick as thought, she cupped her hand over the mare's muzzle, stroking it for a second, whispering in her ear. Ariel had to be…her one true friend.

The pumping adrenaline was making Clea's arms shake but her icy fingers managed to get the halter on and the strap pulled through the buckle. Once she'd led her out—Ari quiet and cooperating as if they'd planned this escape together—Clea took the time to close and fasten the stall door so that, at first glance in the morning, everything would look normal. Every minute she could buy herself was another mile down the road.

Although, now that she had her mare on a lead in her hand, she could kill anybody who tried to take her away. She had another flash of a fleeting fantasy that that somebody might be Brock and…

Enough foolishness. Get out of here.

The other horses were mostly quiet as she and Ari paraded past them, the mare's shoes clinking on the concrete. The smell of fly spray from the automated system burned her lungs and made her want to cough, but she resisted.

Ari switched her tail and knocked a halter against the wire of the last stall they passed, hard enough to make the buckle clink but that was all. No alarms sounded and no voices yelled and no lights went on anywhere.

Once outside, the sultry Texas night slapped Clea in the face. The noises of buzzing locusts, croaking frogs and, farther away, Interstate 20 announced that the wider world was waiting. It wouldn't be long now.

Clea kept to the shadows until they were through the gate to the pasture, then she tied the lead rope into a makeshift rein, led the mare over to the fancy new polyurethane fence, stepped up on it and mounted. Laughter—bitter, terrible, sad, hard laughter—bubbled up in her at the vision of Brock's face, if he could see her now.

But she no longer wanted him to see her. It'd just be a big mess, and if he called in law enforcement, she would lose Ari for good.

Wait. Wait till you cross Red River. In Oklahoma you can celebrate.

One smooch and they were going, heading diagonally across the big pasture, taking approximately the same path through the tall grass Clea had come in on. Her legs and seat melted against the warm horseflesh and she felt the first glimmer of peace flow through her. She wanted so much to squeeze Ariel into a lope and fly away with her, but she took a deep breath and made herself fall into the rhythm of the mare's long, reaching walk instead.

It was hot. So hot that even Ariel didn't have it in her to be frisky. Good thing, because Clea didn't dare use the flashlight now, out in the open. Even if she did, the grass made it impossible to see the ground beneath, so she wouldn't—would *not*—jog or lope, no matter how much her nerves screamed that they wanted to. This was enough. Just to be together again.

Tears sprang to her eyes and she leaned forward on the sleek black neck so she could lay her cheek against it.

"You're my gorgeous girl," she said. "Don't get in a hurry and step in a hole now. Nobody'll see us."

She hoped. She tugged at the black do-rag to make sure it covered all of her pale hair.

A mosquito rose from the grass and dived at her, hanging in the air at her cheek, singing in her ear. Clea hunched her shoulder to rub it off so she could keep her hand on the horse. The feel of Ari's warm flesh against her palm comforted her. She wasn't alone anymore.

And Ariel was safe.

I'll sell your precious damned mare down the road, Clea, and I won't be too particular about who buys her. You can bet your selfish little life on that. If you're gone, then so is she. Maybe to the killers.

Brock's voice was in her head, so real she thought she felt his breath on her neck. She shivered.

Her only comfort while she plotted and planned and waited to get Ariel back into her possession had been knowing that he was too greedy to sell a high-dollar horse for a killer price.

Maybe. His need to control consumed him. She'd been living in fear that it might trump greed in the face of all the inconvenience and money Clea was costing him.

The sudden glow of headlights coming around the curve on the county road she was heading for, jerked her back into the present moment and froze her in place on the horse. She could tell by the moonlit silhouette that it was a big pickup truck with lights across the top and along the running boards.

Would the driver see her rig? And then think *thieves* and stop to investigate? Or call the sheriff? Take her tag number?

She'd done the best she could, but her brand-new truck and trailer pulled up into a ragged bunch of mesquite by the side of the road at three in the morning were not hard to spot. This whole area was slipping fast into urban-sprawl development land and the people who lived in the new McMansions and worked in Dallas usually didn't drive pickup trucks. It must be one of the few farmers or ranchers or horse trainers still holding on in that area. And they were the ones who might get suspicious.

For a minute she wished she hadn't been too worried about scratching the paint on her new vehicles to drive deeper into the brush. But then the truck rolled right on by her hiding place without slowing down; she was safe again.

As safe as she could be while in illegal possession of one of the best hunter-jumpers in the country.

But it wouldn't be long until she was out there on I-20, blended in among the eighteen-wheelers and the RVs, flying north with her darling tucked safely away out of sight—calmly, she hoped—munching hay. Just a few more minutes. They were more than halfway to the road.

Clea turned around to look behind her at the looming white house in the distance and the gabled barn behind it. The sight urged her to lope the rest of the way. She fought it down. She'd come too far to mess up now.

After what seemed a whole night's worth of time, they reached the fence that ran along the road.

Clea slid off, untied the lead and reclipped it under Ari's chin, murmuring nonsense to the mare, keeping the trees between them and the road as long as she could. She gave thanks again that along this side of the property was still an old barbed-wire fence with a section held up by a loop of baling wire to make a gate. No lock.

She opened it and the black mare walked right through the gap, waited for the trailer door to swing back and loaded without a bit of trouble.

"If you'll just haul the same way you loaded, we'll do great," Clea said.

She let herself take a second to hug Ariel's neck before she tied her in the slot prepared with the full hay feeder.

"You be good," she said as she fastened the divider securely around Ariel. "Don't give me any trouble and we'll get to our new home a whole lot faster. You'll love it there. It's nice and cool."

Ari grabbed a mouthful of hay and started chomping. Clea closed up the trailer and then went to put the gate back in place.

Excitement was starting to build deep inside her, pushing away fear and anger, coming up hot through the pool of cold sadness. She ran to the driver's door, unlocked it, climbed in, fastened her seat belt and turned the key. She backed out into the blissfully empty road to head for the interstate. Straight south from here, all the way to the access road, then a right turn and it wasn't half a mile to the on-ramp. The northbound on-ramp.

That was the plan.

But to follow the plan she had to drive past the main entrance to Brock's development, Falcon Ridge. Yes, Falcon Ridge, when there wasn't a falcon or a ridge anywhere in sight and hadn't been for a hundred years, if ever.

It might have been the very first or just one of the first, but soon there were bound to be more of these stupid monstrosities springing up like weeds all over the farm- and ranchland of north Texas. She hated them.

And here it was now, looming ahead on her right, somehow reminding her of an enormous medieval castle and its keep somewhere out on a moor in the middle of nowhere. But no, it was a shining new, self-sufficient small town with its own specialty food shops and spa and convenience store selling gasoline. With its very own gym, coffee shop and guarded gate.

With its fake variety of townhouses, one-story houses, two-story houses, houses with yards and houses without. Fake community. Fake closeness. Well, what could be more natural for Brock to build?

The reckless need to defy her ex-husband drove her. Her arms turned the wheel with no direction whatsoever from her brain and she drove in past the gatehouse where the guard sat fast asleep. He didn't even hear the loud purr of her diesel motor.

She followed her instincts on the streets that wound around for no reason and finally found the last one on the north side, where one of the houses backed up on the acreage she'd just crossed and the barn she'd just burgled. A bitter chuckle rang out, loud in the truck. It didn't sound like hers but it must have been.

Her hand ached to hit the horn and summon Brock-the-Builder and his new wife, both of whom belonged here so unequivocably—he with his fake hair and she with her fake breasts—into the yard or at least to the window so she could wave at them while she drove past. Then, in the morning, when the guys went to feed and discovered Ari was missing, Brock would know who took her.

He would never, ever, in a million years think Clea had done it herself. He might suspect she'd hired someone, but she wanted him to know she hadn't needed to hire to get it done.

She wanted him to know her real spirit was coming back to life. She was stronger now, strong enough to confront him.

But not strong enough to let go of Ariel, now that I just got her. Better be careful.

She slowed more and idled in front of the house—ugly fake Southern mansion, with even the proportions of the pillars all wrong. Just as she'd expected. He had a new wife with fake breasts *and* bad taste.

Clea's foot tapped the accelerator to make the motor growl, a noise she liked to think of as threatening.

Take that, Brock. You'd better not come after my mare.

He would, though. She knew him too well—as opposed to her realization, when she'd finally gathered the courage to leave him, that *he* had never known *her* at all.

Well, honestly, how could he? She hadn't known herself. She'd been afraid to face her real feelings and afraid to assert her own will—when it went up against Daddy's or Brock's. Well, no more.

Get out. You have miles and miles and hours and hours to think about this.

She stepped on the accelerator, laid the gas to her truck and roared her way along the empty street toward the exit of the pretend-town and the still-sleeping man in the guardhouse. A frisson of new excitement mixed with relief zigzagged its way down her spine where the sweat was drying. It carried her to I-20 and kept her wits and her reflexes sharp as she merged into the traffic. She forgot about everything except reminding herself to allow for the length of her new trailer when she changed lanes and keeping her foot light on the accelerator so she could stay within the speed limit.

Of course, *that* was probably the best way to get noticed by a highway patrolman. She seemed to be the only person on the road traveling at a speed less than ninety miles an hour; the huge trucks whipping past made her dizzy. She'd have to get tough—only 1,499 more miles to go, or something like that. Maybe more.

Clea still couldn't believe that she was here, in the driver's seat, for the long haul all the way to Montana. Just like the old cattle drives—Texas to Montana. Well, Charles Goodnight had been one of her ancestors so surely she could do this.

She'd hauled her own horse a few times before on short trips to ride with friends. Also, she'd taken turns driving during the thousands of miles she'd traveled during the serious horse-showing days of her high school and college years, but it was her trainer or his assistant who did most of it. Many times she'd flown while they drove.

However, for this job she couldn't exactly pay her trainer or hire a horse-transport company, could she?

No, she could not. For the first time ever she was on her own.

She gave herself a tight little smile in the rear-view mirror as she checked her surroundings and settled firmly into the slow lane at a solid seventy miles per hour, which she pretty much had to maintain or get hit from behind. The look of that smile lingered in her mind. She'd meant it to be a show of courage and not the scared grimace she'd glimpsed.

Clea lifted her chin and smiled again. This one was better. Scared or not, she wasn't giving up or giving in or giving back. *No way.*

Free at last. Freedom. Free. *I'm free. Free.*

"Free." She said it out loud. After a lifetime of being Daddy's girl and Brock's girl. *Wife* hadn't applied to her because she'd had no more decision-making power married to Brock than she'd had with Daddy. Well, she was growing up now. She would show them she could take care of herself.

The most exciting thing about freedom was that she could do whatever she wanted. She could train Ariel herself and she could buy a trail horse or two to keep Ari company and she could go exploring. She could please herself and not worry about pleasing any man.

She could take all the pictures she wanted and work around the clock at becoming a professional photographer instead of a hobbyist, if that was what felt like the right thing to do. She could do anything, just as long as she had enough money to pay for her keep and Ari's.

And maybe in the process she'd find whatever she was meant to do in her life.

But for now, she wouldn't think that far ahead. She had secretly scrimped and saved for months. Selling possessions, lying about some uses of her horse money, writing checks forty dollars over the total for groceries and taking photos at horse shows for cash. Now she had enough money hidden to get her through a year at the place she'd leased and some things she could sell if necessary.

In two years, when she turned thirty, she'd have access to the trust fund from her mother. Until then, she could get a job of some kind. In the long run, if she couldn't break into photography, which was a tough, tough field to make it in, she'd go into interior design or *something* that would give her a decent lifestyle. For one thing, she was determined to prove to Brock and Daddy that she could take care of herself.

Not in the style to which she was accustomed, that was for sure. She'd be living a lot differently this next year. Her new life would be stark in comparison to the old one. However, being able to breathe free and become her own real self would be worth any sacrifice.

But right now, her *really* most challenging goal was to hide this horse from Brock. He would be livid when he found out she had taken Ari. She closed her eyes for a split second and then concentrated on the traffic to banish him from her mind. She couldn't bear to think about him anymore.

Revenge wouldn't be her biggest satisfaction from this theft. Companionship would be, along with the relief of rescuing the mare. She and Ariel had a five-year history—the same amount of time as she and Brock—and she'd always been much closer to the mare than to her husband, now that she thought about it.

She and Ariel understood each other. Clea *needed* this mare. She loved her more than any horse she'd ever owned, even though she was by far the most ornery, four-legged creature alive—when she wanted to be. Well, maybe not more than Prince-the-Pony, but Clea had been a child then and children loved with a purity adults couldn't match.

Relief flooded Clea then with such a sudden intensity it made her shiver and clutch harder onto the wheel. As if she'd saved her own life along with Ariel's.

On one level, that was true. Right now, clinging to the courage to defy both Daddy and Brock and to try to make a new life alone took every ounce of strength she had.

This wasn't a theft. This was refusing to be robbed a second time. But thinking about the past would do nothing but bring her down. She moved her mind to the future and tried to imagine herself and Ariel in their new surroundings.

The realtor who also managed the rentals at the ranch had described a rustic place with several far-flung cabins, each with its own small barn. The rent included the use of a heated indoor arena—a necessity for anyone who wanted to work with horses in the winter—and a stall in that same building during the winter months. Hundreds of miles of trails. Privacy. Great views, gorgeous natural beauty. Help from him when needed, solitude when she desired.

That man had better have been telling her the truth. Clea needed to be alone so she could sort out her mind. She was planning to do everything online except buy her groceries. Logging on as a guest on her best friend Sherilyn's account, of course, so the people Brock would hire to find her couldn't do it that way.

She'd be at her cabin alone all winter. What would it be like to be snowed in? She'd have to prepare by bringing in supplies of food and books and camera batteries and photo printer paper and plenty of wood to burn in case she lost electricity. Maybe she should get some snowshoes. She already had skis, which she'd shipped ahead with quite a lot of her other stuff. Maybe just surviving would keep her busy.

Clea would have to do her own barn chores for Ari and whatever inexpensive horse or horses she could find to keep Ari company. Most of her barn chores in the past had been done by other people, true, but she knew how. She could do it. She'd helped out at a million horse shows, hadn't she?

Being the wife and hostess of a successful man had given her some skills, but how many paying jobs existed for a woman who could pretend to be fascinated when she was bored stiff—both in and out of bed? She raised her eyebrows to her reflection in the mirror. Well, it *would* be an asset in the oldest profession, which, if she hadn't truly loved Brock—or thought she did at first—she would compare to her position as his wife.

No more. Never again would she give a man that power. Her days of catering to and obeying a man were gone.

Firmly, Clea looked at the road and the traffic. She blocked the past out of her mind one more time. That was another skill of hers—compartmentalizing—and she needed to use it now. No memories. No more. Just adventure ahead.

She concentrated on the sound of the tires on the road and tried to imagine details of her new life while the miles rolled by. A trip to Jackson with Brock to meet some business associates and another to ski at a private lodge near Kalispell were the only times she'd been to Wyoming or Montana. She'd never seen this place she'd leased. There wasn't even a picture of it on the Internet.

She tried to imagine the first day, which she intended to sleep away. After so many miles and trying to sleep in the trailer—pray God she could find a fairgrounds or two where she could get Ariel out for some exercise and maybe even park close enough that she could leave her in a stall overnight—she'd sleep for a week.

Oh, no, she couldn't! Not even for one day and night. She'd have nobody else to do the chores twice a day.

Get it down, C. Real life ahead.

She merged smoothly onto I-35E and, proud of the way she'd handled a crowded tangle of traffic, sped north, headed for Oklahoma. And then Kansas. Then Nebraska. And then Wyoming. All the way, well no, more like halfway west into it and finally north to Montana. Maybe her new home state forever—if she found out that she liked lots of winter.

Clea had intended to stop at the first convenience store she saw after she crossed Red River to buy a cup of coffee to celebrate but instead she just kept on going. Stopping would break her momentum and she felt compelled to continue moving away.

Just past Ardmore, though, the trailer started rocking. It shocked her at first and then she hoped she'd imagined it. But no. Ari was weaving and rocking it. Definitely. Clea could feel it swaying behind the truck, pulling the whole rig to one side, then the other.

Damn. She should've known Miss Ari wouldn't be too good for too long.

Well, who could blame her? She wasn't exactly used to being kidnapped from her stall in the middle of the night or to being without other horses for company.

But that wasn't the reason. Diva that she was, center of the universe as she felt she was, Ariel felt compelled to try to get any bit of control over this whole operation that she could.

Finally, after a mile or two of intermittent rocking and swaying, Clea saw a rest area up ahead and pulled off the road. She turned off her lights because this was still the horse country of southern Oklahoma and north Texas where everybody knew everybody in the industry and someone might stop to see who she was and if she needed help.

Clea got out, walked back the length of the trailer, switched on her little flashlight and turned off the interior lights before she opened the door. She felt like a spy in a movie as she stepped in and shined the light over Ariel, who was still swaying rhythmically.

When the light reached her head, Ariel turned toward Clea with her eyes flashing, lifted a front hoof and pawed, hard.

Before Clea could open her mouth to make soothing sounds, Ari did it again and then started to rear, fighting the rope to try to get her head up, tearing at it with a vicious strength.

A terrible chill bloomed in Clea's gut as she started moving toward the horse, making soothing noises, trying to get her mind together enough to make words. What if she'd brought Ari out here only to have her break a leg and die?

She hadn't tied her tight enough. She'd been too happy to have her—too excited, too scared, too eager for Ariel to eat hay, too much in a hurry and too *careless* to make sure the tie was short enough.

Clea looked at it again. No. It wasn't all *that* long.

She started stroking the mare's muscled rump, over and over, as she started a soothing line of patter and moved toward Ari's head.

"It's just you, isn't it, Ari? You're not happy. You're a problem child, but hey, you've made your point. I should've asked you first if you wanted to go for a long drive. Next time I'll consult you. Okay, baby. It's okay. Calm down now."

The real problem was that this mare loved to be difficult and was under the illusion that she was David Copperfield. She planted her rear feet on the rubber matting and rose even higher on the front end.

Clea wanted to grab the rope and try to pull Ari down but she didn't want to make the contrariness worse. She could hardly bear to watch. *Almost.*

The left hoof almost caught in the feeder.

A broken leg and it would be all over.

Wild thoughts raced each other through her head while she froze in horror. What would she do? She couldn't shoot her own horse. She couldn't pay for a surgery and a long recovery....

Come on, Clea. Stop it.

She set her jaw. She hadn't gone through all this fear and effort to let it all end now, before the mare ever even saw Montana.

Ari came down and stood, trembling. Clea stepped up to the mare's head and took hold of the rope.

"You're working yourself into a fit," she said in her most authoritative tone. "Ariel, settle down."

She stroked Ari's nose and talked to her. She patted her neck and talked to her. Ari snorted, then pricked her ears and listened.

"That's my girl," Clea murmured. "Now listen, sweetie..."

Sweetie threw her weight as hard as she could from side to side, then kicked out behind and swayed again, harder still. She pinned her ears, jerked her head free and tried to rear again, reaching for the wall.

No choice. No doubt. Clea would have to tranquilize the horse so they could get on down the road. They weren't even started on this trip yet and Clea hadn't gone through all her fear and trauma to let it all fall apart now.

Now Ari's eyes were rolling. She made little choking sounds.

Break a leg or strangle. Great choices.

Without wasting any more breath, Clea turned and moved toward the door.

She jumped to the ground and fighting the urge to hurry—hurry that was beating harder in her veins with every sound that came from Ari—she punched in the numbers to open the door to the dressing room, letting its light come on automatically because it was on the side away from the road. She stepped up into it, closed the door almost all the way and took down the first-aid box.

Stay calm. Be deliberate. Ari was excited enough without sensing more fear from Clea.

She found the Ace tranquilizer and filled a syringe, despite her hands shaking a little. She forced herself to think positively.

Thank God, she'd had sense enough to prepare for this. She'd worried about this very thing because Ari had been hard to haul at times, so she'd asked Sherilyn's boyfriend, a veterinarian who didn't know Brock, to sell her the medicine and teach her how to administer it.

Sherilyn was Clea's hairdresser and best human friend, the only person in whom Clea ever confided. The only person she trusted enough to tell about her plans for a new life, that was for sure.

With the needle and an alcohol wipe in one hand and the flashlight in the other, Clea pushed the door open with the toe of her sneaker, stepped down to the ground, went around back and shouldered the rear door aside. The trailer was still rocking.

"You have to settle down, Ari darlin'," she said in as soothing a tone as she could muster. "Maybe take a little nap. We've gotta get on up the road."

She kept on and on with the calm, slow words, trying to calm herself as much as the mare and Ariel did actually stand a bit more still when Clea reached her. Part of Clea screamed to hurry before the mare started pulling against the rope again; another part cautioned her to go slowly and do this right. That tension made her bite down on the little flashlight until she thought her teeth might break.

She found what she hoped was a good spot in a muscle—no way did she have the nerve to try for a vein—and tightened her lips around the torch in her mouth while she wiped her target clean. Through her nose she took in a long, deep breath to steady herself and slid the needle in with hands that felt stiff as wood.

Ariel squatted and pulled back but the needle was in. Clea hit the plunger and pushed it all the way.

She pulled the needle out and with a last pat on the butt, left the mare, closed up the back door, went to the dressing room and put things away. Deliberately. Efficiently. Quickly.

Heart hammering—she'd successfully managed her first emergency of the journey!—she jumped out, locked up and headed around the trailer to the truck. Ariel was looking at her through the bars on the window.

Clea felt a broad smile come over her face—victory and relief all mixed up together. She stopped in her tracks and looked at the mare, who was standing still at last. "You just hang on, my girl, and you'll be a Montana horse before you know it."

She couldn't tell whether Ari's reply expressed excitement or dismay. Whichever, it was a full-hearted whinny that reverberated thrillingly against the rocky walls of the Arbuckle Mountains and echoed up the road.

CHAPTER TWO

THE WIND whipped the stallion's whinny of alarm up from the valley, a sound so wild and shrill that it rang Jake's bones. The harem band fled ahead of the red stud snaking them away from the scent of the wildcat and Jake's own horse danced beneath him. It spoiled his aim.

He used his legs to hold the gelding together and his voice to steady him while he lined up the sight again.

"Stand," he said, surprised his voice could come out this calm with his chest so tight. "Whoa now."

His jaw clamped down. He had one shot to save the foal. It had better be now.

The rhythm of the band's drumming hooves matched the thunder of the blood in his arms. He steadied the rifle, drew his breath, made sure his crosshairs rested on the spot in the middle of the tawny shoulders that were folding into a crouch on the rocky ledge below and ahead of his horse.

For one split second, endless in time, he let the air out of his lungs and slowly squeezed the trigger. The back-and-forth threatening motion of the cougar's long, black-tipped tail kept going. And going.

The shot went off at the start of the cat's leap. At first he thought he'd missed, but its body crumpled in midair and dropped out of sight.

Jake dismounted and walked far enough to look over and down. The cougar lay within twenty yards of the foal, but neither its scent nor the sound of the shot had made the little orphan move more than a few inches away from the mare, who lay as dead as the mountain lion.

He guessed the foal at two or three weeks old. It was red like the stud, although the mare was a pale palomino. The mare must not have been dead too long or it wouldn't still be alive to stand this dogged vigil. Its head was hanging. It wouldn't last much longer.

What had he done?

The lion's body would keep away any stallion that might snap the foal's neck to put it out of its misery. Odds were slim that another mountain lion would come along. Therefore, it would have a slow death unless Jake did something.

If you have a grain of sense in your head, Hawthorne, you'll jack in one more round and send the pathetic little bag of bones to the great grassy pasture in the sky. You'd be cruel not to do it.

True, but he'd already made the decision. He'd sacrificed the mountain lion's beauty and wildness for the foal, so now he'd have to step up and take care of it, no matter how slim its chances. "Well, shit."

He scanned both ways along the steep hillside for any sign of a trail that would take him down. "Come on, Stoney, my man. We're in the nursery business now."

He thought he could see a faint trail that the wild horses made to get down from this ridge, going to water at the small runoff lake at the bottom of the hill. He started down, leading his horse. A rock rolled out from under his feet and Stoney's hind feet scrabbled in the gravel for purchase on the slope.

They'd have to find another way back to the road—that

was for damn sure. This steep grade would be way too hard to negotiate while carrying the foal.

They finally got to the bottom and the baby turned its head to look at Jake. Weakly, it stumbled closer to the mare's body, instinctively knowing that of the four enemies existing for wild horses—man, fire, drought and mountain lions—man was the most dangerous.

It was a filly, huddled here in a little brushy cove protected by the mountains surrounding it on three sides, where the mare had come with her. Maybe she was one of those wild mares that liked to change stallion bands every once in awhile. She'd been killed by a falling rock that rolled about a yard away after crushing half her head.

The foal's knees buckled and she collapsed in a heap. Her spirit was what was strong about her; it showed in her eyes. But her body was dehydrated and weak. She might not even live until they got home.

Jake went back to Stoney and led him over to the baby, picked her up, and laid her, belly-down, over the big gray's withers, feet hanging off on either side. He steadied her with his rein hand as he caught the horn with the other and the stirrup with his toe to swing up into the saddle.

Then he smooched to the gelding and started looking for a way out.

CLEA DROVE with both hands on the steering wheel as if that could make up for not keeping her eyes strictly on the two-lane road. The enormous land and sky overwhelmed her, just as they had that day during the ski trip when Brock had immersed himself in business as usual and she'd driven miles and miles alone in a rental car, exploring Montana.

Looking for something; she didn't know what.

That day had been the beginning of the end.

She'd waked to hear Brock in the other room, dressing down somebody over the phone, cursing and demanding and then changing calls and becoming charming as he tried to make a deal. She lay there and listened to him. From what he said she knew that he'd be at it all day. The last day of the *romantic vacation* trip he'd given her for Valentine's Day.

Which was the first *romantic* gesture he'd bothered to make in ages.

Which was just as well because she could hardly stand him anymore.

She ran from the sound of his voice—into the shower, then into the dressing room where she tried to distract herself by choosing exactly the right items from her extensive new ski wardrobe. Her ski lessons were going well. She liked being out on the slopes in the crisp air and forgetting about everything except learning this new sport.

But as she slid the hangers along the rod, opened drawers and started putting pieces together, the hollow in the center of her body began to grow, inching its way into her veins, pushing her blood aside to make room for the empty tentacles stretching toward her heart with a cold efficiency that promised loneliness would soon own her. She dropped the ski clothes into a bright-colored heap on the floor, dressed in jeans and hiking boots instead, called the desk for a vehicle and walked into the living room of the suite.

Sunlight coming in through the windows lay in stripes on the floor. In the air, dust motes danced in them, held up, probably, by the raw electricity running through every nerve in her body. Brock liked to be in control and he didn't like surprises.

She was past caring what Brock liked. That was new. She hadn't known that before.

"I'll be busy all day," he said without looking up from his Blackberry phone.

"No problem," she said. "I'll be gone."

He glanced at her. Just long enough to see what she was wearing. "You're not skiing?"

"No."

"Why not?"

"I want to go driving."

This unusual stroke of independence made him actually look at her this time. He narrowed his eyes as if this was the most irritating thing she could possibly have said to him.

"I should've had enough sense not to bring you to a resort with no town," he said in the tone he liked to use with her. The tone that implied *You idiot child.* "Gotta be spending my money or you don't know what to do with yourself."

She ignored that and walked past him to find her parka and bag.

"Hold on 'til I talk to a couple of people and then I'll call Jim to fly you down to Jackson Hole. You can shop all day."

"Jackson is the town," she said. "Jackson Hole is the valley."

She slid her arms into the sleeves of the parka.

He actually dropped the phone and stood up.

"What th' hell is the matter with you? You can't go running around by yourself in a place you've never been. That's some wild country out there. This is insane. This isn't like you, Clea."

It sure as hell isn't. But maybe I'm changing.

She didn't have the guts to go quite as far as to say that out loud, but she'd already gotten his attention. He was staring, no, glaring, at her. All she wanted was to be away from him.

"I don't have time for this," he snapped. "Have you lost your mind?"

She'd love to blurt out the truth of her feelings right then but even as she thought about it she knew she didn't have the nerve. He would go ballistic.

And actually, until she had a chance to think, she didn't know exactly what she did feel or want. So as usual, she took the easy way.

"Look," she lied, "I saw an ad. I just want to go look at a horse."

Brock relaxed. This was something familiar. This was something he could control.

"Well, why didn't you say so? When have I ever denied you a *horse?*" He sat down and began dialing the phone again. "Just remember not to use your whole fifteen K for the down payment or the rest of your nags won't eat. I'm not putting another red cent in that account until next month."

Halfway to the elevator, she knew she couldn't—wouldn't—tell lies forever to preserve the accustomed parameters of their so-called marriage. It was a bargained deal that she'd let her daddy make for her.

She'd thought she loved Brock, though. Or maybe she'd just told herself that because she wanted to please Daddy.

She was nothing but Brock's arm ornament and his ticket into some social circles, plus his business alliances with her father. He disdained her really or he wouldn't use that tone with her.

And why shouldn't he? She kept her mouth shut and did as she was told and in return he bought her anything she wanted and gave her plenty of money to support her horse habit. To him, she was only as good as her manicure.

Only as good as her last social performance. Like a rodeo cowboy who was only as good as his last ride.

Clea was barely out of sight of the resort when she began

to really see. The mountains and the sky, cobalt and white meeting in sharp, clean edges. Gray gravel coming through the dirty scraped snow in front of the car. One tan deer bounding across the road into green trees that were as deep as a vertical dream. Yellow sun so bright it made her smile.

This world so huge and wild it filled her heart.

She smiled to herself. Right now, that day with Brock seemed a hundred years ago. Now here she was in Montana again and she was in the middle of the end. It wouldn't be the end of the end with Brock until somehow he accepted the fact that Ariel belonged to her. Rightfully. Morally.

But when had Brock ever cared about right and wrong?

She took a deep breath and pushed the past and future from her mind. She let the land and the sky take her again. Then she realized she was getting close to her destination. She should begin to look for the sign where she would turn in on her road. There *was* one, wasn't there? According to the realtor, there was.

Holding the wheel with one hand, she fished deep into her new chocolate-brown Gucci bag to find the map the man had faxed to her, then slowed while she looked at it. Yes. The sign would be on her right and it read Firecreek Mountain Road.

After two nights, each with no more than four or five hours of nervous dozing in the living quarters of the trailer—which she could never have done without the alarm system and the gun she'd bought when she took the course in home protection—she'd gone right on through exhaustion and come out the other side. A sharp edge of excitement—and quite a bit of fear also, to be totally honest—had wound her up tight.

This was her new world, the one where she would become another person. She could only pray she was strong enough to do that.

These snow-topped mountains, this endless sky, that narrow road that wound up and up, following Fire Creek to its source, as the man had described it, they all were hers now. And she'd be theirs. She'd belong to them and to the log cabin and barn he'd told her were at the top of the first high ridge.

She would not belong to any people.

She drove more and more slowly, looking for the sign, determined not to miss it because if she passed it she'd be forced to find a good place to turn the trailer around. Just the thought of having to drive even one unnecessary mile was more than she could bear. Ariel *needed* to get out of the trailer. She'd been exercised at both nights' roadside rest stops, but that wasn't nearly enough.

A bed would be wonderful, but later. Right now, a shower and something homemade to eat, even if it was only a scrambled egg and toast.

If the realtor had brought in the food and supplies that she'd ordered.

Come to think of it, she hadn't even checked on the cost for that service. She shouldn't have asked for it at all. If she wanted to live for at least a year on the money she had, she had to learn to think differently. From now on she had to do everything for herself, including clean her own house. She had to make every penny count.

And every brain cell. Brock would be beside himself by now and he'd be looking for her. That was a given. She'd slept in the trailer to keep from leaving a trail at horse hotels or horse people's places, so she had to make that sacrifice count, too. She'd ordered a new cell phone no one knew about. She'd brought hair dye—Sassy Black—to cover Ari's white markings. Perhaps she should use it before anybody here saw the mare.

There it was. The sign, Firecreek Mountain Road.

And another one, fancier, that read, Wild Horses.

Right. The realtor was all excited about the wild horse sanctuary. He said that sometimes tourists could see bands of them and sometimes they couldn't, but they could always buy T-shirts and mugs and photographs with photos of wild horses on them and spend the night at the local motels and eat at the cafés in the little town of Pine Lodge.

She only hoped she could get close enough to shoot some pictures of the wild horses for herself. But if they wouldn't cooperate, she could understand—at the moment, she needed her own space with a longing that went to the bone.

However, it'd be something fun to try, a challenge. Taking pictures was her other comfort, besides horses. It soothed her somehow. After her mother died, it had made her feel secure, as if whatever subject she captured would be hers to hold in her hand forever.

Which made no sense at all, since during that time she'd clung to every picture of her mother she could find, yet her mother was irrevocably gone.

That was before she'd learned that *nothing* is forever.

She should've already known.

She took the turn carefully, mindful of the way the trailer was tracking because the gravel road wasn't very wide and the last thing she needed right now was to hang a wheel off the end of the tin horn. Once she'd straightened out the rig and headed up the first rise on the winding road into the hills, Clea let herself believe it. She was here.

And Ariel was here.

Feeling even more efficient, Clea looked at her odometer so she could measure the last leg of the journey and turn in at the correct driveway.

Then she rolled down her window so she could smell this

place. Sage, she knew that smell, and a hint of pine but the dry air carried other scents, too. It was *such* dry air and thinner than she was used to. A whole new world from the ground up.

A chuckle began deep inside, rolled up into her throat and came out as a short but sincere belly laugh.

"Hey, Brock," she said into the enormous space that surrounded her. "Catch me if you can."

She'd told him once or twice that she would love to live—which was true—in northern New Mexico. Live in an artists' colony and do nothing but take pictures in that fabulous light, she had said. He might look for her there.

Or not. Half the time, he didn't listen to a word she said.

She glanced to her left, down into the valley along the river that flashed in and out behind some trees. There was a small ranch house and barn and some other outbuildings. Who lived there? Would she ever meet them?

How far was it on up to her place? She looked at the faxed map again and checked her mileage one more time. Not far.

Here was another hill, another ridge that led on up toward the big mountains with their striped bluffs and trees with snow still on their tops. The first high ridge. That had to be it.

Clea was going into the next switchback when she saw him. She'd turned away from the glare of sunlight off the rearview mirror and there he was, an arm's length inside the fence, riding down the slope on the right-hand side of the road.

Coming out of the trees like a cowboy in a Russell painting, his blue shirt like sky against the green. Exactly like that.

Her heart lurched. *Exactly* like that, with a name like Saving the Baby or Mama's Gone. He carried a small bright sorrel foal in front of his saddle; its long legs dangled off the sides of the big gray horse.

She couldn't take her eyes off him—something about the

sure way he sat the horse, something about the easy way his left hand held the reins and his right one rested on the baby he was rescuing. He had a presence.

Without taking her eyes from him, she slowed the rig still more and grabbed her camera from the slot in the console where she always carried it. Slipping it from the case, she raised it to her eye as she slowed even more.

The rider was looking at the foal. His hat was tilted down, but just as she passed him by he lifted his head and swept his gaze across her rig. She took the shot. Broad shoulders, a lock of black hair on his forehead, a blaze of green eyes imprinted on her mind's eye. Then she was moving again, on around the curve.

It was one of the best photos she'd ever taken. She knew it in her gut. She knew it because she could feel that a huge smile was splitting her face and she was bubbling deep inside. What a moment! What a shot! And she'd been ready!

This had to be a good omen for her new life.

She would name it Montana Cowboy.

The sight of him haunted her as she finished the short drive to the ranch entrance that matched the X on her map. Even as she turned in under the swinging hand-carved wooden sign that read Elkhorn Ranch and started looking for her cabin, she could still see the whole gorgeous scene of the cowboy and the bright foal.

The epitome of cowboy gallantry—rescuing a creature weaker than himself. Sacrificing his time and effort to make sure that this baby would be all right instead of rounding up cattle or fixing fences or breaking colts or whatever other jobs he had to do.

She spotted the cabin sitting up a long driveway in a little meadow with blazing yellow and red leaves on the trees at its back. Fall was a fantastic time of year and one that at home often was either way too short or non-existent. She was going to enjoy this one to the fullest. She was going to love it here.

Clea parked and got out, then reached into the backseat for her jean jacket. The fall wind in Montana carried a bite of coolness that would be months yet reaching Texas.

She checked on Ariel, then left her standing in the trailer while she ran through the grass to check out the barn and the pen around it. Her lungs grabbed for more of the thin, dry air that roused her blood. This was exciting. She didn't want to sleep after all.

The barn door stood open.

Inside, she stopped short and breathed in the smell—like that of any barn but with an overlay of age and seasoned wood. Cedar. Her eyes tried to take it all in at once. It had been built of cedar logs a long, long time ago and it had been well used. It was clean; a little neglected but not bad. The realtor had assured her everything was clean.

She smiled. Talk about different! This barn was as different from any she'd ever used as Ariel was from the horses Clea imagined had lived here before. She loved its atmosphere—all rustic and rough and built to be serviceable. Everything useful; nothing fancy just for show.

Somebody had left some grooming brushes and buckets in the little feed room, but she had her own, of course. Same with the feed in the barrel and the hay. They looked and smelled pretty fresh, so the former tenant must've just moved out.

The water tank in the pen was nearly full, too. She unloaded the mare and led her around the perimeters to let her get acclimated, then left her delirious with freedom to run around inside the pen. Clea went to the back door of the house and to her shock found it unlocked. It swung open into a kitchen with the same look as the barn: functional, rustic and actually—no doubt unintentionally—charming. The furniture was the really rough kind made of logs but there was an old blanket-covered couch in the living room that looked soft and comfortable. She loved that there was a fireplace in the wall that opened to both rooms.

The basic pots, pans and dishes were in the kitchen as promised, but the supplies weren't at all what Clea had ordered. Right then, she didn't even care. She'd go to town tomorrow. And she'd be sure to pay only for what she got and not what she ordered when she went by the realtor's office.

Also, she would point out to him that neither the cabin nor the barn was exactly what he'd described to her. Try to keep him honest.

And maybe talk him down on the rent? What a good idea! She'd insist on it. She had to save money where she could.

Hurriedly, she went through the rest of the house, which turned out to be two bedrooms and a bath. The view from one bedroom was better than in the other, so it would be hers. She smiled. Or if she wanted, she could make the living room do double duty because it'd be great to have a fireplace in her bedroom.

Wood. There was quite a bit stacked neatly on the back porch and more in the yard, but she'd need a lot for a whole winter. Another thing to put on her list of questions for the realtor.

Clea pulled her rig up closer to the front door and started bringing things in. There were sheets on the bed in the room she decided she'd use for the bedroom but she wanted her own, of course. And judging by the breeze, she'd need her comforter tonight. She had to check out the thermostat and maybe get the heat going now before the house got too cool.

That would save money on the electric bill, wouldn't it? She was learning to think like a woman who couldn't afford to be wasteful anymore.

Happily, she worked at making the house hers and brought in most of what she had in the truck and trailer. She was tired, but moving around and using her muscles was energizing her. It was so much fun to create a new nest and watch it come to life, that she couldn't quit until she was done.

The things she'd shipped should be at the freight place by now. When she went to town she'd arrange to have them delivered.

Finally, as the sun started to slide down, exhaustion dragged at her.

All she wanted was something hot in her stomach and to lay her body down. The bed was already made with her colorful serape-striped sheets. The perfect ambience for a new life in the West.

There were eggs in the refrigerator.

She could take a hot shower and….

No! It hit her like a slap. She still had chores to do. There was no one else to take care of her mare.

No sense reaching for the cell phone because nobody was close enough to do her bidding.

Clea dropped down onto the couch and let her head fall into her hands. This was it. She was on her own. It didn't matter one bit how tired she was or what she'd rather do. Poor Ariel had nobody else to depend on.

Her eyes closed. Her body, aching for sleep now that she'd thought about it, longed to turn, lift her legs onto the sofa and stretch out. Just to reach for the blanket over the back of it and cover up….

Clea ripped herself off the couch and onto her feet. "Cowgirl up," she muttered, made a face at herself and headed for the barn.

It took an unbelievable *hour* for her to orient herself, decide on a stall, bring in the feed, hay and bedding that she'd brought with her, bed the stall, set up the water bucket and fill it, catch the ornery Ariel, check her over, brush her down and put her in with her feed. When the mare was happily crunching away, Clea heaved a huge sigh of relief and trudged to the house. She didn't feel like running anymore.

In fact, she didn't feel like anything but a shower and sleep.

Still, there were more chores. She locked up the house and dragged a chair in front of each door. This was out in the middle of nowhere. She would have to get a dog.

Then she took her shotgun into the bedroom and slid it under the edge of the bed; thoughts of outlaws and bears and cougars drifted through her head. At that moment, as she had been those nights on the road, she was very glad she'd learned to protect herself.

Turned out the water was hot, thank goodness, and she stood under it until it ran cold. Drying off with one of the delicious, fluffy towels that matched her sheets, she could barely make her arms move. Her muscles ached. But she took an extra moment or two just to enjoy the luxurious feel of the cotton against her skin.

She wouldn't be able to buy towels like this again for a long, long time.

Finally, she finished up, dried her hair until it was only barely damp, climbed into her new cowgirl retro-print flannel pajamas and fell into bed. Just before her eyes fell closed, she saw by the moonlight streaming in at the window that the open closet—which, like the barn, seemed to have some stuff left in it—was tiny. Really, really tiny. Far too small to even be called a closet.

That realtor was definitely going to come down on the rent.

CHAPTER THREE

SOMETIMES JAKE felt like a man he didn't know, in some place he'd never expected to be. Like now, driving down the road in a rig so new and fancy that it had a closed-circuit TV system between the truck and trailer, meant for show horses but used for wild ones. How crazy was that? If wild horses could survive on the rough, barren ranges where they'd been confined for generations, they could survive a trip down the highway without a babysitter.

But his employer, Natural Bands, was a horse-rescue organization—from California, which said it all. They aimed to keep the horses *in their natural wild state* and babysit them at the same time. And here he was, working for them. He had even gone so far as to sign a contract—and for a year, no less. Usually he insisted on the handshake approach to all agreements. Why do business with someone whose word is no good?

He'd made an exception for Natural Bands, though, because they had such deep pockets. Therefore, he felt like a stranger to himself. Every other job he'd ever had was one he'd taken because it offered him some adventure, or a chance to see some new country, or a big challenge, or excitement. Or because it would give him a chance to learn something.

Which, in his opinion, was the only true way to live.

Maybe so, but it's not the best way you've ever tried, Hoss.

His gut tightened. True. The best way was living with Victoria and her two boys, loving all of them and feeling their love in return. But he'd never live that way again because it depended on other people, and that was a risk. A big one.

A woman might love a man temporarily. She might go back to an ex-husband because of money. Money was a poison.

Yet here he was, where he never would've thought he'd be, tied down for at least a year bustin' his butt every day for Natural Bands and riding other people's colts half the night. For what reason? Money.

Wanting something that cost a lot of money changed a man.

"Listen here, Jake. Don't tell that woman boss of yours we've got that orphan filly. I aim to make a helluva usin' horse outta her."

Jake turned in time to see the conspiratorial wink from his uncle Buck, sitting over there in the passenger seat, scheming his schemes.

Buck's buddy, Teddy, spoke up from the backseat. "Funny thing to me, this *our* orphan business," he said loftily. "*I* might have some claim to that little mustang but, Buck, you shore don't."

"How you figger that?"

"I'm the one raisin' her. I took the night shift last night. So far, you ain't done nothin' but try to boss me and Jake."

"We ain't had her a week yet," Buck said. "She'll still need her milk fer a few more days. I still got time to do more chores than you do."

"Quit lyin'. You won't do a damn thing. You never do. You couldn't make my silly aunt Polly believe that."

Here was something else as incredible as working on a

contract: Jake Hawthorne hanging out all the time with two old men who talked too much and kept nosing into his business. *Living* with them, in fact—but only for a couple of weeks—so he'd have help feeding the little filly he had so foolishly saved. Every four hours. He'd never get anything else done if he had to do all the feeding himself.

So, for that reason it was good that he had let them stay when they appeared in his yard a couple of months ago to announce that they'd come to help him with his new job. "Seeing as how we know all about wild horses and you don't know squat," they'd said.

He still couldn't believe that he'd let them attach themselves to him like that. He was a natural loner and he couldn't tolerate constant company. Even if Tori had stayed with him, he would've gotten tired of her and the boys. And from the minute they'd gone, with tears pouring down their little faces, he'd sworn he would never again take responsibility for the health and happiness of any creature except himself—and Stoney, of course.

Yet here he was with a helpless foal and these two old men on his hands.

Right this minute he was wishing like crazy that he'd sent them packing the minute they showed up. He hated being cooped up in a truck with them when they argued. Which was what they did for fun.

"That orphan baby is Jake's," Teddy declared. "He's the one who found her."

Jake spoke up to try to put an end to this new foolishness. "When she gets a little older I'll probably take her up to the Great Divide for Elle to raise her. Little sister's always been good with young animals. She's the rescuer of the family."

They ignored him.

"She's Jake's all right, but I aim t' trade for her," Buck said.

"Trade what? You ain't got no horses but Topper and you need him."

"I seen Jake throw a jealous glance or two at my old pickup."

Teddy chuckled and said, "You'll play hell gittin' *that* trade done. And even if you did, then you wouldn't have no way to git around."

"You don't understand me, Ted," Buck said. "I'm only tradin' him the right to *drive* my truck some."

That made them laugh. Jake, too.

Sometimes it wasn't so bad having the old guys around all the time.

"Forget Celeste," Jake said. "She knows the filly can't keep up with the wild bands. Even if she could, there'd be no wet mares to feed her—if they would. This is a freak deal, that mare foaling so late in the year."

"Yeah, but remember it's Montana Red that's the sire," Teddy said wisely. "That old devil breeds as he pleases. He probably stole that mare and bred her at the wrong time just so's she'd lose the other stud's baby."

"Surprises me Celeste knows that much," Buck said, ignoring Teddy entirely. "Reckon she knows that white devil we just now hauled to her Cal-i-forn-y man will drive them young bachelor studs outta his band pretty soon and the family won't all be together anymore?"

He and Teddy chuckled over that and shook their heads.

"Them old-time mustangers would laugh their heads off at this whole deal," Buck said. "Whoever heard of tryin' to keep wild-horse families together? Can't even do that for people."

Teddy nodded. "Plus out there on the range, sometimes the mares switch bands. Them old-timers could tell Celeste that, too."

Jake smiled to himself. Teddy and Buck themselves were old-time mustangers.

"I don't care if they put 'em in houses and buy 'em a bed," Buck said. "Long as they keep on payin' us the big money."

That's where you made your mistake, Jake. You shouldn't have started paying them so much. If they were making less, maybe they'd go away.

No, they wouldn't. They didn't care any more about money than he used to. They were helping him for the adventure of it. If he cut off their wages right now, they'd still hang around and help him for nothing until the work was all done. They would finish what they'd started because that was one of the rules of the code they'd lived by for fifty years or more.

"There," Teddy said. "There's our turn up ahead, Jake."

The backseat driving got on Jake's nerves as much or more than anything else about being with the old boys all day.

"Comin' right up, too," Teddy said. "Jake. You just as well to start to shuttin' 'er down."

Sometimes it *was* so bad having the old guys around all the time.

"I've got a handle on it, Ted," he said.

"Cain't tell it from how fast you're drivin'. You gotta slow down now. Ain't that right, Buck?"

Jake clamped his jaw shut. Complaining had never shut Teddy up, so he might as well save his breath and the hurt feelings that were bound to result if he said what he wanted to say.

"Put a lid on it, Ted," Buck said. "You talk too much anyhow."

"You're runnin' *your* mouth right now," Ted snapped back.

Jake slowed the truck and turned up Firecreek Mountain Road.

"What was I thinking when I let you two hook up with

me?" he asked, just to break the cycle of petty sniping. "You sound like a couple of magpies."

"You mean to say 'what was you thinking when you killed that cat that was only doing what comes naturally so's you could pick up that little broomtail scrub for me to raise?'" Theodore's tone sounded so dignified and righteously offended that Jake and Buck laughed again.

"Just hang in there, Ted," Jake said. "It won't be long 'til she'll be on grain and grass. Besides, Buck just told you—broomtail or not—she's gonna make a helluva usin' horse."

He made the turn and pulled the full length of the trailer onto the graveled road before he stepped on the accelerator again and started up the hill.

"I'm gonna stop at my house to pick up some more clean clothes," he said. "Might as well take some of that food in the fridge, too, so it won't go to waste."

"Well, don't think you can stay at yore house," Teddy said. "You're gonna take your turn on them foal feedings just like the rest of us."

"Jake's got colts to ride," Buck said.

"And they're over at the big barn, too, ain't they?" Teddy said. "You jist as well get all your gear, Jake, and move in with us because you already brought us all your responsibilities."

Jake tuned them out and looked at the mountains as the rig pulled the grade and wound its way up the hill. This was a pretty area all right, but to his eye not as beautiful as it was up in the Garnet Range where he was buying his place. If….

No. Not if. *When.* He was in this now and he had the land half paid for. He could finish paying it off in a couple more years if he stayed hitched and worked as hard as he'd been working. He wanted that place like he'd never wanted anything. Well…anything that could be bought with money.

But the thought of settling down in one place scared the hell out of him, too. What else would he do? He'd lost his yearning to roam.

Tori was gone for good and he was *not* making a landowner out of himself to acquire "something to offer her and her boys."

He didn't want her back anyhow, unless he could turn back time to the way things were when she and the boys first moved in with him. He could never take her back now, even if she wanted to come back, because he'd never be able to trust her again. She'd chosen a remarriage with no passion and no love—she'd gone back to the very opposite of Jake—for the sake of security. "He has something to offer me and my boys" was what she'd said when she broke the news.

No, he was *not* buying his own place so that next time *he'd* have something to offer a woman. There wasn't going to be a next time. He would never live with a woman again. The remote, beautiful land he'd bought was going to be a place for himself, a place where he could live alone and raise some horses that would support him so he wouldn't have to drive all over creation shut up in a truck with two garrulous, bossy old men.

He began slowing for the turn as Teddy was still urging him to do, clamping his jaw shut as he took the road into the ranch and then, soon after, the driveway that led to the little cabin he'd added to the rental deal after the old guys had showed up and moved into the big one with him. He'd had to have a private hideout or lose his mind. He just wasn't made to live with other people.

His eyes widened as they neared the house. "Hey, what's this? Looks like I got company."

"Company pullin' a trailer," Buck said. "Reckon it's thieves? Good thing your horses ain't here."

"I'll block 'em in, just in case," Jake said, and pulled up to park so his trailer would be across the driveway.

The front door flew open and a beautiful woman with a shotgun in her hands strode out onto the porch. The surprise of it made all three men draw in an involuntary breath.

Teddy said, "Looks like they're makin' thieves a lot prettier these days."

Jake and Buck both started opening their doors. The woman raised the gun.

"Don't get out," she yelled.

"If she's a thief, she's a damn-sure successful one," Jake muttered. "That vest she's got on is real fox fur."

That and everything else about her screamed money. She was polished and burnished and shiny all over, from the pale hair swinging around her face to the little thread of gold in her turtleneck sweater to the tips of her pointed-toe shoes. Her legs, slim and as long as forever, were wrapped tight in boot-cut jeans with flowers embroidered up the side. The shoes were those killer ones with high, skinny heels that would stab desire into a man's heart with every step they took toward him—and despair with every step away.

He wished she'd take off the fancy sunglasses so he could see her eyes.

Jake hit the button to roll down Buck's window and leaned across him to talk to her. "This is my..."

"You heard me," she shouted. "Stay in the truck."

Then she whirled on one heel and pointed the gun at the ground. Tried to aim it.

Both doors on the passenger side opened and Buck and Teddy stepped down off the running board at the same time as if they were doing some kind of coordinated dance, Buck with his rope, Teddy with a quirt in his hand.

"What the *hell?*" Jake hollered. "You aim to rope a woman with a *shotgun?*"

"Snake!" she screamed. "Get away from it."

Now it was the muzzle of her gun that was dancing, swinging around to point everywhere at once. Holy hell. She could blow them all away.

She took a step forward on the porch, braced her legs apart in a high-heeled fighter's stance, set the gun into her shoulder and—God help them all—propped her right elbow against her ribs to try to steady her aim. She was a right-handed shooter.

The muzzle passed right over Jake. Unless there was a snake in the truck here with him, it was as safe as a church.

He ducked but after a second he couldn't not look and when he did, the wavering shotgun had left him to hover around and above and below his uncle. Buck held his doubled-up rope ready in the air and Teddy did the same with the quirt, both trying to gauge the striking distance of the good-size rattler coiled on the ground between them. They ignored the woman and the gun completely.

"Get out of the way! I'll take care of it," she yelled and then her voice began to shake. "I don't want to hit y'all…"

Well, that told him she wasn't from around here. And everything else about her told him she wasn't the marksman of the year. The barrel of the gun made a big circle and swung back toward the truck again.

Jake threw his door open and hit the ground. He crouched behind the front wheel and yelled, "They've killed snakes before, ma'am. Don't worry about them. Now, put the gun down…"

He could see Buck's feet and he saw the rope slice down to hit the snake right behind its weaving head. The gun roared anyway.

The whole front of the truck exploded with a crash, rattled

and broke into a million pieces. For a second, Jake thought he was dead. He wasn't even hit.

The truck gave one last gasp and died. Antifreeze poured out of the radiator, red rivulets ran from the power steering, and bits of metal twinkled on the ground. Everywhere.

He yelled, "You boys okay?"

For a minute nobody answered. The sudden silence was deafening. Then, faintly from Buck, "Depends on what you mean by that."

Jake yelled again, trying to put a persuasive tone in his voice, "You done shooting, ma'am?"

She didn't answer, or if she did he couldn't hear her.

"Hold your fire," he said, trying for authority instead. "I'm gonna stand up now. Put the gun down."

The recoil had probably knocked *her* down.

He got up and stood behind the truck. Even in the state she was in, which basically was one of a terrible need to let go and crumple to the floor until her legs could regain their strength, Clea knew him. Her Montana Cowboy.

Well, not hers.

He looked her over as if to judge whether she'd take another shot, then he strode around the front of the truck and came up the steps of the porch like a man here to take charge. Who was he really? But if he'd been carrying a foal around on his saddle, he couldn't be a bad guy. Could he?

All she could do was lean against the wall where the recoil had thrown her. She still held the gun frozen in both hands but she couldn't lift it. Her shoulder felt as if she'd been hit by a truck. The instructor had warned the class to hold the stock really tight but she mustn't have held it tight enough.

The cowboy walked straight up to her and took hold of the gun as if he'd decided that she *would* shoot again. Up close, he was even more rugged and handsome than she'd thought when she saw him from the road.

However, he certainly wasn't behaving like the mythical cowboy he'd looked to be.

"Let go," she said, pulling back on her weapon as hard as she could.

"You're liable to blast a hole in the floor," he said. "Turn loose. All I'm gonna do is take this gun and stand it up against the wall."

Whatever happened to a slow, drawling, gallant "Can I help you, ma'am?"

"Don't talk down to me," she snapped. "I took lessons."

A spark of humor flashed in his eyes but his voice stayed grim. "My advice? Ask for your money back."

It might've made her smile if she hadn't felt so...not scared exactly, but yes, scared. And inadequate. The way Brock had made her feel sometimes. She continued to cling to the gun with both hands. He didn't take it away but his grip was so strong she could tell she couldn't stop him if he tried.

So much for self-protection. This was why her instructor always said never let a bad guy get close enough to take your gun away from you. There were scarier things in the world than stealing a horse.

For the first time in her whole life, there was no one in the house she could call on for help.

Could Brock have hired these men to take Ariel away from her? No. He couldn't possibly know where she was. Not yet.

She took a deep breath and took the offensive. "Who *are* you? You have a nerve, all of you, coming in here as if you own the place. You're trespassing. I warned y'all to stay in your truck."

"I'm Jake Hawthorne," he said. "I live here."

It took her a second. "In your dreams. We may be out in

the middle of nowhere and you may have your snake-killing buddies with you but no way are you moving in here."

"I already did."

That flat sincerity startled her into taking one hand off the gun to remove her sunglasses so she could look into his eyes with no barrier.

"Didn't you see my boots and jeans in the closet? My groceries in the kitchen? My feed and hay in the barn? My shorts in the underwear drawer?"

It all became clear.

"I…I'm in the wrong house?" She hated that her voice revealed just how deep her embarrassment went.

He smiled. Sort of. With just the slightest lift at the corners of his mouth. At least he wasn't rude enough to really laugh at her.

"I…I leased a house with a barn for a year…"

He nodded. "But not this one."

He was remarkably calm about her mistake, standing here in the middle of this mess of ruined trucks and dead rattlesnakes, so unlike the yelling, hysterical idiot that Brock would have been if *his* new truck had just been shot to pieces. In fact, she didn't know *any* other man who'd act like this in such a situation.

But who cared what kind of man he was? He might be calm but there was still an undercurrent of steel resolve in him that didn't bode well for anybody's opposing will.

Especially a woman's. Like most men, he saw her as a sex object. His gaze had drifted to her mouth.

She stared at him until he met her eyes.

"I *am* going to get a refund," she said. "I had ten lessons and the best score in the class."

"That's the devil of it," he said. "Most times, lessons can't put a patch on real life."

Real life. The words hit her like a blow across the back of the knees.

Clearly, this Jake Hawthorne could handle whatever real life threw at him. While she on the other hand had just proved she had a long way to go to even get started on a real life. She'd shot up his truck, misunderstood his remark about living there, moved into the wrong house. If this was the best she could do, how could she survive out here? This was a place filled with tough men.

Get tough yourself, Clea. Say what you think. Say what you want. Sound like you intend to get it.

"Is this what you do? Pin a person up against the wall where they can't even move—*after* you tell them to get out of your house?"

"First experience," he said.

He took the gun and stepped away to lean it against the wall.

"I declare, miss," one of the old guys said. "You nearly blowed me and Teddy right out of our boots. How come you're tryin' to shoot your own snakes, anyhow?"

It was the one who'd killed the snake who was stomping up the steps. He had keen, very keen blue eyes that seemed to see everything. His buddy was right behind him.

Both of them were grinning at her but she was in no mood to smile back. She felt shaken now that Jake Hawthorne had finally let her go.

"Because I'm not really fond of snakes," she said. "I thought it might get into the house. I thought it might bite me or my horse. I thought this place wasn't big enough for both of us."

Completely immune to her sarcasm, the old guys headed straight for her. She moved away from the wall.

"Well, o' course that's right," the blue-eyed one said. "Ma'am, I'm Buck and this here's my pardner, Teddy."

They both tipped their hats to her.

"What I was askin' by my question was, where is your man? Are you here by your lonesome, Miss…uh, Miss…?"

"I'm Clea." That was all she intended to tell them.

Teddy spoke to her as if he'd known her all her life. "Well, don't you worry none, Miss Clea. We done kilt that rattler fer you deader than a rock." His faded brown eyes were as calm and steady as Buck's were lively.

"You want us to get Jake out'n' yore hair, ma'am? He can be a real bother sometimes. Won't listen to a word nobody says. Cain't tell him nothin', you might say."

Jake snorted derisively.

"This here's quite a party you've throwed, Miss Clea," Buck said. "I ain't had me such a rousin' good time since the Miles City Bucking Horse Contest the last year I rode."

His twinkle and Teddy's nod of agreement made her smile in spite of all the aggravation of her insecurities. "Usually I entertain at my own house," she said wryly.

They laughed, then Buck drawled, "Wal, this can be your house if you want. Jake can live with us. You oughtta stay here so you'll have a nice mantel board where we can tack up this hide."

He lifted the dead snake. Clea screamed. She hadn't even noticed he was carrying it by his side. Held up in the air at the old man's shoulder, its tail brushed the floor. Its mouth was open with the fangs hanging out. It was a horrible sight.

"He's a beauty, ain't he?" Teddy said. "Might be near as long as Buck is tall."

"Don't worry none," Buck said. "I'll skin him out for you."

The vision of that activity made her whirl on her heel and run into the house. Her stomach clutched. Partly because the snake repelled her so and partly because it had just occurred to her that she might never want to carry her beautiful snakeskin bag ever again.

She got as far as the worn old sofa and collapsed onto it. "Please go," she called, through the open doorway. "And take the snake away."

Nobody answered. Clea let her head fall back onto the top of the cushion. Even with her eyes closed, she saw the snake on the backs of her eyelids. Saw it coiled on the ground beside her truck, waiting for her when she went for the door.

Saw it dead, fangs reaching, hanging from Buck's hand.

What if it had been a mountain lion…or a bear? At least she could stay away from a snake if she saw it soon enough. It hadn't chased her when she went to get the gun.

Voices murmured out on the porch.

Here was another example of her mishandling real life. No, two examples. Screaming and running away.

Weariness flooded her jangled nerves. This was the wilds of Montana. She was here for a year. She felt completely exhausted and she hadn't even found her own house yet.

The scuff of boots against the floor and the squeak of the screened door took the place of the voices. She sat up.

Buck stepped through the door. Holding both hands out to show he was without the snake. "I'm sorry, Miss Clea," he said. "I never thought you might be scairt of a dead snake. Can I get you a cool drink of water?"

It made her feel like a character in an historical novel, a delicate lady who needed a dose of smelling salts. She opened her mouth to say no, but Buck went on to the kitchen.

When he came back with a tin cup of water he called, "Come on in, boys."

To her, he said, "We ain't throwin' you outta this house 'til you git over this little upset. Mebbe not ever. Jake can take the house over there by the lake that you're s'posed to have." He grinned. "Or he can move in with me and Ted, 'cause…"

Jake interrupted, "I'm not goin' anywhere, Buck." He was headed for the bedroom but he glanced at Clea over his shoulder. "You can move tomorrow."

"I'm moving today," she said, shooting the words back at him as briskly as he'd spoken to her.

"Don't rush her," Buck called after him.

Teddy said, "No, don't. But Miss Clea does need to get settled into the right place so's she can get started on her—"

He interrupted himself to come closer to Clea, his kindly brown eyes questioning her as he finished, "Well, doing whatever you come to Montana to do, ma'am."

"Whatever it is," Buck added helpfully.

Hopefully. They both looked at her expectantly and fell silent, giving her a chance to tell them what she was doing here. In Jake's house. With her bright orange cashmere afghan thrown over the arm of the couch and her burled wood bowl with its meandering turquoise inlay sitting on the mantel.

Not to mention her sheets on his bed.

She couldn't help but like the two old-timers who were so lively and curious but no way was she going to get into her story with them.

"Runnin' from the law, more 'n' likely," Buck said with a grin and a wink.

Clea jumped and spilled water on her jeans.

"I'd lay money on it," Teddy said. "Don't she look jist like a hoss thief to you?"

She felt her eyes go wide and the blood rush to her cheeks. "I can't believe you saw through my disguise," she said.

They laughed, loving that she played along with their joke.

"We mind our own business," Teddy said. "So we ain't turnin' you in, Miss Clea, not unless you try to throw your long rope on some of *our* hosses."

"Yore disguise ain't so bad, though," Buck said. "Ain't seen many thieves wear them high-heeled shoes like you got on."

She laughed, too, even if it sounded a little forced, then she finished the water fast and stood up. She didn't want to get involved. She had to be alone to get her head straight and her confidence back.

"All I need is directions to my cabin and I'm outta here," she said.

The old guys nodded. "We'll show you where it's at and then we'll help you with your move," Buck said. "If you *do* move."

Damn, he was stubborn.

Jake thought so, too, judging by his irritated tone. He yelled from the bedroom, "She *is* moving. And remember, Buck, we've got work to do."

Gallant enough to carry a foal around but not to carry boxes for her.

Face it, girl. The real cowboys have been gone for a hundred years. "I don't *need* any help," Clea yelled back at him. "I won't *accept* any help. I moved myself in here and I'll move myself out."

Jake came out of the bedroom carrying a paper sack with a shirt peeking out of the top and a pair of boots in his other hand.

Clea said, "What're you doing? I just told you *I'll* move."

"This's only for a few more nights."

"So's he can take his turn feedin' the baby," Teddy said. "He brought in a orphan foal that we're helpin' him with."

She turned to Buck. "Maybe they could go feed the foal and you could ride with me and show me where I'm supposed to be," she said. "Then I'll drop you at your place."

All three of them just stood and looked at her.

"What?" she said.

"Reckon we'll all have to hitch a ride with you," Teddy said, "or walk. Our truck ain't runnin' right now."

Clea's face went hot. She slapped a hand to her forehead. How could she have forgotten?

How could she survive—anywhere—when she'd lost her memory and most of her good sense?

She found her keys and led the way out across the porch, down the steps and past the ruins of the pickup with Natural Bands, whatever that was, written on the door. It was truly a wreck. Also new and top-of-the-line. How much was *that* going to cost her?

She'd never had to clean up her own messes before. She couldn't call Brock to take care of it and she couldn't call Daddy. There was *no one* she could call.

Not even an insurance agent. Nobody sold policies to protect shooters against their own bad marksmanship.

"First experience," Jake had said. No kidding.

CHAPTER FOUR

CLEA KEPT going, using her longest, most confident strides to make herself feel stronger. She was almost to her truck when she realized no one was behind her anymore. She turned to look and then she leaned against the truck and let her shoulders sag.

Of course. Once again, she'd failed to use her common sense. She'd forgotten that she couldn't get her truck out with the wrecked one blocking her driveway.

Jake was unhooking it from the trailer. Buck was sitting in the driver's seat with the door open.

"Put 'er in neutral," Teddy yelled at him. "I'll give you the heads-up when we're ready to push."

The only answer he got was a light nicker from Ariel.

Clea whirled on her heel to see the mare standing at the fence watching the entire proceedings with ears pricked. Her stomach clutched. She'd prefer that no one ever see Ari, even though she'd dyed her white markings after she fed her this morning.

That was a useless hope, of course. And the disguise was paper thin. She doubted that there were very few horses around this part of Montana at least who were part-thoroughbred and stood nearly seventeen hands, much less horses who moved the way Ariel did.

But no sense in worrying. She didn't even know whether

these guys would pay any attention to or remember the mare. Anybody could go around pulling a horse trailer. That didn't mean they'd know a warmblood from a quarter horse.

Ignoring Ari in the hope that the mare would wander off, preferably somewhere out-of-sight behind the barn, Clea turned back to the truck and started clearing spaces for passengers in the backseat. She gathered up her barn coat and clogs, piled them on top of the metal train case that held most of her cosmetics and balanced all that on the hump in the middle of the floor. She pushed the sack of snacks and carton of soft drinks left over from the trip to the middle of the seat. The old-timers weren't very big. They could fit in here just fine.

She climbed into the driver's seat and looked in the rearview mirror at the long piece of driveway stretching from the house to the road and the nose of the Natural Bands trailer hanging over it. Backing out, she'd have to swerve her own trailer and then get it back on track so as not to go off into the ditch when she reached the road.

Maybe she should unhook it.

She shook her head at herself in the mirror. No, she had to be able to handle all kinds of situations and she'd backed the trailer before. She needed the practice. And she didn't need the extra work of unhooking and hooking it up again to move Ariel this afternoon.

Jake finished unhooking his own trailer and went to help Teddy push the truck. As soon as he got behind it, the truck moved smoothly out into her—no, his yard.

Buck steered, holding the door open with his foot. Debris scattered everywhere and a large piece of shiny metal fell and bounced away into the grass when Buck put on the brake.

Dear God. This was going to take every penny she had

saved. She might as well drive into Pine Lodge tomorrow and apply for a job at a McDonald's restaurant. If they even had a McDonald's. There must a café or two, at least. Could she learn to carry a heavy tray above her head on one hand?

Buck got out, closed the door and started up the little slope toward her. Jake went back to the trailer, picked up his paper sack of belongings from the ground, and he and Teddy followed Buck. Jake's face, what she could see of it from under the brim of his hat, struck her as incredible. Heart-stopping.

Would he let her get some more pictures of him? No. She didn't know him, but she could not imagine him willingly posing for a photographer.

She reached down, turned the key and looked at the protruding gooseneck of his trailer again. She'd better keep her mind on her business.

She looked for Ariel. Thank goodness, now she was nowhere to be seen.

Clea made herself draw in a deep, calming breath. Her insides were still a little shaky from all the havoc of the morning but now that was over. It had just been a terrible shock when she'd seen the snake and then three men rolling up into her yard with a trailer. Men who could easily have been sent by Brock to take Ariel back.

They hadn't come for that at all. Brock still didn't know where she was. She'd take these men to their cabin, find out where hers was, then come back and load up. She'd be settled again by tonight. Everything would work out all right.

Buck opened the door behind her. "All right, Miss Clea," he said. "Yore way is clear. Let's you and me run off and leave them two sorry so-and-so's."

He kept chattering away as he climbed in, as if they'd

known each other for years. Clea had the sudden thought that she might've wrecked the only vehicle they had. What if she had to drive them everywhere they wanted to go until their truck was fixed?

Montana was turning out not to be quite as solitary as she'd expected.

Jake glanced back at his trailer as he walked up to Clea's truck. It wouldn't be easy to get past it without messing up one or the other or both, and one wrecked new vehicle was enough for one day. What a waste!

Natural Bands might have deep pockets and probably had good insurance but he wasn't going to enjoy trying to explain to Celeste how this had happened.

He opened the passenger door as Teddy got in the back.

"I'll drive," Jake said.

Clea gave him a disdainful look. "Why should you?"

"In case you can't drive any better than you can shoot."

Her eyes narrowed. "Get in."

"That trailer's the only one we've got," he said. "And you panicked."

She sat up straighter and glared. "If you want a ride, get in. If not, shut the door."

He held the stare, trying to intimidate her, but she wouldn't give in or look away. Her eyes were blue, instead of brown like Victoria's, but they were just as sure and hard as Tori's had been when he tried to talk her out of leaving him.

Yep, here was another woman too stubborn for her own good. Too stubborn to have good sense. Why was that the only kind of woman who ever crossed his path?

He couldn't by rights throw her bodily out of the seat, therefore he ought to stay on the ground to direct her, at least until she got around the trailer.

But that'd be a good way to get killed, judging by the way she was looking at him now. So, damn it, let her prove what she could do if she thought she was such a hand.

He moved her fancy piece of luggage—one of those with letters and little French symbols printed all over it—to the floor, set his paper sack on top of it and got in.

Clea put the truck in Reverse and her eyes on the mirror, released the brake and started rolling back the rig.

"You can do it," Teddy said from his seat behind Jake. "Just take 'er slow and steady."

"You bet," Buck said. "We'll spot you. You git around that gooseneck, you got'er made."

"You're all right," Teddy said, looking out the back window. "Jist do what we tell you now."

Clea didn't take her eyes off the mirror but she pulled in a deep breath and lifted her chin. The way her hair moved when she did that—so smooth and sleek and shiny, falling back from her perfect face—reminded him of Victoria again, although Tori's hair was dark. Maybe that was why Clea'd irritated him from the get-go—besides shooting the hell out of his truck, she was a spoiled rich girl.

Jake stared out the window and tried to ignore her. The old guys would direct her. He'd just sit here and be ready to grab the wheel if she got in a jam.

"You're all right," Teddy said. "Just keep on comin'."

She was moving at about an inch per hour.

"Cowgirl up," Buck said. "Don't let nothin' git you down on the day you killed your first truck."

She jerked the wheel. The trailer jerked, too. She got it back.

"Thanks a lot, Buck," she said through clenched teeth.

The old guys laughed. Jake shook his head. They'd probably rattle on until they unnerved her completely.

Then she pressed the accelerator and backed a little faster. Another second or two and she could crash into the gooseneck.

"Want me to unhook you?" Jake asked.

"I've backed a trailer before," she snapped.

"Once," he muttered, under his breath.

Spoiled *rotten,* determined to do whatever she wanted whether she knew how or not. Wouldn't listen to reason. He hated that.

She sped up a little more but she was still just creeping. In spite of that caution, her trailer seemed to be going in a more and more crooked path.

"There you go," Buck said. "You're nearly to the hard part. Come on, now."

Clea clenched her jaw even harder and pressed down on the gas a little more. Jake kept his eyes on the outside rearview mirror.

Buck muttered, "Go for it."

"Watch it," Teddy said. "Crank 'er to the right, just a hair."

"No, she's okay that way," Buck said. "Send 'er toward the house, Clea, and then hold 'er there. Straight back."

"You cain't even *see* straight, Buck. You shut up and let me do this. You're..."

A sudden loud whinny cut through the air and a big black mare ran to the fence. Clea sucked in her breath and stepped on the gas a little more.

"Now, you all watch for that trailer," she said, and kept her eyes on the mirror. The whinny rang out again.

"Whoo-ee, and not a white hair on her," Teddy said. "Black as the ace of spades and, what is she? At least near seventeen hands."

"You've got a mighty fancy mare there, Clea," Buck said.

Clea didn't say thanks for the compliment. She didn't say a word.

"What d'you use her fer?" Buck asked.

Finally, she said, "I show her some."

"She one o' them jumpers?"

"Yeah."

"Never could stay in one o' them little postage-stamp saddles," Teddy said. "But I never did try it but the one time."

"Then don't say never," Buck said. "One time won't do it. Maybe Clea'd let you try jumping her mare..."

"Which way is it to your place?" Clea interrupted.

"East," Buck said.

She glanced at him in the mirror to find out which way that was. Jake shook his head. Couldn't shoot, couldn't drive and didn't know east from west.

"Naw, now watch it—you're gonna hit the nose of our gooseneck," Teddy shouted, having suddenly looked back instead of at the horse. "Give it some room. Watch it there, Clea."

She sent the trailer the wrong way again, toward theirs, but brought it back. Almost too quickly. Then she had it off the driveway on the right, the way it had to be, and they were moving past the Natural Bands trailer.

She gave a huge sigh when it was done. Actually, they all did. No crash, no scrapes, no trouble. She maneuvered the trailer back onto the driveway, going for the road.

"You're good now. Give 'er some gas," Buck said.

But she stepped on the brake.

"Hey," Jake said. Damn. Was this torture gonna last all night?

"I've got to get out of this vest," she said and Jake saw that her upper lip was filmed with sweat.

She slipped her arms free and handed the fur to Jake, who laid it across his paper sack. It wafted her perfume to his nostrils, a light, citrusy scent that smelled as expensive as that luggage of hers had to be.

The mare whinnied again, then took off and began to canter down the rail with a beautiful smooth gait that made her look to be floating just above the ground.

"Look at the way that mare goes, boys," Buck said. "She'll reach and get it, won't she?"

Clea shifted in the seat and sat up straighter, then hit the gas and stayed on it until the trailer rolled straight down the drive and across the tin horn into the road. At the critical moment, she almost turned the wheel the wrong way, but she caught herself in time to make it swivel to the west so they could head east.

Applause from the backseat.

"You got 'er done," Buck said.

"Good job," Teddy said.

Jake said nothing. She threw a triumphant glance at him.

"What's wrong, Mr. Hawthorne?" she said. "Did I scare you with my reckless speed?"

"No," he drawled, "I'm scared I'll be too old to get outta the truck by myself by the time I get home."

Laughter erupted in the back and Clea realized the old guys had been pulling for her success. Jake should've been, too. After all, that was his trailer she'd managed not to hit.

He didn't like her much. But he didn't have to show it every second, did he? She stepped down on the accelerator and they roared off down the road with the old guys laughing and whooping and Jake staring out the window again.

Sullen, too. Well, whatever. What did she care?

Buck and Teddy showed her the turnoff to the cabin that was meant to be hers, which was about two miles into what they said was a five-mile distance to their place. She kept thinking about the ordeal she'd just gone through, about *all* the challenging ordeals that had made up this day so far. Living in Montana couldn't be quite this rough *all* the time.

As soon as she dropped these guys off, she'd go back by her new place and check it out. Once she got Ariel hauled over there and her stuff all moved in, surely she'd have some peace so she could get herself organized.

Finally, Buck said, "Next road. There. On your right."

Their cabin looked to be a little bigger than Jake's. It had pens and a small barn immediately behind it and beyond that, just a little higher up at the foot of the hill, a large indoor arena. With real metal walls, not the black curtains like in Texas.

"That there's where your winter stall will be if you want it," Teddy told her. "You can ride your mare in there when the snow's ten-foot deep. All you have to do is figger out how to get yourself over here."

He and Buck laughed at her horrified expression. Jake wasn't listening.

"I like to ski," she said dryly.

"Sometimes it's that or snowshoe in," Ted said. "There's a guy hired to feed and clean stalls when you can't make it, though. Included in the rent for all the cabins."

Buck said, "Let me and Teddy out here at the house and we'll mix up the feed fer the foal. You and Jake go on to the barn and see about her."

Clea stepped on the brake. "I'm just dropping y'all off..."

"Jake oughtta come in and learn to mix the milk," Teddy said. "If 'n' he's really gonna take his turn at feedin' tonight, I don't want him wakin' me up—"

Buck interrupted the diatribe. "Clea, you have to go down there by the barn anyhow to turn around. Let Jake show you our little wild orphan."

He opened his door. "Come on, Ted," he said, in a sardonic tone. "I'll do the work and you kin put yore feet up."

Insisting that he was not lazy, he just wanted things even, Teddy got out and he and Buck headed for the house. Jake was entirely silent as Clea drove on. He seemed to be deep in thought, a million miles away.

"I don't know why Buck thinks I need a place to turn around," she said, with self-deprecating sarcasm, "I could just *back* out to the road."

It didn't get a rise out of him. He was staring through the windshield at the mountains.

Well, of course. *Duh,* Clea. He's worried about his truck, no doubt.

She pulled up and stopped in front of the barn.

"Here you are, safe and sound in spite of all I could do," she said. "I'm really sorry about your truck. Have your insurance people contact me about the damage and I'll take care of it."

She shifted into Park and reached to open the console.

"I'll write down my cell number."

He opened the door and stepped out as he waited for her to write the number down on an index card.

"They'll need your last name," he said.

"Of course," she said, but that hadn't occurred to her. Usually the people she dealt with knew who she was.

Above the number she wrote, Clea Mathison.

Clea Mathison, whom Jake Hawthorne saw as an incompetent idiot—a dumb blonde. Well, she might just let her hair grow out to its natural chestnut.

When she looked up to hand the card to him, she smiled and said, "Again, I'm sorry I shot your truck, Jake."

He barely glanced at her, just took the card with a muttered thanks, closed the door and walked away.

She watched him go, the sunlight bright across the back of his shirt. He didn't hesitate, didn't look back. He no longer knew she was there.

Since she was a teenager, every man anywhere around her *always* knew she was there. Even Brock. He'd ignored her plenty of times but he'd always been aware of her and so had every other man.

Now, to Jake Hawthorne, she wasn't even a sex object.

She didn't want to be one. But to be perfectly honest, at that moment *she* didn't know who she was, either. And she didn't want to be alone.

When she ran away from home to another world, she'd had no clue how alien she would feel.

The old Clea would have driven away and let that feeling get stronger. Especially if that was what she was expected to do.

But the new Clea would do something positive. Whatever her *heart* wanted her to do.

She reached down and turned off the motor. "Wait up," she called.

Jake, halfway to the barn, stopped in his tracks to look back.

"I want to see the foal," she said.

He said nothing, just stood there and waited for her to catch up to him.

"I've gotta ride," he said.

"Just point me in the right direction. I don't expect you to give me a tour. I'll see the baby and then I'll check out the arena and the winter stalls."

He looked as if he didn't know what to think of her. He was wary. Like the shy, lonesome cowboy in an old movie who'd be less afraid of a gunslinger than of talking to the new schoolmarm. Except he'd plainly told her she couldn't shoot and couldn't drive.

Who was he, anyhow? He was going to be her neighbor. He *was* her neighbor. Solitude and self-sufficiency were fine but she'd seen just now that she might need her neighbors sometimes. And they'd have to have dealings about his truck repairs, so they might as well be on pleasant terms with each other. "Have you lived here on the Elkhorn for a long time?"

"No," he said. As if that should put an end to the conversation.

She gave him a nice smile. "So. Where are you from?"

"Never lived anywhere more than a year or two."

"By yourself?"

He gave her a slanted glance that said it was none of her business.

He turned toward the barn.

"Then we're opposites," she said, matching strides with him. "I've never lived *anywhere* new before. You'll have to teach me about living free and on my own in a brand-new place. I need to enroll in How to Start Over 101."

They walked across the graveled drive to the broad doors standing open at the end of the barn aisle. Without another word.

That didn't matter. She didn't care if he wanted to talk to her or not because this was all about her. She was still jangled over the snake and the truck damage. And the reminder that she wasn't quite as able to protect herself as she'd thought.

But the main thing was aloneness. She just wasn't ready yet to drive off and be by herself the rest of the day and all night, moving her stuff and her horse into yet another strange place that she'd try to make look like a home.

She didn't know another soul for fifteen-hundred miles in any direction.

You don't know this guy, either, Clea. Or the two old ones, friendly as they may seem. This is real life, remember?

Clea Mathison stayed right beside him like they were joined at the hip while they walked into the barn and down the hard-packed dirt aisle between the two rows of stalls. She strolled along in those three-inch—or more—heels as easily as if she wore boots or sneakers, with that air of hers as if she owned the place, adding a wisp of flowery-lemon scent and a dab of shine to the old barn.

And something in him kept his eyes on her in spite of himself. He could feel the tug of curiosity but there was something else underneath it. Probably just that she reminded him of Tori. Same kind of woman.

Which means you better run, not walk, the other way, Jake ol' boy.

What was she *doing?* He damn sure hadn't invited her in.

He hadn't invited the old guys, either, and they were still here.

Get a grip, Hawthorne. This ain't about you. She's not moving in here, and she's moving out of your house. She's not staying all day. She just wants to see the baby. All women like babies.

"The foal's in there," he said, pointing out the stall.

"Great," she said, turning to flash him a smile that nearly blinded him. "Thanks. I don't want to hinder your work."

He felt more like he'd been dismissed than like he made an escape as he headed for the tack room to get his saddle. This whole deal gave him a bad feeling. Clea Mathison seemed way too comfortable, whether she was in his house or in his barn. And that was Buck's and Teddy's fault, being so helpful offering to move her and all. Those two oughtta get a life.

He went to find the saddle for Sugar, a filly who was anything *but* sweet. She was one of a string of ten three-year-olds that belonged to a ranch over on the other side of the mountain, young horses he'd been hired to green break for ranch work.

Getting some outside colts like that was adding a healthy amount of money to his Natural Bands salary and bringing him closer every month to paying off his place. His own place. He still couldn't get used to the fact that he had one.

At first when he came out of the tack room, he felt a little shock because he thought she was gone. But then he saw that Clea was in the little orphan's stall with the door closed behind her as if she knew what she was doing instead of standing outside and looking in, as he'd expected. How irritating could one woman be?

They'd already gone to a lot of trouble to save the foal's life. It was high-strung at best and nervous from being closed up in a stall, although it was getting used to people. But the last thing he and the old guys needed was for Clea to get the filly all agitated right before feeding time.

"It's not good to overhandle a motherless young one," she said.

Like he'd asked her. Who did she think she was, anyhow?

"So what are you doing in there?"

She didn't answer.

He walked up to the door and looked into the stall. The foal wasn't running around all over, looking to jump over the wall the way she sometimes did or trying to hide in the corner. She was getting to trust people enough to be curious about them. First thing, Buck and Teddy had put a little halter with a sawed-off rope on it so they could catch her.

"I hope y'all are being as firm with her as her mama would be," Clea said, holding out her hand to be sniffed as the foal approached her. "It'll ruin her if you treat her like a puppy dog and let her be disrespectful. Even now. As little as she is."

"What're you talking about? Are you a veterinarian or something?"

Of course not. Her type of woman wasn't tough enough to get through veterinary school.

The baby snuffed up Clea's scent, then turned away. With the next breath, she slapped her ears flat against her head, whirled like a rocket and kicked out behind. Clea was quick but not quick enough and the filly hit her a glancing blow with both feet.

Clea squealed and lunged like a maniac for that little scrap of rope. She grabbed it in one hand and proceeded to hold the little thing while she spanked the tar out of her with the other hand.

The foal tried to get away but Clea wouldn't let her. She spanked her all over the butt and sides.

"Hey, now, wait a minute here," Jake said, diving for the door to stop the fight before blood flew. "What's the matter with you? Good God, woman, this filly's barely alive and—"

"And you'd better...get a companion...for her before she grows into a...little monster," Clea said, between slaps.

Jake jerked the latch open and stepped in, reaching for the rope.

"You can leave now," he said. "I'm sorry she kicked you. Are you hurt?"

Clea stopped spanking but she held on to the rope. The filly looked at her and Clea returned the look, both of them breathing hard.

"You've probably...been spending...too much time with her," she said. "Handling her too much."

"Well, then, we can thank our lucky stars that you've come to set us straight," he said.

Sarcasm didn't faze her.

"Have y'all been trying to pet her and play with her? She's got to learn that people have to be the boss."

Her calm, superior tone made his blood boil.

"You some kind of expert?" he asked. "You know all about orphan foals? *Wild-horse* orphan foals?"

"Horses are horses," she said. "The wildness is in her bones and, if you think about it, it's in the domesticated ones, too. They're all born knowing that they're prey, so we have to earn their trust."

"And so you do it by slapping her around?"

"And their respect," she said. "Her mother or any other horse would've been a lot rougher on her. She has to learn her manners.

"Come on," Clea said and marched out of the stall, motioning for him to follow.

That surprised him. And irritated him even more. But he went, so the filly could think about her lesson.

And so he wouldn't be trapped in there for Clea to stand in the hall blocking the door while she gave him more lectures on the nature of horses.

He walked past her and went into Sugar's stall, which was next to the foal's, and started saddling.

Clea said, "You were shocked at what I did, but you would've done the same to a bigger horse."

"You said it yourself—a bigger horse," he snapped. "I'm not one to beat up on something smaller than me."

"Her mother would've bitten a chunk out of her. You all can halterbreak this baby, teach her to lead, maybe brush on her a little, but after that let her alone."

This woman made him so mad he could hardly see straight.

"Get another foal in here for her to grow up with," she said. "More than one if you can. It'll make all the difference for her for the rest of her life, because then she'll know how to fit in."

He'd planned to ignore her until she gave up and went away.

He'd decided not to argue with her. But he couldn't keep his mouth shut.

"One orphan baby is all we can handle around here."

"She needs to be with other horses so she can learn how the world works and how to find her place in the pecking order."

"When she's a little bigger I'll put her out with the using horses."

"She needs something her own size. So she can see when her companion's getting ready to kick or bite. So she can learn the body language that she'll need to read her whole life."

He rolled his eyes. "Anything else, professor?"

"Yes. So she'll be more athletic, quicker, more prepared to get out of danger or avoid it. Older, bigger horses tend to be too indulgent with a foal. Even stud horses."

He started pulling up the latigo on his saddle.

"When you do put her out, don't put her with a whole herd all at once. Just do it one horse at a time."

"Sounds like you know everything there is to know about this deal," he said dryly.

She shrugged. "You just have to let them learn to be real horses. They're social animals."

He *could not* talk to her. He *would* ignore her. As long as he talked to her, she'd stay here aggravating him.

But curiosity got the best of him. All this confidence and knowledge was such a contradiction to the way she looked and acted about everything else.

"How'd you come to know so much about orphans?"

"I've raised three of them since I was a kid," she said, leaning back against the stall wall and crossing her arms beneath her gorgeous breasts as if settling in to tell him her life's story. "The first one I did all wrong, but the other two turned out great."

So maybe she wasn't a total incompetent, after all.

But he didn't want her getting all wrapped up in this foal and coming over here all the time to tell him what to do with it. Or asking him how to start her life over in new places. He did *not* need somebody else driving him crazy and sucking his energy.

Not when he was just getting over Victoria. This woman was probably divorced, too. Had to be, since she wasn't used to being *free and on her own.*

He finished cinching the saddle and slipped the bridle on.

The old guys would be here in a minute with the feed and then Clea would be their problem. From now on he would be keeping to himself.

He buckled the bridle and led Sugar out into the aisle. He moved past Clea with a backward glance at her feet, which had shavings clinging to her high heels. "A barn's no place for those shoes."

She snapped back, "I happened to be on my way to town when I saw the snake. Which seems like a hundred years ago instead of an hour."

He could tell by the sound of her voice that she was following him.

He threw an answer back over his shoulder. "Maybe that's because we coulda gone to Canada in the time it took you to back out to the road."

Silence. He led Sugar on out of the barn and stopped to get on her.

Clea walked out into the sunlight. It turned her hair into a halo.

"Why'd you let me do that?" she asked. "Any other man would've tried harder to make me get out of the driver's seat. Why didn't you?"

He looped the reins into place in front of the saddle and

stepped back to mount. But before he stuck his toe in the stirrup, he looked her in the eye.

Any other man. Yeah. She probably had a dozen of them after her all the time. Somehow that thought irritated him even more.

"It's not up to me to *let* you do anything. Or to try to *make* you do anything. I'm not in charge of you. I've already got way more on my plate right now than I ever wanted, and I sure as hell don't want to be responsible for one more living, breathing thing."

Her blue eyes sparked with temper. "You really think a lot of yourself, don't you, Jake Hawthorne? Well, you can rest easy. I'm not trying to attach myself to you—all I came in here for was to see the wild-horse baby. I can take care of myself."

"No, you can't. You're a woman alone looking at wintering in Montana and you don't have a clue how to survive."

"What's it to you?"

"I'm your closest neighbor under the age of seventy."

"So *what?*"

"I would never refuse to help a neighbor. Or a woman. Or anybody weaker than I am. But I've got a job. I don't have time to take you to raise."

"Nobody's asking you to. Nobody *will ever* ask you to take care of me. You're jumping to the conclusion that I'm helpless based on nothing except the fact that I'm not very good at backing a trailer. Is that stupid, or what?"

"*And* based on the fact that you're used to having a man take care of you and buy you fox-fur vests and fully loaded trucks and trailers. Hired hands, too, to wash your dishes and build your fires and carry out your trash, and horse psychologists to teach you about your orphan foals."

"You don't know anything about me."

"I knew that much the minute I saw you. A minute after that I knew you can't shoot well enough to save yourself from a snake, much less a bear."

"Bear?" Buck yelled from a stone's throw away.

Jake looked up. He hadn't even seen—or heard—the old guys coming.

"Somebody seen a bear? Least you could do would be to warn us 'fore we come outside with a bucketful of milk."

Buck and Teddy were laughing as they came, silly as kids.

"Are there really bears around here?" Clea asked.

"Well, we ain't seen none right *here,*" Teddy said, pointing at the ground. "But yes, ma'am, there's black bear and grizzly, too, all over this country."

Jake thought her face lost a little of its color. Good. Maybe she'd go back home to Texas or Oklahoma or wherever it was she'd come from.

CHAPTER FIVE

BEARS? That was all Clea could think about as she drove away. Real life, with bears in it.

Evidently, pickup truckloads of eccentric—not to mention prickly and insulting—trespassers and wrong houses and hours of moving and packing and unpacking and constant barn chores and kicks in the thigh from orphan foals weren't enough for her orientation into real life.

Bears. Her breath caught. She'd better put Ariel in the barn every night for sure. But what about daytime? And what about all those stories about bears tearing their way into cabins? Maybe she should go sleep in the barn with the shotgun if there was word of bears around. But how would she ever hear those rumors? Her *neighbor,* Jake, certainly wouldn't want to be responsible for keeping her informed.

The old guys would come see about her, though. She would bet on it. She'd had a terrible time just convincing them to stay home and let her move by herself.

But she wouldn't let them, not now. Now she had to prove to Jake—in addition to Daddy and Brock—that she could take care of herself.

They weren't her major focus, though. Mainly she had to prove it to herself. This whole morning had been pretty unsettling.

But she would think positive. Dealing with the foal had grounded her some and reminded her that she wasn't a complete incompetent.

She would keep herself positive and *learn* how to be self-sufficient instead of worrying. She had a million things to do before the snow flew. Practice shooting, for one. Right now, if she shot at a bear, she'd probably hit Ariel. At least a bear would be a bigger target than a snake but it was also a much bigger danger. She could get away from the snake when she saw it, but she'd read somewhere that no human being can outrun a bear.

Clea straightened in the seat, took a long, deep breath and hit her fist on the steering wheel. So be it. She wasn't running anyhow. She was here and she would survive.

By the time she got back to Jake's place—*without* going by to see her own house because she was going to move into it no matter what it was—she'd locked bears away in their own compartment in her mind. Tonight, after she was all settled in the place where she was supposed to be, after the physical work of moving had taken the edge off her nerves, then she would go on the Internet and find out where to get the best information possible about how to share the neighborhood with bears.

She parked at the end of the driveway where she wouldn't have to drive past Jake's trailer again, hurried past the wrecked truck in the front yard without really looking at it because it was just too painful and, once inside, changed her shoes and went to work. Too bad Jake wasn't there to see that now she was wearing shoes appropriate for moving.

For a man who acted as if he were on another planet, he certainly had noticed a lot of details about her. Her shoes, her vest, her rig.

As she worked, their conversation cycled through her mind.

What was the deal with him, anyhow? What were his "way too many responsibilities"? He appeared to be single—Buck and Teddy had mentioned him moving in with them and, after all, she was in his house this minute and there was no evidence of a woman's presence, or that of children.

He had extremely few possessions, also. Maybe he was divorced, with three or four children to support. Instinctively, though, she didn't think so.

Had he been talking about the foal? But the old guys were doing most of its care, as far as she could see. He'd probably just said that to make his point.

For a man who basically was the strong, silent type, he could certainly put a person in her place. Using only a very few words, of course.

Smiling grimly at her own joke, she focused on getting out of his house as fast as possible. She took it room by room, starting in the kitchen where she packed up her favorite insulated travel mug and coffee, then fastened a note to the refrigerator with his tractor-shaped, feedstore magnet: I take responsibility for the food I ate. I'll replace it.

In the bedroom, she stripped her sheets off the bed and put his back on it, slapping away random thoughts of how he might look lying in them and what he might or might not be wearing at the time. She was thinking as a photographer, that was all, but she no longer cared whether he'd pose for her or not. She didn't want to spend that much time with him.

When she drove up to her new place, her spirits lifted. It was what the realtor had described to her *of course* and although it was newer and didn't have the atmosphere that Jake's old cabin had, it definitely had a glass-and-wood A-frame charm of its own. The four-stall barn was even newer than the house. It sat at the edge of an acre-or-so that was fenced with peeled logs, which would be a fine turn-out pen. She could use it to ride in, too, when she wanted to practice her jumps and flat work.

The tiny kitchen was stocked with the supplies she had ordered. The view was wonderful in every direction and the loft bedroom with its own balcony made her feel like an eagle in its aerie. It even had an almost-decent-size closet.

Clea skipped lunch to start her Montana life all over again. She kept her thoughts positive as she looked out at the vast space that lay between her and any other human being and wondered idly whether Buck or Teddy carried a cell phone. Or whether there were game rangers in the area who she could call, just in case.

Staying busy had always been her antidote to worry, so she worked from just after noon until nearly sundown unloading everything, taking her time arranging and rearranging the few personal decorative things she'd brought. The furniture wasn't great but it wasn't awful either, with a few old and battered mission-style pieces she really liked. Her burled wood bowl was perfect on the coffee table.

She spent most of her effort on the living room, which was basically the only room. It and the kitchen were all one great room, the loft was open to them, except for its tiny bathroom and the small room that held the washer and dryer in the back of the cabin.

It was by far the smallest house she'd ever lived in. It gave her the same cozy feeling she'd had in the dollhouse Daddy had paid the gardener to build for her when she was a little girl. Cozy and safely in charge of her world. It was the only place she'd ever felt that way.

Long after she outgrew the dollhouse, she remembered that feeling, and as a new bride moving into the McMansion that

Brock had had custom built on the acreage he had bought for its resale value, she had longed to feel that way again. Maybe she would have if she'd married anyone else but Brock.

That really had been her *very* first lesson in real life.

She'd been in Frisco, shopping for hours on end as she did sometimes when Brock was out of town. Early on in the marriage, when she still thought she loved him and when she missed him terribly.

When he'd still treated her with the deference her daddy's daughter deserved and pretended that he loved her, too.

The window of a new interior-design shop caught her attention because the eclectic blend of styles was such a homey-but-sophisticated, interesting-but-soothing creation that it pulled her to the window and held her there until the young fledgling designer came to the door and spoke to her. An hour later, Clea had hired the woman.

The two of them worked together for the ten days Brock was in Houston and she had had the den finished when he got home. For fifteen or twenty minutes, everything was wonderful.

She opened the door. He stepped inside, dropped his briefcase, swept her up in his arms and kissed her senseless. When he let her go, he still kept his arm around her waist to hold her against him.

But it fell away in a hurry when she led him into the den to show him his big surprise.

"You can't be serious." His voice held an edge that sliced away her happiness in a heartbeat. "This looks like crap, Clea. What the hell were you thinking?"

Her lips parted but no sound came out.

Which was fine. She didn't need to say a word, and it wouldn't have mattered if she did because Brock wouldn't have heard it.

He kept talking as he walked around the room. He flicked a finger derisively against a lampshade, then picked up a hundred-year-old Navajo basket and sent it spinning across the room to land on the floor in front of the door.

"Don't tell me you paid good money for this. Did you hire somebody to buy all this trash or did you pick it out? Either way, it stinks."

"I like it."

"You didn't even ask me," he said. "I thought you knew better, Clea. You've gotta run anything that costs more than...well, let's say a couple thousand...by me. Don't make that mistake again."

That night had been the real end of her marriage. She'd wasted another four years of her life on it because she didn't want to admit it was dead.

Because then what would she do? What *could* she do?

It had taken her *four years* to work up the courage to get the hell out.

Clea noticed she was breathing hard and getting a headache, so she pushed the memories away and headed for the barn. She had more than enough reason to keep her mind in the present and she was strong-minded enough to do that.

Brock was behind her, and by the time he found her again she'd be stronger still. By then, she'd know what to do.

When she had Ariel all settled in, she finally called it a day.

Starving and weary to the bone, she showered, dressed in sweats and went downstairs to make an omelet. Pretty soon she had to cook something besides eggs, but she really didn't know how to make very many other dishes. That'd be another thing she could do if she were snowed in—she could learn to cook.

She grabbed a notepad to begin a list for her first trip to

town, wrote *cookbook,* then crossed it out. There were, no doubt, a million recipes with directions on the Internet, free.

Think before you spend. Save the money. Pay for the damage to Jake's truck. You can't be free if you owe somebody.

Then she chopped tomato and onion, sliced ham and shredded cheese. She toasted bread in hot butter in another skillet while the eggs were cooking.

Feeling like a pioneer cowgirl who'd never heard the word *calories,* she put it all on a speckled tin plate and carried it with a mug of hot coffee out to the deck to watch the sunset. There was no table, no outdoor furniture at all, so she sat on the steps and leaned back against the banister post.

The air had begun to chill. It felt cool and crisp in her lungs and it smelled like pine and sage and many, many other scents she couldn't name. As she ate, the sky burst into flame. The clouds burned. The mountains reflected the fire and threw purple mist into it while they drew it down, little by little, to extinguish it at last in the dark, mysterious shapes of the valleys.

Only when the sun had dropped completely out of sight and the light it left behind dwindled to one thin streak of the palest salmon color, did Clea come to herself. Her plate and cup sat empty on the floor of the deck and her arms and legs were covered with goose bumps underneath her sweats.

She pulled up her knees and wrapped her arms around them. Tears hovered behind her eyes but she wouldn't let them fall. She wasn't a crier. If she ever started, she might never stop. Besides, this truth went too deep for tears.

She couldn't go back.

Forget that she wouldn't go back to Texas because she wanted—needed—freedom and a new life. The operative word was *couldn't.*

She had burned her bridges when she took Ariel. Not just with Brock, but with Daddy, too. No, she'd done it even earlier. When she'd "had the unmitigated gall and ingratitude" as Daddy had put it, to leave Brock and "rock the boat."

And she'd put the cherry on top when she'd told Daddy she wasn't going to let him take over her life again where Brock had left off.

She could not go back.

This truth wasn't new, yet it was. She'd known it. She had known this since the minute the word *divorce* had left her mouth, but she hadn't known it in the visceral way she knew it now.

Maybe Jake had been right. Maybe she'd followed him into the barn, not to see the foal but in an attempt to attach herself to him somehow. As a protector or something.

It didn't matter. She would learn to protect herself.

She would learn to do everything for herself. Including *think.*

That silly stunt she'd pulled this morning would have to be her last. She could've wrecked both trailers for no reason except trying to one-up a man she should've listened to. She could have thrown away *all* the money she had instead of half—or whatever it would cost her to fix the truck. That had been nothing but selfish, petty behavior.

Which was a kind of luxury. One she could no longer afford any more than she could afford more fluffy bath towels or new shoes like the ones that had bothered Jake so much today.

She would learn to protect herself and to think and to survive. Because the other truth she'd seen written in flames on the Montana sky told her that she didn't *want* to go back.

Her true heart was here. All she had to do was find it.

JAKE RODE up into Clea's yard yelling, "Hello, the house! Clea, it's Jake."

The young horse he was on didn't like yelling, so began gathering himself to buck.

Jake pulled his head up and started him going in a circle.

"Clea! It's Jake Hawthorne!"

Still no answer. Damn. She was probably in there right now loading her shotgun.

He got the colt straightened out and went around to the back of the house. Maybe she was out on the deck.

As he rounded the corner, he heard a horse. Hooves thundering.

The big black mare. Coming around the far corner of the barn lot at a hard lope with Clea on her back. Then he saw the jumps set up—homemade ones made out of hay bales and barrels and some rickety-looking sawhorses with a pole set across them.

Clea was up on the balls of her feet in the stirrups, her neat butt a little bit off the saddle, leaning forward at the hip, getting ready for the first jump. Her face was what held his eye, though; she looked even farther gone in her concentration than she had been with the wild foal.

She had her head up, looking ahead, her whole body focused on what she was doing. The next instant she and the mare were rising into the air and flowing over the stack of bales like one huge bird. Beautiful. More than beautiful. His heart lifted with them. They landed, headed for the next jump.

The mare tried to veer then, her ears back, wanting to go off to one side, and Jake's breath caught. Too late. They were already committed, going too fast to stop.

He couldn't tell or even look to see what Clea did, but she

held the mare to the course and leaned forward, ready for the jump. If the mare refused it, no way could Clea stay on and they were nearly there, nearly there and then they flowed upward again, over the barrels.

One more to go and the instant message in the air was that Clea was determined to jump it and the mare was not. She pinned her ears hard and switched her tail but Clea didn't give her an inch of room. Straight, straight to the pole across the sawhorses and then up and over it.

Jake let out the breath he hadn't realized he was holding. He rode on up to the fence. Clea passed him without giving any indication she knew he was there, rode around the jumps in one huge circle, headed for the first one and then put her horse over all of them again.

Pretty damned impressive. He would never have thought Clea had it in her.

This time, her blue eyes took him in as she loped—cantered, he supposed—the mare around the pen once more. Then she trotted up to him, pulling off the helmet she wore, patting her horse's neck while she smiled at Jake.

No, she was smiling in triumph. At the horse. At the sunny morning. It wasn't really directed *at him.*

Why'd you think it would be, bozo?

Sweat was beading on her forehead. Her eyes shone. She was sitting very straight in the saddle and breathing hard.

The uncertain, worried, shotgun-toting, trailer-backing Clea was gone. This one was impressive.

"Hi, Jake. You got here in time to see my girl being naughty."

So. She had known he was there all along.

"Seems you know how to handle her."

She shrugged. "Most of the time. She's a regular diva and she keeps me on my toes."

Horses, it seemed, brought her confidence.

It was like she picked the thought out of his head. "How's the baby?"

"She hasn't kicked any more."

She grinned a little. "And how're your partners?"

He shook his head.

She chuckled. "I know they're not okay unless you're doing your share of the night feedings."

"I did two. Then we decided she didn't need 'em. She's fine with it."

"Oooh, sounds like trouble. Buck and Teddy will never let you forget this—as soon as *you* have to get up for the night feedings, the foal doesn't need them anymore."

He felt a little grin turning up the corners of his mouth.

"You got it," he said.

It seemed weird to have somebody who knew what he was going through with the old guys. She liked them, too, he could tell.

"Did you come over to get your overnight bag? I decided you'd forgotten all about it."

"That and give you the bids. We need my truck fixed as soon as possible."

She nodded, then dismounted in one flowing motion, the helmet dangling from her free hand. "Let me just tie her up to think about her sins and I'll meet you at the house."

He rode to the house and tied his own horse to the pipe hitching-rail set in the backyard, then sat on the steps to wait. Clea came across the yard with a long, swinging stride, her hair shining in the sun. Slim and supple in her tight English breeches and high riding boots. What was it about a tall woman that turned him on?

But, hey, that was just another way she reminded him of Tori.

Clea was also wearing a tight top that showed her high breasts to be exactly perfect.

Jake stood up.

"Come on in," she said as she pounded up the steps past him. "I need water."

Inside, the house looked somehow as if it had come alive, as his own cabin had done during those few minutes he'd seen her stuff in it. Weird how a woman could make a difference in a place.

He was losing his mind even thinking about something like that.

"Here they are," he said, pulling the folded papers from his shirt pocket while she put ice in two glasses and poured water from a pitcher in the refrigerator.

"Oh, I didn't ask you," she said. "Do you want a Coke or something?"

He shook his head. "Water's fine."

"Bring those over here," she said, leading the way to the table by the window. "I need to be sitting down when I see the amounts."

He followed her and took a chair, although he'd planned to hand her the estimates, get his stuff and leave.

She drank most of her water, squared her shoulders and took the papers from him. Her face paled when she saw the bottom line on the first one. Quickly, she shuffled through all three of them.

"The lowest one is a place I called in Bozeman after the first Pine Lodge guy figured out what had to be replaced, so it's more of a guess than a final estimate. Plus you'd have to pay towing to get it over there."

She took another long drink of water and when she set it down, her hand was trembling.

"Nearly fifteen thousand dollars," she said, and her voice shook a little, too. "I can't believe it."

"Well, the three of them aren't that far apart," he said.

"Oh, I don't mean it that way," she said. "I just can't believe mechanics and body shops cost so much."

She was quiet for so long, staring down at the numbers written on the papers, that he got worried.

"I wish I could say you can pay it a little at a time, but you'd have to work that out with the guys who do the repairs. My boss doesn't have another truck for us to use and I know she won't front you the money."

That roused her. "Oh, no. No. I want to get it over with so I'll know where I stand. I've got some money coming for a couple of broodmares I sold right before I came here and that'll help."

She tried to smile.

"I'm still getting accustomed to being entirely on my own," she said, lifting her eyes to his. "You probably don't even remember how scary it is."

The words and the unexpected look went right into him, to the lonely place where he lived. What was it about a vulnerable woman that always touched him?

He looked away. Not his deal. She had resources. All appearances said she did.

She looked down at the papers again.

"Basically, these are too close to call," she said. "Just take it wherever you think they'll do the best work. I'll pay the whole thing when it's done."

He looked at the gleam of her hair and drank his water. "I'd say Larry's in Pine Lodge. He does good work and he can do it in a week. Trouble is, he wants half up front to order the parts."

Clea pushed back her chair and went to the stairs, ran up to the loft and came back with a fancy handbag. *Nice* leather.

She sat down again, pulled out a checkbook holder that matched the bag and a slim gold pen.

"I'll give you a check with the payee blank in case you decide to take it someplace else," she said.

"What if I write in my own name?"

"You won't."

"How do you know that?"

"I just do," she said.

She wrote fast, then handed him the check and the bids. They both stood up.

"Once again, I'm sorry, Jake. Is your boss mad at you?"

"Well, she can't understand how I drove straight into live fire. But she'll get over it."

Again, Clea's smile was pretty shaky. He felt he needed to do or say something but he didn't know what.

"What is Natural Bands, anyway?"

"Some call them a bunch of horse-huggers," Jake said, glad for a topic he didn't have to think about. "They want to keep wild horses in a natural habitat. Keep them healthy, keep them in family bands, keep them fed and watered in a drought, keep them safe, keep them wild."

"Sounds a little contradictory," she said.

"Yeah, but we're givin' it all we've got," he said dryly.

"How'd you come to work for them?"

"Money."

He turned and started walking toward the back door. Now they were getting into territory that he *did* have to think about. She walked with him without talking any more. They were out on the deck when she stopped.

"Oh," she said. "Your bag. Let me get it."

She disappeared for a moment, then she was back with his things.

"I would've brought it over," she said, "but I knew you wouldn't want me to take responsibility for you."

Startled, he looked at her closely. Her tone had said she didn't hold any grudges. There was a glint of humor in her eyes.

He felt heat come into his cheeks. For no reason. He hadn't been rude or out of line in telling her he wouldn't take her to raise. He'd simply told her something that had to be said.

It had made her mad at the time, according to the way he'd read her expression. But if she could laugh about it now, so could he. He wouldn't let her think he was a bad sport.

"I got your note about the food," he said, "so I knew we were on the same page."

It came out sounding heavy and stuffy and not funny at all. What the hell was the *matter* with him?

"No problem," she said.

Then she looked at his horse. "Is he one of the colts you're breaking?"

"Yeah."

"The paper sack might be a problem," she said. "If you think it will be, I'll bring it by this afternoon on my way into town."

That hit him wrong. Was she saying she thought he couldn't ride a horse through a problem as well as she could? "No, thanks."

He wanted to say something else but he couldn't quite figure out what it could be. He touched a finger to the brim of his cap, which, to be downright honest about it, he should've removed when he went in the house. Living alone had destroyed his manners and a few days with the old guys sure as hell hadn't brought them back to life.

"I'll bring your food on my way home," she called, as he ran down the steps.

He pretended not to hear. He wasn't up for any more conversation. He didn't even know what'd been said in the one he'd just had.

On the way home, he decided he'd never been so confused in his life.

Mainly by his own thoughts, he had to admit. Why did he care what she thought of him, anyhow? His manners were none of her business, because *no way* was he trying to impress her.

Well, the answer was that he was concerned about his reputation. And his self-respect. After all, he had his code to live by and he meant to live up to it every day. That was it. It was what he thought of *himself* that had brought the subject of manners to his mind.

Bullshit.

He shifted in the saddle and threw the bay colt a little more rein.

It kind of surprised him that Clea didn't try at all to prolong his visit. He'd been leery about going in the house, because some girls would've made up some excuse to keep him around, like trying to give him something to eat or asking him to help them lift or carry something—maybe a couple of bales of hay or a sack of feed. Judging by the way Clea had followed him into the barn the other day, he would've bet good money that she was that type. That she was trying to hook up with him.

But no. Her behavior today just proved she'd taken him seriously when he told her to take care of herself. Which was the result he'd been looking for.

It'd surprised him that she could tease him about it now. He wasn't used to anybody kidding around with him except for the old guys.

Duh. He hardly ever *talked* to anybody but the old guys.

Celeste and all her volunteers always took him seriously

and treated him like the last moody cowboy in the West. He played up that image because he didn't want to spend any more time than he had to with any of them.

Clea was like them—from the same class of people—but different somehow. For one thing, she didn't seem to have a cause like saving wild horses or outlawing logging or preserving the rivers.

Plus she *could* ride and, evidently, work with orphan foals.

He deliberately shook the sack and made as much noise with it as he could but the colt didn't turn a hair. Just wait. At any minute, he could see his shadow, spook and come completely unwound. With this horse, you never could tell.

Just like Jake.

What had that been all about, feeling sorry for her? She was rich. It was written all over her and everything she owned.

But it'd sent that old cold chill through him the way she'd reacted to that fifteen-thousand-dollar price tag on her bad marksmanship. She hadn't been acting. She'd been sincerely shocked and scared about finding that much money.

He knew how bad it felt to owe money you didn't have. To really *need* a large amount and not know where to turn to get it.

That's exactly what she'd been feeling when she sat there across that table from him and looked down at those pieces of paper.

And then looked up at him as if she really *knew* him. Knew he understood. Knew it'd be all right to let him see her worry. Her fear.

He kissed to the colt to tell him to pick it up a little.

His imagination was running away with him. No doubt about it—he'd been too long without a woman. Just let a tall one with beautiful breasts, long legs and soulful eyes come around and he'd turn into a babbling blob of sympathy.

And desire. If he was going to be honest with himself, he had to admit that played a part in it, too. He had to get over that. He didn't know this woman and he didn't want to. She had trouble written all over her.

He needed to get home and do something really physical, like get on that live-wire gray filly for the second time. Something exciting that'd make him stop thinking.

Something that'd bring back his sanity.

Because he had to be far gone if he was sitting around manufacturing sympathy for a rich girl's bank account.

CHAPTER SIX

SQUINTING THROUGH the haze of morning sunlight streaming into the kitchen, Clea scooped coffee into the pot. Then she switched it on and dashed to the corner under the coat rack, which she'd made into her mudroom by laying a mat from the truck on the floor until she could buy a sheet of plastic or a rug. She stuck her sock feet into her barn clogs, grabbed a jean jacket to put on over her pajamas and was out the door.

Worry about the state of her new bank account after she'd given Jake that check had kept her awake and at her computer half the night, researching winter survival, wild-horse photography, Montana in general and bears in particular. So once she'd finally gone to bed and had slept until midmorning, Ari was beside herself. People who did the feeding chores for animals couldn't sleep half the day.

People who wanted to develop a career couldn't sleep half the day.

People who had to make their own living couldn't sleep half the day.

This afternoon she needed to take her camera over to the wild-horse range. She also needed to call around and find her winter supply of hay and firewood. Those were the two most important essentials, except for her own supply of food.

Her mind was running on down the to-get list: a battery-powered radio for communication, snowshoes, more shooting lessons...when she stopped in her tracks. She finally focused on what she was seeing. There was the box from last night's Lean Cuisine dinner crumpled at her feet. A potato chip bag, paper napkins, an old newspaper from when she'd cleaned out the truck, the large brown paper bag she'd used to carry it all out in.

Other trash that wasn't hers. Trash that had been half filling the burn barrel last night.

She looked at it. It had been turned over and its lid lay five feet away, leaning up against the trunk of a tree as if it had rolled there. An animal must've....

Bears.

That thought chilled her blood but the next one froze it.

Ariel!

She whirled to look at the barn but saw nothing. Listening, she could hear nothing. Was Ari in there—dead in her stall? Surely, if she were waiting for her breakfast, she'd be banging her bucket against the wall, as usual.

Noise. Experts said to make lots of noise to let bears know you were there and to scare them away.

She whirled back to scan the yard, ran to the far side of it to pick up the barrel lid and then hurried to get a stick from the small stack of firewood. Banging it against the lid, she headed for the barn at a run.

Singing. The article had advised hikers to whistle and sing in bear country.

No way could she do either. Her mouth felt dry as dust and her heart took up her whole chest until her lungs had no room for air.

She made the drumming noise louder when she got to the door but she didn't slow down. If she did, she'd lose her nerve and not have the courage to go in.

But two steps later, she threw down her weapons. Ariel was standing there, perfectly normal, hanging her head over the stall door and staring at Clea as if she'd lost her mind.

Clea stared back, drinking in the welcome sight. "Thank goodness," she said, swallowing as the saliva flowed in her mouth again. "Oh, Ari, there's been a bear here."

Ariel stepped back, grabbed the lip of her bucket in her teeth and slammed it against the wall.

Laughing like a maniac, her limbs weak with relief, Clea went to get the feed. If there were a bear anywhere around right now, Ariel would be telling her.

Once Ari was munching, Clea saw she still had plenty of water and threw her some more hay.

"We'll ride later," she told her and picked up the lid and stick of wood on the way out.

Buck and Teddy were hurrying toward her across the barn lot. They stopped when they saw her and she stopped, too, shocked to see them. They looked her over carefully.

"You startin' up a band, Miss Clea?" Buck asked. "I kin play the mouth harp."

"I told him that there's your new weapon," Teddy said. "And all because him and Jake made fun o' your marksmanship." He shook his head sadly. "Honey, I hate to tell you but that ain't no way to try to kill a snake."

"I could hug your necks," she said and started walking toward them. "I am so glad to see somebody."

"I don't quite know how to take that," Buck said. "Would you be that glad to see just *anybody?*"

"Not even a possibility," she said and, laughing, they fell into step on either side of her to walk toward the house.

"So," Teddy said, "what really is going on here?"

"Did you look at my backyard?"

"You gotta do something about your trash," Buck said.

She stopped.

"Don't you think it was a bear?"

"Is that what you thought?"

"Of course. Haven't y'all ever read the Internet? Bears tear into people's trash."

They stared at her again. "The *Internet?*"

They laughed all the way to the house and she couldn't get them settled down until they'd hung their hats on the rack, washed up and pulled up chairs to her table, coffee cups at the ready.

"I didn't hear a thing," she said as she poured coffee. "And I was up until nearly two, but it happened during the night. Everything was fine when I took my trash out about seven o'clock last night."

"Two o'clock," Teddy said wonderingly. "That's nearly time to get *up.*"

"Coulda been a raccoon," Buck said. "Or a coyote, even. You've just got bears on the brain, Clea."

"You're the ones who first told me there are bears around here."

"That don't mean it *was* one that dumped your barrel."

"I know it was."

"We'll look for tracks in a little while," Buck said. "I'm a pretty good camp cook. Want me to make you breakfast?"

Teddy brewed another pot of coffee and they talked her into having something to eat as soon as she got over her fright and her nerves came back to normal. While Buck mixed up some flapjacks, Teddy explored the house.

"I see you've got some cameras here," he said. "Take a lot of pictures, do you?"

Clea smiled, thinking about their probing polite hints to know her reasons for coming to Montana.

"I want to take some of the wild horses in the sanctuary," she said. "I'm thinking about a career in photography."

The two old guys exchanged a quick, significant glance.

"Well, it's about time you told us," Buck said. "We've guessed about everything under the sun."

Clea laughed. "You two are the nosiest people I know. I thought real Western men never asked another person their business."

"We didn't," Buck said. "Think back. Did we ever ask you a di-rect question about your intents and purposes?"

"Takin' pictures of horses is a lot better for you than tryin' to steal 'em," Teddy said dryly. "We had done decided that you was serious about bein' a hoss thief."

"Easier, too," Buck said, as he poured some batter into the sizzling pan. "Better to limit your thievin' to the broke ones."

"You oughtta hire us as your assistants," Teddy said. "You know, like on TV when they go around with them big cameras on their shoulders. So's we can be on TV, too."

"Yore ugly mug'd ruin her pictures, Ted."

"I mostly take still photos," she said, as Teddy came back to the kitchen to refill his cup. And hers. They were sweet to coddle her like this.

"Them wild horses most likely won't be still fer you," Ted said.

"Except when they're hiding from you," Buck said. "You better hire us to find 'em. We'll take you out and introduce you to Montana Red."

"Who's he?"

"Nobody but the sneakiest, smartest, fastest stud horse *we* ever seen. And we've seen some. You can write that down in yore little black book."

"Red dun," Ted said. "Bright sorrel red. Dorsal stripe, leg stripes, striping on his withers. And he *is* what you'd call a striped sight, too. He's one o' them that can read your mind."

"He's a stalker," Buck said, shaking his head in wonder as he lifted the pan to flip a flapjack with a practiced twist of his wrist. "Me and Ted set on a side hill one time and glassed him on the next ridge. Ol' Red stole a mare from another band and run off with her before that stud ever knew what hit him."

"Let me tell it," Teddy said, talking fast like a little kid trying to take over the floor. "There's a rancher over on the other side of the Fire Creek drainage that lost a bunch of mares and foals to Red. He didn't see him do it, but he swears it was Red *broke down the poles on the pen* and took 'em. That was before Natural Bands bought the range and made it a refuge."

"Makes no sense to say it was before that range was a refuge," Buck said tartly. "It's not like they fenced it or nothin'."

Clea smiled to herself. Buck sounded like a little kid, too. Jealous because Teddy had told the best story about Red.

Buck pulled out three plates, took the pancake up on one and started cooking another. He glanced out the window.

"You got a pet doe?" he said. "Maybe there's your garbage girl."

Clea got up and went to stand at his shoulder. "I don't think she could turn the barrel over, do you?"

"'Course she could."

That got them back on the subject of Clea's living alone with the woods full of varmints and her not able to hit the broad side of a barn with her shotgun. "Gotta have a bear-proof place for your trash," Ted said. "And your barn's not it.

You need a metal container. Suspend it from a branch of that pine out there."

"Even if you had a garage, you couldn't keep it in there," Buck said. "Bears've been known to tear through a wall into a house."

Then he glanced at Clea's face and said, "But the best thing for you to do is learn to really use that gun of yours."

Ted nodded as he poured another cup of coffee.

"Ask Jake for shootin' lessons," he said. "He's the best shot I ever seen with a long gun of any kind. And I do mean *ever.*"

Clea stiffened. "I'm not asking Jake for anything. I told him I can take care of myself, and I can."

She took a drink of coffee and set the cup down with a thud. "He said I can't survive on my own and I'm going to prove him wrong."

Buck turned around from the stove and grinned at her. "I'm thinkin' that any woman who'll go after a bear with a stick of firewood *will* survive. But think about it this way. It jist might be a whole lot easier to shoot a bear than to beat him to death. He might not hold still for that."

Teddy was nodding agreement. "Don't cut off yore nose to spite yore face, missy. Takin' lessons from Jake ain't even on the same range as him takin' care of you. Learn to shoot and you *can* take care of yoreself in the long run."

"Yeah," Buck said, "and he'll shore not turn you down, 'cause he's tryin' to gather up a lot of money."

Clea, her blood cold from imagining trying to beat a bear into submission, stared from one man to the other. "Thanks, guys. I'll consider it. I just want to do as much for myself as I can."

"You survive winter in Montana, you'll get to do plenty," Buck said dryly. "But we *all* have to have help sometimes.

Even Jake. That's the only reason we're here on Fire Creek right now. To help Jake. Ain't that right, Ted?"

"It is," said Teddy. "Clea, you tell that to Jake if he gives you any more grief. Now, first thing we need to do is to go outside and look fer signs around that trash. That gol-durned Internet ain't gonna teach you to read tracks, Miss Clea."

"First thing we gotta do is eat," Buck said. "I ain't makin' these pancakes to feed to the birds."

"I was *talkin'* about after we eat," Teddy said disgustedly. "You know *that* much, surely."

"I knowed you was too much of a pig to miss a meal," Buck retorted. "Me and Miss Clea'll do good to get one flap-jack apiece. That's how come I'm stackin' 'em on our plates to start with."

Clea got up to find the butter and syrup, racking her brain for a way to get them to stop arguing.

"So," she said, "what else besides tracks do I need to study for my wilderness education?"

That worked like magic.

"Well, you gotta be able to ride fer hours at a time when you go huntin' wild horses," Buck said. "You cain't jist drive up to 'em in a pickup and snap a picture. So you gotta be tough."

"Gotta learn to shoot and hit what you shoot at," Teddy said. "There's animals out there and people, too, you might get crossways with."

"Wouldn't hurt nothin' to know how to rope," Buck said.

Clea shook her head as she set the table. "I don't have that kind of time," she said. "Not before the snow flies. Shooting and tracking will be plenty for now."

"Wal, and judgment," Buck said. "But I ain't sure that's somethin' that can be learned. Maybe you gotta be born with it."

"Gotta have a sense of direction," Ted said. "So's you won't get lost. At least not *entirely* lost."

"I'll get a compass," Clea said, and that made them laugh.

While they were eating the flapjacks, which turned out to be delicious, the men made plans for Clea's education and enlightenment. There were enough different subjects on the list to make her dizzy, not to mention the fact that she'd have a lot to learn about photography, too, if she had any hope of bringing in money from her efforts.

They finished the meal and started carrying the dirty dishes to the sink.

"You wash, I'll dry," Teddy said to Buck.

Clea shook her head. Already she was exhausted, even though she'd slept half the day. If she could learn skills for one-fourth of what they wanted her to do, it'd be a miracle. She could only hope that she wouldn't have to be an expert at every single thing in order to survive the winter.

The real challenge would be paying for everything she'd need. She needed to be alone to get a deep breath, assimilate all this information and plan.

"I'll take care of the dishes later," she said. "I know y'all probably have lots of work to do today."

"Keepin' your camp neat and in order is one o' the rules of survival," Teddy said. Judging by his tone, he was winding up for another lecture. "You gotta know where everything is all the time and not have clutter to trip over if you need to go after something in a hurry."

"I'll wash them as *soon* as y'all go on your way, I promise," she said. "Oh, something else I need from you two is leads on where to get hay for the winter and a good supply of firewood."

She wrote down the names they gave her while they went

to get their hats and jackets. Then, hesitating, she thought about the advice they'd given her. Shooting lessons had already been on her list before they got here. If she'd gone through all this hardship to save Ariel from Brock, she'd be nothing but an idiot to lose her to a bear.

Paying for lessons was hiring Jake, not accepting a favor from him. So she said, "And tell me Jake's cell number. I'll ask him about those shooting lessons."

They recited it in unison, beaming with relief.

"Yep," Ted said happily as she joined them. "You got good sense, girl. Learn to shoot from Jake, then fall in and ride with us, Clea, and a year from now you'll be as good a cowgirl as Montana ever sees nowadays."

Buck held the door open for them to go out ahead of him.

"There is a difference there," he said. "I'm sorry to say it, but none of you girls comin' up in this day and time can compare with the cowgirls we knew growin' up. When we was young. A lotta them girls was *cowboys*."

"But you'll be right up there with the best of what we've got now," Teddy said, like a promise. "Guaran-damn-teed."

She said, "I believe it. I can't imagine having any better teachers than you two renegades."

That tickled them, but they tried not to show it.

With a snort, Buck said, "Humph. Renegades."

Then he turned and gave her a devilish grin. "I reckon we might teach you something about throwing a long rope, too, if you wanta stick to yore old hoss-thievin' ways."

Clea laughed, shaking her head. How'd this joke get started, anyhow? They'd be shocked to the core if they found out it was the truth.

They were right. Everybody had to have help to learn skills they needed but didn't know.

And everybody, no matter how much they needed freedom and privacy, also needed a couple of friends.

She realized she couldn't stop smiling.

And every little girl who loved horses, at one age or another, wanted to grow up to be a cowgirl.

JAKE DROVE up to Clea's house in his own battered pickup and parked beside her shiny new one in the open area between the back of her house and her barn. The first thing he noticed was an old tub filled with yellow and purple flowers she'd put on the deck. Brightened up the whole place.

She came out of the door and ran down the steps, wearing a backpack and carrying her shotgun, ready to get down to business. Looking good. A quick thrill of desire ran through him—just from one quick glance.

He'd been thinking about her too much. He wished he'd never seen her in her tight breeches taking that strong-willed mare over those jumps.

Any man would be drawn to that. But even more than that picture in his mind—he did *not* intend to get sexually involved with her in any way—he'd been concentrating on trying to figure her out.

Really, his main interest in her was simple curiosity. That and helping her get the skills to be self-sufficient so he wouldn't have to spend his winter over here building her fires and digging her out of snowbanks.

Yep, that explained it. He always felt better around people he didn't know when he at least had them pegged as to what *kind* of people they were, and underneath that beautiful exterior Clea was more complicated than Tori, more contradictory than he'd first thought.

And now, here she was, jogging toward him with that shotgun, acting as confident as she had in the saddle, even though the last time she'd used it she'd done fifteen-thousand-dollars worth of damage.

"You ready to use that on some deer?" he called.

The surprise on her face made him grin as he went around to the passenger side where he'd put the target and the ammo. She walked up to him.

"I'm not going to shoot Bambi. Or his mother. Plus, I don't think most people use a shotgun to hunt deer."

"I'm thinking about when the deer start eating those new flowers instead of your trash."

She smiled. "I'll fire into the air to scare them off."

"I also give lessons in cleaning and dressing out game, in case you hit one by mistake."

Her wry grin told him that she did have a sense of humor.

"Well, thanks a lot for that reference to my past shooting skills. I won't be making any more of those mistakes after today, since I have my own shooting instructor."

Her own.

Remember that, Jake ol' man. You're one of the servants now. Just like you were the tough cowboy toy for Tori until the money man called her back.

"Hey," she said breezily, "I think I found the spot you were talking about down on the creek."

He turned to face her, the ammo in one hand and the target in the other.

Which was good, because he wanted to touch her. At least to brush away the hair blowing across her mouth.

Tight top again, pulled even tighter by the backpack. Fit her like a second skin, plus matched her eyes. Exactly the same shade of blue. Tight jeans, with cowboy boots this time. Battered, but very high-dollar, cowboy boots.

"Got your shootin' clothes on, I see," he said and then wanted to bite his tongue.

Way to go, Jake. Slightly familiar remark, coming from the help.

"You bet," she said. "Pretty soon I'll be able to shoot a dime off a fence post at thirty yards without breaking the bottle it was balanced on."

He shook his head. "Good thing I brought the target. Balancing dimes'd take so long you wouldn't get in twenty shots before dark."

He slipped the strap of the ammo bag over his shoulder.

Get the job done. Give her a shooting lesson. Then tell her goodbye and go home.

"Let's go see if you found the spot I was thinking about," he said and started walking at a good pace.

She fell in beside him and kept up easily.

"I brought some bottles of water and snacks," she said.

She'd surprised him again. He'd had water in the truck but forgot all about it. Evidently, just the sight of her had rattled him. Bad sign.

He flashed her a wry grin, "Sounds like you're expecting it to take a while before you hit the bull's-eye."

She scowled at him. "Enough," she said. "You need to be encouraging me instead of bringing up my past failures."

He raised his eyebrows. "There was more than one?"

"See? There you go again. Now tell me why you want to use that particular spot on the creek for our lesson."

"It has an earthen hillside to stand behind our target and catch our rounds and a good flat place for us to stand at different distances from across the creek."

"Sounds good."

She glanced curiously at the cast-iron target—a swinging tongue hanging from a top-rail set on two legs. "It's not very big."

He nodded. "So if you can learn to hit it, you're pretty much guaranteed to hit a bear."

"You're not including the fear factor," she said. "I might be shaking too hard."

"Not after Lesson Two," he said. "That's when we find some bears and practice defense against the real thing. That'll get you past the fear."

Her blue eyes widened and she stopped walking to stare at him. Then she laughed. "Good try," she said.

"What? Don't you think that'd help steady your aim?"

Her eyes darkened to a deeper blue.

"What would steady my aim would be Ariel in danger. She's the main reason I'm worried about bears."

She started walking again. "I mean, I certainly don't want one to attack *me,* of course, but I worry more about her out there in the barn and the turn-out lot. She's my buddy, and I love her more than any horse I ever had. Except for one."

Well, good. Maybe she'd tell him enough that he could get a handle on what kind of person she was. Maybe if he got her all figured out he could stop wondering about her.

"What horse was that?"

"Prince-the-Pony. My dad sold him."

"Your first pony?"

"Yes. And I didn't even know he was going to be sold until suddenly he was gone. I still haven't gotten over it. Do you have any idea how much a loss like that can hurt a kid?"

He gave her a long look.

"Well. *Do* you?"

"I lost every pet I had every year," he said. "Ranches always have animals running around, but my dad looked for a better ranch job all the time, so we moved every year. I lost my cats, dogs, goats *and* horses, my school and the place where I lived."

"So you got accustomed to it," she said flatly.

As if losing his whole world every year hadn't hurt him as much as losing one pony one time had hurt her. Yep. Everything was all about her. Like everything had always been about Tori.

"Yes, I got used to it," he snapped. "Everybody does, Clea. Loss is part of life. Everybody knows you lose your childhood pony."

"Maybe," she said hotly. "But not without being told in advance."

His scornful grunt echoed in his own ears. "Do you think my dad told us in advance before he tore up our lives? You think he didn't just walk in one day and tell us to start packing? You've been so protected all your life you don't know the world you're in."

"You don't know my world *or* my life," she said hotly. "Some people keep their childhood ponies out to pasture for the rest of his life. *Lots* of people do. Or they lend it to some other child—not sell it because it'll bring a good price."

"Maybe your dad needed the money."

"No way. He's always had tons."

"That's how he got it," Jake said. "Taking every good offer when it came along. The world runs on money. Haven't you noticed?"

"No," she said. "The world runs on control—most of which comes from money, I'll grant you—and it was a control thing for him to sell Prince. He's always controlled me."

She really did have a beautiful face, even when she was angry, which she was now. Remembering.

He waited. She was breathing hard and it wasn't from how fast they were walking.

"My therapist helped me realize that I thought Prince got sold because I hadn't been a good enough little girl. So I've been trying to be a very, very good girl ever since. Big mistake."

Shocked, he looked at her. "You thought your dad sold your pony not for the money, but to make you more obedient?"

She shrugged and shifted her shotgun to her other hand.

Jake shook his head. "I don't know. That's just life, Clea. People who can make money make it."

"Daddy knew it'd work that way on some level. I doubt it was a conscious one. He's just instinctively good at getting control."

"Money gives control, but it controls people, too," Jake said. "Like a habit does."

She nodded. "It can be a god, an obsession, a temptation, a goal. It's the main thing in the lives of lots of people."

"Yeah," he said.

"Like you," she said.

He whipped his head around to look at her. "*Me?* I've always just wanted adventure and challenge. New colts to break and new places to see."

"But you're working for Natural Bands for money, you said."

"Well, yeah..."

He snapped his mouth shut and walked faster. How'd she do that? How'd she go straight to the core of his dilemma? She didn't even know him.

Clea was looking at him, waiting for him to go on.

"Yeah," he said again. "Life's full of surprises."

They walked on in silence. She took a deep breath and seemed to relax.

Jake looked ahead. It wasn't much farther. Thank God.

Get this done. Work at your moneygrubbing. Get this over with and be a few dollars richer. Working for a dollar, just like a regular Joe.

A dollar to buy a place of his own, just like a regular Joe.

"So," she said, "you moved every year when you were a kid and you hated that, but you still are renting a place to live?"

Well, damn. Double damn.

He jerked his head around and stared at her. How'd they get on the subject of him and his life, anyhow? He wasn't going to answer such a nosy question.

But then he snapped, "I've bought a place. I just don't live there."

And could he ever, even after it was all paid for?

Well, if he could work a silly job like teaching this woman to shoot straight and like the one for Natural Bands for money, he could do anything. Even something he'd never thought he could do, like settle down in one place and give up his wandering ways.

She must've decided that she'd crossed a line, or else she got bored with talking about him, because she didn't say any more until they reached the spot on the creek. Neither did he. The less said between them the better. He couldn't tell her anything without having it used against him.

The sun was coming through the red and yellow leaves, spangling the creek. The creek was chattering, the water so clear a person could see every rock in its bed. It was fall, a glorious fall. The wind was more of a breeze today, which was a pleasant change, and it carried a crisp edge of promise.

He hadn't even been aware of any of that before. He hadn't seen or heard anything, really, except Clea, and she'd stirred his mind so much a bear could've crossed the trail ahead of them and he wouldn't have seen it.

He shook his head to clear it. It'd been months before he and Tori had shared any confidences. Tori never had been able to see straight into him like Clea had done.

He took off the ammo bag and set it on a flat rock.

"I'll set up the target over there," he said, gesturing at a spot across the creek. "Wouldn't want you to get your feet wet."

She gave him a smiling glance as she laid the gun beside the ammo bag and unzipped it.

"You're saying I'm too clumsy to walk on those rocks?"

That was more like it. Lighthearted banter.

But he didn't let himself really smile back. Keep it business.

When he had the target placed where he wanted, he crossed the creek again and showed her how to load the slugs into her shotgun, making sure that their hands didn't touch any more than necessary. All of that went fine and they both focused on Clea's learning what she needed to know.

"I saw something on the Internet about a pistol some people carry for bears," she said as they both straightened up and she lifted the gun to her shoulder.

Jake went to stand right behind her. "Probably the .454," he said, his tone crisp and efficient. Distant. That's right. Keep it that way. "Lots of recoil, though, and too heavy for a woman to carry."

He put his hand on the elbow of her shooting arm to lower it just a hair and reached around her with the other to slide her left hand back some on the barrel. Her scent was like some exotic drug to his senses—lemony flowers of paradise.

He was definitely losing his mind. Her hand was soft and small and warm and…in no hurry for him to move his away.

He closed his arms tighter around her to use both arms to sight in the gun.

"And I already have the shotgun."

Did he hear a little catch in her breath, or did he imagine it?

He had to think for a second to remember what she'd just said.

"Right. It's best for you. These slugs're so heavy they'll do the job."

He bent his head to get her line of sight and that put his face beside hers. Nearly touching. He wanted them to touch. Wanted to feel his skin against hers.

She'd tied back her hair but his cheek brushed her temple and he felt the silkiness. He wanted to set it free.

"I read that the Forest Service recommends pepper spray over any kind of gun." She spoke very softly in a slightly absentminded way.

And yes, she did have a little catch in her voice. He forced himself to focus. "Yeah," he said, pulling the gun a little to the inside. "But you have to be within fifteen to thirty feet of the bear for pepper spray to work."

She shifted and her butt brushed against him. He felt a quick response in his groin. His chest curved around her shoulders and sharp regret sliced through him. He wanted to be really *holding* her.

"Oooh," she said. "Talk about *fear* at fifteen feet! I'd be lucky to hold still enough to press the button."

He didn't say anything. Then he gathered the sense of the conversation again. "Yeah," he said, his voice coming out low and rough.

"Jake."

She turned her head to drown him in her blue, blue eyes. Her mouth was so close he could feel her breath on his lips.

"Look, I'm not sure what's wrong," she said. "I'm sorry if I said something wrong—I didn't mean to imply that you didn't hurt when you lost your pets…"

He tried not to listen to the sweet sincerity in her voice, tried to hold on to his resentment, tried to look up, look away, tried to drop his arms and step back.

But here she was, encircled by his arms, looking into his eyes as if she could see straight through to his soul.

So all he could do was kiss the rest of her words away.

CHAPTER SEVEN

LIFE'S FULL of surprises.

Such as the shy cowboy who was really as bold as a bandit.

Then that thought was gone, lost with Clea's mind in Jake's hot kiss. It replaced her feelings, too, with its own deep heat and rousing, sweet shock.

Shock that opened her whole body to him entirely by instinct, hungry—ravenous—in the space of one breath. A shiver ran through her as he took the whole weight of the gun from her hands. She turned in his arms to face him completely, while he laid it down on the rock behind her.

His hands had the same melting heat as his mouth. They held her by the shoulders as if to keep her from getting away and burned the strength of his long fingers into her skin.

She ran her hands up the back of his neck and into his hair to make sure he stayed right where he was, too, and twined her tongue with his. She looped her arms around his strong neck and melted against him. He was destroying her defenses, taking the strength from her legs, but not from her mouth. It was begging him, imploring him to keep on doing what he was doing.

He answered her with long, throbbing caresses of his tongue. He drew the very life out of her and then poured it back in, while his hands began to wander, rubbing her shoulder blades, exploring the valley of her spine. He wrapped one arm around her rib cage and pulled her hard against him, her breasts straining against his broad chest.

The muscles of his forearm flexed against her flesh through the thin shirt, another kind of power he possessed. She'd never been kissed by a man like this.

Muscle power. Sexual power. She absorbed the heat from both, desperately, as if he'd found her just before she froze to death.

Yes. Desperate she was. She'd never known it until now, this minute. Ravenous. For more. More of *this*.

She pressed closer still. More closeness. She needed intimacy, sex.

Even more.

His hands shaped her body, then cupped her bottom to bring her against his hardness.

She wanted—needed—everything.

What she really needed was love.

The thought raced through her, almost as much of a shock as his kiss. It scared her.

She wasn't steady enough to look for love or to take it if she found it. Her real self was still too new, too needy.

Needy meant vulnerable. After such a long time and so much heartache, hadn't she finally learned that need was the root of all her troubles?

She had to remember that. She had to be stronger than that so she wouldn't bring on new troubles. Besides, her real self also knew that love was probably nothing but an illusion.

She tore her mouth free.

Yet he didn't loosen his hold on her at all. He let his heavy-lidded eyes drift sensually over her face as if he didn't want ever to look at anything else.

"Jake."

Her lips felt swollen, tingling with sensation, stiff with wanting to kiss him again. And again. More. She needed more. More than she'd ever needed anything in her life.

"Mmm?"

"I...I uh...we have to...stop...this. It's too much..."

He gave her a slow smile she'd never seen before. A smile that made her knees go even weaker. It was a good thing his arm was holding her up.

She stiffened her legs and pulled back. He let her go.

But not with his eyes, not with that green gaze that stayed on her face.

"Tell the truth," he drawled. "It'd take a whole lot more than one kiss to be too much."

She felt her eyes flare wide. He knew how much she'd wanted him, how drawn to him she'd felt, how truly needy she was.

Her lips parted to deny it, but then she couldn't say a word.

There was a world of wanting in his eyes. He knew exactly what she was feeling and he was feeling the same.

Bold as a bandit and a passionate man.

That was bound to be a dangerous combination.

JAKE DID the chores by himself for the third time that week. He might as well have kept on living here with Buck and Teddy because he seemed to spend all his waking time at their place, anyhow. Most of it was riding, but if he kept on doing their chores, too, he was doing nothing but wasting gasoline driving back and forth to his cabin.

Which was a bad place to be.

No, alone was the worst place to be. Alone with his thoughts. *That* was why he'd been looking for the old guys to drive in from town—not so they'd do their share of the chores, but because he wanted them to *talk* to him.

Surely not! Unbelievable. How could it be, when all he usually wanted was to make them *stop* talking?

Jake threw the last flake of hay to the last waiting horse as the truth hit him hard: he wasn't hanging out over here for any other reason except distraction from thinking about Clea. And maybe a little news about her.

It'd only been a couple of days and *he* was wanting to call *her* about another shooting lesson.

You'd better get a handle on it right now, Hawthorne. No way do you need another Tori in your life.

He shook his head, walked to the open doorway and forced himself to focus on the here and now. On the beauty.

The air crinkling cool in his lungs, the sun coloring the sky and the valley as it began its drop toward the mountains, the wind dying down, the horses settling in for the night. Nothing like horses crunching slowly on their sweet feed and snuffling in their hay, sighing a little and stamping once in a while to make it seem that everything would be all right.

And for them, right now, it was.

People needed to take more of a horse's view of life. That's what he usually did, what he'd done all his life. He'd always really lived each day instead of thinking into the future. He'd learned to do that as a very little kid when he realized the future meant a move nearly every year.

But now, foolishly, he was stuck in the past. At the creek, at the shooting lesson. Remembering the kiss that had blown him away.

And thinking about the contradictory woman he couldn't quite fit into the slot he'd thought was hers. After that kiss, they'd both thrown themselves into getting down to business. Clea had worked as hard as anybody could, sighting and firing and holding up the shotgun until her arms had been shaking. She'd reminded him of his sister Elle, for sure. Full of grit and determination and fire in the belly.

Come to think of it, he and Clea had both worked very hard—at not kissing each other again.

He'd completely lost his old habit of staying in the present. If it wasn't the past, he was thinking about the future. Ever since he bought his place he'd been thinking about the future.

Another way that his desperation to accumulate money was poisoning his life.

Past, future, either one could drive a man crazy. Thing to do was just what the horses did. Get the very most out of the present moment.

Go back to what he'd learned as a five-year-old. He couldn't take his secret hideouts, his swimming holes and his pets with him and he couldn't stay with them. He couldn't *keep* anything. So best bet was to wring the most out of everything while he had it.

What he used to do was enjoy the day, every day. He'd work hard and then really relax when he rested. He'd use his muscles and feel the pleasure of his strength; he'd feel the comfort when good, hot food hit his belly.

Now he wasn't even aware of what he was doing half the time.

What'd happened to him? He didn't even know what he'd eaten for lunch today and he certainly hadn't been aware of any pleasure or comfort it brought him.

He'd been too busy thinking and planning ahead, and too busy remembering a kiss with a woman he shouldn't touch with a ten-foot pole.

Yes, it was the land purchase that'd started this change in him.

Maybe he wasn't meant to be a landowner. Maybe gathering up a lot of money and spending it on a place of his own wasn't worth the trouble, if it sucked all the living out of life. He'd been a happy man roaming all over the West all these years. Maybe, like his dad, he was meant to wander.

Her words still rang in his ears. You moved every year as a kid and you hated it, but you're still renting a place to live?

None of her business. He should've either told her that or else something meaningless like, *I guess it got to be a habit.*

Normally, he would never have been defensive enough to say he'd bought a place. And he had done so this time, because he'd thought he heard a trace of condescension in her voice, and he'd hated it.

You sure you weren't trying to let her know that you have something to offer a woman? The way Tori's ex-husband had something to offer her?

Jake hated the thought that Tori's leaving him was affecting his behavior a year later, but it was probably true. Really though, what was driving him crazy enough right now to wish Buck and Teddy would come home and talk to him was this stupid obsession with wanting Clea in his arms again.

To feel her, to breathe her in, to taste her.

Buck's old rattletrap truck was still gone. Jake turned around and gave the barn one last look, then walked on down to the house. He'd get a Coke or something and wait for the old guys to come in.

They might have stopped at Clea's on their way home. Teddy and Buck liked excitement as much as two little kids, and they thought it was exciting to hang out with a pretty woman and teach her to be a cowgirl and show her what all they could do. Well, they were right. But they ought to be old enough to know that showing off for a pretty woman was a prime path to trouble.

Jake grinned, imagining them at that moment, helping Clea swing a rope or build a fire. They'd give her a challenge, that was for sure, despite the fact she was well...he'd guess her age to be in her late twenties...so she was nearly fifty years younger than Buck and Teddy.

He only hoped, when he was their age, he'd be able to ride as hard all day long as they could.

What he really hoped was that when he was their age he'd laugh and joke and be as happy to be alive as they were.

Fat chance of that, Hawthorne. You don't exactly bounce back from disappointments. Life's full of them.

He felt his grin widen because—no, in spite of the fact—that was true, and then he reached up to stretch out his shoulders as he walked.

The phone was ringing when he opened the door. He first thought he'd ignore it. After all, he didn't live here.

But Buck and Teddy might've driven off into a ditch somewhere, so he'd have to answer it.

In fact, knowing them, they could have even gotten on a couple of broncs and let themselves get thrown over the moon and into the emergency room.

Or it could be Celeste. He'd left the cell phone she got him at home because half the time it didn't have a signal anyhow.

Then he finally had a positive thought. Maybe it was Larry, the mechanic, saying the truck was ready.

He picked up. "Jake Hawthorne."

"Hey, Jake. This is Carl Baker. What's going on out there on Fire Creek?"

A couple of times, the sheriff had called to ask him and Buck and Teddy to keep an eye open for a poacher or for unauthorized campers in the wild-horse sanctuary, or maybe for some cattle that had strayed.

"Nothin' much," Jake said, "unless you know something I don't."

"Well, there just might be somethin' goin' on out there that you'll like. Got a job for you, if you want it. Pays good and it's right down your alley."

"What's the deal?"

"You seen a woman with a horse, rented a spot out there on the Elkhorn somewhere? Name of Mathison?"

"Yeah."

"What's that horse look like?"

"You're looking for the *horse?*"

"The owner is."

Stunned, Jake took that in. "She's not the owner?"

As the words left his mouth, he remembered the way Clea had gone all tense that day when she was backing her rig down his driveway and the big black mare appeared at the fence. Unlike most proud horse owners, she had *not* wanted to talk about her. Now he knew why.

Disappointment stabbed him. And a sharp hurt. Damn it—she hadn't been honest with him. Therefore she shouldn't have kissed him like that.

You're losin' it, Jake.

No, it has nothin' to do with the kiss. I just hate crooked people, that's all.

"Not according to the papers I just got through my fax machine."

"Whose horse is it?"

"Registered to a Mr. Brock Burlingame down in Texas. Man works for him told me on the phone that Mr. Burlingame is Ms. Mathison's ex-husband. Looks like she took back her maiden name before she stole the horse outta his barn."

Jake stared at the juniper tree just outside the window. Ex-husband. So that was the sugar daddy who'd paid for all that gloss and gleam. *And* that mare. He didn't know anything about jumpers, but he knew good horseflesh when he saw it, and that mare would bring some bucks.

A horse thief. Damn it all. There was no kind of crime lower.

Another ex-wife still messin' with her ex-husband's mind. Just exactly what he needed.

Yet he couldn't help wanting details.

"How'd he find her, way up here?"

"Hired a P.I. that must've bribed somebody in the cell-phone business, because that's how they got a line on her. She's got a new one in this 406 area code. Thought her ex wouldn't find it, I guess, since nobody knew where she was headed."

"So if you're going to arrest her, why're you calling me?"

"Mr. B. basically wants the horse. Doesn't want to press charges, but damned sure will if he can't get the mare. Doesn't want the scandal of an ex-wife who's a runaway and a horse thief. Thinks it'd make him look bad."

Baker paused and took a sip of something—coffee, no doubt. He had a well-known habit of carrying a mug of it with him all day long. Cold, hot, fresh or stale, that made no difference.

"You ask me? I think the guy might be just a little embarrassed that the little woman put one over on him and don't want folks laughin' about it."

"Sheriff, what's all this got to do with me?"

"Or me," Carl Baker said wearily. "I've got seventy-five-thousand square miles to patrol and three men to do it with. I've got meth labs and poachers and cattle rustlers and at least one arsonist. I don't have the manpower to chase down stolen horses and haul 'em back to their rightful owners."

Jake waited.

"Damn sure wish I did, though," the sheriff said. "This Texas dude's offering fifty grand for the job."

Fifty grand?

A little chill ran through Jake. Fifty thousand dollars would knock a huge hole in his debt.

Maybe this was a sign he *was* meant to be a landowner, after all.

"Insane," Jake said. "How much is the mare worth?"

"I get the idea that don't matter," Baker said. "Evidently it was a pretty nasty divorce and she took the horse for revenge. Plus, like I say, he's humiliated. He aims to get that mare back if it costs him the farm."

"And you want me..."

"To go get the mare—I'll deputize you—and haul her to Texas. Upon arrival, you will be paid a cashier's check for fifty big ones. Or cash money, if you prefer."

Jake stared out at the tree some more but what he saw was Clea, up on Ariel, flowing like water over those jumps. It wasn't her horse?

Not if the registration papers said it wasn't. Not even if she and the mare became one creature when they went over a jump.

I've never loved a horse like I love Ariel....

He did feel sorry for her.

But how childish and stupid was it to steal a horse to get back at her ex-husband? *That* was why she was in Montana, planning to spend the winter.

Hiding the horse. Playing games. She was trying to spend the winter in Montana instead of in jail. Nothing honest about her.

Maybe she'd turned in his arms and looked at him like she'd done so she'd have a protector for her and her horse. And then in the spring, she and her ex would kiss and make up and he'd buy her a new rig and a new house to come back to.

"Jake, I don't get paid to work for out-of-state millionaires. You want the job or don't you?"

Why wouldn't he? Fifty thousand for three or four days' work? And it was perfect timing. He wasn't doing anything for Celeste right now.

Clea did love the mare, he'd seen that with his own eyes....

Just the fact that you're hesitatin', boy, is proof she's gettin' under your skin. You may not know what you need for the rest of your life, but you sure as hell do know what you don't need.

This is meant to be. Take her horse back to her ex-husband and she'll cut you off at the knees. You won't even have to worry about resisting temptation.

Plus, the law was the law.

Nobody should have his horse stolen from him.

"Hawthorne? You there?"

"Yeah."

"Whaddya say?"

Fifty thousand. Then only ten thousand more and he could pay off his land. He'd clear that and more from Celeste by the end of the season. Another couple of months.

If he took this job, he could start out the new year owning his own home free and clear. He'd have a piece of his dream: a sweet, beautiful place of his own and no debt. His horse business would be well on its way to reality.

He didn't owe Clea one damned thing.

"Swear me in," he said.

IT TOOK half the morning to go into town for the paperwork at the sheriff's office and to have his truck serviced and a new tire put on his trailer, a three-horse that had seen many a mile.

It'd be a comedown for the big black mare compared to Clea's rig, and she wouldn't have air-ride or air-conditioning. But it'd get her back home to Texas.

If he called Celeste and told her what he was doing, she'd tell him to take the big trailer with all the bells and whistles. But this was his deal and he wanted to keep it that way. A smaller trailer would be better for his truck to pull anyhow.

He'd wanted to be on the road south by ten o'clock, but it was closer to noon by the time Jake drove up into Clea's yard and cut the motor. The big black mare was in the turn-out pen by the barn, running around with her head up, all excited about something.

Buck and Teddy had told him Clea was a photographer, so she probably was working at that and not riding every day. Too much high-powered feed and not enough exercise made a lot of show horses hyper. Clea ought to know that, being that she was a hotshot rider of jumping horses and thought he couldn't ride a green colt and carry a paper sack at the same time.

Maybe Ariel had already let off enough steam that she wouldn't kick the trailer all the way to Texas.

As he opened the door and got out of the truck, the mare trotted with her head up to the far corner of the pen and strained her neck over as far as she could, looking into the distance beyond the cabin's backyard. Nostrils flaring, she danced in place and called out, loud and long. As if to another horse.

Well, she'd better be saying goodbye to whatever it was. Some scent on the wind, no doubt. The wind was plenty high today—he'd fought it ever since he turned off the highway.

Jake hesitated a moment to choose front door or back, decided on back and started around the house.

"Clea," he called. "It's Jake. Are you home?"

He hoped to hell she was so he could tell her what he was

doing in person. Her truck was here. He'd feel like some kind of a coward to leave such bad news in a note on the door.

But if she did find a note on her door instead of a horse in the pen, it shouldn't be too much shock to her. After all, she did know the horse was stolen.

Jake made a disgusted sound and stomped up the steps to the deck. It made him mad every time he thought about her being a horse thief and then acting so innocent and helpless and pitiful. And sexy.

As if she owes you or Buck or Teddy the secrets of her life. Only because she happens to be your neighbor. Or only because she kissed you. Get a grip, Hawthorne.

"Clea!"

But the sound of her name was lost in the high, rolling bugle of a horse's voice and it wasn't the mare's.

It cut the morning in two. It swiveled Jake around on the heel of one boot and drew him back down the steps like he could do something. His gut knew what was going on before his head did.

Then the horse was just there in the yard, bursting like a huge bright flower out of the gray-blue shadows of the trees, coming at a high gallop.

Montana Red.

Jake had both feet on the ground and running—toward the mare, across the yard, when he looked, really looked at his rival.

The first clear sight of the stallion stopped the man in his tracks.

Eyes fixed on his prize, lip lifted, teeth bare and ears pinned, Montana Red was here to get the girl.

Deep in the back of Jake's mind, the stories stirred. Some said this horse was a man-fighter. He sure didn't spook at being this close, which most wild horses would've done.

Ariel still ran the fence, calling for him, but when he got

to it, she stood for a minute, dancing and trembling, pulling back, then sticking her head over the fence again. Red touched muzzles with her, spoke to her, then thrust his head over and bit her on the neck.

She screamed, whirled on the front end and kicked the fence hard enough to knock a pole loose as she raced to the opposite side of the pen. He ran, too, up and down the fence, demanding her return.

From a flat-footed stop, the mare headed back like a rocket. Jake saw the intention to jump just before she started to rise. She flew over the fence like a great, black bird.

Montana Red bit her on the rump as her feet touched the ground and she whirled in a circle once. Then she straightened out and he drove her ahead of him, their hooves pounding hammers on the ground, their legs flashing wings carrying them into open spaces. The mare was fast and with his teeth, Montana Red made her even faster.

They vanished before Jake could draw a whole breath, Ariel's blackness drawing Red's bright sunlight into the shadows of the trees like night falling. After that was the drum of beating hooves and then nothing.

They were down the slope and gone so fast it seemed they were never here at all.

But the air still trembled with so much testosterone it roused Jake's own. He could hear his own heart beating. The adrenaline pumping into his veins made a lightness in his head as if he too were running fast across a ridge that rose high against the sky.

The magnificent wildness was *in* his head. It would be etched on the backs of his eyelids and surging in his blood, living in his bones every time he thought about this sight for the rest of his days.

It took another minute for him to come back to earth. He had gained a memory that most people would never have, but it had cost him.

Fifty thousand dollars. He turned and ran for his truck.

CHAPTER EIGHT

CLEA RAN out onto the deck, screaming for Ariel, knowing how useless it was even as she opened her mouth. She bolted down the steps then, screaming for Jake to stop, which was just as stupid as yelling at the mare.

He had backed his truck and trailer out into the road just in the few seconds it'd taken for her to run down the stairs, through the house and out into the yard. But he had seen what happened. From the loft, she'd seen him see it.

The least he could do was stay and tell her whose stud horse that was so she'd know where to go get her mare. She was shaking all over, she was so mad. And scared.

The last thing Ariel needed was to get bred by somebody's backyard stud. Somebody who wasn't even responsible enough to build decent facilities that could contain a stallion.

That was unforgivable. She would sue, she thought, as she ran to the barn for her whip and a rope. Absolutely, if Ariel were hurt or with foal, either one, she would sue the stallion's owner.

Would it make any difference that her hussy of a mare had jumped the fence to him and he hadn't come into her pen? No, it shouldn't. But she could wring Ariel's neck just the same.

Maybe she could stop it. Maybe it hadn't happened yet.

Fat chance of that. She ran in the direction the horses had gone, afraid that was as useless as her screaming had been but running anyway, thankful that she'd put on her sneakers when she got out of the shower, thankful that she'd run at least three miles a day for the past year. Maybe she could whip him off her if they'd stopped anywhere near.

There weren't many stallions who would attack a person, but she didn't think that would hold true when they were in the throes of passion. It was too late, it must be too late. If he were going to breed Ariel now, he would've already done it. Wouldn't he?

Fury rose in her throat with the thought. Ariel had never had a foal. She was seven years old and sometimes it was hard for an older mare to have a first foal. What if this idiot horse bred her, she caught, and having the baby killed her?

Clea wrenched her mind from such morbidity and kept running.

This was a perfect example of somebody keeping a stud horse who didn't know what they were doing. A man, no doubt, who felt like a bigger man somehow because he owned a stud. She'd never understood that, but she'd seen it more than once. They lived vicariously through their horses or something. She would like to just wring his neck, as well as Ariel's.

For a second, as she ran through the trees where the horses had gone, her mind tried to escape this horror. What was Jake doing here, anyway? Could he possibly have come for still more money for the truck repairs? Or to suggest another shooting lesson?

Who cared? Ariel was gone.

And after all Clea had gone through to get her back! To save her from being sold to a bad person! Ungrateful wretch that she was!

Damn! If Brock knew what had happened, he'd be laughing his head off.

She emerged from the trees into a meadow that sloped

steeply down to a nearly dry creek. On the other side of the rocky creek bed, an even steeper hill started another bench of mountains backed by another and then another.

Clea stopped in her tracks, gasping for breath, and stared.

There they were, the horses, just leaving the creek bed and starting up the big hill, heading for the top at an angle that let them climb faster, and it wasn't just the red stallion and Ariel. There were six, maybe seven, other mares and some foals. The red stud was driving them all, with his head down, nipping and biting, rounding them up from behind, keeping them together as they ran.

She planted the stock of her whip on the ground and swore.

It had to be a wild bunch. In the research she'd done on photographing them, she'd read about how there was always a lead mare—which would be that white one out in front—and that the stud horse stayed behind so he'd be between his harem and danger, and so he could keep them together and moving.

What other but a wild stallion would be running amok through the countryside with a whole harem? The answer hit her like a blow. Montana Red? The notorious Montana Red who broke down pole pens to steal domestic mares?

Well, with Clea's girl he didn't have to. She'd always been an incorrigible hussy when she was in heat.

Save her from Brock and lose her to a *wild stallion.* What an irony.

The horses were growing smaller and smaller against the hillside, climbing higher and higher by the minute in the fading light. Soon they'd be around those big rocks and gone. Ariel *was* gone.

And she would regret her slutty ways. She had no clue what she was getting herself into. She would break a leg running on rocks. She'd starve eating only grass and leaves. She'd get caught by a cougar. She'd start fighting Montana Red's domination, and he'd kill her.

Clea turned and ran for the house. She'd havc to have another horse to go after them.

Even if there were some roads in the wild-horse refuge, she'd never get close except on horseback. The Natural Bands people were the ones she should sue. If they were going to protect wild horses, they ought to protect the neighbors *from* the wild horses.

Somebody would help her get her horse back. There were agencies responsible for the land and another for the forest and a wilderness something or other. Plus there were sheriff's deputies and emergency people who fought wildfires and all kinds of divisions of the government who had some jurisdiction out here in the boonies. She knew there was a National Park Service, but it was the Natural Bands people who owned the refuge. Buck and Teddy could tell her the number of that Celeste, or whoever it was who managed the wild horses.

The one person she would not call was Jake.

He'd seen what happened and rushed away—hopefully to try to get Ariel back. If that wasn't the reason, she certainly wouldn't ask him for neighborly help. Not ever.

In fact, now that she thought about it, she hoped he wasn't out looking for the mare. If he was, it was only for some nefarious reason. Jake Hawthorne wouldn't be going to all that trouble because he empathized with Clea's feelings.

No way. Not if he could kiss her with a kiss so hot it melted the taste of him into her lips forever and then never call her again.

CLEA DROVE up to Teddy and Buck's cabin and then past it to the barn, searching as she went for any sign of their whereabouts. That light-headed feeling of disconnect was threatening her—the one that the counselor had said was part of the panic attack she'd had the first night she'd spent alone when she'd left Brock—but she was beating it back.

She didn't have time for that. This was an emergency more important than any she'd ever faced. Except for the night of her mother's fatal heart attack, when she hadn't known anything about it until the ambulance came screaming up to the door. At least she'd had Daddy to handle that. Now she was the one in charge.

Finally, through the open door, she caught a glimpse of Buck pushing a wheelbarrow down the barn aisle. She slammed on the brakes, pulled up in front of the barn and parked.

By the time she got the motor turned off, herself out onto the ground, and the door slammed, Buck and Teddy were both coming to see what she wanted.

She blurted, "My mare just got stolen by a red stud. I think it might've been Montana Red."

"Jake said it was," Buck said. "He seen it."

"I know he did!" she cried. "I couldn't believe he ran off like that."

"He was in a hurry 'cause he's gone after her," Teddy said. "Come roarin' in here and saddled a good colt and we helped him pack his saddlebags. Didn't stay thirty minutes. He means business."

That news shocked Clea into silence. Then she said, "Why? Does he think I'll pay him or what?"

She tried to figure it out. Was Jake doing this for *her?* For no pay? Because she'd told him how much she loved her mare?

Clea, do not lose your mind along with your mare. This is real life, remember?

"I came down here to borrow a horse because I'm going

after her myself. Jake can't touch her, anyhow. She's really difficult with people she doesn't know."

They stared at her, seemingly unable to absorb what she'd said.

Buck recovered first. "Now, Clea," he said, in the pure voice of reason, "this is one of them cowgirl things where you'd need a little coachin' before goin' off on a wild hair all by your lonesome."

"Yeah," Teddy echoed. "Think for a minute. You seen Red?"

She nodded.

"Well, then, how're you gonna get your mare away from him? He ain't exactly prone to givin' back what he took. And he outweighs you by about a thousand pounds."

"And how you gonna find him?" Buck said. "His range covers several-hundred square miles."

"I've got to get her back before she gets killed or permanently lamed," she said.

They nodded. They waited for her to say something more.

"In fact, she's such a diva she probably won't put up with his bossing for long. She's likely to fight back and then he'll kill her."

"Jake'll find her," Buck said.

The two old men exchanged a glance she couldn't read.

"I'm not *letting* him get her, even if he could catch her. I don't want to be obligated to him. I know I don't know how to find her, but I do know if y'all will help me, I'll go get her myself. Ariel will come to me and she won't to anybody else."

They shook their heads at the same time.

"Don't even think about it," Teddy said. "That's some rough country and some wily stud horse you're talkin' about. You ain't up to it."

"Jake's probably thinking I'll pay him," she said, sounding nasty and hateful, even to herself. "He thinks I have a lot of money and that I can write him another check for fifteen thousand dollars for a big reward, but I can't."

There went that glance again. They were consulting each other. But about what? Did they know that was Jake's motive?

"Go with me," she said. "When we get her back, I'll find a job and pay y'all a good wage—more than Natural Bands pays. I know you two know how to catch mustangs."

This time, they looked at each other for a long time. It seemed forever to Clea.

"We'll go," Buck said, at last. "But you better stay here. Somebody'll have to do our chores."

Clea straightened up. "Find somebody. I'll pay for that, too, but *I'm* going or y'all don't get paid."

They stared at her, then looked at each other while she held her breath.

She shouldn't have said that. She couldn't hold to it. She had to take every chance to find Ariel.

If they wouldn't take her, then she had to go by herself and try to figure out how to survive. She'd been camping before. She'd try to remember what the outfitter and his helper had done and imitate that.

She had to. She couldn't possibly sit around worrying or she'd lose her mind.

But no. That outfitter had carried some kind of a stove around and he'd had pack mules and....

These two had to go with her.

"What was all that big talk about y'all going to make a cowgirl out of me? Was that nothing but a lot of hot air? A brag?"

They looked at her. Buck shrugged and raised his shaggy eyebrows again as if to say she had a point there.

"If you're so hot to get on the trail, how come it took you an hour and more to get down here to hire your help?" he asked.

"I ran after them on foot for quite a way," she said. "And then I was winded and had to walk back."

She didn't tell them that when she'd gotten back to the cabin she'd looked online for the numbers of the Forest Service and the Bureau of Land Management and the sheriff only to realize while dialing the first one that calling in any kind of authority was a bad idea. Chances were slim that her name or the description of the horse would ever come to the notice of any Texas official Brock might've alerted, but who knew? Why take chances when Teddy and Buck, the old mustangers, were already here and teaching her to be a cowgirl?

She looked from one of them to the other.

"So," she said. "What's it gonna be? You two are mustangers. That means you *are* in the horse-recovery business. Do you want me to call around and find two or three other guys who know how to catch wild horses? A couple of cowboys who maybe aren't, as we say in Texas, all hat and no cattle?"

The looks that came over their faces sent relief flooding through her.

"We ride at first light," Buck said. "You go home, get your warmest clothes you brought up here from Texas, and your most comfortable saddle. Jake thinks he can git this done in a couple of days, but I dunno. We'll take a pack horse and plenty of grub."

"Otherwise I ain't goin'," Teddy said. "I'm hungry right now."

Buck ignored him and kept his eyes on Clea as if to make sure she was getting her orders.

"Git your stuff and then get your butt back down here and learn to make a pack."

"It's hot," she said. "I don't need my warmest clothes."

"The weather's gonna change," Buck said.

"I haven't heard that."

"Neither have I, but it is. Git your long johns."

THEY RODE and rode, and with every mile, Clea felt more aware of the wind, the dust, the shades of green of the juniper and sage. The buff of the dry land and the blue of the sky. But mostly of the distance.

The vastness of the earth and sky pulled her in, as it had from that very first drive in Montana, but now its power made her throat go dry and the back of her neck prickle. Any minute now, her hair might stand on end.

This enormity was about to swallow her up. Just as it must've swallowed her mare. They'd been riding since daylight and now it was two o'clock in the afternoon, and they had not found the slightest trace of either Ariel or Jake.

When they rode up over still another ridge and looked out into mile after mile after mile of more of the same—except that the hills were getting steeper and their rocky bluffs added stripes of red and ochre in front of the blue mountains that were coming closer—she felt a stab of despair.

Buck and Teddy had been quiet for so long, they must be feeling hopeless, too. She couldn't stand it. She stopped her horse.

"We've gone the wrong way, haven't we? Jake must've found their tracks and that's what we should've—"

"Montana Red will go back to his range and we're on it right now," Buck said.

The careless unconcern in his voice made her feel a little better.

"Well, why didn't you say so? I was about to give up."

Clea grabbed her binoculars and started looking at the valley below.

Buck bent from his saddle and spit some tobacco juice on the ground.

"You young'uns think you oughtta get ever'thing you want *right now,*" he said. "Well, pull yore hat down tight, Miss Clea, and grab a deeper seat in yore saddle because his range covers a whole lotta square miles. You ain't done ridin' yet, and you better not even *think* about sayin' another word about givin' up."

Just the words going into her ears made her legs scream to straighten out and her tired bottom beg to dismount and walk around. But they stiffened her spine and stirred up her courage, too.

The wind picked up, and Clea felt a hint of coolness touch her face.

"I think I might even smell rain," Buck muttered to himself. Then he said, "Whoa. Let's move on down that way now, right along there where we've got them trees for cover. I thought I seen somethin'."

Clea and Teddy followed him along the scraggly line of trees, staying behind them so as not to be silhouetted on the high ground. After they'd walked their mounts to the end of the cover, they stopped. Clea tried to see what Buck was seeing.

"Yep," Teddy said. "I see it."

"Where?" she said. "What is it?"

All day, she'd been amazed at what was there in the distance every single time that she couldn't see at first. Sometimes she never could see whatever Buck and Teddy were talking about.

"West end of the valley," Buck said. "See there? Up on that little rise. Might be a small band of horses."

"All I see is a cloud of dust," she said.

She stood up in her stirrups to give her bottom a break while she looked some more.

"Wait a minute," Buck said. "They're just millin' around a little. Now, Clea, remember that from a long way off, too far to tell a cow from a horse, if it looks sorta square and boxy, it's a cow critter. Rounded lookin', it's a horse."

"Or a round bale," she said dryly.

He chuckled. "Most times hay don't have legs."

"I'd probably not be able to see any legs, anyway."

She kept staring through the binoculars, trying so hard her eyes watered.

"It jist takes time to get your long-distance eyes on," Teddy said soothingly. "Sorta like getting your sea legs if you was on the ocean."

Finally she saw that the blur was indeed a small bunch of horses. Or she thought she did. She wasn't quite sure if the shape was round. Or if she was seeing anything but rocks.

Damn! If she didn't get better at this she was going to have to get her eyes examined.

"It's a harem band, all right," Buck said. "Let's get closer so we can see if it's Ol' Red or not."

Clea dropped back into the saddle, kissed to the gelding they'd loaned her, a roan they called Freckles, and started down the slope.

"Naw, naw," Buck said. "Come on back here, Clea. We better ride the back side of this ridge."

"Don't wanta spook 'em," Teddy said with a smile as she turned her horse around to come to them.

She held her head up and tried not to show her embarrassment.

"I really did hear y'all this morning when you told me about getting close enough to see without scaring them away," she said. "I just forgot to think for a minute."

"Aw, you didn't make no mistake," Teddy said. "We ain't

close enough to spook 'em right now and we're downwind, anyhow."

"Jist wanta give you a little lesson in stalkin'," Buck said.

They were being so kind to her, Clea concluded that her face must be red.

How they could tell under the dust she must've accumulated on her sweat, she didn't know. She pulled out the bandana they'd given her, pushed back the cowboy hat they'd loaned her, and wiped her forehead.

Once again, the breeze's touch was definitely cool.

She tilted her head and squinted at the sky. Gray clouds were forming along the tops of the mountains.

"Look," she said. "Do you think it'll rain?"

"Might blow in tonight," Buck said. "Hard to say when."

They lined out at a trot along the back of the ridge, Buck in the lead. Freckles was sure-footed over rocks and around brush and he stepped over fallen logs without slowing his pace, so Clea gave him his head. She watched the open area for a glimpse of bright red or shiny black horse hide.

Every minute that went by, that dictator stallion might be picking on Ariel. Knowing that mare, she could lose her temper any minute and get into a fight with him that would be the death of her.

Couldn't she? Stallions fought with other stallions, but did they fight with mares? Did mares ever have the nerve to confront them and disobey their orders?

She would ask Buck and Teddy, but it was too hard to talk now, strung out like this. Teddy was behind her, keeping an eye on her, watching out for her. This order was how they'd ridden all day, whenever they went single file.

She owed these two tough old cowboys. Big-time. Not just the money she'd promised, but for all the extras, too. Mainly for letting her come with them. If they hadn't, she'd be out here alone making one mistake after another and never getting within a mile of any wild horse, much less Montana Red's band and Ariel.

At last, Buck decided they were at the right place and they started riding uphill again. They stopped before the top of the ridge, then got off their horses and tied them in a juniper thicket.

Clea's heart began to beat a drumroll in her chest while a voice in her head chanted *Please let it be Red. Let Ariel be with him.*

She had Ariel's halter and leadrope in her pack, ready to put on the mare. Should she have brought them with her right now?

Clea got to the top, climbed over and stood leaning against a tree while she looked down at the bunch of horses. They'd moved down into the valley and were grazing on the thicker grass along the creek.

She looked them over quickly, then used the binoculars to look again, stopping to check out each of the three black horses in the bunch individually, even though she already knew. Buck said it for her, shaking his head.

"None o' them black mares is yours. See that buckskin over yonder by hisself? That's the stud horse watching over his mares. He's brought 'em over here 'cause of the drought, prob'ly."

"Ariel's used to alfalfa and grain," she said. "Can she survive out here?"

"We'll find her," he said absently.

He was searching the hill across the valley now and then he moved his glasses to the one to the west.

"See that bluff up there? The red and sorta grayish one? Right there, the one closest to us?"

She nodded.

"There's a lake at the base of it where Red likes to take his bunch to water. There's another watering hole about five miles north of here that he uses. We need to check 'em both out today before they find a spot to huddle up and wait out the weather."

He looked at the sun.

"Quicker we find her, the better. But it'll be dark before we can hit both places."

"She's already bred, no doubt," Clea said. "She's in heat, big-time."

He nodded. "And she'll want to stay with them because she's been by herself ever since you left Texas and horses need a herd. But we won't let that stop us."

"Look," Clea said, her excitement starting to rev up again at the thought of actually catching Ariel. "Let's split up and we can check both watering holes before dark."

Buck and Teddy exchanged a questioning glance.

"Why not?" Buck said. "You gotta practice bein' on your own sometime."

Teddy nodded. "If he ain't there by dusk, he ain't comin. On the other side of the bluff, not a quarter mile from the top you can see right now, there's a cabin where we'll meet you."

"There's a trail up from the lake and it'll cut a road that'll take you to the cabin," Buck said. "Sometimes the refuge people rent it out. You can't miss it."

Clea's thoughts swirled like the dust in the wind, which had turned hot again. Every nerve in her body had come to full alert. She was thrilled. She'd never felt so strong.

Buck let his binoculars swing from his neck. "Here," he said. "Hand me that stick so's I can draw you a map in the dirt." He talked to her about it as he went, let her study it and repeat the directions, then he threw down the stick and they started back down the hill.

"Soon's you get there, make sure there's plenty of firewood in where it won't get wet," he said.

Clea said, "I'll do that first thing."

Mixed excitement and trepidation made her fingers clumsy as she untied her horse.

"You have a lot of faith in me," she said. "I appreciate it."

"I wouldn't try to send you all the way back home by yourself right now," Buck said. "But you can ride straight to Moose Lake and Perry's Cabin with your eyes closed. You can nearly see 'em from here."

They sat their horses and watched her go. The second time she turned to see them, nobody was there.

She faced west again, her heart hammering.

She was on her own! All she had to do was stay calm and keep her wits about her and her eyes on the red-and-grayish bluff in front of her.

Now she was leaving her old life behind forever.

CHAPTER NINE

THE RAIN camc with such suddenness that it sucked the air out of her lungs and sluiced cold water down her skin inside her clothes. She might as well have been naked for all the protection they gave her.

It took so much out of her so fast, both body and mind, that she couldn't get her saddle strings untied to put on her slicker. They were getting wet, too, just as fast as she was, the knots tightening and shrinking until she couldn't get her fingers into them. She'd already broken a nail. She shouldn't have done everything Buck and Teddy said. She should've folded it and put it in her saddlebag the way she'd started to do, no matter how much space it took.

On top of everything else, the rain was blowing into her face, reaching in under her hat brim, blinding her. She ducked her chin, pulled her hat down tight and hung her tied reins around the horn. Then she twisted in the saddle to fight the ties with both hands, leaving Freckles to his own devices. He kept up a steady trot as if nothing at all was happening in his world.

Lightning cracked and changed that. He jumped sideways, she jerked around to grab the reins and a new sheet of rain came with a rolling wave of thunder that rattled her teeth.

Her whole being craved shelter. She couldn't think what to

do, she knew only what she *needed* and that was a roof over her head. Tempting as it was to ride into the trees for a little protection from the deluge, she was too afraid of lightning striking.

The cabin. She had to find that cabin, even though it was up on top of that bluff and closer to the sky. Poor Ariel, out in the elements with no dry stall to hide in. No doubt the mare was totally terrified, but right now Clea couldn't help her and she couldn't let herself think about her. She had to help herself.

Finally, after the lightning and thunder had slowed down, she took the chance of stopping beneath a low, heavy branch of a pine tree to open one of the saddlebags the old guys had loaned her and then the small zippered cosmetic bag she usually carried in her purse to find her manicure scissors.

She cut one set of saddle strings and pulled her slicker out of the others. Struggling into it was another trial, but she managed it without scaring Freckles and took up the reins again with a whole new urgency. This was worse; the plastic holding wet clothes against her made her skin crawl. She felt colder than ever, too, because the temperature was falling with dizzying speed.

If it kept going at this rate, she could freeze to death covered with sweat.

She fought to get her thoughts in order, to make a plan.

They'd been headed uphill for a while now and the bluff was so close she'd been trying to glimpse the lake at its foot when the storm came in. Now she couldn't see much past Freckles's ears but she could see the ground, so hard from the drought that the water ran off the top in most places instead of soaking in.

Judging by the ground, they were still going uphill and the bluff had to still be on her left. She would head straight for the road. She could see Buck's map in her head. The road.

For a little while, just as suddenly as it had started, the rain let up. But not for long. The wind blew harder and colder.

Then she discovered that good news truly did warm a person's heart. Because during the second hard onslaught, just when she'd thought that there wasn't enough air left between the sheets of rain for her to breathe, Freckles's next step was onto gravel. Clea leaned over for a better look, just to make sure.

The road. The cabin was at the top of the bluff. She laid the rein against Freckles's neck and turned him left, uphill. Thank God, this wasn't all happening on flat land or she'd probably be lost by now.

She felt her stiff lips try to smile. Her whole face felt stiff, as if the water had frozen into a shell on it already, but everything inside her started loosening up. She felt that hot strength again that she'd felt when she'd asked to try this job on her own. Some kind of determination that she didn't know she had.

Not to brag, but she'd done very well today. She wished she could check out the watering hole at the lake before going to the cabin, as planned, but in this storm she'd have to be within arm's length of the horses to see them.

They would never let her get that close. Besides, they were probably huddled in some protected nook of a mountain valley by now and they'd stay there until the storm was over.

Didn't a person have to think for herself and make good decisions in order to survive in the wilderness? Too bad Jake couldn't see her now.

JAKE CLAMPED his legs tighter around the bay colt's sides and tried to see what was immediately ahead. The instant he lifted his chin, the sleet slanted in under the brim of his hat and hit him in the eye.

The bay colt jumped sideways as if it had been *his* eye.

"It's all right," Jake said, keeping his voice level and soothing. "Steady, boy."

The wind was rising by the minute and the rain was turning to sleet as cold as the devil's heart, so he really couldn't blame the colt for wanting to bolt. He'd been steady up to now, in spite of his squirrelly nature.

But still, Jake'd give a lot to have faithful, sure-footed old Stoney underneath him now. He wished he'd put on his coat along with the slicker. This sky looked full of snow and sleet.

It's a drought, Hawthorne. Gotta be glad to see moisture coming in.

Yeah. But damn that Montana Red. Ornery sucker just *had* to steal Jake's fifty-thousand bucks on the day the first storm of the season came rolling in from Canada. Clea would probably be worried about her mare being out in it. Her *ex-husband's* mare.

The bay colt's front end left the ground. He pawed at the sleet in the air, snorting like he wanted to attack it. Jake stuck to him, instincts wiping out thought, willing him to go back down.

Nothing killed a man faster than a saddle horn through the chest. The colt's hind feet were slipping….

Then he finally did come down and his front feet hit the ground with a thud and a scatter of gravel.

Jake took firmer control with his hands and his legs. Talking to the colt, he pushed him on. The light was starting to fade, partly because the sky was lowering but also because the afternoon was going. He'd like to be at the cabin by dark because this was no horse for a night ride. What the *hell* had he been thinking when he saddled him for this trip?

That the experience would help finish breaking the colt.

That he'd never ridden the bay down to the point where he was really tired, so he had more stamina than the majority of horses. And that Stoney's back was sore, so he would not ride him.

They were just getting settled into a steady trot when something blew past the bay's nose, rising from the ground like a flushed bird. The colt went up with it, but with all four feet this time, and Jake rode him in a swirling circle of gray air with a vague impression of the red-and-yellow scrap of plastic paper that had put him there. A potato-chip sack? A piece of a tarp? What the hell?

The colt sucked in more air and the cold in it sent him straight up, then down. He reared again almost before Jake could get a breath, came down again, then started bucking his heart out in all four directions at once. His neck was like iron against Jake's attempts to get his head turned to one side.

He flung his front end into the air again and tried to climb the rain.

He rose higher and higher, reaching for the invisible sun, now seemingly forever hidden, his hind feet scrabbling in the gravel and shifting every second, trying for purchase, finding it, losing it again. Jake sensed the colt's whole back end slipping downhill an inch at a time.

His mind was spinning, like the horse had been trying to decide what to do. He should get off before the colt fell on him but he didn't want to be left afoot out here....

But he didn't want to be dead, either. They were straight up now, not slipping for an instant, but he could feel the colt starting over backward.

Instinctively, Jake kicked out of the stirrups and launched himself sideways as best he could, praying to get both legs out from under the horse, praying that the colt wouldn't fall sideways on top of him.

The only other thought he had time for before he hit the ground was that now the colt was loose with Jake's pack on the saddle.

Then he landed in a nest of knives, hitting so hard the force knocked the breath from his body and sent his shoulder, then his back, tearing on the blades, trying to move him past them, but the momentum gave out and they held him still. He lay there so shocked he couldn't even close his eyes to keep the sleet out.

Finally, he managed to turn his head and open his eyes.

Another potato chip sack, caught in the long tangle of barbed wire, waved at him. He must've fallen in a ditch or a little ravine, because the colt was on a higher level, somehow. He could see all four feet.

It was barbed wire, tangled in with a couple of beer bottles and some old feed sacks and a greasy red rag. Some lazy, stupid son of a bitch had cleaned out his truck here.

Jake stared at the circled loops rising out of the ground darker than the darkening sky. An evil, curling vine coming out of the ground. He couldn't turn his head, couldn't close his eyes, so he stared at them until the sight of each barb was engraved on his eyeballs. He blinked but they didn't go away.

At last, he breathed. The pain began coming to life.

He gritted his teeth and tried to sit up. There was no place to put a hand down without cutting his arm and getting tangled more, so finally he tightened his abs and sat straight up, which made him have to bite back a yell so as not to scare the horse.

The wire came loose in some places but it hung so tough in enough other spots that it came up with him. He couldn't get hold of it.

The bay colt was standing up there—looking down at him—innocent as a baby.

"I'd give you a good cussin'," Jake muttered, more for the sound of his own voice than anything else, "but we're jammed up pretty good now and I don't wanna make you mad."

The horse pricked his ears at the wry, calm tone of voice and took a step closer, trailing the reins. One of them fell down into the ditch.

"All you gotta do is come untangle me from this mess," Jake said, hard as it was to keep getting enough air in his lungs. Maybe he wasn't afoot, after all.

He sucked in some air and twisted as far around as he could, clamping his jaw against the pain, trying to get the barbs out with his left hand. Good thing he was wearing his leather gloves.

Rain and sleet, sleet and rain, soaked his head and ran down the back of his neck but he could barely even feel them.

"Damn," he said conversationally to the bay, "I lost my hat. You seen it?"

There it was, an arm's length away, held by the wind against the side of the ditch—a shallow, rocky ravine surrounded by scattered juniper trees.

Jake struggled to his knees to reach for his hat, the wire tearing more of his flesh, but still clinging only where it had gone deepest. A gust of wind got under the hat's brim and lifted it. He lurched to keep it from blowing away and some more of the wire came loose with a fiery pain that spread all through him.

Damn! How many barbs had gotten him?

He slapped the hat onto his head with his left hand, pulled it down, and then made himself move his right arm to tie it on with the big silk wild rag he wore around his neck. If the temperature kept dropping this fast, he'd freeze without a hat.

If he moved that arm again with the last barbs still in his

shoulder, he'd scream and cry whether it would scare his mount or not.

The bay colt wanted to come even closer but he was hesitant to walk down into the ditch.

"There's not room in here for both of us," Jake told him. "Hang on right there and I'll be with you in a minute."

He worked at the wire and made himself think about something besides the pain. This mess had been thrown here recently, or Celeste would've found it and had it cleaned up.

Jake made himself concentrate on who might've dumped the garbage. Celeste would've strung up the son of a bitch single-handed if she'd happened along here when he was doing it. This was a fairly out-of-the-way spot but it *was* on the road to the cabin.

Jake gritted his teeth. There was one barb left and both ends of it had gone in, each in a different direction. This would not be pretty.

Surely none of the people who rented the cabin for a wilderness weekend would act like such pigs. Those people drove SUVs instead of pickups and they didn't haul barbed wire or baling wire.

He reached around under his right arm and up onto his shoulder blade, trying not to cut his arm too much, and worked the buried barb quick and fast.

Must've been one of the guys Celeste hired to change out the fence around the perimeter of the refuge. Too lazy to haul the old barbed wire away, as they were being paid to do. Had to be.

His back would be hamburger, but he was nearly free.

"Hang around," he told the colt, who was looking at him and sniffing at the air.

Jake could smell blood, too.

"Don't let it spook you," he said, forcing his voice to be calm and even through his clenched teeth. "I'm nearly done."

He finished tearing the wire from his flesh by pure force and made himself stagger to his feet on the strength of the pain. He stood, feet braced apart, amazed at how light-headed he was. He gave himself a second to settle so he wouldn't make any sudden movements, then slowly reached with his left hand for the trailing rein.

The colt stood like a trouper while Jake worked his way up out of the ravine, forcing his legs to hold him. He only shifted around a little bit when Jake reached level ground and laid the reins along his neck.

Jake clung to them as he grabbed the saddle horn and stuck the toe of his boot in the stirrup. The sleet mixed with rain stung his back through the holes in his slicker and when, after his second try, he got enough momentum with his legs to clamber into the saddle, he saw the liquid running pink on the ground.

He kissed to the colt, who was now dancing around more than a little, and moved on out, checking to make sure they were headed uphill toward the cabin. He had his cell phone but he wasn't certain it would work from there. He wouldn't need help anyway.

All he needed was a mirror and some water and some kind of disinfectant. He had a small bottle of betadine in his first-aid kit, but from the way his back felt cut all over, it might not be enough.

Jake wasn't sure how long he rode with the rain stinging and the sleet needling and the shredded plastic scraping his back like sandpaper. His flesh felt as raw as if it'd been through a grinder.

For the next few minutes he debated whether he should take the time to unroll his pack, replace the slicker with his coat and let it get soaking wet or endure this and have at least one warm, dry garment to wear. It was shaping up to be a cold night.

WAS THIS what people meant by an out-of-body experience?

Clea could no longer feel any part of her body, and she definitely was watching herself from a distance, so maybe it was. Also, what she had just seen herself do surpassed anything she'd ever thought possible.

A year ago, six months ago, just *yesterday,* she would've sworn that she couldn't have ridden however many miles she'd ridden today. She'd say that she would never have volunteered to go off all alone in the wilderness, not even to look for her mare. She'd admit that, even though she'd always had a good sense of direction, she would've been too scared in that circumstance to ever find the cabin.

She would've been wrong. She had done all that.

But her proudest accomplishment was that she'd denied herself the comforts of warmth and shelter in order to take care of her horse. She was proud that she'd figured out how to get water for him and even though she was shaky with fatigue had carried it to him. And that she'd rubbed him down even though her fingers were numb.

And that she'd had the foresight to draw another bucket of water and set it by the door to bring in for her own use. She'd come back and get it in a minute. Before it froze.

No. This wasn't an out-of-body experience.

Because when she pushed open the door of the cabin for the first time and staggered through it under the weight of her saddle and saddlebags, she *could* feel. She could especially feel every one of the tears of gratitude that welled up in her eyes.

What a relief! She was inside shelter under a roof. She had

a fireplace with a stack of wood beside it. There was a lantern on a table, so she wasn't caught by the rapidly falling dark.

Tears of fear had threatened her when she had had to ride through a creek, when she got turned around and lost the bluff where the cabin was and when she realized that Ariel might die in this weather because she didn't have a long coat, but she had held them back. She couldn't indulge them now, either. She had to get that lantern turned on and build a fire before dusk turned to dark.

The lantern turned out to be easy. A shiver, a hard one, took her when the light illumed the room. She was glued into this horrid plastic raincoat and she had to get out.

The most heavenly thing she could think of was to be dry again.

Shivering, she took off the slicker and dropped it on the floor as she crossed the room to the bunks. There were two of them built into one wall. She tore one scratchy blanket free and began to strip. She shivered more, much more, so much that her teeth really did chatter, and wrapped herself in the blanket even before she peeled off her boots and socks.

She warmed for a few minutes, then she shifted the blanket to under her arms, like a strapless dress, found a hair clip in her things and fastened the edges of it with that. Then she put on her jean jacket to try to keep her shoulders warm and began to seriously start looking at what she had to make a fire.

The wild-horse refuge rented this cabin out, Buck and Teddy had told her, or let big contributors stay there when they wanted to try to see or photograph the horses. So there was wood and kindling already inside. Enough for tonight, at least, according to her judgment.

She picked out some sticks, then knelt in front of the fireplace opening. She wished for somebody to teach her how to do this.

Like Buck and Teddy. Until now, she really hadn't had time to worry about them, but the thought of them hit her like a blast from the wind. The rain hitting the windows pinged against the glass like sleet.

Surely they'd be here soon. Surely they would've realized, just as she had, that they couldn't find the horses in such weather. If so, they'd have turned around and headed for the cabin about the same time she had.

She glanced at the door as if they might come through it at any minute. If she had a good fire going, they'd be so proud of her. Well, they would when she told them it was the first fire she ever built.

They were probably only a few minutes away, braving the sleet to meet her here as they'd promised. Buck and Teddy with all their knowledge and experience and survival skills.

But she didn't wish them here only for herself. She didn't want them to be in any danger. It was weird to think about, but she'd already begun to feel attached to them. Fond of them, even.

She realized she was smiling. She couldn't wait to hear what they'd have to say about her finding the cabin and building the fire on her own.

There was a metal rack to hold the wood inside the firebox. She fought the blanket out of her way as she picked out three sticks of firewood, which was about what it would hold side by side.

Fire had to have air to burn. That was about all she knew.

She made sure those sticks had plenty of room between them, put two more at an angle on top of them and added the amount of kindling she thought would be right. Then she reached for one of the fire-starter things that looked like an extra-long cigarette lighter. After two clicks, a flame flared out and she held it to the kindling until it caught fire. The flame tried to flicker down a couple of times, but she blew on it and finally it was burning merrily.

Smiling at her success, she left the fire, went to her packs and carried the saddlebag with her clothes to one of the beds. Dry things, especially wool socks for her freezing feet, would be wonderful. She pulled on her heaviest pair and sighed with pleasure. The blanket was scratching her skin raw but she needed to warm up a little more before she dressed. She wished she'd brought towels.

She found a couple of small ones in the kitchen corner where there was a wood-burning cookstove. At least, that's what she thought it was. But it would have to be. There was no electricity. When Buck and Teddy had told her that, they'd laughed at the expression on her face.

Maybe there were more towels in the bathroom....

Her heart sank. There *was* a bathroom, wasn't there?

She opened the back door and saw it a few yards away, connected to the house by a wood-shingle covered stone path. The little building was new and all stone and cedar, much like the ones she'd seen in the national parks.

Evidently, the wild-horse guests didn't want *too* much of a wilderness experience. Clea was grateful for that.

She also appreciated that it hadn't been built onto the cabin, which would ruin its authenticity.

Her feet freezing through her socks, she turned back to find the other boots she'd brought. Her breath caught and she coughed. Again. She smelled something... Smoke! The cabin was filling with smoke.

Her fire. Something was wrong. Panicking, she ran to the fireplace where her kindling was flaming merrily and one of the logs was starting to burn. But none of the smoke was going up the chimney.

Clea threw herself to her knees to peer up into it. The smoke was too thick, the heat wouldn't let her get close enough, and it was all black up in there anyhow.

She pulled back and looked around, frantic. Was something blocking the chimney? She should've looked up it before she built the fire. But now she couldn't. She should put out the fire.

But how? If she threw water on it she'd make everything so wet she'd never get another one started. She had to have a fire tonight or maybe freeze to death.

The windows. No, the door. Just for now, just until she could think, she would open the door and try to….

It slammed open with a blast of cold rain.

"Buck?" Her breath caught in her throat. "Teddy?"

The wind. Probably, just the wind.

Coughing more, she started toward the door, then stopped when a man loomed up in it, a bigger man than either of the old guys; she could see that through the smoke. Yellow slicker, dragging a saddle in one hand, saddlebags in the other.

"What the hell? *Clea?*"

The same second she recognized the voice, she saw that it was Jake with his hat tied on.

"I made a fire," she said and started coughing again. "I can't get the smoke to go up the chimney."

"What are you doing here?"

He sounded as if he had a bad cold, all raspy and gruff. And angry. Angry to see her.

For fear he'd have to take care of her, no doubt. Damn! Why'd he have to arrive when she was in trouble?

She glimpsed the terrible look on his face as he dropped his stuff where he stood, then strode straight to the fire, not even glancing at her as he passed. He bent over to check the fire, swaying a little on his feet. He must've been riding for hours. He reached to support himself on the rock of the fireplace with one hand and stuck the other into the blaze. No, he was reaching up....

He had something splattered all over the back of his slicker. Or was it shadows from the lamp? She walked toward him. It looked all torn...it *was* torn up. It must be mud....

But no. Colored water was dripping off him onto the floor. Bloody water. He was swaying on his feet because he was bleeding.

She stared, disbelieving.

Jake's sleeve dripped water onto leaping flames and made them sizzle. He jerked on something up in the chimney. Some of the smoke immediately went up. He pulled again, then turned around and flashed her a glittering look of disgust on the way back to his bags.

"Don't give me any more of that noise about how you can survive on your own. Damn sure can't if you can't make a fire."

His teeth were clenched. Not exactly the Jake who'd kept his cool when she shot his truck to pieces.

But still the same Jake who sneered at the thought she could survive on her own. Right this minute, after her big mistake, she was a bit afraid he might be right.

Nothing personal. She must remember that. He was mad because *he* was the one who needed help.

Well, she knew all about a man who lashed out when he couldn't control a situation.

"I *made* a fire," she said calmly, as much for her own benefit as his. "And I remembered a map and found this place after I rode for miles through a storm."

"But you didn't bring a slicker."

He carried his saddlebags to the bed and dumped them, then stood there for a minute with his feet spread apart and his back turned to her as if that could make her go away. Even from across the room, it was plain that he wasn't steady on his feet. A hard shiver ran the length of his body.

She ignored him while she fanned the smoke toward the open door. The wind was flinging drops of rain and sleet all over the floor.

Finally, she closed the door halfway and turned to look at him.

"What happened to you? You're shaking worse than I am and you have on all your clothes."

Dear God, what's happened to him while he's been out looking for my horse? But I didn't ask him to do it.

He didn't even turn his head. "Look, Clea. I've already got my plate full."

"What part of 'I am not expecting you to take care of me' don't you understand?"

He ignored the question and jerked more stuff out of his bag.

"Did you have a fight with a bear?"

He found what he wanted, which was a first-aid kit in a metal box, glanced at the fire—now sending all its smoke up the chimney—and began untying his hat. He turned with the box in one hand and his hat in the other to glance at the hat rack on the wall. After a moment, he hung the hat on the end of the bed instead. His scarf slid to the floor as if his fingers had lost their strength.

He stepped away from the bed and walked toward the door to a spot where the wooden planks were already wet and started to pull off his slicker. His jaw set, he pulled out one arm, then the other, switching the box from one hand to the other. Even in the bad light, she saw his face go even paler when he tried to push the coat off his shoulders.

She went to help him.

He snapped at her, "Get away."

He tried again to drop the slicker but it stuck to his back.

"Stand still," she said and to her amazement he did as she said.

Because he was hurting so much. His jaw was set hard enough to break it.

She took hold of the collar with both hands and started peeling the plastic down, biting her lip to distract her from the sick feeling rising at the sight of his blood. His tattered shirt stuck to the slicker.

She spoke softly. "What did this?"

For a minute she thought he wouldn't answer.

Then, tensing more when she hit a bad spot where the blood had glued his clothes to his skin, as if to distract himself, he muttered, "Barbed wire. Why are you out here?"

"Hunting my horse."

He gave a derisive grunt.

"I heard that's what you're doing, too," she said, working loose a shred of plastic and one of cotton that was buried deep. "But she won't let anybody catch her but me."

He made another scornful noise that was almost like a laugh.

"I hired Buck and Teddy to help me." She said it calmly, although her stomach tightened with fear again. "They should be here anytime."

"Good," he said.

"I was surprised when they said you're looking for Ariel," she said. "You do realize nobody asked you to go after her? That nobody's going to *pay* you a reward to bring her in?"

He didn't answer.

At last Clea drew a deep breath of relief when she dropped the slicker onto the floor. But a little chill of helplessness ran through her when she saw how hard it would be to get his shirt off.

"Thanks," he snapped. "I'll take it from here."

He walked to the table swaying only a little bit and laid the box down, then went to warm by the fire. The shivering went through him again. If he passed out there, he could fall into the fire. Even if he didn't, she couldn't get him up by herself.

Well, she'd dealt with two difficult men, Daddy and Brock, for years. Jake, though, was a different kind of man.

"Look," she said, trying to be brisk and light instead of gentle because he obviously wouldn't accept gentleness from her. "Let's get this job done now. Then we'll have something hot to drink and get warm."

Most of the smoke was gone, so she went to close the door. But first she looked out.

"It's raining too hard to see past the yard," she said. "I hope Buck and Teddy are close by now."

Jake didn't answer.

She crossed the room and stood by him.

"You can't even *see* the damage to your back, much less work on it," she said. "Let me just check out how much skin you've got left. That must've been a pretty rank pile of wire."

He answered with a grunt and then he just stood there, feet set wide apart, doing nothing but dripping water and blood as if he'd forgotten what else he'd intended to do. Her own legs were shaky with weariness, but he truly was on the edge of collapse. She was going to have to take charge.

"Must've been a pretty rank horse, too," she said, keeping her tone brisk and light. "You must have been thrown into the wire to get your back cut up like this. Right?"

To her shock, he started opening the buttons down the front of his shirt. Her spirit lifted. Maybe she'd be good at taking care of people. This must be like dealing with a recalcitrant child. Maybe she'd be a good mother.

She startled. Now *that* was a thought she'd never had before. Where had it come from?

She moved behind him and took his shirt off as he pulled out his arms.

"Jerk it loose," he said. "I've got to sit down."

She did that as fast as she could. Then she let it fall to the floor.

"Oh, Jake," she said.

In a voice that wasn't brisk at all.

CHAPTER TEN

IT SOUNDED bad. From the way she caught her breath and said his name with her breath quivering, he judged he looked like two hundred pounds of freshly ground meat. He certainly felt like it.

"This is gonna sound like a movie where someone's having a baby…" she said.

His head jerked around to look at her but he couldn't turn it far enough, since every muscle in his body felt stiff as the wire that had ripped him up.

"But we are going to need a lot of hot water here. You've got all kinds of dirt and gravel in these cuts and little pieces of yellow plastic, and so much blood I can't see how deep they go and what else is in them."

Her voice sounded a little thick. More than a little uncertain.

He was in a helluva mess. Buck and Teddy couldn't get here too soon. Clea wasn't the kind of woman to even look at anything ugly, much less try to take care of it—even a blind man could see that she was one of those high-maintenance women whose full-time occupation was taking care of herself.

Too bad he hadn't been bucked off on his front side so he could take care of himself.

"You can't do it," he said, and damned if his teeth didn't chatter on every one of those words. The shiver went all over him, head to feet, like a small tornado wrapping itself around him.

All he knew was, he'd better find a chair. And quick.

"Well, *you* sure can't," she said, with a new edge to her voice that was both anger and fear. "And there's nobody else here but the horses."

Another tornado, but this one warm. It came around him in a sudden wave and stayed.

"Don't turn around," she said and he realized it was a blanket. The blanket she'd just been wearing.

"Sorry if it scratches you," she said. "But you're probably in shock and you have to get warm. I remember hearing that shock makes a person freezing cold."

She held the blanket at his shoulders until he took its edges in his hands. He had a sudden vision of how she must look without it, standing right there touching him. Battered and bloodied or not, his body responded. Well, at least she was a distraction.

"I'm going to stay right behind you while you walk over to that chair by the table where the lantern is," she said. "You'd better sit down before you fall down."

He took a step. His head went all dizzy so he stopped, swaying on his feet. Clea gave a shocked little cry and grabbed one of his elbows through the blanket. He set his jaw and started off again.

"As soon as I get you settled, I'll go put on dry clothes and get you cleaned up. We don't want those cuts to get infected."

She was making a gallant try at *sounding* like she knew what she was doing, but it was all pretend. He could hear the fear and fakery in her soft voice.

"You're doing great," she said. "I'll steady you if you get dizzy again. Don't forget we can stop and rest if you need to."

Yep. Talk. She could talk a good game, but that's all it was—talk.

And while she talked she was wearing nothing at all, walking along right there behind him, pretending she could catch him if he fell. She was beautiful no matter what she wore, but with no clothes at all....

Hey. Get a grip. You don't already have enough trouble?

"I can walk," he said and it came out a growl. "Go put on some clothes."

"You're not peeking, are you?"

And she laughed a low, sexy, little laugh that made the whole thing worse. Actually, it sort of made him mad. Didn't she trust him? Did she think he was too much the rough cowboy to act like a gentleman?

Oh, yeah, she should trust you, Hawthorne. Like when she asked why you're chasing her horse and you were so quick to tell her.

Did she think that because he'd kissed her once they had something going between them? Well, he'd told her the truth when he said one kiss wasn't enough, but he wasn't gonna do anything about that.

It was mighty tempting, though. Good thing he already had this horse deal going that would make her hate him forever.

"You may be used to playing hide-and-seek in your birthday suit down there in Dallas," he snapped, "but I'm just an ol' country boy who's never even been to Las Vegas."

For some reason, she thought that was funny, too. He thought it was pitiful. He must be going out of his head.

"Don't worry," she said, "I hear the wild-horse refuge is just like Vegas. Whatever happens here stays here."

"Never thought you were shameless," he muttered, which was just as pathetic as that first remark of his.

He snapped his jaws shut and didn't say another word.

He got to the chair as fast as he could, grabbed it by the back and twisted it around to straddle it. When he did, he accidentally caught a glimpse of her, just in profile as she turned away—the graceful swing of one long leg and the curve of her hip, the lift of her full breast and the delicate bones of her shoulder and neck.

He closed his eyes but the sight was imprinted on the back of his eyelids.

He gripped the top of the chairback and sat. The movement of his muscles pulled his back into agony and he was glad. He needed to get his mind on his predicament and try to get some kind of a handle on helping himself.

"Stay still," she said. "I'll be right back."

He crossed his arms across the top of the chair and gradually, so it wouldn't be too sudden to tolerate, lowered his head to rest on them. It was swimming so bad he could fall off the chair.

Cowboy up, Jake ol' man. You've got a job to do. You've got fifty-thousand big ones to collect. Can't let a few little wire cuts slow you down.

He grabbed that thought and hung on to it. Better be ready to ride by the time the weather cleared. Better figure out how to do that. Better not think about the naked woman rustling into her clothes over there in the corner.

"Better get you out of your jeans just as soon as we can," she said. "I know that sounds shameless for me to say, but they're stuck to your skin and you can't afford to catch a cold while you're fighting infection."

He didn't say anything. All of sudden he felt too weak to take off his pants—even if she didn't have hers on. He couldn't even raise his head.

He heard a zipper and then a rattling sound.

"That is, assuming that *you* brought a change of clothes," she said. "Which I hope you did, since you criticized me when you thought I didn't."

Rattle, rattle, and then the zipper again.

"By the way, it's okay to look now," she said.

He *was* able to lift his head. She walked toward him with her sexy sway, carrying a black bag with a picture of a big pink flower on the side of it and another one with plastic bottles sticking out of it.

She wore pink suede knee-high boots with furry linings and jeans that were as tight as her skin. Tight as the pink thermal-underwear shirt she had on.

His eyes lingered on it just a little too long. She caught the look and they locked gazes. Sort of talking without words. Sort of remembering that kiss together.

Despite his misery, a shot of heat hit his loins. She was beyond beautiful.

A dozen different thoughts flashed through her blue eyes. He couldn't read any of them except to know that he wasn't the only one feeling this shimmer of heat in the air between them.

All of a sudden she looked younger than she was, sort of innocent and uncertain and not quite sure what to say.

He tore his gaze away and stared at the wall. No way could he afford any kind of involvement with her. Even that one long look meant he truly was out of his head. This woman was another Victoria, just with blond hair instead of dark. Same type, same class, same cushiony life and the same need for the money to keep on living that life.

Clea talked a good game of being self-sufficient, but so had Tori. Then what had she done? She'd chosen security instead of passion and gone back to her ex-husband. Clea was the same kind of girl. She wouldn't stay with this wild-horse chase very long, no matter how much she loved that mare.

This thing she had about moving to Montana was nothing but a winter's vacation from her real life.

In fact, she could be back in Texas before he even got there with Ariel. Or afterward, she'd use Ariel for an excuse to go back to Brock or whatever the hell his name was and his money. The guy had plenty if he could offer fifty K for a reward.

"This may take a while," she said, laying the bags on the table beside his first-aid kit. "But don't you worry about a thing. Nurse Clea is here."

There she went again with that pretend-I-know-what-I'm-doing tone. She was trying to encourage herself as much as him.

"Look," he said, "you don't owe me a thing. Especially not this ugly job of cleaning up my blood and guts."

"I'd expect you to do it for me if the tables were turned. Now tell me how to work the damper on that stove—if it has one—so I can put some water on to heat."

He started to push up out of the chair but she touched his good shoulder to hold him down. A feather could've held him down. His knees were like a newborn foal's. Had he lost that much blood? Surely not.

Since he didn't want to end up in a heap on the floor, he stayed in the chair and told her what to do. By the time she had a second fire sending its crackling sounds through the cabin, his head had settled down and he was beginning to stop shivering.

But he hated like crazy to move a single muscle. Only when he was perfectly still could he keep the pain down to a dull roar.

"There's a half-bottle of whiskey in here," she called. "I'm gonna soak my tweezers in it while we wash the blood off."

"It'd make more sense to let me drink it," he said.

"Good try," she said, "but we'd better keep it on the outside of you. I've heard alcohol expands your blood vessels or something like that, and it might make you bleed more."

He grunted a laugh. "Doesn't sound very scientific to me. Good thing you're not a surgeon."

She clinked the bottle against something.

"I'm not, but I *will* have to do surgery on you," she said. "Sort of like getting bullets out. But in your case, they're plastic and gravel instead of metal."

"You could use fire to disinfect your tools," he said, trying to keep the talk going just to keep from thinking. Or feeling. "Save the whiskey."

"I'll save all of it I can. Before this is over, I may have to drink it myself."

"A true nurse would give the anesthetic to the patient," he said. "Now. Before he suffers."

"I'm not only shameless, I'm selfish, too," she said. "But I *am* your nurse. You'll find out in just a minute."

He groaned.

"We don't have a whole lot of germ-killers between us," she said in a fake-cheery voice. "I'd hate to have to use nail polish remover."

"Ow," he said.

When she returned, she lifted the blanket off his shoulders and dropped it on the floor. One good look at the damage and he would bet money that Nurse Clea would announce she was done.

But instead she said, "Scoot your chair around where I can have more light."

She moved the lamp. She seemed very efficient.

However, when she began to wash away the drying blood,

she made a little noise deep in her throat that sounded like a cross between a sob and a whimper.

"Look," he said. "I know it's raw. Get me a mirror and I can…"

"You couldn't take care of this if you were a professional contortionist," she said, hooking another chair with her foot to drag it to her.

She dropped into it and pulled it up behind him as close as she could, propping her feet on the rungs of his chair, one long leg on each side of him, seeming not to notice that her thighs were embracing his. A new heat ran through him in spite of his shivering. It was an oddly intimate place to be. Somehow, almost more intimate than being in each other's arms, kissing like there was no tomorrow.

More like riding double. Bareback.

What a shame his body was blazing with pain. What a waste.

What a slippery slope. Get over it, man.

She was saying, "And if I don't get this done now, by morning you'll have an infection setting up. Next time you get thrown, try to land in a haystack."

The cold in the room hadn't really been touched yet by the fire. It seeped straight through his hurting flesh and settled into his bones, carrying the truth of her words with it.

She began to wash his wounds, touching him carefully but firmly, using warm water to soak off the blood, then following it with the sting of the betadine. Doing nothing but sitting here, submitting, made him feel restless, helpless, trapped.

He lifted his head and turned it the other way. Pain rippled through his muscles like needles in his blood.

She hit an especially tender spot and he set his jaw harder. He could feel it was a deep cut. Clea made a little gagging sound. He hoped this didn't take much longer.

But he hoped even more that now that she'd started, she could finish the job. He could try to keep her mind busy so maybe she wouldn't have time to think about how gross a job this was. He had to try to stay in control, even if he couldn't do the work.

"You're always trying to get me thrown," he said.

"What're you talking about?"

His eyes tried to close but he forced them to stay open. His only concession was to rest his head on his hands on top of the chair. Clea was clinking her tools like she knew what she was doing. He caught the smells of whiskey and the betadine cutting through the scent of smoke that lingered in the room. He *would* keep his wits about him.

"You predicted my paper sack'd cause a rodeo," he said, sipping in some air instead of gasping the way he wanted to when a new shock of pain hit him.

She was picking at a wound in the very tender middle of his back between his shoulder blades.

"And now that I've had a wreck, you're already planning the next one."

There. He managed to say it all without showing any sign of pain.

"Well, somebody needs to," she said, pulling a piece of something out of his back that didn't want to let go. "Left on your own, you make a lot of bad choices."

She finally took her infernal tweezers away and something dropped, rattling, into a bowl on the table. New pain flew through him like a crowning forest fire.

"Like what?" he muttered.

"Like diving into a bed of gravel," she said. "That was a stone big enough to put in a rock garden."

"Felt like a boulder," he said.

"Hey. You complaining about my work?"

"No, no. You're doing fine. Just fine. I'm lovin' it. Don't quit now."

They both managed to chuckle a little, although she sounded pretty grim. She was a surprisingly good sport to be doing what she was doing—she was trying to distract him, too.

"Some of this plastic is ground into your muscle halfway to the bone," she said after a new minute of probing and poking that had him clenching his jaw and trying to rip off the back of the chair.

He tried his damnedest to think about something else but unfortunately all that came to mind was the image of her in nothing but her silky skin.

"Oh, lord, I'm making it bleed again," she murmured, talking to herself. "But I know there's a lump of dirt in there. I saw it. If I can just get hold of it, oh, if I break it up, I hope the blood will wash it out..."

The warmth of her legs left his. Her chair scraped back and fell over as she jumped to her feet and, hand over her mouth, ran toward the door.

She rushed outside and left it open. He heard the sound of retching, saw her arm wrapped around the post, her bright hair swinging out into the freezing rain as she vomited off the porch.

He raised his head slowly, so as to manage the dizziness, and got to his feet using only his legs. He had to help her. He'd been right—she wasn't tough enough for this ugly job.

He moved through the amazing stiffness that was already settling into his muscles, dumped the stuff off the towel and carried it out the door. She was vomiting again and when she saw him coming, she tried to wave him away.

Instead, he put a hand under her forehead and held it in

spite of the pain tearing through him like claws. It was the least he could do to even the score.

She threw up one more time. Then she straightened and reached for the towel.

Pressing it to her mouth, muffling her words, she said, "Get back inside."

She led the way, pointing at his chair as she passed it, gesturing like a stern teacher for him to sit, and went on to the kitchen where she dipped some water from the bucket into the basin. He followed her.

"Jake, please go sit down," she said, holding the wet towel to her face. "Without a shirt, you truly will go into shock."

"You're not cut out for anything like this. There's a shower out there in the bathroom. I'll go stand in it to wash my back."

But he swayed on his feet as if the wind was trying to blow him over. Which it was, because they'd left the door open.

Clea grabbed his arm and led him back to the chair, then ran to close the door.

"I'll pour that bottle of betadine over it and it'll be fine," he said.

He was dizzy again. He took a harder grip on the top of the chair.

He would rest for just a minute and then he'd go get in the shower.

Clea dragged her chair up behind him and went right back to work.

"I *am* cut out for this," she said, clipping off each word. "Just because I've never done anything hard and ugly doesn't mean I *can't* do it. That's why I came to Montana."

Jake wanted to ask her to explain that but it was too hard, too much trouble, to open his mouth. It was going to be all he could to hold on to consciousness.

Maybe he ought to just let go, because the one thought in his mind right now was one he'd just as soon lose. Clea was doing all this for him and he was going to repay her by taking her horse away.

But he was in the right. No matter what she did for him, she was still a horse thief.

CLEA WOKE into a silence so pure it filled the room. She lay still, knowing from the first glimmer of consciousness where she was and who was with her.

The cabin on the wild-horse refuge. Jake.

Who, she had to say, was one tough hombre. Not a sound had come from him while she probed and poked at his back, although it must've hurt like crazy. Besides that, he'd had enough iron control to come out onto the porch and hold her head while she vomited.

That had touched her inordinately. Brock had never done such a thing, even when he was in perfect health.

She sat straight up.

Jake had stopped muttering and thrashing around in his sleep. She couldn't even hear him breathe. *That's* what had waked her.

The cold slammed into her from all sides when she threw off her covers but she ignored it, grabbed her tiny torch light and ran across the freezing floor to see about him.

Oh, God, please let him be all right.

She bent over his face, which was resting sideways on his arm. He *was* breathing, lying on his side to keep his weight off his back.

His blankets were half off the bed on the floor, and his flannel shirt, which they'd agreed was the only garment soft enough to wear, was half off his body. A strip of curly black hair showed on his chest.

He had to be utterly exhausted or unconscious not to know how cold he was. She reached for the blankets trailing off his hip and onto the floor, but the sight of his face held her still.

Pain was pulling his tanned skin tight against his already-chiseled bones, making him look like the hardest of hard men. Except for the long, black lashes spiking on his cheek and the sleeping vulnerability of his mouth.

His mouth. Just looking at it made her breath quicken.

She wanted to touch it so much right then that the need dragged at her heart. Just with the tip of her finger. Just to trace the shape of that full lower lip.

And then kiss it until they both were senseless.

He groaned, muttered something unintelligible and lifted his arm, sending the blankets sliding farther. Instantly, she switched off the light so as not to wake him and dropped the string of the torch over her head to free her hands so she could retrieve them. Shivers were starting at her center and more were coming up through her feet from the frozen wood of the floor.

No telling how long Jake had been uncovered. He had to be freezing, too.

She bent over and picked up the blankets lifting them with both hands to lay them over him. Gently, so he wouldn't wake.

He muttered, stirring in spite of her carefulness, and the next thing she knew she was falling back onto his bed pulling the blankets over both their heads.

"Cold," he mumbled, pulling her against him. "Come on over here."

Dear God, it was his right arm. He'd make every wound bleed again. She couldn't jerk away. But she couldn't have gotten loose, anyway. His grip was irresistibly strong and relentless in spite of the fact he was hurt.

She couldn't even sit up against the force of it. He laid her down and curled his long body around her back. Warmth from him and more from the blankets settled into her and the shivering slowed.

"Better," he murmured and tucked his chin in against the top of her head to hold her there. "Tori," he said, the word trailing off into a sigh.

Tori? Was that it? Had she heard that right?

He thought she was someone named Tori. Must be his girlfriend.

Maybe it was a former girlfriend. Despite herself, she hoped that was it.

Why, Clea? You're not ready to get involved with a man, remember?

Instantly, he went deeper into sleep. He proved it with a snore.

She needed to get up, get out, get away, even if it woke him. That surely wouldn't put any more strain on his wounds than he'd already done.

However, even with both of them dressed in two layers of clothing, his body and hers fit together like spoons as if they were supposed to be just exactly where they were. As if they'd be hard to separate.

But she shouldn't be here. This was wrong. He didn't know what he was doing or even who she was. This could start a whole lot of trouble, increase the longing for another one of his killer kisses.

Actually, they'd both been very strong and had shown a lot of character during all the rest of that shooting lesson, because that kiss had shaken him as much as it had her. She guessed. By the way that, ever since that day, he'd avoided her as carefully as she had him.

In this cabin, there was no way they could avoid each other. And what if he was hurt too much to ride tomorrow? She couldn't leave him.

Was he feverish, delirious? Maybe that was the source of the talking.

Tentatively, she found his hand, since he had her arms in a vise grip and she couldn't reach his forehead. She could touch the inside of his wrist. Wouldn't that be hot if he had a fever?

It wasn't hot. In fact, it was as cold as the room that surrounded them, therefore, she needed to be there. She was doing him some good. Hadn't there been a study just recently that proved getting chilled could actually cause a person to catch a cold, just as mothers had warned their children for centuries?

Her own mother would certainly be ashamed of Clea if she could see her now. This was a dishonorable thing, like taking advantage of a drunk person. Jake had no clue she was in his arms.

But it wasn't sexual. There was nothing sexual about it. This was survival. The temperature obviously had been dropping like a rock all night long and the fire had gone out.

That truth hit her hard. Of course.

That was the *other* silence that had waked her—the fire had stopped crackling and snapping. From here she could see that it was down to a few glowing embers. There was no sound from the cookstove at all.

But she could not make herself get up to rebuild the fires. It was too warm here and too cold out there.

Jake snored again. He muttered softly, moving his chin against her head.

He shifted his arm to hold her around the waist tighter against him and when he did, she freed her arm. But what did she do with it? Only tucked the blanket in so they'd both be warmer.

She had only *thought* she was becoming a stronger person. She wasn't strong at all. Her temporary comfort was more important than doing the practical, necessary thing for physical survival.

She'd better be strong enough to do what was necessary for her *emotional* survival. This instant, her body was tuned to his, wanting more contact with his.

As soon as they both were really and truly warm, warm all the way through, she'd get up and build the fire that they needed so much. Then she'd go back to her own bed.

At least it wasn't a situation where they had to have the remains of the old fire to start the new one. The cabin had those firestarters and if they failed because of the cold, she had matches in her pack. Buck had told her to bring them.

Where were Buck and Teddy? She prayed they were not freezing to death somewhere right now. She *ached* for them to come. Just for them to arrive so she'd know they were all right. Jake had said there were caves and other cutbanks where they could take shelter, but what if they didn't find wood for a fire? There *was* no other shelter from cold.

Even the thought made her feel guilty about the warmth that was beginning to seep through her blood now.

Jake's arm, heavy and strong around her made her feel not only warm but safe, too. Which was so nuts, since he thought she was somebody else.

What did Tori look like? What kind of woman was she? Was she a cowgirl?

Clea would try to get Buck and Teddy to talk about Tori. Those two would tell anything.... No. She'd ask Jake himself.

The new Clea was more assertive, she was able to speak her mind and say what she wanted. And ask questions of whomever knew the answers.

Her eyelids drooped. The orange embers and the pale window faded away as her eyes closed. She was getting too warm to think. Tori was none of her business.

And neither was Jake. This was simply a life-or-death rescue situation. The new Clea was ready to be assertive but she definitely wasn't ready for another man.

She was not looking. Not for at least two or three years. Not until she found her new, real self growing even stronger.

She smiled as sleep pulled at her. The self she'd found last night had done really well with the emergency first aid. She was proud of how she'd stuck it out, even through the vomiting, to doctor Jake's back. Proud and surprised.

He'd been surprised, too, she could tell.

Her stomach was still sore from throwing up so much.

It might be that she hadn't been brave so much as stubborn. That was what had carried her through—her determination to prove to Jake that he was wrong about her.

Now, even though she had just slept a few hours, she was exhausted all the way to her bones. Every nerve and every muscle in her body ached. She needed to sleep some more.

Assertive or not, she didn't want to be in charge anymore. She wanted Jake to wake up feeling fine and take over until Buck and Teddy could get here.

No, she didn't want him to wake up. She wanted to stay right where she was, warm and still, and sleep until noon tomorrow.

He might be bleeding again right now. He might need help and not even know it.

No, he was holding her close with his face in her hair and sleeping deep.

She would let him sleep and she would sleep until full daylight came. That wouldn't be long now.

CHAPTER ELEVEN

JAKE THREW his leg over hers and caressed her flat belly. She snuggled closer into the curve of his body. His hand slid higher. He found her breast and cradled it. The warm weight of it comforted him and stirred his blood, pulling him toward pleasure, away from pain.

The hurting clawed at him again, though, faster. This time it dug so deep he had to try to get away from it. When he moved, she made a little protesting sound in her throat and clung to the pillow—his pillow—to hold it in place. She always stole his pillow.

Vague needs started sharpening in him. Her skin. He needed to touch her skin. He dropped his hand to her waist to scoot her even closer into him, settled her little butt against his growing hardness, found the bottom of her shirt and slid his hand up and under.

His consciousness sharpened, too, but he tried to hold it at bay. This woman's scent wasn't Tori's.

He touched her in slow, slow circles. Her skin was the sleekest, softest he had ever felt. Sleeker than the muzzle on the filly foal he'd saved from the mountain lion.

Dim bits of images, pieces of memories flashed in his brain, then the feeling of her sweet, hot kiss flooded his hurting body. Clea.

This was foolish. But she was in his bed.

He couldn't get enough of just feeling her skin. Until he reached her breasts and had to choose. He held one, then the other, moving his thumb lazily across the taut nipples.

His lips ached for them. As if she knew that, she sighed and lazily turned flat on her back to give him free access. He pushed her shirt up more, scooting down in the bed so he could get his mouth on her.

The pleasure was growing so much, so fast, that the pain faded back enough for him to prop himself on his elbow. He bent his head to suckle her, but she thrust her fingers into his hair and took his face in her hands, guiding his mouth to hers.

Here it was again. That kiss. But real, not a memory.

The same but different. Here was a whole, warm world where there wasn't any cold, sharp air biting at his back. And something about the way her hands cradled his face talked to him, deep down.

Her lips and tongue already knew his so well they teased and drew him on in a dance that both soothed and fired him. Then all the soothing was gone, and she was tantalizing him so desperately with her breasts against his chest and her mouth trying to draw out his very soul, that he drove her deeper into the bed, kissing her harder until he had to have breath.

He pulled back, their lips still clinging together, not letting her go, but tasting again, taking time to feel the perfect fullness of her lower lip with his tongue. She met it with the tip of hers and the sweet, hot taste of her and the citrus-flower scent of her filled him up with wanting.

But when he resumed the kiss and his hand went to her breast again, she let go of his face and pushed at his shoulders, making little noises that sounded like she was trying to say no. He tore his mouth away from hers and opened his eyes.

"That's enough," she whispered.

He looked down into Clea's blue, blue eyes. Her cheeks were red, her smooth blond hair tousled from his kiss.

But it was the look she was giving him that went straight to his gut.

There you are. I know you. I know you, Jake Hawthorne.

She did. They knew each other. The loneliness that had always been deep inside him lived in her, too.

"Who's Tori?" she said.

He wanted to turn away, get away, not deal with this, not answer. But she was a fellow traveler on the lonely road.

"I knew it was you," he said. "Maybe not at the very start, but I knew it was you."

She didn't answer. Her eyes held steady on his. Looking *in* his.

"Nobody kisses like you do, Clea," he said.

Finally she said, so low it was almost a whisper, "I have to say the same about you, Jake."

Trouble. Big trouble. Inside, he was shaking as bad as when he'd staggered in at that door yesterday.

Even though they'd lived together, Tori had never been able to see into him like that.

He jerked away from her and hit the wall with a blow that sure enough woke him up. Pain shot through him, hotter now than the pulsing desire.

"I'm *sorry,*" she said, scrambling to sit up, hurrying to untangle her legs from his. "Let me get out of here so you'll have more room."

She gasped when the cold air hit her, swung her long legs

out of the bed and stood up. Then she turned to catch his gaze, which was glued to her little butt in her tight jeans.

"If you knew who I was, weren't you getting a little carried away?"

Quick anger stung him. "If that's the way you feel, weren't you a little out of line getting in my bed?"

"You had to have blankets. You were so restless you kept throwing them off."

"And I should've known you're a one-kiss-only kind of girl," he said sarcastically. "How come I didn't learn that at the shooting lesson? Because you never said a word when you kissed me like there was no tomorrow and then broke it off in a heartbeat."

That made her mad. She started to turn away but then her blue eyes were back, blazing at him.

"Lay it on me," he said. "I can take it."

"I'm not used to talking about my feelings," she said. "That's why."

"So you meant it when you said that—" He gestured at the spot where she'd lain. "About nobody kissing like I do?"

She gave him a frown of disgust, while those blue eyes bored into him. Even then she was beautiful.

"I don't lie," she said. "I've quit lying."

Which is more than you can say for yourself, Hoss. Kept your mouth glued shut yesterday when she asked why you were going after her horse, didn't you? That's called a lie of omission.

She danced on the cold floor in her sock feet, turned and went for her boots—ridiculous, knee-high, pink, silly things that they were. She sat down on her own bed to pull them on, taking time first to rub her feet and warm them.

She looked at him. "You still haven't answered my question, Jake."

"I don't remember a question."

"Who's Tori?"

He stared at her. "Me first. Why'd you get in bed with me?"

"*You* did it," she said. "You said, 'Come on over here' and pulled me into your arms. You're really strong, Jake and I..."

"Couldn't you tell I was talking in my sleep?"

"Well, yeah, but the fire'd gone out and I didn't want to get chilled through while I built another one and—"

"And was I *walking* in my sleep, too? I walked to your bunk and said, 'Come on over here'?"

"No! I *told* you, you kept throwing off your covers. You were about to freeze to death in the night! And you were feverish and hurt—"

"So I kidnapped you and then what happened? I was talking in my sleep and what else was I doing?"

"Nothing. Good lord, Jake, I have my jeans on. You have your jeans on."

She was starting to recover now, pulling on her boots. Standing up tall. And gorgeous.

"Okay. So what did we do with our jeans on?"

"Well, you snuggled me in against you and I was grateful because I was already chilled pretty bad, and you were sleeping hard and I felt secure and I could go to sleep."

A note in her voice, *underneath it,* really, struck the same one deep in him.

"You have trouble with that?" he asked.

"Sometimes. I'd *been* asleep, though, because I was so tired, but before I did go under—"

She clamped her lips—her beautiful, full, soft lips, still swollen from his kiss—closed, fast, as if she didn't want him to hear the rest of it.

"What? What before you did go under?"

"Nothing."

He had to know. It hit him like a freight train that for some crazy reason he needed to know this piece of her. Nuts. He'd never pried into somebody else's business. That went against his code.

It was because *he* sometimes had trouble falling asleep.

"Tell me," he said.

"When I first went to bed, I lay there for a long time thinking about the huge sky raining and sleeting outside on this enormous land, and these mountains that just go on and on. About how here is where I was…am…and how far out in the wilderness *here* is and how far from Texas…"

He nodded, and wouldn't let her look away when her eyes met his.

She swallowed hard. "I thought about how *I* don't even really know where I am and nobody—like my daddy—who ever loved me or said they did, knows where I am. No one could find me even if they tried."

Your ex-husband already did. Did he love you? Or just say he did?

Yes. She knew what lonesome was.

She had come to him in the night so as not to be alone in the wild.

"You let me…touch you," he said. "I wasn't trying to take advantage of you."

The color in her cheeks heightened but her eyes didn't waver. She believed him.

"I know."

He couldn't stop looking at her, with her full lips still swollen from his kiss.

"So why…"

"Look," she said. "I'm just not the kind of woman who

can...make love lightly. If I sleep with somebody, it's...important to me. It...has to mean something."

So you think it'd mean something with me?

What the hell is the matter with you, Jake? Damn. You don't want anything that means something, for God's sake.

"I'm not looking to get involved with another man," she said. "Not for a long time. Maybe never."

He said, "Then you'd better not be climbing in bed with any."

She raised one eyebrow and gave a little nod to concede him that point.

Then she said, "So. You never told me the other day if you're single or not. And you never told me who Tori is."

He laughed. Not many things made him laugh these days, but he laughed out loud.

"I thought you said you're not looking to get involved?"

"We can be friends," she said. "You're hurt. We don't know how long we'll be here. And we're neighbors."

She fixed him with a commanding look, standing with her hands on her hips.

"And you said, 'Me first.' That means that if I answer your question, you'll answer mine. You've asked lots of questions and I've answered."

"Tori used to be my girlfriend," he said. "We lived together for a while. But it didn't work out."

"How long ago was that?"

"A year or so."

He gave the look right back to her. "I don't have another girlfriend and I am not looking for one. I'll *never* love another woman. That's definite. No maybe about it."

"So we *can* be friends," she said.

She smiled at him, turned, grabbed her coat and shrugged into it while she vanished out the back door. Jake stared after her. How could they be no more than friends when she smiled at him like that? After she'd kissed him like that?

No sweat. It'll all be over when you haul her horse away, Bucko.

HOW COULD SHE do that—just be just friends with him?

She was running so hard she didn't even turn and exclaim to him about the snow. Instead, she made footprints in it down the steps and onto the path leading to the bathroom, all the time thinking about his hands on her and the taste of his mouth.

In Texas, snow was always cause for excitement. In Montana, snow would have to take a number and get in line.

Why *had* she let Jake pull her into his bed?

She'd never been daring, never been a risk-taker. Growing up, she'd always been just a bit shy, sort of an observer of life because her mother wasn't there to explain it to her.

And because she'd wanted to please Daddy every minute.

Grown-up, she'd been so good at pleasing other people and hiding her real feelings that finally she hadn't known what they were. She'd had the facade down to ultimate perfection: Southern woman with perfect manners and unfailing charm in every social situation.

But somehow, with Jake, that was all gone.

Because she'd spent such a long time working on his gorgeous, broad-shouldered, muscular back that tapered down to his slim waist? Her fingertips touching his naked skin?

Or because she'd sat so long with her thighs pressed against his hard ones, the muscles flexing under his tight jeans?

She skidded a little on the icy walk and had to flail her arms to catch herself, but that didn't distract her. It must've been that that contact with Jake had made her body want more.

Simple lust. That was her problem. Jake brought it out in her.

No big deal. She just wasn't accustomed to letting her body tell her what to do. But gurus and therapists and counselors were always saying people should listen to their bodies.

Even so, she and Jake were going to be friends only. That was all settled now.

Breathing in air so cold and fresh it made her lungs feel raw, she rushed into the incredibly cold bathroom, then back out into the morning sunlight. It would help warm some by noon, but not much. Even the sun was colder up here.

Despite all that, she was *still* melted at the core of her, still heating in her blood when she thought of Jake's hands on her. She ought to throw herself full length into the snow and make a snow angel to cool off.

Letting him pull her into his bed tied leaving Brock as the most daring thing she'd ever done. She'd gone from zero to sixty on the risk-taking scale in only a few months. But that was the end of it. Running around all over the wilderness and catching Ariel would be enough risk for a while.

It had been foolish, but she'd really been living in the moment. Somehow she knew that she'd have the vivid memory of Jake until she died.

The horses were outside the lean-to shed, standing in the sun. Freckles threw up his head and whinnied at her. Jake's horse, the bay colt he'd ridden over to her house that day, joined in.

"I'll feed you two in a minute," she called to them cheerfully.

But the thought that hit her then wasn't quite so lighthearted. She was probably drawn to Jake because, even though she wanted her freedom and needed to become a strong and independent woman, she also wanted somebody to take care of her. A handsome man to be her hero and fight her battles for her.

Oh, well. Wasn't that true of most women? Wasn't that why we had fairy tales? Did any woman manage to have both? Was that possible or did we have to choose?

She'd never really had either. Daddy and Brock had taken care of her financially, but neither had fought any real battles for her.

Maybe a man and a woman could both be strong and independent, yet deeply in love and willing to fight battles for each other.

Yeah, right. Talk about a fairy tale.

She went to pet the horses.

JAKE WAS on his knees—that hurt less than sitting on his haunches—holding a match to the kindling and wood he'd laid in the fireplace when the back door burst open and Clea blew in.

"It snowed," she called. "Did you see?"

"Yeah," he said. "But just a few inches. First snow of the season."

"I'm going to feed the horses," she said, heading for their saddle bags. "You have grain in your packs?"

"I'll do it."

"No," she said. "You don't have your boots on. I'll be right back."

Jake watched her go, surprised that she'd take her nurse duties as far as doing the horse chores. But he appreciated it. Every inch of his back hurt as he got the fire going and then hoisted himself to his feet. He set his jaw against the pain and walked to the window. There were her small footprints leading from the house to the horse pen, where she was petting the horses and pouring the grain.

Ruining her silly suede boots. Wearing a puffy pale yellow jacket the color of her hair. It made him think of lemon ice cream.

She turned quickly then, as if she could feel his eyes on her, and he hoped she didn't see him. Why, he didn't know.

However, he didn't step back so she wouldn't see him, either. Instead, he stayed still and watched her some more, not sure why he had to look. She was one frustrating woman.

What he *did* know was that he wasn't going to think about her all the time after he rode away from here. He could still taste her and he'd never forget the feel of her skin under his hands, but he wouldn't think about it. One thing he was good at was controlling his thoughts.

Wasn't he? He didn't think of Tori anymore except on rare occasions when something brought her to mind. Or when he happened to see a cute little boy in a cowboy hat that made him miss her four-year-old and six-year-old so deeply it wrenched his heart.

Clea Mathison. Victoria Jensen. Different, but a lot alike, too.

Except that he doubted Tori ever stole a horse.

Remember that, Hawthorne. She's a horse thief.

And you're here to take that horse back to its owner.

Sudden restlessness hit him. Hard. He needed to get out of here, get on horseback, get out in the open.

No, it was fear. What if he was hurt worse than he'd thought? What if he couldn't ride until he healed a little more? Right now, he sure as hell wouldn't want to. Maybe moving around would loosen him up. He had to go to the bathroom anyway.

When he grabbed his coat he felt some of his wounds pull open. Some bled a little, he could feel it. He put his coat on anyway and stood still for a minute. All his muscles were stiff and he hurt in every corner of his body. He tried not to make any sudden moves as he went out the back door into the bright morning and headed clumsily down the paved path to the bathroom.

"Jake!"

He turned to see her in the horse pen, brandishing a hoof pick in one hand.

"Are you sure you can you walk all right by yourself? You feeling okay?"

It irritated him. But somewhere in the back of his mind, it pleased him, too.

He raised a hand to show he was good.

But if she could get in his business, he could get in hers.

"Don't bother that colt while he's eating."

"I wouldn't," she said. "I'm only doing Freckles now. I was too wiped out to do it last night."

Jake nodded and went on his way, careful not to slip on the icy spots. He didn't need any jolts or jerks on his back.

He got back to the house before she did. When he passed by, she was still in the pen, bent over one of Freckles' hooves, cleaning it out.

Which proved she really was more useful and competent around horses than anywhere else. He had to be fair, though. She was a pretty damn good nurse, too. Working on his wounds, she'd shown a lot of grit for a woman like her.

Except there aren't any other women exactly like her.

She came back in all flushed from the cold and smiling. "Isn't it great out there now? You're right—the snow's only a few inches deep. Buck and Teddy shouldn't have any trouble getting here."

She was putting a pot of water on the stove.

"I hope you like oatmeal," she said. "I found some in this tin. And I have raisins in my pack."

He turned and went to check on the fire.

"If they stayed at the caves, they oughtta ride in by noon," he said.

They'd damn sure better. He needed some space and some time to himself. He had a lot to think about.

She left the stove and went to the table where she'd left all the medical supplies.

"While the water boils for our breakfast, let's check out your back," she said. "See how good a nurse I am."

It had to be done. Jake thought he could ride but he was sore as hell and could still feel a trickle of blood here and there. He didn't want to head out alone and start bleeding again in a spot where he couldn't reach.

He straddled the chair as he'd done last night and took off his shirt.

"Hmm," she said. "I'm gonna hang out my shingle. Looks pretty darn good to me. You've got a spot or two bleeding again, but I'll get that stopped. How does it feel today?"

"Like I fell into a tangle of barbed wire."

And then slammed up against a wall.

He could still feel her lips on his. Could still taste them.

He wouldn't think about that.

"Anything look infected?"

"Hmm. A couple of spots are reddening. I'll put betadine on all the wounds again. Then as soon as we get with Buck and Teddy, you should go into town and let a doctor see if anything else needs to be done."

No way. He had a job to do. A job that'd put a stop to all the wild fantasies floating in his head.

He kept catching the scent of her perfume. Or her hair or her skin or whatever it was. Each time she touched him, so gently, with a bare fingertip, a profound longing went through him.

"After I catch your horse," he said.

She went still for a second, as if she'd forgotten.

"Why are you chasing her? I don't understand why you'd take time away from your work, Jake, but I think it's really sweet of you."

He was the one who went still that time.

Forget it. The mare doesn't belong to her. You don't owe her anything.

"Remember you told me you have a job to do and no time to take me to raise," she said, in a soft, conversational tone, while she dabbed something stinging on his wounds and cleaned up the bleeding. "I understood that."

Tell her. Spit it out. Tell the woman you're working for her ex.

She touched his shoulder with her bare fingers, then pressed a cotton ball to that deepest cut in the center of his back. It burned like hell. He sucked in air and then didn't move a muscle, not even to clamp his jaw.

"I'm just curious," she said.

Damn, she was persistent.

"It seems to me that going to all this trouble to get my horse back could be construed as taking me to raise."

That honeyed tone of her voice was like a caress asking, "Are you doing this for me?"

He damn sure didn't want her to think that. But he couldn't risk her reaction to the truth. *Where* were Buck and Teddy?

"We really ought to stick together from now on," she said. "Because I truly think I'm the only one who can catch her."

No. That'd be bad. He needed to catch her alone and be on the road south before Clea knew....

Coward. You can't let her keep worrying and searching.

The truth might bring on a hysterical crying fit.

That was the reason he wasn't telling her. And what man *would* risk that?

Even the gutsiest guy in the world wouldn't do it. What was that saying about a woman scorned? Hell hath no fury?

She would see it as betrayal; he just knew she would.

It'll be even worse if you let her believe this until you actually catch the mare. Tell her now.

His lips parted. Damn! What a mess!

He said, "If the old guys aren't here by noon, I'll ride out a little ways and see if I can spot them."

And keep on riding.

But he couldn't just go off and leave her here alone. She might burn the house down. Or break a leg out in the horse pen and freeze to death.

Her scent was drifting to him every time he turned his head. He faced forward and held it there.

Buck and Teddy couldn't get here too soon.

Thank God she'd quit questioning him.

"Jake? Are you still with me?"

Well, no. Maybe she wasn't letting it go.

"Yeah," he said and to his everlasting shame, he winced as if he were hurting even worse than he was.

It did distract her as he'd hoped it would.

"It won't be much longer," she said in a soothing voice. "I've done everything but your shoulder."

She started talking to try to help him keep his mind on other things, as if he were a little kid and she was afraid he might burst into tears. He felt lower than a snake.

"Where are those caves you said Buck and Teddy may have used last night?"

He jumped on the new subject of conversation.

"Over at Shelf Mountain. It's probably eight or ten miles from here as the crow flies."

"I can't help but worry about them."

"Ah, they'll be along pretty soon now. They've slept out many a time when the weather was worse than last night."

"I'm just going to clean this one cut," she said, and he felt the cold sting of the antiseptic, then the heat of it. But she kept the pressure light and moved on.

She was very gentle. She'd make a good mother.

So what? You're not a little kid—you're just acting like one.

"Put your shirt on," she said, when she was done. "It won't take five minutes to make the oatmeal. Let's have some coffee and something to eat and you'll forget how I've tortured you."

She was still torturing him, but she didn't know it. She made him sit and watch her while she moved around the corner kitchen in her tight jeans and shirt, trying to act like she knew what she was doing.

"I'll make the coffee first," she said, "and then hope we have enough hot water left for the oatmeal. I like mine dry and not mushy. Do you?"

She stood for a minute with the sack of coffee in her hand, staring at him with those blue, blue eyes.

"Hmm? Oh, uh. Yeah. Dry's great. Don't like mush."

Get a handle on your head, Hawthorne.

She went back to work. "I'm just learning to cook," she said, ladling coffee grounds out of the bag with a spoon. "But there's some honey here that we can use lots of if I burn the oatmeal or put too much water in."

Clea gave him that look again. "Do you like honey?"

At last the question soaked in. Jake startled. "Yeah. Uh, sure do. Love it."

"When I got to Montana, I couldn't cook anything but

eggs, but now I can fix oatmeal, make vegetable soup and bake chicken strips in lemon juice and butter."

She looked at him with her brows raised, smiling a little smile, inviting him to share her big accomplishment. Typical pampered rich girl. Thought she'd really done something.

He realized she was expecting him to react.

"Hmm," he said. "Sounds good."

She poured hot water over the grounds she'd put in the coffee pot.

"I don't see any other way to do this," she said. "I guess this is right."

Her butt was exactly the perfect size and would just fit his hands, like her breasts had. Which he was not going to think about again.

He stood up and walked to the front door, opened it and looked out. In all directions. No sign of horses anywhere.

Buck, Teddy, hurry up. Quit your yappin' and ride on in here.

He stepped on outside and stood in the sun for a minute, but they still didn't show up.

"Breakfast is ready," Clea called, "and I don't think you'll need *too* much honey."

She'd cleared all the medicine off the table and set it with two bowls of oatmeal, two cups of coffee and a little plastic bear full of honey.

"Sorry if you take cream in your coffee," she said, "because we don't have any. We do have sugar."

She looked so proud of herself that he couldn't help but smile back.

"Black's the only way," he said. "The blacker the better. Cowboy coffee."

"You got it, cowboy," she said, with a smile that went right through him.

He would've sworn that she was thinking about kissing him.

He went against his promise to himself and thought about kissing her again, too.

Then he forced himself to forget about everything else, relax and enjoy listening to her and looking at her and feeling hot food and coffee in his belly. She got up and refilled his bowl and his cup, and he let himself enjoy being waited on. He could get used to this.

So, when they'd finished eating and he'd carried his dishes to the dishpan in spite of her protests, he said, "Thanks for breakfast, Clea. It was great. I'm gonna ride out now."

CHAPTER TWELVE

IT WAS A fantastic day—cool, fresh, a breeze that held some warmth and snow glittering like crystals in the brilliant sun in the places where the melting hadn't yet begun. Jake had been right when he said it wouldn't last long. But Clea didn't even want to go out.

Or stay in. Inside or out, everything felt empty and weird after Jake rode away. She was used to being alone. She'd been alone lots of times throughout her life. This was silly beyond belief to feel that everything was empty just because Jake had gone.

And silly to have this vague sense of foreboding that he wasn't well enough to ride out by himself. His wounds had looked surprisingly good this morning. Even the bleeding ones showed signs of healing.

She was worrying for the sake of worrying. It must be the altitude. And the fact that talking about finding Ariel had focused her mind where it ought to be, painful as that was. What if she never saw her again?

Clea straightened her shoulders as she began to clean up the kitchen area. Corner. Whatever. She was about to get too attached to Jake. She'd been in danger of that ever since the shooting lesson, and it was all because she had had no affection for too long.

So? Nothing new about that. Get over it.

Ariel was the reason she was here. Somehow, the same was true of Jake. He'd said he liked adventure and challenge. His reason was probably as simple as that.

But *could* he be doing it for her? For no reason but empathy for her love for the mare?

Clea let herself think about that on one level, while she tried to distract herself by working out a system for washing dishes without running water.

No. But that might be. He might not be as shy as the cowboy myth would have him be, but Jake *was* the lone cowboy who had to be on horseback all the time—proven by what he was doing this very minute. Even if he *had* lived with that Tori person for a while.

Jake's motive had to be the oldest, most durable one of all: money. He knew horses and he'd seen what a great horse Ariel was. And he'd seen Clea write a check for thousands of dollars out of her bank account.

She'd better not fool herself for one minute. Jake thought she had money and he expected a reward when he brought Ariel back to her.

And he would deserve one. However, to get it she'd have to find a forgotten gold mine up here in the mountains.

She heated more water on the stove and used her new system of wash and rinse in a dishpan, which had to be emptied by throwing the dirty water out the back door. While she did that, she tried to banish Jake from her mind.

She was acting like a high school girl, thinking about him and remembering how it'd felt to be in his arms and reliving his kisses. Keep this up, and she'd be drawing hearts everywhere and writing their names in them.

Instead she made herself think about the winter ahead and

preparations for it, while she looked out the window at the glittering snow cover on the world. She made the biggest production she could out of cleaning two bowls, two cups, two spoons and a cooking pot, but then she was finished.

Clea checked on both fires, then wandered to the bunks and straightened them, smoothing the covers while she held back thoughts of going to sleep and waking up in Jake's arms. Neediness was a terrible thing. She was really looking at the huge hollow inside her for the first time. When she'd cared about pleasing Brock and Daddy, she couldn't confront that emptiness—because if she did, she'd have to do something about it.

She'd learn how to fill it now that she was determined to take care of herself, but not now. Someday.

Most men—a man like Brock—would've pushed her this morning and really taken advantage of her. Truth be known, she'd wanted more—wanted it as badly as she'd ever wanted anything in her life, but she'd known from the first kiss that sex with Jake would only made her needier and more vulnerable in the end.

To survive, she had to be strong instead.

Jake had acquiesced to her wishes like the gallant cowboy she'd seen that very first time when he rode out of the trees with the foal.

A friendship with him would be nice. And they could have that. All they had to do was not touch each other.

And of course, Jake would have to accept the fact she couldn't give him a reward *if* he did manage to catch Ariel.

She smiled as she tucked the blankets in along the edge of her bunk. *If* he'd put that accomplishment in the adventure-and-challenge column of his life.

It'd be really nice to have another friend besides Buck and Teddy. It had always been so hard for her to trust people, so hard for her to make real friends because she couldn't confide her deepest feelings the way lots of women did. Acquaintances she had by the dozens, but she had no friends she really trusted except for Sherilyn.

Was that sad or what? She'd never really thought much about it: her only real friend was her hairdresser, whom she never saw socially.

But that was how they *could* be friends. Sherilyn was in a totally separate part of Clea's life, one where none of her social acquaintances ever went. Where Brock never went. Or Daddy.

She finished with both bunks, walked to the front door and out onto the little porch. She drew in great gulps of the crisp air.

They were not only thousands of miles away—Sherilyn, Brock and Daddy—but they were in the past. They didn't figure in her life anymore. This was Montana.

She stood there for a long while, looking out at the mountains, at the myriad shades of purples and blues that went on and on forever, showing colors beneath a few white tops that were always covered with snow. She'd never lived in the mountains before and every time she looked outside and saw them, she was still surprised. Still overwhelmed by their beauty, their power.

Montana, the last frontier. The last best place.

Because it had the most space and the most freedom for a person to do and be whatever they wanted.

What I want is a life where the person I live with is my best friend. The one I tell my secrets to. If I ever live with anybody again.

If I don't, let me at least acknowledge all my secrets to myself and know my deepest feelings. Nothing wrong can be fixed if I don't admit the truth of it and look it in the face.

She flashed on Jake's face at the breakfast table. Something about that piercing green gaze made her feel he'd been looking for her secrets. But that couldn't be true. Men didn't think like that.

He had looked at her that same way, except even more intensely, when they were in bed this morning.

Freckles trotted to the wood-rail fence of the pen and whinnied, long and loud, trying to call Jake's horse back to keep him company.

Clea turned and went back into the cabin to get her sunglasses and her coat.

She found her gloves, tied her scarf around her ears and dug in her saddle bag for a brush. The perfect cure for all this thinking would be to go hang out with Freckles.

He came to her and was glad to see her but not effusive about it, being the seasoned working horse that he was.

"You've probably never even seen a horse behave like Ariel-the-Diva," she told him. "You're a good boy."

He stood for her to brush a couple of strokes down his back, but then he pulled away and ran to the other end of the pen. Head high, scenting the air, he whinnied again.

When he stopped to listen for an answer, Clea listened, too.

A faint whinny rode on the breeze.

An unreasonable happiness touched her. Jake was coming back!

But that wasn't the direction he'd gone. Had he had time to ride a big circle?

Had he found Buck and Teddy? Maybe it was all three of them. He'd said it wouldn't take too long for them to get here if they'd started at daylight from where he thought they might've spent the night.

Freckles whinnied again.

Clea ran across the pen to him and climbed up on the rails, trying to see over the curve of the land. Another thought hit her: maybe it was Ariel!

She threw her leg over Freckles and sat on him bareback, trying harder to see while her heart beat faster. Maybe Ariel had escaped from Montana Red....

Maybe, if he'd bred her—which he surely had—she hadn't caught....

That didn't matter. It didn't matter. Even if she weren't bred to a suitable stallion, Ariel could have a baby just like any other mare and it might even be good for her. Maybe becoming a mother would make her less of a princess....

The whinny sounded again, much closer. Freckles whipped around and ran down the rail again, he was so excited. Clea dropped the brush as she lurched halfway off, then she grabbed his mane, righted herself, clamped her knees, and hung on. Her heart was what dropped to the ground.

That whinny wasn't Ariel's.

The next time Freckles called, the new horse appeared, slow trotting over the rise, reins trailing. Clea took one look and slid off Freckles to run open the gate. It was Buster, the horse Teddy had been riding.

Her blood froze. She watched him trot on in and go straight to the old rubber pan under the overhang to clean up the stray feed Jake's colt had left. No horse followed him.

What should she do? What had happened to Teddy?

She closed the gate and ran to Buster's tracks, following them down the slope until she could see over the next roll of the land. The snow was starting to melt everywhere the sun hit it. She couldn't see the end of the trail of hoofprints and she couldn't see a person, another horse or anything that the old guys might have used for shelter.

She turned and looked in the direction Jake had gone. Nothing there, either.

She walked a little farther down and tried to memorize exactly where in relation to the clump of evergreen trees at the end of her vision Buster's hoofprints ended. The closest mountain peak rose just to the right of it.

Shaking her head, knowing already that that would be very little help, in fact none, because everything would look different the closer she got to it, she walked back up to the pen and searched Teddy's saddle. The saddlebags were there but the bedroll was not.

Clea noticed her hands were shaking. She'd give anything if she had a way to reach Jake.

She talked to the horse just to hear a voice.

"Have you been loose all night? Why didn't the old guys unsaddle you if they took the bedroll? Or were they saddling you this morning and hadn't tied it on yet?"

Maybe that was it. Maybe they would come in riding double in just a few minutes.

That thought made her feel better. She decided to unsaddle Buster so he could rest better, although he was already dozing off, head hanging. Working horses were used to being saddled for long hours at a time.

She unbuckled the cinch and pulled the saddle and pad off together, then carried them into the cabin. Her gut kept telling her something was really wrong. Was this the reason for the foreboding she'd felt when Jake rode away?

When she'd walked out there and tried to memorize where the hoofprints led, she hadn't seen any trace of two men riding double headed this way. She had not seen one movement of one living thing.

She hadn't even brought her cell phone because the old

guys had said there was no service. If only she could call emergency services!

But she had no clue where they should look.

She dumped the saddle onto the floor and started going through the bags. At the bottom of the first one, she found Teddy's pistol. Both of them had told her they would be armed, so she need not bring her shotgun.

Remembering that teasing remark made her smile and tear up at the same time.

She was a worse shot with a handgun than with the shotgun, which was the reason she hadn't bought a pistol at the end of her self-protection courses. But she did know how to use one.

Three shots, right? Wasn't that the signal? To ask for help? To ask whoever heard it to come? At least it was in all the old westerns.

Something had to be wrong. Otherwise, surely Buster wouldn't have left Buck's horse. And he certainly wouldn't be running around alone with his saddle still on.

The pistol was loaded. She walked out again over the rise to look, but nothing stirred. No sign of Buck and Teddy. She turned around in a complete circle but saw no sign of Jake, either.

She took off the safety, used both hands to point the muzzle to the brilliant blue sky and pulled the trigger. Waited the count of ten and pulled it again, then once more. Three shots.

Then she went back inside to get her things together.

If Jake didn't come back in half an hour, she'd leave him a note. She couldn't just sit and do nothing.

She packed her saddlebags. It might be a long way to wherever the old guys were. She debated about Jake's first-aid box and finally took it. If he were this long, he could come after her. He'd *have* to follow her—this might turn out to be something she couldn't do by herself.

She felt scared but brave. She had absolutely no choice, because she'd never forgive herself if she could've helped Buck and Teddy and didn't.

She felt scared but determined. No choice.

Once packed, she smothered the fire in the fireplace with the tin dishpan. If Jake had to stay here, he could build another one. The one in the cookstove was going out on its own. She took a box of raisins from the kitchen shelf.

Her fear was growing so fast it was about to eclipse bravery and determination. What if she got lost? What if Buster's trail was all gone and he didn't retrace his steps? What if Jake couldn't find her?

Clea panicked then because she realized she had neither pen nor paper in her pack. Finally, she saw there was a drawer in the table and found it magically held a pen. No paper.

She started going through everything again. She couldn't wait for Jake and she couldn't leave without letting him know what had happened.

In the bottom of her cosmetic bag she found a brochure about the new kind of moisturizer she'd bought, took it to the table and began writing in the margins. She'd barely written Jake's name when he rode into the yard at a high lope and slid to a stop that threw snow in a plume up onto the porch.

He threw himself off the horse and was in the house the next instant.

His eyes blazed at her, took her in, sitting at the table with the pen in her hand, and swept on past her to each corner of the room. To the bunks. To the kitchen corner. In two long strides, he was beside her.

"What the *hell,* Clea? Was that you firing shots? Nobody else is here?"

He looked pale around his eyes, somehow. He was furious.

No, relieved. A dozen more feelings flashed from him in rapid succession too fast to read but he didn't care if she saw.

He dropped to his haunches and looked into her eyes so fiercely she caught her breath. Time stopped.

"Clea," he said, low and rough.

"I'm all right, Jake," she said. "I'm all right."

BUCK BENT his knee and struck at the hillside with the heel of his boot, digging it in, trying to find purchase. To heave Teddy up another notch toward the top, he had to have a place to stand and another handhold higher on the bluff. Helluva mess. The snow was melting, yeah, but the ground itself was clay and it was wet and slicker 'n' snot.

"Bad thing about it is the lack of vegetation," Teddy said. "I need a tree to grab onto, not this here baby brush."

Buck grunted. "From yore end that might be the bad thing, but from here it's draggin' a hunnert and seventy five pound dead weight by the collar with one arm and scrabblin' to find a tree to hold on to with the other."

"I never weighed that in my life," Teddy said.

"Damned if you don't. Maybe as much as two hunnert."

"No more than one-sixty soakin' wet."

"Which you come close to bein' at this very minute."

Buck found a tree root with his fingers, sucked in a lungful of air, pushed with his heel and heaved Teddy upward. He estimated they gained about a foot.

"It's jist the back o' me that's wet," Teddy said, "since I got my chinks on. Them and my vest kept me dry on the front even though I fell facedown."

"Well, that's a relief," Buck said, through his gritted teeth. "Good thing for me you're wearin' all the clothes you got and *them's* wet."

"You're the one draggin' me through the mud and snow," Teddy said in an accusing tone. "And me with a broke leg."

Buck laughed. He tilted his head forward a little more to try to keep the sidehill from knocking his hat off. Ted had lost his when he fell and it was completely out of sight, somewhere at the bottom of this ravine.

"Yeah, I like it. It's 'bout as much fun as I can ever remember," he said.

Toward the top, there was a little bit of an overhang and the way was a good bit steeper, so they both quit talking and used their breath to push on upwards. Teddy was helping as much as he could with his hands and his good leg, but the whole deal was a train wreck.

"More work than wrasslin' calves," Buck pronounced, gasping for a good breath as he pulled Teddy over the top and onto flat land. "I oughtta jist set my horse up here on top and throwed a loop down to rope you."

Teddy tried to keep on helping, there at the last, but what he did was pretty feeble.

"I can take you the rest of the way, now," Buck said.

But Teddy shook his head and sat up. "I got one leg. Just get me up and I'll lean on you."

Buck scooted him over to a rock big enough to lean on, got under his shoulders, and after a couple of tries they managed to stand Teddy up on one foot. Buck got under his shoulder and they hobbled back to the cave where they'd spent the night.

"Wonder where Jake's at," Teddy said after Buck had him sitting on his bedroll, leaning back against his saddle.

Buck went over to the remains of the fire they'd just smothered out before Teddy started chasing his frisky horse and went over the rim.

"No tellin'," he said, starting to lay a new one with the wood they hadn't used during the night. "Who I'm wonderin' about is Miss Clea."

After a minute, Teddy said, "Buck. You'll have to go find her. What if Buster went to the cabin? If he headed that way and got wind of Freckles, he likely did just that."

"Gotta splint your leg first. Clea's a smart girl. She knows the way home. She'll wait for us a day, maybe, and then head out to get help in the mornin'."

"Splint this leg," Teddy said. "And we can ride double to the cabin."

"Yeah," Buck said. "But first we gotta get you warm through. If it keeps warmin' up, we'll move you out in the sun."

Teddy looked like a damn ghost. "Maybe the weather sent Jake to the cabin last night."

"Mebbe so," Buck said. "But we don't need Jake."

However, he was thinking something else.

Like hell, we don't. You ain't in no shape to ride fifteen miles and I ain't in none to hold you on a horse, after the workout my arms have jist had.

He hated that. It was downright hell thinking about the differences that getting a little age on him could make in a man.

"I still think we oughtta say somethin' to Jake when we do come across him," Teddy said. "I cain't believe he'd haul Clea's mare to her ex-husband for money."

"I done told you a hundred times we gotta mind our own business," Buck snapped. "And I've wished *more* than a hundred times that you hadn't called to tell yore *girlfriend* goodbye when you oughtta been helpin' me and Clea make the packs. If you'd jist do yore share of the work, Ted..."

"I couldn'ta jist *disappeared.* No tellin' how long we'll be out here. I had to tell Thelma where I was goin'."

"You're whinin' like a love-struck kid and I ain't puttin' up with it."

"But Jake'd be betrayin' a friend—"

Buck interrupted. "Clea's our friend, not Jake's. They been crosswise since day one."

He thought about that. "Except, to hear 'em both tell it, the shootin' lesson went pretty well. But that was a business deal, not friendship. And she *did* steal the horse, Ted."

"You seen her and that mare together," Ted argued. "You know it's her horse."

"Not if it's true her ex-husband has the papers with his name on 'em," Buck said. "And Jake needs money t' pay fer his place. Don't you wish you'd saved your money all these years and now had a little ranch of your own?"

"Nope. If a man don't move around some he gits in a dog-gone rut. I do wish, though, that Jake would reconsider. When a man like him lets the law trump loyalty to a friend, that proves it—the whole world's headed for hell at a high lope. I'm plumb disappointed in him."

"What I wish is that you'd quit your flirtin' with Thelma Jo McCartney," Buck said. "Or else that she could learn to keep her big mouth shut. I don't know why Carl Baker don't fire her and git a secretary that won't tell the sheriff's business to the world. Thelma's old as the hills, anyhow."

"Ain't as old as you," Ted snapped back at him. "And he keeps her on 'cause she knows everything about everybody and everything *on* everybody and he ain't lived in this county but ten or fifteen years."

Buck struck a match on the sole of his boot.

"What *I* know is that I shoulda left you to slide right on down the side of that bluff. I done worked up a sweat and risked my own neck this mornin', and it ain't got me nothin' but the privilege of listenin' to you give me nothin' but grief."

He threw the lighted match into the kindling as he turned to go out and hunt for something he could use for a splint.

"Mind your own beeswax and try to learn to stay on a horse."

CLEA'S SOFT voice broke into his thoughts but he didn't quite hear what she said. He shifted in his saddle and looked at her riding beside him, opening his mouth to say something—he didn't know what—before he saw that she was looking at her mount and petting him on the neck.

Jake clamped his lips together. Close call. In another heartbeat, he would've made a fool of himself for the second time in as many hours.

Why should he care? Why the hell should he spend one instant caring what she thought about him? It wouldn't be long until she'd hate his guts.

Talk about a waste. What he needed to be caring about was finding the old guys, making sure they were okay and giving her over to them. Right now, he could cheerfully throttle them for even *thinking* about bringing her out here.

She was putting herself through what must be misery to her—bloody wounds and hard rides and horses coming in with empty saddles and panic over her expensive mare—all for the purpose of getting her horse back. And he was here, fighting barbed wire and babysitting, to take her horse away from her.

And his own panic when he'd thought she'd been shot. What the hell was *that* all about? He must be losing his mind. Guilt. He had some kind of a weird attitude toward her because of guilt.

But there was no reason on earth to feel guilty. If she didn't own the horse and if the man who did would pay him, then he had every right to take that mare back to Texas. This was nothing but business.

But the way she'd looked at him when he went bursting into the cabin was not.

And neither was the fear that had torn him up inside when he heard the shots. But he would've felt that for anyone. Any other human being who was as helpless as she would be against a sudden intruder.

But then where did this come from, this unspoken tension riding in the air between them as if it had a horse of its own?

"Is this the best way between the cabin and those caves? Is it possible they would go another way?"

It took him a second to realize that this time she was talking to him.

"If they're not between here and Shelf Mountain," he said, "we'll head back from there to the spot where you left them. We don't know how long Buster's been loose. They may have never made it to the caves."

"His saddle didn't have snow on it and the seat wasn't really wet when he came in," she said, glancing at Teddy's horse, who was now tied to one of Jake's saddle rings and was carrying a pack of extra supplies they'd taken from the cabin. "Does that mean anything?"

He let himself meet her gaze. He'd been trying not to look at her too often.

She must think he was an idiot. He should've been worried about the old guys instead of her the minute he saw Teddy's horse in the pen.

Something was *really* wrong with him. He hadn't cared about anybody else's opinion of him or his behavior since he was ten years old. It used to drive his parents crazy and Elle, too.

"Probably it means that he got away from Teddy this morning," Jake said. "Otherwise, he would've had to have found a really protected spot somewhere for the night. Even underneath a thick tree, snow would've fallen into crevices in the saddle.

"Buck and Teddy are two of the best," he said. "Not just at catching wild horses, but in the wilderness in general. Something probably just spooked this horse this morning and he got away."

"I keep thinking we'll meet up with them any minute," she said. "I'm doing a one-eighty scan all the time."

"It'll slow 'em down quite a bit, riding double," he said. "If they did stay at the cave for the night, they probably wouldn't have made it this far yet."

"I know you're worried," she said. "And I want you to know that I'm just sick to my stomach over what might've happened to them. They're so funny and so good to me. I'm just realizing, riding along here, that they've already sort of wormed their way into my heart. Past friendship even."

He looked at her carefully. She meant it. She wasn't just trying to be polite or sociable or compassionate for his sake.

"At first I didn't think they'd let me come with them—or even that they would come to look for Ariel by themselves, since you were already out here. I really think they gave in because they saw how upset I was and they knew I'd go crazy trying to sit home and wait. I'll be thrilled if I could help them in anyway."

Her voice suddenly sounded as if she might be close to tears. It tightened this pull he felt toward her and so did the fact that she had real feelings for Buck and Teddy. They were a couple of chattering old magpies but he—and Clea, too, evidently—would be lost without them if suddenly they weren't around anymore.

"They're a couple of pretty tough old birds," he said. "Right now, I'm more worried about you being sick to your stomach than I am about Buck and Teddy bein' short a horse."

That made her laugh. Which made him feel like a pretty powerful guy.

"I'll give you fair warning," she said. "I promise."

CHAPTER THIRTEEN

LAUGHTER ALWAYS made people feel closer. Clea could feel a smile lingering on her lips that matched the one on Jake's. They were still exchanging glances, sort of waiting for something as if one of them would make another joke any minute. Or as if they both wanted to keep talking, but suddenly neither knew what to say.

She said, "Is your place anywhere near here?"

He looked a little startled. Maybe he thought that was a nosy question. At first, she thought he wasn't going to answer, but then he shook his head. "No. It's over in the Garnet Range."

"What do you plan to do with it?"

Again the glance, the hesitation. This must be a private subject with him.

"Breed horses. Start some colts."

"What kind?"

"Quarter. All-around ranch horses. Maybe an emphasis on cutters."

"I love to try to figure out what to cross with what," she said. "Every time I've bred one of my mares I got completely caught up in trying to create the perfect horse."

He chuckled. "That's the dream."

"And this time I didn't even get to choose. I'll have a

Thoroughbred/warmblood crossed with wild. Thanks to the unintentional broodmare."

Jake looked at her, then looked away.

"Don't you think?" she said.

He turned to meet her eyes. He'd lost the smile and looked about to say something serious.

It turned out to be only, "Maybe she won't catch."

"I hope not," she said fervently. "I pray not. Ari's pretty old for a first baby."

They rode for a while, each lost in private thoughts and not saying very much. Clea wanted badly to be the first to spot a sign of Buck and Teddy so she could be the hero and not always the ignorant greenhorn, but the land was overwhelming and beautiful and complicated and there was more to see with every change in the landscape than she could take in.

It was so enormous she felt completely insignificant. Buck and Teddy would be hard enough to find in all this space, much less Ariel. At least, Buck and Teddy would be trying to find her, too.

Would Ariel be glad to see her? Was she scared of being out in all this openness?

"Once, a long time ago when I first got into horses," she said, "my trainer took me with him to a sale where he was offering some two's he'd raised that he thought weren't gonna be good enough to show. A man from Wyoming bought one of them, a mare named Dee-Dee, and as he led her out of the stall into the aisle, he slapped her on the rump and said she'd never see the inside of a box stall again."

Jake turned to look straight at her. Questioning, as if to ask the point of the story.

"I couldn't stop thinking about that," she said. "He said

she'd be turned out for the *winter* loose in a forty-thousand acre pasture."

He grinned and her heart turned over. She forgot what she was talking about.

"Clea," he said. "There are thousands and thousands of horses who have never seen the inside of a box stall. They've survived just fine."

She felt a little foolish. "Well," she said. "I just keep thinking about Ariel. She's never known anything but luxury."

She waited, but he didn't say, "Don't worry, I'll get her back for you." Or, "It won't be long now and she can survive it for a little while."

"Horses are like humans," he said, "in more ways than being a herd animal. They, too, can adapt to nearly anything."

But I can't adapt to losing Ariel forever. I have too much other adapting to do. I don't have the strength for that now.

She didn't say it, though. Cowgirls don't whine.

They rode for what seemed a long distance, Clea thinking about Ariel, worrying about her delicate legs and her lack of a thick haircoat, and her rebellious disposition that could make a stallion really hurt her if she refused to obey him.

But how could she be so selfish as to be worrying about herself and her mare instead of Buck and Teddy?

She tried to steady herself by standing up in her stirrups and stretching her legs, then sitting back down in her saddle again with her shoulders squarer and her back straighter. Now that she thought about it, it was as if the whole world had tilted at her first glimpse of Buster trotting over the rise into the cabin yard with an empty saddle and it still sat sideways.

Especially when it came to Jake. When he'd come rushing in fired up with worry about her safety, she'd felt a closeness with him, but now he seemed as remote as that faraway mountain several ranges away with its white cap shining against the sky.

He was gone into his thoughts so far he seemed to have disappeared.

How selfish could she *be?* He was worried sick about Buck and Teddy, no doubt.

Pray God nothing serious had happened to them.

The rolling land itself was changing constantly and she felt as if it were shifting beneath their horses' feet. The sun was warming fast, like Indian summer, melting the snow away in all the high spots. That made the uneven ground into stripes of tan grassy brush and white snow, with clumps of green scattered here and there. That variety made it hard to see everything at once.

Even two men on one horse could be lost down in one of the shallow draws and then come into sight a minute later.

Riding at an angle down a gradual slope, her horse went a step or two past before she realized Jake was stopping.

"Whoa up," he said. "Listen."

The sound was on them, then, like a huge rock rolling down a hill, a hollow thrumming that came closer, fast. She'd only just recognized it as hoofbeats when the horses plunged over the rim of the hill about fifty yards away, coming down through the snow, throwing it everywhere in plumes up behind them.

Wild ones. Nobody had to tell her that.

Heads up, eyes bright, manes and tails flying like flags, they ran bunched together directly at Clea and Jake, who were frozen in place watching them come. For one long minute it seemed they would run right into them, but the horse in the lead, a gray already furry for winter, spotted the human intruders and began swerving away.

In spite of that, though, they shook the ground beneath her

and agitated the air around her so much it stirred her hair. She thought she could smell their good horsiness over the cleanness of the snow and the spiciness of the pine. She *knew* she could feel the ancient wildness in them, see the free joy in their hard flashing hooves and flying round bodies.

They took her breath with them onto the pristine path they were breaking through the snow and carried it on up the savage slope, striking rocks and tearing them loose to roll. None of it slowed them a bit.

It was when they topped out and plunged down the other side that they took her heart. No hesitation allowed. Up, over and down into the great unknown without a pause. Without a fear.

Later, when she ran the whole vision through her mind again, Clea could not believe it could possibly be true, but it was: during that first thrilling minute in shock, she hadn't even thought about Ariel. The wild band had been nearly to the top of the ridge when she looked to see if there was a black horse among them. When they were closer to her, she didn't think about Ariel at all. She couldn't. She could only *be.*

Because they were only *being,* too, pouring all the force in them into that run. All their being, all their force, all their mystery.

She couldn't move until the sound of them was gone. Jake was still, too, staring at the place where they had disappeared.

"Were they running for joy?" she asked. "Or were they scared of something? They didn't look scared."

He turned and she saw her own feelings mirrored in his eyes. The look lasted a long time.

TO JAKE, it was a conversation without words, like one he might've had with Elle.

Like one he *did* have with his little sister long ago when he was ten years old. They'd ridden far up into the hills on the ranch where their dad was working and spotted some wild horses.

They'd climbed off their mounts and, lying on their bellies, hidden at the top of a ridge, they'd spent half the afternoon watching two stallions carry on a long, protracted fight while the mares and babies had grazed and played as if nothing was going on.

Clea's wondering look was the very same as Elle's was that day. Another thing about this Texas princess that reminded him of his little sister.

His little sister at six years old and this grown woman had the same innocence, somehow.

Clea finally said, "Jake?"

"Joy," he said. "I think they were just feeling good."

He kissed to his horse and they started moving again.

"Now I know why Ariel went with Montana Red," she said. "I wanted to go with that bunch we just saw."

"They're something else," he said.

"Doesn't it break your heart to catch them? How can you take them away from such freedom?"

He squinted a look at her as they rode out into the sunlight.

"That bunch we just saw was about to starve out when we brought 'em over here. They look a whole lot better now."

"Well, yeah, but there's a limit to how many this refuge can take, right? Sometimes you catch them and they live in captivity the rest of their lives."

Her tone wasn't accusatory, just wanting to know.

"Lots of 'em make good usin' horses. And in captivity they get plenty to eat without scroungin' for every bite. For centuries we've pushed them onto worse and worse land—sorta like what happened to the Indians. In a drought or a hard winter, it's really hard for them to survive."

"I'm still seeing the wild ones in my head," Clea said. "They went so fast. Was that the stallion behind them or ahead?"

"The buckskin bringing up the rear. The stallion follows to keep everybody together, no stragglers. *And* so he'll be between the mares and young ones, and any predator behind."

"At first I thought it was the stallion in the lead. That horse seemed so sure and full of power."

"That was the lead mare. She's the boss for everything except a challenge from another stallion, or when it's time for the young studs to be driven out and stuff like that."

"Well, then, that gives Ariel two bosses," Clea said, chuckling at the thought. "She may be ready to come home after all, unless she's already in a fight to take the lead mare's place."

"If she is, she'll be cut up and bruised pretty good when we find her," Jake said.

"That's a bad image but a good sign," Clea said with a smile so sweet he couldn't look away from it. "You said *we.* Maybe Buck and Teddy will be just fine when we find them and we can all work as a team."

He answered with a noncommittal grunt. No sense ruining the moment with a big argument.

"I could just wring Ari's neck," she said. "If she hadn't jumped out of the pen, Red couldn't have taken her."

"He might've. Montana Red's famous for tearing down a corral fence to steal a bunch of mares."

She nodded. "Buck and Teddy told me."

He felt her eyes on his face as they trotted down into the valley. "I was watching the whole thing from upstairs and I got so mad you didn't do anything to stop him," she said. "But now I see why."

"Why?" he asked, turning to look at her as if this were some kind of test for him.

"Awe," she said.

He chuckled. "Yeah. And fear. No animal's more dangerous than a charging stud horse."

"Did you really think he'd charge you?"

"Hard to say. Rumor is Red's a man-fighter but who knows? Anybody who's ever had any dealings with him likes to tell a big story about it, so there's as many lies floating around out there as there are truths."

"Did you know I was watching you and him when he stole Ari?"

He gave her a sharp glance that told her nothing and shook his head.

Jake didn't say anything. What did she expect from him? Why did she keep talking about that moment when he'd been outmanned by the stud?

"I knew you weren't going to 'take me to raise' as you put it," she said. "I thought that might fall into the category of helping a neighbor in need, but it didn't. So I was really surprised when I got to Buck and Teddy's, and they told me you had gone to get Ari back."

So *that* was what it was about. Again. She sensed something. She *was* one determined woman.

This is your chance. She's begging you. Spit it out, boy, and it'll be a load off.

He couldn't even open his mouth.

"I couldn't figure out why," she persisted, forcing a casual, easy tone to encourage him to answer when he could sense the edge beneath it. "I still can't."

Jake lifted his reins and rode on ahead.

"Look," he said. "Any horseman would hate to see a mare like that ruined."

Hypocrite.

Well, it's not a lie.

"Keep your eyes peeled," he said. "We're getting close enough that Buck and Ted could've come this far by now. For sure. We're nearly to the cave."

Clea let the question go. Thank God.

They rode over a couple of rolling rises in the land and then up out of the shallow valley onto a hillside that was higher than the ones they'd just crossed.

"The other side of this is what's called the Shelf," he said. "It has a couple of caves, one with a smoke hole in it. Best shelter for miles around and just downstream from that watering hole Buck and Teddy were telling you about."

He led the way up and then around the side. They weren't up too high but it definitely felt as if they were on a shelf above the rocky river that ran below. The trail they were following was about three horses wide and well-worn.

Jake was looking ahead. "Yep," he said. "There's smoke. If it's them and they're still here this time of day, something's wrong."

"Hello," he yelled. "Anybody home?"

For the longest time he got no answer. Anybody could come out of that cave, maybe with a weapon. He and Clea didn't have much room to turn around and get out of there if they needed to.

He didn't want to scare her by saying that but he did want to protect her. He moved his horse forward on over in front of hers, and said, "Stay behind me." They rode closer and closer to the cave opening.

Then Buck's rough voice sounded and he appeared, bent over in the mouth of the cave. "Well, speak o' the devil," he said.

Jake slumped with relief in the saddle and he heard Clea let go of a long breath. Buck seemed calm and at least *he* was unhurt.

"Whoa," Jake said and, standing in the stirrup to dismount, called, "you two gettin' too old to catch your own horse?"

Buck walked out to meet them. "Ain't I done told you I'm gittin' plumb riled at you makin' fun of us old folks all the time?"

Clea dismounted, too. "Oh, Buck, I'm so happy to see you," she said. "Is Teddy all right?"

Buck took the reins of the horses.

"Surprised to see you two have run into each other," he said, looking them over. "Well, you three, countin' Buster. Looks like a dad-gummed reunion and me and Teddy missed it."

"Where's Ted?" Jake asked. "What's wrong?"

"I've splinted his leg, but I reckon the real trouble's in his head, as usual," Buck said.

He walked off with all three horses, taking them onto the shelf of open grass that curved back into the mountain on the other side of the cave's entrance. Jake glimpsed Buck's horse there on a stake rope. The drop-off to the river was steep, even if it wasn't more than eight or ten feet high.

Clea went in first, ducking her head to get through the entrance, with Jake at her heels. The entrance was wide and the smoke hole a natural opening of a good size, so they had plenty of light to see Teddy sitting propped against Buck's saddle, wearing his coat and a blanket with one bare foot sticking out from under it. His hurt leg was mostly uncovered, splinted with strips of wood, a feed bag lying limply on the calf.

"Snow," he said, gesturing at it. "To keep the swellin' down."

He pulled at the blanket when Clea came closer. "Don't feel quite decent," he said.

"You're covered," she said. "You think it's broken?"

She was using her crisp nurse voice. Jake couldn't quite suppress a smile.

He shook his head. "I broke bones before. I know it ain't. It's nothin' but a sprain. It's jist swole up to where I can't get my foot in my boot yet, that's all."

"And I'm sure it'd hurt like crazy hanging off a horse," she said.

He sat up straighter and nodded, thumping his thigh for emphasis. "I'll keep it cold, take this swelling down tonight and by morning I'll be ready to ride."

"What happened?" Jake asked.

"Slipped on a little spot of cotton-pickin' ice and slid down the bluff nearly to the river," he said. "Chasin' that damn stupid Buster. Spooked right out of my hands—at a shadow, like a two-year-old, even though he's going on ten—with me trying to tie my bedroll on."

Buck came in.

"I damned near left him where he lay," he said. "Had to drag his worthless carcass with one hand and climb with th' other."

He went to stir up the fire. "Not to mention I had to climb down *again* and git his hat."

Clea saw Ted's hat sitting on top of his empty boot to dry out near the fire.

"Maybe we should haul you into town and see what Doc Fuller thinks," Jake said, squatting on his haunches beside Teddy.

He moved the sack of snow and looked at the swollen ankle.

"And maybe not," Teddy said, his grizzled face turning red. "We come out here to catch some horses and we done seen 'em, and I don't aim to miss the fun."

Clea's gasp of delight made Jake's heart race like the wild horses they'd seen. She was squatted beside Ted, too, but she stood up fast and looked at Buck for confirmation.

"You saw them? Ariel and Montana Red?"

He winked at her.

Buck said, "In the flesh. They was leaving this watering hole ahead of the storm yesterday evening. Me and Teddy got here jist in time to see 'em."

"How'd she look? Do you think she's all right?"

"Looked like a big, black mare to me," he said. "Looked fine. Moving right along while they crossed that flat out there, actin' like she knowed where she was goin'."

She turned back to Ted, who said, "They was hightailin' on out of here at a pretty good pace, huntin' shelter from the storm."

"Which way did they go from the flat?"

"Uh oh, no you don't," he said, laughing at her. "You may be in cowgirl school, but you ain't graduated yit. Settle down and wait fer me and my boot. We'll all go after your mare at first light."

JAKE RODE OFF and left them first thing the next morning.

The sky was turning pink-and-yellow in the east and the wind was gentle, for once, as the four of them rode single file down off Shelf Mountain and started across the flat. On the other side of it, Jake abruptly stopped.

"I'm going on ahead," he said. "I'll check out Blue Streak and meet you at the Dog Creek crossing around noon. It'll save Teddy a long ride for nothing if Red's bunch isn't there."

Then he turned his horse and rode off at a long lope.

Clea's stomach knotted even harder than it had been when she woke up that morning. She looked from Teddy to Buck, both sitting their horses and staring after him.

"Will he really meet us?" Her voice squeaked, so she cleared her throat and tried again. "Or is he trying to dump us and catch Ariel by himself?"

"Didn't wait for us to say yea nor nay nor kiss-my-foot," Buck said. "Well, I'll be damned."

"Will it really save a long ride if the horses aren't at that canyon?"

"When you're chasing horses over thousands of acres there ain't no way of *knowin'* how to save a long ride," Teddy said.

Buck nodded and started his horse moving. "Mebbe we was gittin' on his nerves. Jake likes a lot of time by hisself."

"He don't need to treat me like some helpless old man," Teddy said. "By damn, I can ride as long and fast as he can."

"He's on a younger, faster horse," Buck said. "So right now, you can't."

They rode three abreast over the rise.

"Nothin' to do but head for Dog Creek," Buck said.

"I kept up with him all the way from the cabin to the Shelf Mountain without complaining and never asked for a rest," Clea said. "I don't understand why he left us."

"He may be dumping us," Teddy said. "He shore tried hard enough last night to talk us into going home. Think about that, folks."

"Jake's a man of his word," Buck said. "He'll come to Dog Creek. Whether he'll stay with us after that, I don't know."

"Well, it makes me mad," Clea said. "Why didn't he tell us earlier? Wouldn't it be easier to catch Ariel if he had some help?"

Truth be told, she was scared more than mad. Somehow, even though Jake had come to her hurt and nearly helpless, she had started to depend on him. Deep down.

"He can't catch her," she said. "I'll have to be there. Ariel will come to me."

She hoped and prayed that was true. What if the contrary mare was still besotted with Red?

"Him ridin' off like that makes me feel like a little kid gittin' punished," Teddy said.

"Me, too," Clea said.

"Well then, kids, I reckon that makes me the grown-up. I'll be the one to boss you babies around."

"That's nothin' new," Teddy said. "Is it, Clea?"

But she wasn't listening. She followed as Buck led them around a stand of pine trees and down into the little valley.

"I think Jake just needs time alone," she said. "He'll probably stay with us after we meet at Dog Creek."

She was missing Jake.

Until this minute, she'd had no idea how much.

CHAPTER FOURTEEN

JAKE HELD THE binoculars close against his face so he wouldn't give in to the temptation to drop them and stick his fingers in his ears. Buck, Teddy and Clea made so much noise trying to be quiet that he couldn't even think.

"If you ever git done glassin' that valley, Jake, I'd like to use them binocs," Teddy said, in a loud whisper.

Jake gritted his teeth.

Forget meeting them at Dog Creek Crossing at noon. Why couldn't they have gone straight there as he'd told them to do? Instead, they'd arrived at Blue Streak only a little while after he got here.

He should've sent the old guys packing the minute they showed up all those months ago. And for having the unmitigated gall to bring Clea out into the refuge in the first place—well, he should've wrung their necks the minute he got to the cave.

Now the three of them were surrounding him, spread out along the rocks at the top of the canyon, checking out the horses. He kept wanting to stick out his elbows and push them away, even though nobody was that near to him.

This horse hunt was turning him into a sour hard-ass and he hated that.

"Let me have them glasses," Teddy said again.

Jake glanced around and saw that this time Teddy was harassing Buck.

"Not yet," said Buck. "Shoulda thought to bring your own."

"Well, that pair *is* mine—"

Clea interrupted. "You can use mine in just a minute, Teddy...in just...a...minute...I think she looks good. Really, she's grazing along there as if she's pretty content...oh, I hope she doesn't want to stay here..."

"Good God, what *she* wants! She's a *horse,* Clea. You want her back, don't you?" Jake snapped his mouth shut and clenched his jaw until it hurt. Why'd he have to say that? Clea wasn't going to *get* her mare back.

"I just mean it could make her harder to catch," she said.

She'd tried for a hard tone of voice but it came out shaky, like she might cry. Damn.

Exactly why she shouldn't be here. Now that she'd seen the mare, she'd cry if he missed the catch and if he didn't miss, she'd cry even more.

"I'm sorry," she said, more firmly. Much more firmly. "Seeing her makes me a little bit emotional."

She swept her blue eyes away from him to Buck, then to Ted. "I really think I can call her to me when we get close enough for her to smell me."

"Yeah. Right," Jake snapped. "As if Red might not have something to say about that."

She lifted her chin and threw her hair back, cutting into him with a hard stare. "You'll see."

Her look was such a challenge he almost believed she could do it.

What if she could? What if she did? What would he do?

"I brought her halter," she said.

As if she knew what he was thinking. For fifty grand could he rip the leadrope out of her hands?

The old guys should never have brought her out here. This was all their fault.

Firmly, he brought his mind back from Clea and put it on his job. The horses were still there, still grazing peacefully, still unaware of any danger. They'd be going to water late this afternoon.

He would catch the mare.

Damn! He wanted this horse hunt over. Finished. History.

Which was entirely the wrong frame of mind for getting it done.

"All right," he said, squinting at the sun. "Let's start working our way down and into position. As long as the wind blows against us, they'll come right on in to water."

They mounted—Teddy was so wrung-out Jake had to give him a leg up—and as they rode downhill and around the edge of the grassy valley to the creek, he talked them through the plan.

"We'll stay mounted and hidden in the trees, separately, but all with the wind right. The pool's got plenty of cover. After they've got their bellies full, when they start moseying back out of the little cove and back to the trail, I'll ride in and throw my rope on the black mare."

Damn. What would he do then? Tell Clea to kiss her horse goodbye? Wait until they'd all ridden out and back to the ranch, after Clea had had her big reunion with her darling and her mind set that they'd be together from now on, and *then* tell her?

He pulled his thoughts up short. He had to, damn it, he *had* to stop worrying about Clea and focus on catching the mare.

"What you're there for is to drive her toward me if I miss and she makes a break. Don't be too picky about trying to single her out. Drive 'em all to me if she's in a bunch."

He looked at Clea. "Don't rush them. Keep quiet until I ride out."

"There must be fifteen horses in the band," Clea said.

"No, I counted thirteen, including Ariel," Jake said. "The stud, five wild mares, three foals and three yearlings. It's a big band. They'll come and go to and from the water pretty much single file through the trees until they hit the open about twenty yards from the pool."

"So you want to catch her in the open?"

"Right. I'll be carrying two loops, just in case."

CLEA SAT ON Freckles in the hiding place Jake had assigned them, thinking the time would never come. She couldn't see much except the pool itself and the hills on the opposite side of it. The horses had been somewhere over in that general direction when they'd looked at them earlier. The trees were thicker over there and the bank of the creek steeper. So far, no movement anywhere.

Jake had assured her that the herd would use this trail because that's the way all the wild animals in the area approached this water. The bank on this side was low and open, which meant the water was more accessible, predators could be seen sooner and escape would be much easier than if they used the steep bank on the opposite side.

Freckles let out a small snoring sound and then shifted to rest a different foot. Clea wished she could doze off, too, and escape for even a few minutes from this roaring emotion inside her. Excitement, hope, fear. Excitement, hope, fear.

Fear Ariel would get away. Fear Ariel would be hurt by the rope. Fear Ariel would fight to stay with Montana Red.

Think positively. Send good vibes. Send it out into the universe that you're getting your horse back. That Ariel will run to you.

The first indication she had was a rustling noise in the trees. Her heart began to race. She turned her head and there was the lead mare emerging into the open. The gray looked around a little but she wasn't worried. The rest of the band came on quickly behind her—Ariel next.

Clea smiled. So did that mean she *was* in contention for the position of lead mare?

Maybe. She had some bite marks on her hindquarters and neck that might be from a fight with the gray mare. Or they might be from when Montana Red stole her.

Montana Red. The selfish old bastard. Then the lord of them all followed his band into Clea's line of sight and stopped her heart.

He halted at the edge of the water. Head up, nostrils flaring, he snorted at the air a little and looked around, wary thief that he was.

Bad to the bone.

The wind came out of the west and red streaked the sky. He took them both for his own—his tail and long, rough mane lifted in rhythm with his breathing, his color deepened with the light.

He, too, had savage bite and kick marks all over him, and he wanted the world to know he was proud to bear them. His stance, every line of him, emitted such a pure masculinity Clea couldn't help but respond. He was magnificent.

Dangerous. The naked need to possess, to rule, rolled off him in waves.

He was much quieter than the overexcited stallion she'd seen in her yard, yet somehow he seemed far more savage. Wildness and dominance were coiled in him now, to be unleashed at any time, his presence so strong there was no power but his.

Clea couldn't break it, even to look at Ariel.

The horses in the band relaxed and spread out along the bank, eager to drink. Finally Clea tore her gaze away from the stallion to search for her mare.

The way they settled in, with two of the other mares between her and Ariel, she could see only Ariel's hindquarters fairly well—because she was taller than the others—and her head when she lifted it with the water running off her muzzle.

She looked good considering what she'd been through. Surprisingly good.

Clea's eyes returned to the stallion. He had walked out into the water and was drinking deeply.

They all took their time, while Clea tried to control her excitement, which was building by the minute. The foals drank all they wanted and began to play, splashing in the water, pretending to fight, chasing each other along the bank and up onto a grassy hillside, stopping to sniff at the snow still frozen in the low places.

She smiled at them, loving it when the smallest one sniffed at the snow, touched it with his muzzle, and then jumped back in mock fear and ran to his playmates. Now, that was what Jake's little orphan foal needed.

When Clea got back to the ranch, she'd call around and try to find a companion for Montana Red's other baby. She'd been born at such a weird time of year it wouldn't be easy, but surely there'd be something near her size. Thinking about that now, visualizing the orphan foal in Jake's barn and her own new cabin home, seemed like dreaming of a completely different world.

As for Texas, that was a different lifetime. She would never have even imagined being where she was this very minute.

For what seemed to Clea an endless hour, the horses hung around and played or rested. She couldn't help but watch

Red most of the time. Finally, he and the lead mare both showed signs of getting restless. The gray horse turned away from the water and headed for the trail. Ariel hung back.

The mares nickered to their foals, who came running, and followed the lead mare.

But Ariel didn't. She looked around and then wandered at an angle through the rest of the horses who were drifting together to leave the water. She was coming straight toward Clea's hiding place! Closer. She raised her head and looked so straight at Clea it was hard to believe that she didn't see her through the trees.

Surely, on some level, she sensed her there. Their old connection was *not* broken!

Montana Red got behind a dun mare and nipped at her to get her moving but he hadn't noticed Ariel yet. Soon he would. She was still headed in Clea's direction. Clea edged out from behind the trees hoping she'd see her.

Montana Red lifted his head. He turned and fixed his eye on Ariel. He started toward her….

Instinctively, Clea did, too, just a little more…. Ariel lifted her head and looked in her direction, so Clea leaned forward.

Ariel turned her head toward the stallion. No!

"Ariel!" Clea called. Then louder, "Ariel!"

Everything exploded into confusion and, in a heartbeat, into panic. Horses scattered in all directions, mares calling to their foals, the foals squealing back. Whinnies of terror rang out against the mountains and Montana Red bugled orders.

Jake rode into the middle of the madness, his loop over his head and whirling, whipping the air with a menacing sound that carried even over the whinnies and hooves striking rocks and pounding toward the opening in the trees. Clea couldn't see it all except there was still space between Ariel and the other horses….

Ariel threw her head even higher, Jake's rope hovered over it for one breath and then her ears vanished and Montana Red was at her, nipping her butt, snaking her onto the trail to follow the others streaming after the lead mare now. Vanishing so rapidly they were already nothing but shadows up the trail.

That picture stayed in Clea's mind. That and when she turned, the fury on Jake's face that had made it pale under his tan and put a fire in his green, flashing eyes so hot that it burned her to look at it.

"IT'S BEEN nearly twenty-four hours and he ain't got over it yet," Teddy said, turning to glance across the distance at Jake. "I never seen him so riled."

Buck nodded. He'd been thinking the very same thing.

He and Teddy separated to ride on either side of a little rock outcropping while they kept an eye on Clea and Jake riding ahead. Way ahead. But not *with* each other. Jake wasn't speaking to the poor girl except to tell her what to do.

They'd already crossed the river on the wooden bridge. But not together. They stayed as far apart as they could get and still do the job—Clea way on Buck's right, Jake off on Teddy's left.

All four of them were spread out along the north side of Montana Red's band, which was also on the other side of the river now. They were gradually drifting the horses south. Slowly, slowly, so as not to alarm them. Staying out of sight almost all the time, only appearing on the horizon once in a while to keep them moving on.

It had taken a good while for the band to settle down after that little rodeo at the watering hole. If Buck and Teddy and Jake hadn't known their habits so well, they'd have had a hard time even finding them again in just one day.

But they were doing fairly well now, since nobody was

even trying to get close. Even if they hadn't had that scare, it was best to take it easy. Horses can concentrate on only one thing at a time, so if they were moving in the direction a man wanted them to go, it was best not to distract them by pushing too hard.

Once Montana Red's lead mare had taken the band into the narrow valley on the other side of Wister Ridge, the humans would split up. From there, two people could guide them into the funnel that would lead into the old horse trap, after the other two had gone on ahead to check on its fences and open the gate.

They'd have to use the trap now that the roping hadn't worked.

"Damnedest thing," Teddy said as they came back together again. "Like you said, Jake don't generally hold a grudge."

"He's wantin' to get outta here. How would you feel if you was fixin' to have to look into them big blue eyes of Clea's and tell her she couldn't have her horse back? Which she's just gone through all this hell to git."

"We shoulda stayed home," Teddy said.

"It wouldn'ta helped any. She'da come out here by herself and got lost and mebbe even killed."

"I don't like this," Teddy said. "I don't wanta see it. We'll have to take her all the way back to the ranch, Buck. Reckon she'll bawl and squall the whole way?"

Buck's stomach tightened with dread. He'd already thought of that. He wanted to change the subject. Teddy always got one bone of a thought and worried it plumb to death.

"I cain't see Clea right now," he said. "I hope she don't wander too far and git lost, jist from tryin' to stay away from Jake."

Teddy ignored that.

"Reckon we should warn her?"

Buck's whole body tightened up on that one.

"None of our business," he said. "Cain't git into it, Ted. You know that as well as I do."

"It's our business if we have t' hear it, though."

"Mebbe Jake ain't gonna tell her until we git home," Buck said.

Teddy just shook his head and they rode quiet for a heartbeat or two while their horses' hooves struck the bridge in a steady rhythm.

"That'd be worse, 'cause then she'd be even more settled into bein' reunited with her mare," Buck spoke up.

"Wonder if Jake knows that?" Teddy asked. Then he answered himself, "He wouldn't want to hurt her anymore than he has to, I know that."

He gave Buck a hopeful look. "Maybe he won't do it," he said. "Maybe he'll change his mind and let Clea keep the mare."

"After him bein' this mad at her? I don't think so," Buck said. "And he's wantin' that money. *And* not to put too fine a point on it, she *don't* own the horse, Ted."

Teddy nodded. "I cain't let it go, though."

"You never can," Buck muttered.

Teddy shot him a hurt look, but criticism didn't stop him. It never did.

"Somehow it jist don't quite seem Western to me, though," he said. "Puttin' the letter of the law over what's real. That *is* Clea's mare—you know that when you see 'em together fer five minutes."

He stopped his horse to rest his hurt leg a minute so Buck stopped, too.

"In my book, Jake's walkin' a fine line here," Ted's words rolled on. "I know he's blood kin to you, and he's nearly that to me, so it hurts me to say it. But in this deal, he's skatin' mighty close to puttin' money over friendship."

They started the horses moving again.

"It feels that way to you because you and me don't have no debt and no ranch, I'd say. *And* bein' a tad bit older and all, we have fatherly feelings for her and want to take care of her," Buck countered.

"*He's* got feelin's for her. And not fatherly ones, either, would be my best opinion."

Buck turned to look at him. "You seen it, too?"

Teddy nodded, looking him in the eye.

Buck held the gaze, then looked off into the distance, thinking.

"You done give me a idea, Ted," he said.

They rode on.

Finally, Teddy gave in. "Well," he said, "you gonna tell it to me or do I have to reach over there and slap it outta you?"

"First let me say that this here may look like gittin' in his business when I been sayin' I won't."

After he thought about it a minute, Teddy said, "All right. You've said it."

"And let me say that I think the world o' my nephew and his little sister and his brothers."

"That's said, too."

"What I'm tryin' to do is keep him from makin' a mistake that he might always regret. From doin' somethin' that he might look back on when he's the age I am now and think, 'I'd give everything I've got if I hadn't've done that.'"

Teddy waited a second or two and then he said in a coaxing voice, "You still ain't told me what it is you're doin'."

"Tryin' to give him th'opportunity to see things a different way. You might say, a chance to change his mind."

"You done built my curiosity up to a fever pitch," Teddy drawled. "You can spit it out now, Buck."

Buck kept looking at the mountains, letting them soothe his eyes while he thought it through. "Reckon what'd happen if we kinda made ourselves scarce sometimes?"

After a minute, Ted said, "You mean—"

"I mean I seen how Clea looks at Jake once in a while, too," Buck said.

Teddy considered the thought. When he'd made Buck wait long enough, he said, "Hmm. The old Hawthorne sneakiness at work."

Buck didn't jump right on it. He waited as long as he could while he was holding his breath, dying to know if Teddy would cooperate.

They rode up to the bridge and started onto it, their horses paying no attention.

"Sure is good to be astraddle of a seasoned horse, ain't it?" Buck said. "I thought for damn sure that colt of Jake's was gonna throw him again when he hit this thing a while ago."

But still, Teddy didn't come back with more on his favorite subject.

Finally, Buck said, "Ted. You still ain't told me what you think."

"I'm gonna git you a diaper and a bow and arrer," Teddy said. "And a pair of little wings. What do they call that little feller?"

Buck grinned so Ted wouldn't see his words had stung. What the hell was the matter with him? Was he makin' fun of this whole idea? Didn't he have no imagination?

He was supposed to be so sympathetic to Clea. Well, didn't he want to do something that might help her?

"I reckon you mean Cupid," he said. "But I already got my angel wings. Cain't you see 'em?"

Teddy gave him a good long look and what might be called a smirk.

"What I see is you ain't got the sense God gave a wooden goose," he said.

Buck picked up the pace a little, his horse's hooves striking the bridge with a stronger ring. He oughtta just ride off and leave the aggravating old fart.

"Fer somebody talkin' such a good game about stayin' outta Jake's business," Teddy went on—although nobody had asked him to— "you're fixing to mess with the very most dangerous part of his life. By that I mean women."

Buck gave him a scornful glance and drew himself up to be dignified.

"I ain't worried. Jake ain't riskin' that heart of his again. Not after Victoria. All I want is fer him to really *look* at Clea. See she's a good person. Git to know her. Make friends so he'll reconsider this re-ward plan."

Teddy was not about to be out-dignified. He looked down his nose at Buck.

"I thought you told me he needs to be outta debt. That he's smart to buy a place of his own like *I* didn't have sense enough to do when *I* was his age. You're talkin' outta both sides of your mouth, Hawthorne."

Buck got hot. That was the same as calling him a liar.

"You jist listen to me, you hillbilly hog-caller, you," Buck said, through his gritted teeth. "If'n you ain't gonna help me in this here en-deavor, just make up your mind to stay the hell outta my way."

Teddy narrowed his eyes at him in his most infuriating gesture. Buck had always hated that look.

"I mean it," Buck said. "You interfere, you go against me when I say somethin' to Jake and Clea, like tellin' them we gotta split up and go off somewhere else, and you'd jist as well to start huntin' you a hole to hide in. I can take you in a fair fight and you know it."

"How do *you* know it? Since when did *you* ever fight fair, Buck Hawthorne?"

Buck could've snorted fire. "Whoa up," he said.

He stood in the stirrup and threw his leg over.

"Git down before I pull you off that pitiful cayuse you call a horse," he said. "Crippled up or not, I aim to whup yore ass. I aim to mop up this bridge with you, Theodore Smith."

He stepped off his horse.

And into the river.

CHAPTER FIFTEEN

CLEA TURNED in the saddle, then stopped her horse to listen. It *was* a person's voice. Somebody was yelling.

It came again. A frantic note in a human voice.

The old guys were behind her and she couldn't see Jake right now.

She turned her horse to head toward the sound. It was the old guys who were in trouble. Jake couldn't have doubled back and gotten that far behind her since she saw him last.

Another cry.

As she swung Freckles around, she saw Ariel and the wild horses down in the valley start to run. At least this time she wasn't the one causing the commotion that scared them.

The voice came again and this time it sounded like, "Help!"

She pushed Freckles harder and she was close enough for the next cry to know it was Teddy. When she came in sight of the river, it took her a minute to take it all in.

Teddy was limping up and down along the bank, yelling his head off. Pointing his pistol to the sky with one hand, while he tried to throw the loop in his rope into the water with the other. He'd had the presence of mind to tie the other end to a tree, but now he seemed completely crazed.

Buck was clinging to a rock out in the middle of the river. His head was turned toward Teddy and his mouth was opening and closing but no sound came out, at least none that she could hear.

Three shots went off as Freckles carried her closer. One. Two. Three.

With a pause in between each, the same way she'd fired them when Buster had come alone to the cabin.

"Help! Jake!" Teddy hollered. "Clea!"

When he saw her, he turned and pointed at the river with the pistol.

One glance at Buck's face and she could see how scared he was.

"He. Cain't. Swim!" Teddy yelled.

IT SEEMED to take forever before she could get Freckles stopped and dismount but finally, at the end of the bridge, Clea pulled him up and threw herself off, unzipping her puffy jacket the instant she hit the ground. The weirdest hollow feeling had seized her at the sight of Buck in danger.

She needed him, and not just to help her recover her horse. Strange thoughts raced through her mind as she started struggling out of her boots.

It's a good thing the old guys carry ropes on their saddles…I'm already getting attached here, Buck and Teddy are the grandfathers I've never had…I'm a strong swimmer…Buck isn't really a big man, not nearly as big as Jake. He couldn't be that heavy.

With the rope for him to cling to, she could save him.

He was slipping, grabbing for a hold higher on the rock as he did. Clea had no idea how deep the water was. The current looked fairly swift.

She got the other boot off and looked up to see that Buck was slipping more, still trying to get his feet up. No doubt his boots were full of water and heavy. He still wore his coat, too.

"Hold on, Uncle Buck!" she yelled. "I'll help you. Hold on."

She ran to the rope.

"Clea, I cain't swim neither. Wait for Jake!" Teddy said.

"No time. He'll fall and be carried downstream."

She dropped the loop around her waist and ran into the water, moving as fast as she could so she wouldn't hesitate, knowing it'd be cold.

No, she had never known anything of the kind. It was all she could do to keep moving. She wouldn't even have been able to *imagine* this wall of frozenness if she'd tried, because it immediately stopped her blood in her veins and every thought in her head.

The only way to get warmer is to keep moving. The only way to warm up is to keep moving. The only way to live is to keep moving....

Move, move. Arms, legs, move, move....

Her brain shut down and she went on automatic.

She couldn't even think enough to turn and run for dry land and sunshine.

Somehow she kept swimming, heading for the rock that now looked like salvation. The current was strong, almost too strong for her, and it dragged her heart down with her body. Panic shot through her as she fought to get out of them both—deep, rushing current and paralyzing fear. The river carried her toward Buck and then all of a sudden nearly past him.

She gasped and kicked and grappled for the rock, her ears full of the noise of the river. The current would've won except that Buck reached out and caught her by the arm, just before she swept past. He had more strength than she would've thought possible. Once there, Buck and the river's power held her against the rock with him.

He was shivering and blue and his teeth chattered so he could hardly turn to face her. She dragged in several breaths of air and prayed for Jake to come soon.

Why hadn't she listened to Teddy? What if Buck went down *because* she was here? He was still holding on to her in a death grip. Fear folded over inside her.

Hard as they were clinging, she felt the pull of the river come between them and the rock. Buck was wearing so many sodden clothes it'd be only a matter of time until they took him down.

And her with him.

She tried to think how to get out of his grip enough to loosen the rope, pull it off and put it on him instead. Or should she try to get it around both of them? Would he panic and fight her? Both in the loop wouldn't work because she wouldn't have room to swim.

She was nearly too numb to move and he'd been in the water longer than she had. He would die. They would both die. Freeze while the sun shone down on them.

No choice. All she could do was hang on.

"Clea!" It was Jake. "Buck! Hold on!"

The yell, the *relief* of it, almost knocked her off the rock.

Thank you, God.

She tried to twist her head to see Jake but she almost lost her grip and Buck's fingers clamped her even harder, so she hugged the rock and prayed without words. She couldn't think and she couldn't hold on much longer. Neither could Buck. He was slipping, fast.

Jake appeared in her line of vision as she glanced over her shoulder, then suddenly, he was there, big and solid as he came up out of the water. He pressed against her body from behind, encircling her with his arms to help hold his uncle up. She wanted so badly just to let go and let him hold her and warm her.

Instead, she pried her teeth apart and muttered as best she could with frozen lips, "Take him…first. He's…wet…longer."

Jake managed to push them harder against the rock and somehow peel her away from Buck enough to get the rope he wore around his waist over his own head and then over Buck's and down to *his* waist. When she turned her head, his sharp green gaze went through her like a blade. Water dripped off him onto her.

"Hold…rope," he said. "Stay…on…rock."

Jake drew the rope tight and lifted his arm in a signal. To Teddy, she realized dimly. She tried to make her brain work. To pull on his rope?

"Go," he said to Buck, and then, "I'm…right…behind."

In one swift motion, as Buck moved away through the water, Jake picked Clea up and set her on top of the rock.

She was so numb she couldn't even feel it beneath her and she scrabbled with her aching hands and feet to balance herself.

His eyes met hers and held. He would come back for her.

She jerked a nod that she understood. Shaking and shivering, trying to soak up the sun, she watched him swim away, helping Buck stay up. That rope was tied to Jake's saddle horn. With Teddy at his head, the horse kept backing up. Slowly at first and then faster.

Buck stumbled up onto solid ground, Teddy ran to help him the rest of the way and to take the rope off him. They threw the loop to Jake and he dropped it around his waist before he started back for her. Clea couldn't think but she could want, and all she wanted was to be safe and dry and warm.

She slid down off the rock and started swimming to meet

him. The frigid water possessed her again, doubling the cold already in her and she wasn't sure she could do it, but Teddy ran to her rope then, leading the horse that was tied to Jake, and started pulling her rope in. Jake swam straight to her and stayed right beside her as Ted reeled her in.

When they got to the bank, Jake put his arm around her and they staggered out of the river to collapse on the wet grass. In the blessed sunlight.

Jake's arm stayed around her. It must be so numb hc couldn't remove it.

Breathing hard, they stared at each other.

He'd been so furious with her for scaring the wild horses, he hadn't even looked at her since. His green gaze was still fierce, but now there were a dozen different feelings in his eyes. Relief was the only one she could read.

"Outta them clothes, Clea," Teddy yelled.

He could yell all day and it wouldn't matter. She couldn't move.

Jake sat up, then squatted beside her, looming between her and the sun, water still pouring off him.

"Good job," he said. "You did good but you can't rest until you're dry. Come on. Teddy's getting your clothes."

He helped her sit up, his hands insistent and strong and not to be denied. She slumped in place, trying to gather her hair and pull it to one side to wring water from it. He pulled it all together for her, then dropped his hand away when it touched hers.

"You're shakin' to the bone," he said. "I wish you'd waited for me to go for Buck."

"No...no time," she said, through chattering teeth. "He...was slipping."

He scooped her up to carry her to the trees.

"Teddy's making you a dressing room," he said. "He's throwing your bedroll over a limb."

His arms tightened around her and he let out a long breath that was almost a sigh. "You were both slipping," he said.

She didn't intend to, but she clung to him then, just for a moment, and he let her, arms around his neck, her skin plastered to his by the river, both their bodies seeking all the heat they could get and give.

Safe. She *was* safe.

Thanks to Jake.

She smiled to herself. Spooker of wild horses or not, at least he didn't hate her enough to let her drown.

JAKE MADE himself quit looking at Clea and focused on his uncle instead. But his thoughts stayed on her and how scared he'd been when he saw her in the river. Of course, he'd been scared for Buck, too, but Buck was tough and he'd survived far worse over the years.

Really, though, he shouldn't worry. His fear for Clea wasn't really personal. He'd have felt the same way about any greenhorn in that situation.

He concentrated on listening to Buck. Later. Later, he'd think about his reaction or maybe he could forget it completely.

"Ain't no cowboy worth his salt that *can* swim," Buck was saying, holding forth while the four of them sat around the fire and drank the coffee that was warming their insides like a miracle. "Long time ago when they was comin' up the trail, they hung on to their hosses' tails was how they crossed the rivers."

"Reckon you forgot yer hoss when you went in then," Teddy said. "Write that down for the next time you pick a fight in the middle of a bridge."

All of them laughed, including Buck.

Even Clea, who'd been really quiet. Maybe that scare was making her lose her nerve. Maybe he'd help her, get her to talk about it….

No. What he should do was use it to send her home.

Jake turned away and set his cup down. He didn't even want to be around her anymore. He didn't want to remember the relieved smile in her eyes when she'd come out of the water. That relieved, grateful, admiring smile or the fact that it had made him feel ten feet tall.

Damn it. He just didn't want to think about her at all, especially the trusting way she'd clung to him when he'd carried her.

For a spoiled rich woman—and he must remember *that*—she had guts. He had to hand her that much.

If she hadn't been there to hold Buck up, Jake would've been too late. He'd seen that when he topped the hill.

She deserved to hear that. Maybe that would help her hang on to her courage. That was the least he could do, and he would tell her. But it needed to be when they were alone, because Buck was already embarrassed enough about getting into such a jam.

That's only an excuse. You're thinking about that morning in the cabin. You want her alone for more than talk.

No. How low-down would that be, considering what he intended to do with her mare?

You're drawn to her because of that one, long look that said she knew you. That she recognizes another lonely soul when she sees it.

No.

Yes.

He needed some space. He needed to get away from all this chatter and get himself straightened out, once and for all.

"God only knows where those horses are now," he said. "I'm thinkin' why don't I get on their trail and you three just head on home to dry out? Clea's too tired to talk. She's not strong enough to keep up this chase."

She whirled around and glared at him with those big blue eyes that were suddenly telling him to go to hell. With her delectable lips parted in surprise.

"No, I'm not," she snapped. "I'm recovering more every minute. I'd talk if I could get a word in edgewise."

"Buck talks too much," Teddy said, nodding sagely. "It ain't me."

He and Buck argued a minute, then Jake said, "No, I mean it. You two take Clea home and..."

Furiously, she was shaking her head no. One strand of damp hair clung to her cheek. He wanted to brush it away, even if she was blazing defiance at him, forcing him to accept the message. She wasn't going.

Buck wouldn't cooperate, either.

"Git yer head straight," Buck snapped. "And stop wastin' your breath. You got sense enough to know Red'll never let you close enough to use a rope now. You cain't git 'em in the trap by yourself, without takin' the rest of yore natural life to do it."

Jake snapped back. "If they haven't run all the way to Wyoming, I can trap them in four or five days."

You knew they wouldn't go when you started this. But a man has to try every last-ditch effort to save himself.

I don't need saving. I'm in no danger of falling for her.

"And I can wrestle a bear and live to tell it," Ted said sarcastically.

For half a minute, it seemed Ted had heard Jake's mental argument.

"We ain't goin', Jake," Buck said.

Then he looked at Clea. "Unless you want—"

She interrupted. "I want to stay. I'm *going* to stay, even if nobody else does."

She meant it.

Jake said wearily, "You can't stay alone. You couldn't find the trap on your own. That mare isn't going to come when you call her, Clea."

He hadn't meant to sound so hard but…she was filling up his mind, with her shiny blond hair drying in the sun and the blue fleece shirt she'd put on that was the color of her eyes. That fit her like a second skin.

Filling up his mind with the realization that he'd let her devil him into talking a little about Tori, which he *never* did.

And with her declaration that they could be friends. Nothing more.

She met his glare and gave it back. "So what?" she said. "My partners know where everything is. We'll go—"

"We all will," Buck said, and stood up to throw what was left of his coffee across the ground. "If Red and his bunch kept driftin' south in the right direction after Teddy fired the shots, we'll find 'em soon, maybe even today."

Jake growled, "I shoulda left you in the river, Buck."

But something treacherous in him was relieved that they refused to obey.

He was only thinking of their safety. None of them, really, should be out here without him.

And to tell the truth for once, just saying the words to tell them to leave him had made him feel beyond lonesome.

THEY WERE fortunate in that their mounts were refreshed by the rest at the river and ready to cover some ground, and also because Montana Red's band had continued going south. They were almost to the Mule Deer Valley.

"We can push them on into the valley before dark," Teddy said. "In fact, we won't have to. That's where they'll water this evening."

"They might go on and put themselves in the trap if we'll just leave 'em be," Buck said.

Clea stared at Ariel through her binoculars and let her hopes run wild. "You're a prophet, Buck," she said. "You predicted they wouldn't change direction."

"Don't brag on him too much," Jake said. "He's already got the big head because he started that popular expedition into the river."

She smiled and kept on trying to see every inch of Ariel and to figure out the mare's position in the pecking order of the band. The guys had been teasing each other mercilessly all afternoon. She'd decided it was their way of celebrating that everyone was safe and in relatively good shape.

And they were together. It was weird, considering how different they all were, but they really did have fun as a group.

Buck was slumped in his saddle because he was basically exhausted. So was she. The same was bound to be true of Jake but he showed no signs of wear and tear.

"Me and Ted can hold this band in the valley tonight," Buck said. "Easy. And after they water in the morning, we can push 'em into the funnel. Why don't you two kids head on out and check the trap? You kin camp down there and have it all ready for us to run 'em on in."

Clea's heart gave a sort of thump against her ribs at the thought of being alone with Jake. She lowered the glasses and looked at him. He was already looking at her.

He was talking to her again so it wouldn't be too unpleasant.

But it was Buck who was talking to her right that minute. "Closing the gate when we get 'em penned is a job for young, fast people," he said. "You two head on out now. We don't have no idea how much work the fence on that trap might need."

Clea kept waiting for Jake to object to partnering with her. But he didn't.

He nodded to her and with a tilt of his head motioned for her to come with him. Just as if he were a little kid and Buck was his parent. Very unlike Jake.

She flashed back to that moment in his arms just before he'd put her down on the rock. He'd suddenly held closer for just a second as if to reassure himself that she was really safe.

But they were friends. Nothing more.

The great thing about this arrangement was that he could teach her things. Like how the trap worked and how to fix the fence if it needed it and how to cook over a fire on the ground. Buck and Teddy had been doing all that for her.

What was that saying, something about *you don't know anything until you find out how much you don't know?* Well, this little expedition was teaching her that she had a *lot* to learn before she could even begin to be completely independent.

JAKE RODE off way ahead of her, but Clea caught up with him before they got out of sight of the old guys and stayed right there beside him from then on, as if having old Freckles match his horse step for step was some kind of point of honor with her. Was she wanting to talk?

No, evidently not. She was riding along without saying much at all, looking at the mountains and the rolling valley they were riding through, relaxed, enjoying the country like they were old friends out for a pleasure ride. After the day they'd had, that proved she had a handle on herself.

Which seemed a little weird considering how terrified she been only a few hours ago, clinging to him with her arms hard around his neck. She was, bar none, the most contradictory woman he'd ever met.

"You must be about ready to crash," he said. "You've gone through a helluva of a lot today."

She turned and gave him a look that included a definite twinkle in her blue, blue eyes.

"A helluva lot for a soft, out-of-condition, spoiled woman who's accustomed to having a man buy my fox vests, and hired hands to wash my dishes and pick my stalls?"

Well. She must've been paying more attention to him than he thought. From the very first day they met.

He let his gaze sweep over her perfect breasts to her pert little butt so firm in the saddle, and on down her long, long leg to the stirrup.

He drawled, "I never said 'out-of-condition.'"

She laughed. Why did it always please him so much to make her laugh?

Probably because he didn't bother to make jokes all that often. Buck was always telling him he was too serious, solemn as a judge.

"Now *that's* something I do for myself," she said, "I stay in shape. That's about all I accomplished this last couple of years."

Was that after the divorce?

None of your business, Hawthorne. You don't want to get to know her.

Won't matter. We catch her horse and I tell her my plans and she'll never speak to me again.

"What else was going on in the last couple of years?"

Even his mouth felt weird to say that. He never asked personal questions. Never. It was against his code.

"I was growing a backbone," she said.

He set his lips together and kept back the next question. But he held his eyes steady on hers and she read it in them.

That was the strangest thing. This woman could read his mind. Like she knew him so well, even though that couldn't be.

She said, "I was facing the truth that my marriage was a travesty and I had to get out of it. Admitting to myself that I had to make myself a real life if I was ever going to have one. That or die young from *existing* in the same house with Brock."

He couldn't look away when she said that. The pain in her eyes and the grit in her voice made him want to know more. He must be turning into a nosey old gossip like Buck and Teddy.

What kinds of trouble did you two have? What kind of guy is Brock?

None of your business, Jake-o. All you need to know is he's rich and a horse owner. Owner of a mare named Ariel.

Tears glinted in Clea's eyes. She smooched to Freckles and loped on ahead.

Understandable. He needed some time to himself, too, every time he remembered Tori.

He waited for the stab of pain that always cut him at the thought of her.

It didn't come. He said her name out loud, which he hadn't done for a year, until that morning at the cabin when he told Clea that little bit about his past.

"Victoria. Tori."

Nothing. No pain.

Tori was fading from his mind. The hurt was leaving him the same way she had.

That made him feel a little lonesome, somehow. Hollow inside where it used to be. Had he really been that attached to feeling sorry for himself?

Damn! Maybe Buck and Teddy had been right when they'd tried—without getting into his business, of course—to let him know he was stuck in a pit of self-pity.

He smooched to his mount and loped after Clea, who'd slowed to a long trot now. He shook his head. She was still riding out there ahead like she knew where she was going.

He smiled. You couldn't expect a woman who'd jump into a cold, fast river to save an old man who couldn't swim to slow down just because she didn't have detailed directions.

When he caught up to her, she turned and gave him a sweet smile. You might say a welcoming smile. No sign of tears.

"How'd you pick Montana for a new start?"

Hawthorne. Shut up. What the hell's the matter with you?

"Montana," she said. "Itself. The land, the sky, the gorgeous natural *forces* that they are. I was here one time, only one, and the simple act of looking at this place and trying to take it all in changed my whole way of seeing my life."

He thought about that. "I guess I can imagine that. I grew up with it, so I can't say."

"So all your many homes were in Montana?"

"Pretty much. Some in northern Wyoming."

"Did your dad do the same kind of work all the time?"

"Ranch foreman, mostly. Or ranch hand. Anywhere they'd give us a place to live. On the side, he traded horses and mules and broke out a few."

"So you got your horsemanship from him?"

"And from the hundreds of horses I've gotten on."

They rode along in silence for a minute or two.

He looked ahead at the purple, white-topped cone of Turkey Mountain standing against the blue sky.

"Are you excited about someday living on the ranch you bought?"

He could feel her gaze on his face.

"Do you plan for that to be soon?"

Surprised, he shot her a keep-away look. Yet a minute later, his mouth opened and he answered her.

"I hope so."

They were quiet for a little way, then she said, "Have *you* had a lot of different kinds of jobs?"

"Some," he said.

"Name some."

"Shoeing mules, for one."

She twisted in the saddle to stare at him in disbelief. He laughed.

"Mules?"

"Firefighting mules. Did you know they still use 'em? I was at the Ninemile Remount Depot last summer shoeing mules and training a fcw young ones and fighting fires. My sister, Elle, stayed with me for a while."

"Was she shoeing mules, too?"

"Normally she would've been, but right then she was too lovesick to do much of anything useful. Never saw anybody so crazy over somebody who could still deny it with every breath."

She smiled. "I love the affection in your voice," she said. "I can tell you love your sister. How'd her romance turn out?"

Good. This is good, Hawthorne. Talk about Elle and keep it away from yourself.

"They're married now. Happy. Living on his ranch up north, not too far from Helena."

"So he's a rancher."

"And bucking bull and bronc breeder. Chase Lomax. If you've ever heard—"

"The bronc-riding champion," she interrupted. "I don't see many rodeos, but I've definitely heard of him and I've seen him ride on TV at the finals in Vegas. Is Elle a barrel racer?"

"No, a bullfighter. Her real name is Farrell."

"Of course! Farrell *Hawthorne*. I hadn't made the connection with you. I've heard of her, too. Is she still doing it?"

"Yeah, but not for much longer. She says she'll quit when they start their family, and Chase says he'll be too old to deal with teenagers if they wait too long."

"You sound like you like him."

"He's a great guy."

Great. Keep going. Tell her all you know about Elle and Chase. Don't ask her another personal question. Don't let her ask you one.

Clea said, "I admire Elle for being so brave."

Jake blurted, "You remind me of her."

Her jaw dropped and her eyes blazed blue, searching his face for his meaning. Asking if he meant that. Asking if it was a joke.

"Me? Do we look alike?"

"Not looks. Think about it, Clea. You jumped into forty—more like thirty—degree water in a swift-running river today to save somebody else. That took a barrel of bravery."

"But I didn't 'git 'r done,' did I? And you did. *You* saved *two* somebodies."

"Buck outweighs you by at least fifty pounds."

"I was trying to read you the whole time we were drying out and talking about it," she said. "I know you said good job, but I knew you'd also be mad at me for doing it."

Because it scared me out of my mind when I first saw you out there about to be swept away.

"I was," he said lightly. "How would *you* like to come riding over that hill and see you were gonna have to jump into that breath-sucking icy water?"

"I did exactly that," she said, mimicking his teasing tone. "And you'll notice that I've been a real cowgirl about it because, unlike this one guy I know named Jake, *I* haven't complained even once."

He liked the way she said his name in her Texas accent. Ja-ake. Soft and slow. It worked on his skin almost like a caress.

She made a face at him. "And next time, *you'd* better not complain, either, if you still want to be a cowboy."

He scowled at her. "There'd better not be a next time. If there is, I'm gonna ride right on by and pretend I never heard you two troublemakers yelling for help."

"Ha. You already told me you live for challenge and adventure. Buck and I are only trying to give you a fix now and then."

He shook his head. "No way are you two getting away with that line of talk. You both did it because you wanted attention."

She smiled and shook her head to mock him.

"We were only thinking of you. Pretty soon, once you settle down, you'll miss your adventures."

Dumbfounded, he stared at her. She'd hit on his deepest fear.

How did she do it? How could she see right into him? Right through him?

It was downright scary. It attracted him like metal to a magnet.

He didn't really have to worry, though. All this friends stuff would be history when he caught her horse and hauled it away.

Tonight. Once they got the trap checked and supper over, while they drank that last cup of coffee sitting around the fire, he would tell her what he was going to do with Ariel.

CHAPTER SIXTEEN

HE WAS DOWNRIGHT irresistible in the firelight. This would make another great photo featuring Jake Hawthorne as mythical cowboy—camping on the trail, fire glowing under his enameled coffeepot, horses cropping grass behind him, dusk falling across the mountains and throwing shadows from his hat brim across his face. But they didn't conceal his fierce green eyes.

Clea took another bite of what the dried-food package had promised was beef-and-vegetable stew, and let him hold her gaze a moment longer. It was truly a stupid thing to do. This silent flirtation had sprung to life all on its own earlier while they'd done the fence inspection and built the fire. Now it seemed to be taking over.

She tried to think about that instead of pondering the fascinating bones in Jake's face—the way his jaw jutted out and his cheekbones emphasized the tan of his skin.

They weren't flirting. This was just a closeness inspired by having common goals. They were becoming friends, the way they'd agreed to at the cabin after those unexpected kisses and….

He had bedroom eyes. He really did, with heavy eyelids and an unquenchable heat in his gaze. Which, right now, was drifting lazily over her face as carefully as if he'd never seen her before. It caressed her mouth.

They *were* flirting. Probably nothing but a natural result

of the near-drownings this morning. Like an encounter with death caused a need for sex and life.

Because that need had been there, trembling in the air, ever since he'd come up out of the water behind her and set her up on that rock.

Talk, Clea. Don't let this get past friendship. He'd be a hard man to forget.

"Tell me how you chose the land you bought for your horse ranch," she said. "I've never gotten to pick my own place. I'll have to do that someday."

He picked up his mug and drank some coffee and she thought he wasn't going to answer, but then he shrugged and said, "It's off the beaten path, but within a decent distance to drive for supplies. Beautiful mountain valley. River with a natural lake. Good meadows. National forest on one side."

"Sounds gorgeous."

"Yeah. But affordable. Price had to come first. I hate debt."

"No payments would be nice."

He raised one brow. "Well, I'm not there yet. Shouldn't be too long, though."

He seemed about to say something else, but then he didn't.

"How far is it to get supplies?"

"Twenty-five, thirty miles back to Pine Lodge."

"Do you have any neighbors?"

"Closest one's about ten miles."

Clea tried to imagine it. "You're gonna be lonesome out there, Jake. If you get snowed in—"

"That's a given," he said.

His tone held such an unconscious note of acceptance that sudden tears stung Clea's eyes.

She wanted to lean around the fire to brush back that rebellious lock of black hair from his forehead. She picked up her tin mug of coffee from the ground beside her instead. They were sitting cross-legged on their folded saddle blankets, facing each other, so close their knees nearly touched.

That was as much closeness as she could bear without doing something foolish.

"Then why'd you do it? Why not get a place closer in? Where your customers could come to look at your horses?"

"I told you," he snapped. "Price. I can take loneliness a whole easier than I can take debt."

He took another drink. "My dad was the same way. That's why we never had a place of our own—he couldn't stand to be in debt."

Clea nodded.

"I'm used to bein' alone a lot," he said. "I just don't know how good I'll do stayin' in one place."

She heard real fear in his tone this time, but again he didn't know it was there.

"You never have, have you?"

"No."

After another sip of coffee, he blurted, "Well, I take that back. I settled in with Tori. But then she tore that up."

He held the cup in both hands and stared into the fire.

"Why did she?"

She realized that she wanted—way too much—to know the answer to that question. He had really loved Tori. She'd known that from the minute he said her name in his sleep.

"Money," he said bitterly, still looking at the fire. "Money as poison. Her ex-husband had more to offer her and her kids, was the way she put it."

Yes, she'd wanted to know, but now, just as suddenly, she wanted him to let it go. She wanted him to look at her again.

"There you go," she said lightly. "You say money's poison

to relationships and career choices, and I'm just wishing I could get my hands on more of it."

"I miss those boys as much or more than I do her. I'm not fallin' in love with any more women *or* kids."

He looked up and gave Clea an irresistible grin, his teeth flashing white in the firelight.

"*That's* how I know it won't be so bad bein' by myself."

He was breaking her heart. He had no idea. He might be used to living alone and she wasn't, but they were both pilgrims on the same lonesome road. And they'd both known that since they woke up in his bunk together.

What harm would a little comfort do?

They were all alone in the middle of nowhere. They had the whole night ahead of them with no work to do and no distractions. She felt wired to the max with a dozen emotions flying in every direction inside her.

Where was that exhaustion of the nearly-drowned when she needed it? There was no sense letting this escalate into something foolish they would both regret. He was still in love with Tori Whoever, as well as with her boys, and Clea didn't need yet another complication in her life.

He'd reached the same conclusion, evidently, because he changed the subject.

"It's a good thing the fence didn't need much," he said. "I really didn't think it would, since it hasn't been that long since we used this trap to catch the white stud and his band."

He drank the last of his coffee and set down the mug.

"We were coming back from hauling them the day I drove into my own driveway and nearly got my head shot off. The day I *did* get my truck shot all to pieces."

She felt a grin come over her face. "Did you *have* to mention that? What is this? You're trying to make me feel guilty so I'll do all the work around here? So I'll roll out your bed for you and leave a mint on the pillow?"

He leaned toward her.

"Speaking of bed," he whispered. "It's going to be a full moon. We'd better stay close to the fire tonight."

Clea laughed. "I love it! I think I hear a scary story coming on."

"There's not an animal anywhere that's not affected by a full moon."

She leaned toward him, so close their heads almost touched.

"A full moon always makes me restless," she murmured.

A spark flared in his eyes, and his gaze held hers.

"That's what I mean," he said. "It's universal."

"What kinds of animals are around here?"

He answered with a slow grin. Her heart turned over.

What *was* it about the smile of a man who didn't smile very often that made a woman feel so powerful?

Jake. What *was* it about Jake?

"Any wolves?"

"Don't worry," he murmured. "I'm here to protect you."

"Oh," she drawled, "so it's all a ploy. You're trying to make me leap into your arms. I must warn you, sir…"

The firelight danced across his face and threw its heat into his eyes. No, they were already burning.

You scare me more than the thought of any wild animal. You make me scared of myself.

Dark was gathering deeper. His gaze moved over her in the shadows, making love to her already, lingering on her breasts and then on the vee of her legs, open to him.

The look might as well have been his hand. It set her on fire. She couldn't move.

He reached out, took her cup from her hands, set it aside,

and pushed her hair back from her cheek. Barely, barely brushing it with his calloused fingertips.

"I don't need a ploy," he drawled. "Clea."

His low voice went all through her and settled in the very places where his gaze had caressed her.

This was too scary. She liked him too much. She *wanted* him too much. She could, dear God, forever listen to the sound of those low tones saying her name. In the long run, this couldn't be good.

But who cared? There might not *be* a long run. She could've died today.

She put her hand on his face, then thrust her fingers into his hair and went to him, into the cradle made by his long legs, her own on either side of him, sitting on his boots while she wrapped her arms tight around his neck and crushed her breasts against him. He pressed her face to his, cheek to cheek, and murmured in her ear.

Just the one word, rough with need, "Clea."

She loved the way he said her name. She could listen to that over and over again.

His hands cupped her bottom, lifted her, brought her need against his hardness and held her there.

While he found her mouth and kissed her. While she kissed him back.

While they kissed each other absolutely senseless and still stayed desperate for more.

Finally, he pulled back and asked the question with his eyes.

Against the falling dusk, the green gaze glowed in his tanned face.

A shadow fell across it. "Clea," he said, "I should tell you—"

She laid two fingers across his lips.

"Don't tell me anything. Just say my name," she said. "The last time you kissed me you called me Tori."

The fire in his eyes deepened.

"Don't worry," he said, his voice husky, "I could never forget who you are."

She took his face in her hands and kissed him until her whole body trembled.

Until, as if they were reading each other's minds through their bodies, she leaned back to pull him over on top of her and he put his hands on her waist and lay her down.

He broke the kiss. "I'll get blankets—"

"No."

She found his mouth with hers but he laughed and pulled away, saying, "You'll freeze."

"Not if you'll kiss me again."

He did, setting his lips at just the right angle on hers, giving her his tongue and taking hers, pouring that liquid fire that was his power into every corner of her being, pooling it in her woman-core that was already ready for the hardness of him. They sat up and shucked jackets and tangled arms and legs trying to help each other with the rest, working on boots and buttons and zippers and tight jeans without breaking the kiss.

Finally, though, Clea's fleece shirt had to come off over her head. They pulled apart and Jake took it off her, peeling it slowly up and up, holding her gaze with his. Then only her bra was left.

He looked at it, shining dark pink satin and lace, in the lowering darkness. He dragged his fingertips over her nipples, straining hard toward him, and her insides melted under his touch. He looked into her eyes.

"Now," she whispered. "Come on, Jake…"

But he tortured her by doing it again, by bending to kiss

the swell of her breast where it met the lace, by kissing her neck and then making a trail with his hot tongue all the way from there into her cleavage. Then he undid the hooks and turned her so the firelight fell directly on her.

"Look at you," he said, lightly touching one hard tip. "I told you you'd freeze."

She smiled slowly, holding his eyes with hers, and pushed her hair back behind her ears. "That's all your doing and you know it," she said. "Why don't we see what else you can do?"

He laughed deep in his throat and, never breaking the look, cradled one sensitive breast in his calloused palm, already beginning a light caress with his thumb across the nipple.

"Well, I do love a challenge," he said, and dropped his head to take it into his mouth.

Pleasure shot through her, so sharp and fine that it took her strength. Dissolving, she lay back, thrusting her fingers into his hair to hold him where he was, pulling him with her, the saddle pad scratchy against her back, his lips and tongue velvet on top of her. Sweet madness swept her out of her mind and into her body's deep places, places that she didn't know existed.

He moved to the other breast, but kept that one in his hand and she writhed beneath him until he worked his way back up that still-burning line on her throat, added a light kiss on her chin and then suckled her mouth with a primal power that stole her ability to breathe. His kiss was a life force, like the land and the dark sky that surrounded them.

The sweet smell of smoke from the fire wrapped them in their own warm world, and the scent of Jake's skin mingled with it as she took in a long, shaky breath that might be her last. She didn't need air anymore. All she would ever need was his hot mouth, taking her deeper and deeper, and his hard, lean body under her hands. She couldn't get enough of him and languorous as the kiss made her feel, her palms kept moving, memorizing every inch of him she could reach.

Dangerous. Now the feel and smell of him would be a part of her forever, just like his taste.

He kissed her until she knew nothing at all, then moved his mouth—with one last, thoughtful kiss at the corner of hers—along the line of her jaw, to just beneath her ear, then down and down the sensitive side of her neck, creating a new trail of fire with slow, lingering lips on her skin that sent desire like she'd never known flaming through her. Making her desperate. Making her truly reckless and wild.

Taking away her breath now, for sure. Maybe forever.

"Jake...please..."

His mouth came back to hers, his lips hot against hers.

"I need you," he whispered, and she held the power of the universe in her arms.

He pulled back, them, hovering over her. The bite of the cold air came between them. Her skin stayed hot, grew hotter still. Every defense she'd ever had fell away and for that moment, there were no secrets between them.

"Darlin'," he murmured, "why are you trembling like that?"

Through the dizzying dark she could see the trace of his crooked smile.

She smiled back, reached up, and deliberately laid her arms around his neck growling, "I thought you were the strong, silent type but you can't stop talking."

He chuckled low, wrapped her in his arms again, fast and hard, and took possession of her mouth as if he would never let her go. This was a whole new kind of kiss. A whole new way of holding her.

It set a beat going in her blood that pounded itself into her bones.

It was the beat of his heart against her breast, pulling her heart into its rhythm. He owned her then, in a way no man ever had or ever would again.

Clea didn't know how she knew that about the future, but she did.

And she wanted more, more, more of what she had now. She wrapped her legs around him and reached between them to take him, hard and hot into her hand.

Jake groaned, and his "Oh, Clea" came from deep in his throat. She opened her eyes to see his eyes blazing at her and the full moon starting to rise over his shoulder as he entered her.

After that, she couldn't hear and she couldn't see. She could only feel him filling her, moving with her, his two rough hands on her back protecting her skin from the prickly wool. Then he took one away, dragged a piece of clothing underneath her and proceeded to bring her to a white-hot rushing climax that would have carried her right off the face of the earth and into the dark night if she hadn't clung to him like the moon to the sky.

He collapsed with his face in the hollow of her neck and rolled over to his side with her clasped so tightly in his arms they were melded together. They lay without moving, without speaking, until the sweat began to dry on their backs and let the cold of the fall night spread over their skins.

"Let's get to bed," he said, his voice still low and rough with feeling. "You're not used to this."

She laughed as they scrambled up and ran for the sleeping bags still rolled and tied behind their saddles. "And you are? You're accustomed to sleeping outside naked?"

He laughed, too, and got his off his saddle first.

"One's enough," he said. "Agreed?"

"Yes."

All of a sudden she couldn't say more than that. Because even now, this soon, desire was moving through her again. More. Still, she wanted more.

Jake stirred the fire and added a stick or two while she unrolled and unzipped the bag, laying it out a little distance from the rock-ringed firepit.

"Don't want to get too far from the fire," she said. "That full moon's already riding the sky and I thought I heard something rustling through the trees."

"Now who's using a ploy?" Jake asked, laughing.

She slipped into the bed and looked at his magical naked body as he laid one more stick in the fire. He walked toward her.

"Like a fine man once said to me," she said, "'I don't need a ploy.'"

He laughed again as he climbed in beside her and she felt his skin against hers again. "Damn straight you don't, Miss Clea."

WHEN JAKE WOKE it was long after midnight, judging by the position of the moon in the sky. The giant, pale yellow moon. The full moon that always made Clea restless.

He looked down at her head on his arm. She was anything but restless now. That made him smile. Having her here in his arms made him smile. Remembering making love to her made him smile.

And right now, this minute, he was going to enjoy this and think about nothing else. He was going to fall right back into his lifetime habit of not thinking about the past or the future. Living in the present was a skill that had saved his sanity more than once.

Clea's hair, shining bright the same color as the moon, was flung over his arm and shoulder spilling onto the dark cloth of the sleeping bag. She was sleeping deep.

He moved his arm gently to roll her a little bit closer. The curves of her naked body melted into his and she settled in with her hand on his thigh as if they'd slept like this many, many times before.

She was so much more than he'd thought she'd be that first moment they met. Brave and beautiful. Coolly private and hotly passionate.

Looking at her sleeping in the moonlight was like looking at a sunrise. He shifted a little, easing more onto his side and shoulder so he could see her whole face.

She made an incoherent little noise. Her eyes opened.

Dazed with sleep, it took her a minute, but the smile she gave him then struck straight to his heart. So trusting.

"Hi," she said.

"Hey," he said. "I didn't mean to wake you."

She looked around, at the sky, the moon. "This is so awesome. And the wind's died down, too."

"All for us," he said. "It'd be a whole lot colder with the wind."

"I think I can see the shadows of the mountains."

"It's a bright moon."

She glanced at him then, and held the look. "I can't believe the big day is nearly here. It'll seem weird for the hunt to finally be over."

"Yep."

"I almost wish they'd get away from us again," she said. This woman had an impish grin when she wanted to use it. "I don't remember who I am when I'm not a wild-horse hunter."

Fifty thousand dollars. Remember that.

"But if they got away again, that'd mean many more adventures with Buck and Teddy," he said, making his voice light. "Think about that. Think about how cold that river was."

She grinned again. "Right. I was thinking more about the adventures of Jake and Clea."

He felt himself begin to grow hard again.

Whoa. Can't go down that road. Gotta keep the goal in mind.

"Likely they won't get away," he said. "Buck and Teddy'll keep 'em bottled up pretty tight tonight."

"Has Montana Red ever been in this trap before?"

"Not that I know of. This is his home range that Natural Bands bought, so I doubt he's ever been caught or hauled in at all."

Clea nodded and propped her head on his shoulder, snuggling another bit closer.

His arm tightened around her. Desire stirred more, just under his skin where it had hardly slept at all.

But she sighed with contentment and looked out into the enormous night toward the back of the natural trap where the bluffs formed a solid wall.

"He'll be in the next roundup, though," Jake said. "Celeste is determined to get them all checked by veterinarians next fall."

"How old do you think he is?"

"I'd guess fifteen or so. There've been tales about him for a long time. Stealing mares. He comes from a long line, according to Buck and Ted."

"Of legendary stallions?"

Jake nodded and his cheek brushed her hair. Its scent went right through him.

"Legendary *red* stallions. Even the name is passed down. Since before statehood, there's been a wild stallion named Montana Red."

"I thought it was *white* stallions. The legendary white stallion of the plains who could never be caught."

"The *Southern* plains. On the Northern plains, it's Montana Red. Farrell St. Clair, my great-great-grandpa—or however many greats—was a famous one-armed bronc rider. My mom said he passed down a story about one Montana Red who ran over a cliff and killed himself so he wouldn't be caught."

"Is your mom still alive?"

"No. She and my dad were killed by carbon monoxide poisoning."

"How old were you?"

"I was grown. We were all grown. Elle was in college."

"My mom died when I was ten. She had cancer."

His arm tightened around her. "That'd be tough. Ten years old."

She stared at the moon. "It was. It marked me for life."

"We're all marked," he said. "That *is* life."

She grasped his arm that crossed her body just below her breasts and made a funny little sound between a chuckle and a sob. "Thanks, Jake. Somehow, that makes me feel better."

That made him feel even more powerful than he did when he made her laugh.

"Believe it," he said.

They lay like that for a long time, with Clea holding on to him with both hands, lightly, but as if she'd never let him go again.

He could live with that. Her naked skin against his. Her lemon scent in his nostrils and the curve of her firm breasts resting on his arm.

But he couldn't live with it forever without making love to her again.

"I love this," she said. "Brock never, ever cuddled with me

like this and just held me and visited with me without wanting sex. It's my very favorite thing."

Disappointment shot cold water through the heat of the desire building in Jake. Damn.

Listen to that, Hawthorne. Lighten up. Forget about getting hard. Remember, just enjoy the moment here. You can't disappoint her now.

But that wouldn't be easy. He wanted her more with every sound of her soft voice. He wasn't sure he could keep his voice even, but he did.

"Is that so?"

"It is *so* true. And I'd bet that at least ninety-five out of one-hundred women would say it's true for them, too."

"Being held and talked to is what they like best? About being in bed with a man?"

His voice did crack a little when he said that.

"Well now, don't sound so hurt and horrified," she said, twisting her neck to look at him and chuckling a little. "I like sex, too."

She used that blinding smile he loved. It definitely made things worse for him at that moment.

"But holding and talking just...mean more, somehow," she said.

Huh?

"I asked Brock for it a few times early on, but he blew me off. Then, finally, I couldn't stand to be in bed with him at all."

Well, buddy, you still got a chance. You're doin' okay so far.

What a deal. Women. Harder to understand, *way* harder, than any other animal, wild *or* domestic.

You got lucky, Jake. Wantin' to know more about her, wantin' to hear her talk. Way to go, man.

Clea innocently went on with their visit.

"So Farrell's named for your bronc-riding great-great-grandfather?"

"Yeah. Mom saved the name until she had a girl. Something about wanting to give her power in a man's world. My mom never had much say about where we moved to or when we moved. Never a paying job of her own or anything like that. Not much decision-making power at all."

"Well, it worked. Did your mom live long enough to know her daughter was a bullfighter?"

"No. That came after."

"I have to tell you, Jake," Clea said, squeezing his arm affectionately, "you gave me a lot of power when you compared me to Elle. Nobody ever said I was brave before. Not in my whole life."

And I'm brave, too. You have no idea how heroic I'm being right now.

"I meant it. Ninety-nine women out of a hundred would've been running up and down the bank screaming for me instead of jumping in and trying to do something like you did."

She rolled over half onto him, which made his problem a *whole* lot worse, and gazed into his eyes, adding that smile, which piled torment on top of pain on top of misery. Her skin was a silk instrument of torture and her breast brushing his chest took the air out of his lungs.

"I mean it, too," she said. "Ninety-nine *men* out of a hundred would've yelled at me for being foolish, for doing something as stupid as jumping in when I didn't know how cold and swift the water was, for not thinking how much Buck weighed and how hard it'd be to tow him."

"Hmm. Thanks."

"But you said I was brave," she said. "You said, 'Good job.'

That gives me so much confidence, Jake. Now I *know* I can learn enough skills to survive the winter. Thank you."

That smile again. Torture was *way* too small a word for what he was going through.

But he *would* not disappoint her. He *could* not disappoint a woman with a smile like that.

There *was* a God, though. And He was paying attention as the magnificent moon made its way across the endless sky.

Clea's satin hand caressed his chest and moved down his rib cage. Circled on his abdomen.

Down. On down. Go on, Clea....

But she was starting on his chest again, circling her palm in the swirl of hairs in the middle, where his muscles crossed. She was deliberately tantalizing him, but he was too far gone to retaliate. All he could do was beg.

He had no idea if he could talk, but he had to try. His voice did come out sounding sort of strangled. "Clea. What d'you say we forget about all those ninety-nine other men and women and just concentrate on the one of each we've got right here?"

She trailed her hand lazily down his frame and wrapped her long, firm fingers around the hard erection he'd finally quit trying to fight. Then she looked him right in the eye and smiled at him in the moonlight.

CHAPTER SEVENTEEN

CLEA WOKE to a sliver of sun in her face and Jake's rough, tender hand smoothing back her hair, then shaking her shoulder with growing urgency.

She knew who he was but not where they were, then she surfaced to the point that she could hear and understand words.

"Clea, get up."

She must've been mistaken about the tenderness in his touch. There certainly wasn't any in his voice. Straightforward, commanding, no-nonsense. It too was urgent, come to think of it.

Last night must've been a fantasy. Had she dreamed it?

She pulled the bag over her head and slid as far into its down-filled warmth as she could. A few more minutes. Just let her have a few more minutes to believe the dream.

"Clea," Jake said again, this time with a great deal of feeling. "Get some clothes on or we'll never live it down."

"Hel-loooo the camp! I hope you've got breakfast on the fire by the time I cross this creek!"

She sat straight up, holding the sleeping bag to her chest, blinking into the sun, looking around.

"Is that Buck? He's here?"

"Cle-a..." Jake was pleading now.

It all came together in a heartbeat. Clea flew out of the

sleeping bag like she'd been shot from a rocket launcher, the cool morning air on her skin turning every inch of it to goose bumps in an instant. She grabbed for cover, trying to hold the bag to her, scrambling for her clothes, which seemed to be scattered all over Montana, dancing so neither of her bare feet would be on the cold ground too long. Her teeth started chattering anyhow.

"Uncle Buck! Go on down to the ford to cross," Jake yelled. "I'm not in the mood for a rescue this mornin'."

"All right. But I want flapjacks. Clea, you know how. You seen me make 'em at yore house."

She gave up on modesty *and* warmth, dropped the bag to sit on it and pull on her jeans. Jake wasn't looking at her anyhow. He was busy clanging the coffeepot around and adding a little wood to the fire.

She jerked her fleece shirt on over her head, her mind racing.

"This is ridiculous," she said. "All you had to do was yell back to Buck that I wasn't dressed."

He threw a frowning glance at her over his shoulder. "And have him yell back that anybody with a grain of sense would've slept in their clothes last night?"

Clea jammed on her boots and got up, moving fast to bring herself fully awake, blood pumping, nerves twanging.

Jake poured water into the coffeepot. He still hadn't said a personal word to her. Maybe she *was* remembering something that didn't happen.

But flashes of it were coming back to her—very real flashes—that made her weak with desire all over again.

She wanted the closeness back. He'd cuddled with her, talked to her. She wanted more of that.

"I'm going to wash up," she said, although he didn't seem to care, and went to find her cosmetic bag in her packs.

Buck rode in while she was looking for it.

"Mornin', Clea," he called, waving to her. "Looks like you got this roustabout up makin' the coffee."

"I've never drunk his coffee," she called back. "Is it any good?"

"'Bout like stump-water," he said. "But don't tell him I said that or he won't let me have a drop."

She laughed and vanished into the trees, grinning to herself as she heard Buck say to Jake, "Hey, son. Looks like you've done put your vest on wrong side outermost this mornin'."

Maybe he'd ask Jake how that could be if he'd slept in his clothes like anybody who had good sense would've.

Clea washed up fast in the cold waters of the creek, stretching to try to warm up her muscles, sore from her ordeal in the river the day before. And probably from other exertions.

By the time she got back to camp, the two men had started packing up.

"Hey, wait," she said. "What about a leisurely two…or three…cups of coffee? What about something hot to eat?"

"Looks like it's jerky on the run again," Buck said, turning to look her over with a smile. "But the coffee's nearly done."

Jake was bringing in the horses from the grassy spot where they'd been staked for the night. When he got there, he dropped the ropes and left them to go get his saddle.

Clea shoved her cosmetic bag into her pack and went to get her saddle, too.

She wasn't going to sit around and let him take care of her. Especially not in this mood he was in.

As they saddled up, Buck left them alone and walked over to the fire to check out the coffee.

Jake settled his saddle onto the colt and bent to reach under him for the cinch. The colt looked back to nuzzle his shoulder.

"Hey," Jake said gruffly. "Stop that."

He still hadn't talked to her. He could at least acknowledge her presence, even if he did regret last night. She couldn't think of any other reason he'd be so withdrawn. Or maybe he wished he hadn't talked to her so freely.

"That colt loves you, Jake," she said. "There's nothing more loyal than a horse who loves you."

"Yeah," he drawled sarcastically, "that explains why he dumped me in a barbed-wire pit."

She laughed. There was a pleased note under his sarcasm that said he was glad the colt had connected with him.

"Ariel really hurt my feelings. I always thought she was loyal to me, but she jumped the fence without a backward glance. I guess romance always trumps friendship."

He straightened up and flashed her a sharp look across his saddle. Only then did she realize her words could be applied to the two of them, as well.

She felt heat come into her cheeks, but she held his gaze.

"Yeah," he said, "a good horse who loves him is all a man ever needs. A horse is a damn sight more loyal than a woman."

Hurt, anger, embarrassment, all slapped her in the face and shot words out of her mouth. "A man needs a woman just like a woman needs a man. We proved that on more than one level last night. Be honest, at least with yourself, Jake."

She glanced over her shoulder to see that Buck was still at the fire and paying no attention to them. When she turned back to Jake, she couldn't read the expression in his eyes and she couldn't stop her tongue.

"Loyalty's my strongest trait," she said, keeping her voice down. "It nearly did me in because I was loyal to Brock for so long. It'd take a lot to make me love another man but if I ever did, and if he loved me I'd *never* leave him. I don't lump all men together as cheating bastards, and you don't need to say all women are disloyal, either."

He stared at her as if she'd lost her mind. Which maybe she had.

"Coffee's done," Buck called.

"One cup," Jake said. He swallowed hard. "There's extra hot water. Help yourself to instant oatmeal."

They finished securing the saddles in silence, then they left the horses ground tied and went to the fire.

Buck poured her a cup and handed it into her cold hands. "Let's git 'r done," he said.

She hoped he didn't notice she was a little shaky. She kept both hands around the mug to warm them while she raised it to her lips. *What* had she been thinking, going into such a rant? She hadn't. She hadn't thought at all. She'd only been feeling.

She took a deep breath and gathered herself. "I'm gonna go get Teddy," she said, pretending to pout. "I need somebody on my side. He and I both hate rushing around in the morning."

"Teddy's the *reason* I've gotta hurry," Buck said as he stirred oatmeal in another tin mug. "He's gittin' so old he's liable to go to sleep in the saddle and let Red and his bunch escape."

Clea made a face at him. "So why were you yelling at us about flapjacks, then?"

"Naturally, I thought you'd already have the fire built and somethin' good cooked," he said.

Jake made himself oatmeal, too. Clea wasn't hungry, but she made a mug full of cereal, because she needed hot food in her stomach and she had no idea when lunch would be that day. They all stood around the fire and ate quickly.

"I just have to force this down," she said, making conversation so she couldn't think. "I keep telling myself that this time tomorrow I'll be home eating real food and Ariel will be the one eating hot mash, safely tucked away in her own stall."

She looked up just in time to see a strange look pass over Jake's face.

"What?"

He shook his head and pretended great interest in his food. Maybe he was afraid now that the time had come that he couldn't catch Ari after all.

"Buck," she said. "Was Ariel still with the bunch when you left them this morning? Isn't she right up there in the valley this minute with Teddy keeping an eye on her?"

Buck nodded. "Yep."

"Are you all thinking driving them into the trap won't work?"

"It'll work."

She looked at Jake. "Then *what?*"

Buck looked at Jake, too, but he only frowned, threw out the rest of his coffee and started rinsing out the two mugs he'd used. Buck looked at Clea again.

"Cain't count yore wild hosses 'fore they're caught, though," he said. "Jist keep yore fingers crossed, Miss Clea."

"Did I break a superstition? Should I not have said where Ariel will be tomorrow?"

"No superstition," Buck said. "Take it one step at a time. Right now, don't think about nothin'. Nothin' at all past us runnin' them by you and you closin' the gate."

THE SUDDEN POUNDING of hooves set Clea's heart going so fast, beating so hard she thought her blood would come through her skin. The power of the wild horses took over the air and filled it, bounced back from the snow-covered peaks way beyond the canyon walls that formed the bottom of the natural trap and paralyzed her with awe.

You have to close the gate, Clea. You have to close the gate. Just close the gate. Don't get excited and don't think.

They came into sight in a blur of colors, tightly bunched in a dead run, hurtling down the slope where the way narrowed, and then past her hiding place faster than seemed possible for mortal creatures, manes and tails and untrimmed fetlocks waving like flags in the wind they made. She thought she glimpsed a black mane, a black head above the others, but they flowed past so fast, she couldn't be sure of anything. Except that they were so wild and beautiful, they took her breath.

Buck and Teddy flew behind them, yelling and whooping. Jake rode out to join them as the leaders plunged through the gate.

Close the gate. Close the gate.

The men stayed on the heels of the little herd, but it wasn't even necessary because the horses were flying too fast for any of them to think of turning back. They were in.

Clea rode out from behind the canvas-disguised-with-brush wing of the trap and leaned down from the saddle to close the gate. Freckles wasn't excited at all. He'd seen this before. He stood completely still until she'd slid the latch into the slot in the post and turned it down. Now all they had to do was get a rope around Ari's neck.

Clea wished she were inside the trap so she could see better but she was scared. Montana Red was rearing and striking the air, then dropping to all four feet, driving his harem around and around the stone walls and past the gate again, looking for a way out.

Furious as she'd been with him, Clea felt an overwhelming relief that he and all the horses except Ariel would be set free to roam the refuge again. How would Jake and Teddy and Buck bear it if they were all to be kept captive forever?

Of course, if they all stayed free, many would starve. She had to remember that.

They were slowing and she picked out Ariel, taller than the others. The mare started to slow even more, looking around her, seeing the mounted men.

Clea didn't try to get her attention. This time would be different. This time she was going to do her job—she had done it—and trust Jake to catch the mare.

This time would be the charm.

Buck, Teddy and Jake sat in the middle and let the horses run until they began to slow. They'd already come quite a long way from the valley where Teddy had held them, and they needed to stop.

Finally, they slowed and started sort of milling around as far from the men as they could get in the trap. Jake, Teddy and Buck moved slowly to separate them and box Ariel in, away from the others. They were very skillful about it and Clea was glad, because, deep down, she'd had a fear that suddenly roping her at a run might cause her to jerk away and break her neck.

Ariel stood with her back to the rock wall, facing the men, blowing, sides heaving for air. It was nothing short of a miracle that she wasn't lamed from all the running and the rough terrain where she'd been living. It'd be interesting to see whether she still had all her shoes.

Jake was carrying his loop down by his side, so as not to alarm her. It flicked up and out, Ariel threw up her head to look, the rope flew over and settled around her neck. Quickly, quietly. A masterful job.

As far as Clea knew, the mare had never been roped before. But she only pulled back once, not hard, and then she stood again. Jake had the rope tied to his saddle horn and he moved his horse closer. Apparently, he was talking to her because she kept watching him with her ears pricked.

Teddy moved his horse a little closer, too. Buck dropped back and sat his mount between Ariel and the wild ones. Jake leaned over and rubbed Ariel's beautiful neck, then moved closer and scratched her poll.

Clea was aching to get her hands on Ariel herself. She was just beginning to let her heart believe this was all really happening and she could think of their reunion as a reality. Ariel was caught. Clea was getting her horse back at last! She couldn't take her eyes off her mare.

After another minute or so, Jake unbuckled a halter he carried over his saddle horn and put it on Ariel. He attached a leadrope. Now the mare wore two restraints and stood with her head up, still blowing some but not agitated.

Well, not *too* agitated.

Clea decided that the mare was looking straight at her.

You'd better stick with me, girl. Don't you believe that now?

Jake nodded to Buck, and Buck rode toward Clea, signaling for her to open the gate. While she did that, Teddy rode around Montana Red and his band, bunched together and still moving. Buck drifted to one of the flanks to help get them moving toward the open gate.

The lead mare saw the opening, threw up her head and began to run. Red drove the rest of the harem after her but that was mostly unnecessary because none of them would think of leaving the safety of the band. The drumming of their hooves gained speed and volume, then they melted into a beautiful blur again as they ran past Clea and up the slope that led back to the valley.

Gone. Clea looked after them, feeling suddenly poorer somehow. Bereft.

Even though she ought to be happy to see the last of them.

Ariel gave a high, ringing whinny as she, too, stared at the spot where they'd disappeared. Another long call for them to come back.

She wasn't fighting the rope. But she *was* dancing around and looking for the other horses.

Once Clea got Ariel home and secured—a subject on which she'd have to get some advice in case Red came around looking for her again—she'd like to come back to the refuge with her camera. She knew enough about it now that she could find Red's range.

But this was now and she had her horse back, at last.

She laid the rein against Freckles's neck, smooched to him and rode into the trap.

"I think she got attached to them," she called to Buck, who was waiting for her. "Ari misses her new friends."

As if to confirm that, the mare whinnied some more.

"Callin' her buddies back," Buck said. "You'd better git over there and remind her all about her box stall and her alfalfa. She's done forgot what it's like to be home."

As soon as she and Buck rode up to Jake, Teddy and Ariel, Clea dismounted and made herself walk calmly, instead of running to her mare as she wanted to do.

Ariel gave her one low throaty mutter of a greeting but she didn't much care if Clea was there. She had her head up and her ears pointed, looking and listening for her wild bunch.

"You rascally girl," Clea said, running both hands through the mare's thickening fur, feeling for injuries, picking up her feet, trying to see all of the horse at once.

And trying to make the mare hers again. She wanted to touch every inch of her.

"I can't believe that a few days away with a handsome stallion have made you forget me," Clea said.

Ariel nuzzled her shoulder and blew on her cheek as if to say it wasn't true.

Clea hugged her neck, then glanced up at Jake as she worked her way along Ari's side, feeling for wounds that might be there.

"She's really getting her winter coat in a hurry," she said. "It's a good thing I'm not planning to show her any time soon."

He nodded, holding her gaze for a long second. "Yeah," he said. There was something strange in his voice. She couldn't tell whether he meant to be sarcastic or not. Too bad if Jake thought showing horses was a useless thing to do.

She stepped up close and stayed with the mare, even when Ari stepped sideways and away, examining every inch of her she could reach.

What did Jake think about anything? Today he was back to being a stranger to her.

But he'd roped her mare for her, so she could forgive him anything.

She patted Ariel on the hip and stroked her, waiting for her to calm down a little more. Then she ran her hand down over her left hind leg.

"Oh, no," she said. "She's got a cut on this hock. It's still bleeding."

She straightened up. "Let's get this rope off her neck, take her back to our camp and wash it in the creek, then I'll put salve on it and we can start home with her."

For an instant nobody spoke.

"You have to get your camp stuff anyhow," Buck said.

"I'll pony her down there," Jake said. "And leave the rope

on her while I do because I'm taking no chances. Gotta give Red a little more time to get completely gone."

As if she recognized the name, Ariel danced around and let out a loud whinny.

"She's my horse," Clea said, trying to keep her voice calm. "I mean, you caught her for me and all, and I truly am thankful for that and I'll figure out a way to show my appreciation, but I don't want you to pony her with that rope around her neck. She might sit down and pull back."

"Probably not more than once," Jake said dryly.

"*I'll* pony her," Clea said, moving to the rope while Ariel skewed her body to one side. "I'm taking this rope off."

But Jake said, "Watch yourself, Clea." Then he kissed to his horse and left her standing there while he rode away with her mare.

Ariel seemed happy to go with him because they were heading for the same gate Red and his band had gone through. She was calling for them again.

Clea turned to Buck and Teddy, but they were already moving off, too.

She ran back to Freckles and threw herself into the saddle.

"Can you all *believe* it?" she demanded as she rode up between them. "He's got a hell of a lot of nerve. After all, she *is* my horse."

They both looked at her. For a minute, they didn't say anything, then Teddy said, "He don't want her to git away."

Clea said, "She could jerk back and really hurt herself."

Buck just grunted.

They followed Jake to the creek. Clea went directly to their camp to the gear they'd left off their saddles until the capture was over. She got out the antibiotic cream and the wipes, and then took out the pink thermal underwear top she'd worn for warmth. She needed a rag. That wound needed water run over it before any medicines.

Clea dug into her other pack, then, got out the custom-made halter with Ariel's name on it, hung it over her shoulder and bundled the rest of the supplies into the shirt. This should be enough to get the mare ready to go home.

She started to walk the rest of the way, then on impulse, rode Freckles instead. By having him with her when she was ready, there'd be no reason she couldn't be the one to pony Ariel home. By then, surely the mare would be more settled. Right now, she was still calling for the wild ones every few minutes.

She noticed with relief that finally, at last, Jake had taken the rope off Ariel's neck, so he must think she was beginning to settle down. He was holding her by the lead rope, bending over to look at the gash in the mare's leg.

"Jake, bring her over here right by the water, please," she called. "I want to wash that out really well."

She laid her things out, then wadded up the shirt and dipped it in the water.

Jake led Ariel to her and held her head while Clea washed the wound. She hadn't even removed the dried blood and mud before Ariel pulled away from the coldness of the water and kicked out.

Clea stood up and they both tried to soothe her.

"I can't wait to get her home," Clea said. "I guess I'll have to keep her in her stall for a few days until she forgets about the red devil."

"Clea," he said. "There's something I have to tell you. I'm taking this mare to Texas."

She dropped the shirt and stared at him.

"What are you talking about? This is my mare."

"Not according to her papers."

"When did *you* ever see her papers? What are you *talking* about?"

"A fax was sent to the sheriff's office. Legally, your ex-husband owns this mare."

It took a minute for her to even hear him. Her mind simply refused to wrap itself around the words.

She realized she wasn't patting Ariel anymore. Her hand was frozen, tangled in the thick hair of the mare's coat. She was pulling it. Ariel, luckily, didn't seem to notice. Clea stopped pulling and just held on to her mare.

"What does my ex-husband or the sheriff have to do with you?"

"The sheriff thought I might like the reward," he said. "Your ex is offering fifty grand for the safe return of the mare. That's enough for me to pay off my place by the end of this year."

Her stomach got tighter and tighter and tighter, the longer the words rang in her ears. She could barely get a breath.

"I knew he'd find me," she said. "Brock has to be in control, no matter what, and I knew he'd find me. He has the money to do it. I just didn't think it'd be this soon."

"He still may press charges against you for horse theft," Jake said. "It depends on whether or not he gets the mare back. Word is that he doesn't want the scandal of legal action against you, but that's not as important to him as possession of the mare."

"I don't *care* what's important to Brock," she said, fighting the intense rage that was starting to form in her gut. She had to hold on to her mind. She had to think. She had to make Jake see reason. "I knew he wanted Ari. I knew he'd find us, too."

"Clea—" Jake said, but she talked over him.

"But I didn't think it'd be *this* way," she said. "I expected him to hire somebody to *steal* her away from me. Not *bribe* somebody who was my *friend*."

Jake closed his face against her.

"He owns the mare," he snapped.

"I cannot *believe* you'd do this to me."

"You did it to yourself. You stole the mare. That makes you a horse thief."

"She's mine."

"Not according to the law."

Clea looked around for Buck and Teddy, as if they could somehow resolve the argument. They were busy finishing the breakup of the camp.

"I hate it, Clea," Jake said, and she could hear the pain in his voice for a millisecond before he covered it up. "But I don't often have the chance to make this kind of money."

He sounded so definite. So determined. So set on his purpose that he couldn't be swayed.

"Well, then, just hold her," she said, taking satisfaction in the fact that her voice stayed steady.

Her thoughts were racing as she moved back to Ariel's leg again, ran her hand down it and then looked at the wet shirt in a heap on the rocks.

"Hold her," she said again. "I have to rinse this out. I don't want to get dirt in the wound."

Aggressive. She had to assert herself and attack, not fold the way she'd done so many times with Brock.

She had to think and not crumble inside because this was such a betrayal after what they'd had together last night.

But that hadn't meant anything. It had been of-the-moment lovemaking between two consenting adults that included no declarations and no promises. She was on her own and out in the world, and that's the way things worked.

So it *wasn't* a betrayal, and she'd make a fool of herself if she accused him of that.

What *could* she say or do? She was cleaning and putting medicine on the wound, while her mind was going like a hamster in a cage but coming up empty. Where could she get fifty thousand dollars? Would he trust her enough to wait two years for her to get access to her money?

No. She knew that now.

There *had* been pain in Jake's voice, though. He really *did* hate this. Maybe she could make him hate it too much to follow through with it.

She finished with the ointment and stood up. He was staring off into the distance, his jaw set hard as stone.

Let him think about it. Pick your time to lay the guilt on him.

Clea moved closer to him, petting Ariel. The mare pulled at the restraint and Jake gave her the rope to turn her head to Clea. She muttered a greeting at her.

"Finally, you talk to me!"

Clea threw her arms around the mare's neck and pressed her face into her dusty, messy mane, fighting tears again. She had to keep her dignity. She might try to manipulate, but she would not beg.

Which wouldn't work anyway because he didn't care about her feelings at all. Except...she'd sensed he'd felt sorry for her about the money for the truck that day he brought her the estimates.

"Look," he said. "We can't stand around here all day..."

Clea lifted her head and looked at him straight. "Give me some time," she said. "I can get a job in Pine Lodge and I could give jumping lessons, and I have money coming from some horses I sold, so if I made payments to you and you used them to pay off your land..."

Was that pity? Did she see a glimpse of empathy in Jake's eyes?

He shook his head. "You'd be in jail. If Brock doesn't get the mare back, he'll have you arrested for stealing her."

She searched his face. It had been so handsome last night in the moonlight, craggy in the firelight, and it was drop-dead gorgeous now. But it was the face of a traitor.

Hurt, anger, despair all rose in her like a tidal wave.

She bit her lip to hold back tears of frustration. The anger. She had to get hold of the anger and will it to rule.

To give herself a minute so she could talk without crying, she turned her back on him, picked up Freckles's reins, and started back toward camp where Buck and Teddy were packing up. He brought Ariel along and walked beside her.

"Look," he said. "I'm a sorry coward. I was trying to tell you this last night but…I…"

She stopped and made herself look at him, made him hold her gaze.

"But you didn't want to ruin the moment," she said and was amazed at the nasty, cutting tone of voice that came out of her mouth.

It made her feel better. It made her feel stronger. So she kept using it.

"You were all hot and bothered and you wanted relief, therefore, you kept your mouth shut with no regard whatsoever for my feelings."

"No, I—"

But she was on a roll. "You've known this the whole time we've been out here in the refuge, Jake Hawthorne, and you haven't breathed a word of it. So that makes you a coward—and a liar."

"Clea—"

"You've been stringing me along just to get me in bed with you. You waited until the last night and made it happen."

His face flushed red.

"I have *not!* I—"

But she was a woman and words came faster to her and she was in the right and he was floundering in his rightful guilt. She narrowed her eyes and kept up the attack.

"You're the worst kind of liar, Jake, the *very* worst kind. Because you're lying to yourself, too. What's all that noise about how you don't think it's right to work just for money? Well, what other reason do you have for doing this?"

He turned away in disgust and started walking again. She stayed right beside him.

"Justice," she said sarcastically. "I'll bet you're just trying to bring justice to the world and wipe out horse thievery everywhere."

He clamped his jaw so tight the bone stretched the skin. He walked faster. So did she.

"Look at yourself," she said. "Your life is *driven* by money. First, the Natural Bands job and now this. Money as poison. Don't you *dare* ever say another bad word about Tori and the decision she made."

She shouldn't have encouraged her anger. It was consuming her now. It felt so good to stand up and say what she thought and felt for once in her life.

And he was silent. Maybe she was getting to him.

"I don't want to hear it," he snapped. "I took the job. I'll finish it."

She wouldn't give up. She *couldn't.*

Yet despair was already forming at the core of her, overcoming the anger.

Jake was right. The law was on Brock's side. It was all hopeless. If he didn't get Ariel back, he *would* have her arrested.

How could she fight him? She couldn't without Daddy's help, and she was *not* going to call him.

Then they were in camp. Buck came to see about Ariel's injury. He patted the mare on the rump, ran his hand down her leg and picked it up to look at it.

"It's not deep," he said. "It'll heal fast."

"That's what I thought," Clea said. "Buck, would you take Freckles? I want to change Ariel's halter."

"What's wrong with this one?" Jake asked.

"It's too big. This one's made for her, so she might as well wear it."

She looked at Buck, then at Teddy, as she slipped the halter off her shoulder and walked over to take Ari's leadrope from Jake. "Did y'all know that Jake's taking Ariel back to Texas? To my ex-husband?"

They both met her eyes, but only briefly. They said nothing.

Yes, they'd known.

That made her feel left out and plotted against. For a minute. Then she realized they couldn't and wouldn't and *shouldn't* have told her.

She might as well try to make them feel better. They both looked so hangdog sad that she wanted to cry for them as well as for herself.

"Y'all were right when you were teasing me about being a horse thief," she said. "I can't believe you accidentally hit on that, can you?"

They lifted their heads and looked hopeful again.

"You ain't mad at us?" Teddy asked.

"No," she said. "It wasn't y'all's place to tell me. This is Jake's business and it *is* business. There's a reward out for her safe return and he's going to get a lot of money."

"That's better than a reward out for *you,* dead or alive," Buck said.

He twinkled at her and she made herself smile back, but they couldn't quite laugh. There was sympathy in the look and in his voice, too. He hated this for her. So did Teddy.

Jake was unbuckling the halter he'd put on Ari. She was offering her muzzle to Clea now, wanting to be petted. Jake slipped off the halter and stepped back to keep his arm and the leadrope looped up around her neck as a signal for her to stand still while Clea put the other one on.

Immediately, Ari dropped her head over Clea's shoulder in an affectionate embrace she'd used only with Clea for all these years they'd known each other.

"Oh, Ariel," Clea said and threw her arms around the mare's neck.

She nuzzled her face into it and held on. The haircoat was getting thick, and its roughness against her face seemed weird, but the good horsey smell that was only Ari's had not changed. Not at all.

A high, wild whinny cut through the air.

Ariel reared with no warning, ripping herself out of Clea's arms and lifting Jake off the ground. The sudden violent move threw Clea onto her butt, helpless and looking up at the twelve hundred pounds of horse and two shod hooves hovering over her. Ari looked two stories tall.

Jake fell back, too, but he still had the leadrope that he'd thrown over her neck without tying it, and he held on to both ends of that. Ari came down on all four feet, whirled fast, and left the rope in his hands.

Another ringing whinny. Clea recognized that call before she even looked up. In fact, she'd known it the first time.

Along the closest ridgeline on the west, stood Montana

Red. Pacing up and down, head high, his mane and tail tossing in the wind, he was announcing he was ruler of the world.

He lifted his head and called to Ariel again.

The last glimpse Clea had of her was blurred by the high-splashing waters of the creek as the mare dashed across it at a run.

CHAPTER EIGHTEEN

JAKE AND CLEA sat in the dirt and stared at each other, stunned. Montana Red bugled his victory one more time.

Buck and Teddy began to laugh.

"Damn," Buck said, gasping for air. "I wish you two could see yoreselves. Now, if that ain't a pitiful sight—the two best young horsemen, horsepeople—in the whole damn state settin' flat o' their butts in the dirt, and the hoss that put 'em there ain't even *wild!*"

They were bending over now, slapping their knees.

"Losin' yore touch, Jake," Teddy said, when he could get his breath. "Reckon you're gittin' too old fer the job?"

That set them off again.

Jake and Clea shared an instinctive glance. *Aren't they the two most aggravating human beings on the planet?*

But then that brief glimpse of their shredded friendship was gone. Reality set in. They got up off the ground, Clea's heart twisting bitterly. So close and yet so far—it hurt even more to lose Ariel for the second time, especially after holding her pretty head in her hands and feeling close to her again.

Especially after finding out that she was going back to Brock.

"At least *this* time, thank goodness, it's not all my fault," Clea said, dusting off the seat of her jeans. One hip was already throbbing from the hard landing. She'd have a huge bruise.

"You were the one saying the long goodbye," Jake snapped. "Even though you and the mare would've been together all the way from here to the ranch."

"She belongs with me and you know it."

Jake ignored that.

"Buck," he yelled. "Ted. Sober up and help me remake the packs. You three are heading home. I want all the extra supplies."

"You can't catch her by yourself."

Clea said it automatically, a knee-jerk reaction to the need to be there, to stay as close to her mare as she could, even though now it made no sense.

"Why do *you* care? Didn't you hear me? She's not yours and I'm not catching her for you."

"What kind of monster do you think I am? I love her. I don't want her to get hurt and I have sense enough to know she can't live out here indefinitely."

Jake flashed her a furious look. "Have you noticed that with three people to help me, we've lost her twice?"

Clea turned away. She couldn't talk to him anymore, she couldn't look at him anymore. She *didn't* want to help him go after Ariel again. She wanted to crawl into bed and pull the covers up over her head.

And that didn't mean she wasn't tough, either. The old guys were still joking and laughing, but they were bustling around already doing what Jake asked, and there was no way she could go against all three of them and live, now that she knew what it took to survive out here.

No one ought to be out here alone for any length of time.

Not even Jake, as he and Buck—and Teddy with his falling off a cliff—had already proved on this trip. She had proved it, too. Rope or not, she'd never have escaped from the river if it hadn't been for Jake.

She was just worried because she didn't want to be the one responsible if he got hurt again or got in a bad situation.

That makes no sense at all, Clea. You didn't turn the mare loose on purpose. And you certainly never asked him to come out here to catch her!

He stalked beside her, not even looking at her, as she walked over to the old guys.

"Buck. Teddy. I need you two to swear you'll take Clea home," Jake said. "Even if you have to tie her on her horse."

She wheeled and stared at him. He ignored her.

"You both know from the way she jumped in the river that she's just gutsy enough to try to get away from you two and follow me," he said, his stern look moving from Buck to Teddy and back again. "Swear you'll take her straight back to the ranch."

"And then what should they do?" she asked sarcastically. "Lock me up in the spare bedroom?"

"We don't have one," Buck drawled. "But there's plenty of stalls in the barn."

"Don't flatter yourself, Jake," she said, standing tall in spite of the fact she wanted to drop in a heap. "And don't bother looking over your shoulder. I won't follow you. You're right. Ariel's not my horse and you're not trying to catch her for me. Go for it. For the mare's sake, I wish you good luck."

She turned her back on him.

"Buck, you and Teddy go with him. I can find my way home, and I'll go straight there."

Without waiting for an answer, she went to her packs and started arranging them to tie on her saddle.

Behind her, there was still Jake's voice. "You got Dakota to do the chores?"

Buck said, "Yep."

"Tell him I'll pay him extra to ride my colts some. I thought I'd be back before now."

"No animals left over at your cabin?"

"Nope. And my good tack's at your place, too."

You'd be home riding your own colts and taking care of your own tack if you'd minded your own business. Meddler.

She was glad to be away from him. She needed some time alone. She looked forward to the ride. She'd give what little money she had if she didn't have to talk to or listen to another living soul for days and days.

She needed solitude, and after that, she needed to sleep in a bed and eat some decent food.

"*Gutsy's* the word all right," she heard Buck say. "Surprised you, didn't it, Jake? And she's right. She kin git home on her own..."

"I'm taking *nobody* with me." Jake's voice. "Let me have some of those energy bars and..."

Clea laid her forehead against Freckles's warm, horse-smelling neck and shut her ears. They could argue all day as long she didn't have to listen. All she wanted was for them all to go away.

She put one arm over the gelding's neck, pressed her cheek to it and fought back tears. But she didn't have the strength to cry. She was done. Wiped out. A bowl of jelly without a will.

Except to take care of herself. To depend on no one.

Especially not Jake. She wasn't even going to *think* about Jake.

But pure determination was not going to bring Ariel back to her. This was the end of her and her ornery, talented, beautiful mare.

She didn't know how long she stood there before Jake walked up behind her.

"I can take care of myself," he said angrily. "Don't feel responsible for me. You're *not.* I was the one stupid enough to cut the mare loose from my horse."

But you asked me to do it. I did it for you.

He didn't say that, but they both knew it and it made Clea furious with herself. They probably *would* still have the mare if she'd been tethered to his colt.

She whirled on one heel and lashed out at him.

"Hey," she said. "It's Ariel I'm worried about. And I'm the one who has a right to be mad here. I'm the one losing my mare."

He nailed her with that fierce green gaze. "Not. Your. Mare."

THOSE WORDS rang in Clea's ears long after Jake had taken off after Montana Red and Ariel, and she and the old guys headed back to the ranch. It was true. And it would take her a long, long time to get used to the fact.

Despite what she'd said to him, she knew Jake would catch the mare. He was that kind of man. He had no quit in him, as Buck and Teddy would say. He might be a skeleton living on roots and berries by the time he came in with her, but bring her in, he would.

And then he'd take her to Brock.

What Clea had to do was keep telling herself that Brock would sell Ariel. And that whoever paid the price she was worth would take good care of their investment.

And that maybe, when two years had passed and she had her trust fund, whoever that person was would sell her back to Clea.

Ari's legs couldn't hold up to this life. Honestly, she'd be better off with a new owner or even with Brock, than with Montana Red.

Especially if she'd stuck when he bred her—she was old for a maiden mare and would probably need help foaling out.

"I hope you ain't mad at us," Teddy said, startling her out of her thoughts. "I told Buck we might oughtta try to warn you. Help cushion the shock an' all."

"I hope you won't hold this agin' Jake forever," Buck said.

They were both frowning worriedly at her, their eyes so kindly that she didn't have the heart to tell them she didn't want to talk. Or listen.

She noticed the sun. It was nearly noon. They'd been remarkably quiet and patient a long time. Or they'd been their usual talkative selves and she hadn't even heard them because she'd been so far into herself.

So far into the yearnings that kept bringing her back to wondering where Jake was by now, and then to replaying everything he'd said and done yesterday and last night. Those memories were enough make her go weak in the knees every time.

She had to stop it. All of it. She might as well talk. Get her mind fixed firmly on something else.

"No, I'm not mad at you two," she said, as she rode along between the two old guys. "And, I guess I can't hold this against Jake, either. I'd love to. I'm trying to. But legally, I don't have a claim."

And no claim on Jake's loyalty, either. Welcome to the real world, girl.

"With my head I understand that people do all kinds of things for money," she said. "It's just that my heart somehow feels he's betraying our friendship."

They trotted along in lockstep. For once, neither of the old guys said anything. They knew she was talking mostly to herself.

The three of them picked their way across a patch of shale and down into the ford of a creek with a treacherous, rocky bottom and a surprisingly deep current in the middle where every step was a slipping, sliding, rolling adventure. It took such a long time and was so scary that she was desperately glad to be mounted on the imperturbable Freckles instead of Ariel.

When they were all safely across, she wanted so much to get down and just stretch her legs and loosen her nerves for a little while. But she'd sworn to herself that she wouldn't ask for any breaks or any concessions, and she didn't.

It wasn't just the brave cowgirl thing. She wanted to be alone. She wanted to be in her new little home alone, where she could cocoon and start working on her new life again. Rethink it all, now that Brock knew where she was and she wasn't hiding anymore.

She just bit her lip, stood in the stirrups to rest her hip that was getting more sore by the minute and let herself be carried along by these two tough men who were her only friends. She needed to think about how lucky she was to have them to teach her to survive. All that work would make her stop thinking about Ariel.

And Jake.

Making love with him had been a one-time experience but she could never call it a one-night stand. It had opened something inside her that had been closed all her life. Now she was both weaker and stronger in a way she couldn't describe. She needed to be alone and sort it all out.

"About Jake, Clea," Buck said, as he picked up the speed to a long trot. "I know he don't like puttin' money ahead of a friendship. He's jist got a chance of a lifetime and a dream he's tryin' to make come true."

Clea sighed. "I know. He told me about wanting to pay off his place, and when I stand back and look at it from a distance, I truly cannot blame him for grabbing this way to do it."

They both looked at her, then across her at each other. Teddy raised one eyebrow and nodded at Buck.

"What?" she said.

"Aw, we've had a argyment goin' about how you'd take it when you found out what Jake was up to," Ted said. "We was dreadin' the tears and the wailin'."

"Or the screamin' and cussin' and throwin' rocks," Buck said, grinning. "Or the gittin' out the old shotgun and sprayin' the countryside for miles around. We couldn't decide which it'd be."

"Did you two know the whole time we've been out here?"

They nodded, both of them looking sheepish.

"I figgered there was always a chance he'd change his mind," Teddy said. "No sense you worryin' 'til you had to."

Clea shifted in her saddle again to get off her sore hip.

"Go on, Teddy, tell the truth," she said. "What you really mean is, no sense listening to me cry and scream until *you* had to."

They laughed.

"Are y'all surprised I can act like a grown-up? When you thought all along I was a big, spoiled baby?"

They laughed again.

"No, we knowed you're tough," Buck said, "but that scares us, too. It could mean you're plottin' revenge."

Clea narrowed her eyes at him. "Yes, it could. Watch your back."

"Hey," Teddy said. "We never promised to tell you ever'thing."

Buck chuckled. "No and I wouldn't be surprised if you ain't got a few secrets of your own."

Clea whipped around to look at him. What had he seen when he rode up on her and Jake's camp?

But his sharp old eyes flicked to meet hers and told her

nothing. Neither did his weathered face. Then he smiled and she couldn't resist smiling back.

Uncle Buck, mysterious wise man. Somehow, just riding along between him and Teddy made her feel much better. She wasn't completely alone in the world.

THE SUN had almost disappeared under the mountain behind the indoor arena when the three of them reached the ranch the next day. The lights were on in it and in the barn.

"Light and warmth waiting in the dark," Clea said. "That looks weird to me now."

"Does it look welcome, too?" Teddy asked. "Or do you jist love that sleepin' on the ground?"

She didn't want to think about that.

They rode in a ragged line up to the door of the barn and dismounted. The creaking of their saddles, and the stomps and snuffles of their horses, plus the even homier sounds of feeding time coming from inside, filled the dusk.

"I feel like I've spent a lifetime in another world," Clea said, stifling a groan when she threw her leg over and stepped down.

If the old guys weren't complaining about saddle soreness, neither would she.

"This here's the world fer sissys," Teddy said.

"I don't care. I can't wait to sleep in my bed."

Dakota, the teenager who'd been hired to do the chores, came to the door of the barn with the manure pick in his hand.

"That you, Uncle Buck?"

"Yeah, son. How's it goin'?"

"Pretty good, except that little foal in there just bit me on the arm and it bled all over everything. I was playing with her and she just grabbed me."

"Did you find the first-aid kit in the tack room?"

"Yessir. It's okay now."

Clea looked to see the damage. He had his sleeve rolled up and a bandage on his arm.

"Has she been kicking you, too?" she asked.

"No, ma'am. She ain't kicked out behind, but she reared on me a couple of times."

She'd mourned for Ariel and thought about Jake so much that she'd forgotten about this baby the whole way home. How *could* she have forgotten? It was a godsend.

"Uncle Buck, I want that baby," she said, as they led their horses into the barn and down the aisle to their stalls. "She may belong to y'all, but I want to take charge of her."

"Fine with me," he said. "Looks like she needs it."

"Put a fine point on it," Teddy said. "It's Jake's filly."

Buck threw him an irritated glance. "I'll speak fer Jake."

Clea went to the foal's stall and looked in. The baby lifted her head from the hay she was eating and looked back at her. Her eyes were bright. She left the hay and ran around the stall.

"She needs freedom and exercise," Clea said. "But let's leave her in here tonight so she won't be in an unfamiliar place in the dark."

She looked around for Buck, who was unsaddling his horse.

"Buck? I'll come over here in the morning and put her out. Do you have a crotchety old gelding around here anyplace? I need that and a pen where I can put the two of them."

"You got 'em."

On her sore, shaky legs—she'd never ridden so many hours in a row in all her life—she led Freckles into a stall and started unsaddling him.

"But what're you gonna do with 'em?" Teddy asked. "A geldin' and a pen?"

Clea turned to see Teddy, Buck and Dakota all curious, all listening.

"Feed and water him and the foal together so he can teach her some manners. She doesn't even know there's a pecking order in horses. She doesn't know anything about living in horse society, and that's her strongest need."

Dakota repeated, "'Horse society.'"

Clea smiled at him. He was a cute kid.

"They're really social animals," she said. "You know that."

"I'm thinkin'," Teddy said. "Tricky might be a good one to use."

Buck scowled at him. "First you say it's Jake's foal, so leave it alone, and the next thing we know you're tryin' to tell us what to do with it. Just butt out, will you?"

"We're all tired," Clea said soothingly. "We can decide what gelding in the morning."

"Dakota," Buck said, as he finished unsaddling. "You know that bald-faced gelding we call Boss?"

"Yes, sir."

"He's in the creek pasture. Run down there and bring him up here for me."

"Yes, *sir!*"

Clea took her saddle to the tack room and brushed Freckles down, her arms growing heavier by the minute. Never, ever had she been this tired, not even after the long haul up from Texas.

She broke off a couple of flakes of hay for him and filled his water bucket, then she went to get the grain Teddy was scooping up, all the while glancing in at the foal when she passed her stall.

She was dozing now, lying curled up in her leftover hay. Worn out from playing with Dakota, no doubt. And biting him.

But she wasn't kicking out behind, at least. Clea smiled.

Already, she'd taught her one good lesson, and Boss would teach her a lot more.

Here was a problem she could solve. Here was a purpose she could use as a piece of happiness when she woke up every morning.

She'd concentrate on the foal and move on. Move on with her life in every way.

Her horse was gone, yes, and she definitely still needed her—Ariel-the-Diva. Like children, one horse could never replace another. She would miss Ari for a long time. Forever. But right now, this little wild thing would be way better than no horse at all.

JAKE RODE through the low hills that rolled on and on until they built into mountains again and rose into the sky. The sky and land were seamless and enormous, eternal and mysterious. What the Spanish used to call The Northern Mystery.

There was no better unspoiled place in all the world. He'd been deeply happy when Celeste and her people had put this chunk of the Gallatin basin into one of those perpetual conservation trusts or whatever they were called. This country was so magnificent it deserved to be preserved forever.

But today he was having trouble remembering exactly how it felt to be deeply happy. Or even slightly pleased.

Usually he loved every minute of a ride like this, loved the beauty that took him out of himself and into something bigger, loved the fact that no other human being breathed this same air for many miles in any direction. Today, he felt like one small speck on the face of the earth who didn't have the power of an ant.

That was mostly because of the horses. The wily old lead mare and Montana Red both sensed his presence every time he got close enough to have the ghost of a chance of laying a rope on Ariel. He already felt stupid enough because he'd let her get away twice before.

Which was really Clea's doing.

Forget that. You knew better. Both times you could've managed the woman better and caught the mare.

Well, he had managed the woman now. He'd wanted her gone and she was gone.

And at last, he'd had the guts to tell her he was taking her mare to Texas.

He loved being alone. He was a loner. He was born a loner and he'd be one until he died.

So how come he wasn't riding along here "singin' with his tail up" as Uncle Buck would say?

Probably he was in a funk, not because he was alone, but because he didn't know how long it was going to take to outsmart Montana Red and catch this mare on his own hook. Maybe he should've told the old guys to come back and help him.

Forget that, too. You want the money, don't you? You want your own place free and clear, don't you? So go get it.

CLEA DROVE down the main street of Pine Lodge looking for a parking place, but going so fast she missed a couple of them before she saw them. She needed to settle down instead of running around like a scared chicken.

Which she wasn't. Not anymore.

She had realized that the minute she walked into her little cabin after her wilderness experience. Something was different. The shadow hanging over her, the dread lurking in the back of her mind, was gone.

What did she have to be afraid of? Brock knew where she

was. He would tell Daddy—probably already had told him. What else could he do to her? Ariel was gone.

Brock wasn't big on keeping his word, so he could still try to have Clea arrested, even after he got the mare back, but so what?

Hey, Brock—they don't hang horse thieves anymore.

He wouldn't. He wouldn't want the publicity. A lot of people would laugh at him.

She took a deep breath, put both hands on the wheel and one eye on the diagonal row of parked cars along the main street and slowed down. She wanted to get back to the ranch and start working with the baby, but she had to have supplies or starve.

And she had to have distractions or go crazy. She wanted to be busy, busy, busy, she wanted movement and noise so she couldn't miss Ari too much.

Ariel is gone. When she let herself think, all she could think was those three words. It was so unfair for Brock to have her.

But life was unfair. It was time for her to accept that that rule held true across the board. She'd known it when her mother died. And when she'd realized the true nature of her husband and her marriage.

And again when Jake had chosen money instead of her.

The magic that they had together in bed—and, even more important, that incredible way they could read each other's real self with one deep look—meant they could've been soul mates. Or at least really good friends. It was beyond unfair that he had thrown that away.

No, they couldn't ever have been just friends. She wouldn't have been able to keep her hands off him.

Get over it. He's a loner. He doesn't want a soulmate or a friend.

Clea turned at the corner with the drugstore on it, drove

around the block, which to her surprise was residential on the back side, and onto the main street again. She made herself go slowly and halfway down the first block with parking spaces, she saw an empty slot angled in front of the gift shop. She took it.

She got out and closed the door of her truck, snuggling deeper into her coat against a sudden sharp gust of wind. On the sidewalk, she walked slowly as if she had to get her bearings to walk on the boards—part of the effort to, along with the rustic fronts on the shops, give the town a really Western air—instead of on uneven ground. A few days roughing it had made town seem like an alien world.

When she reached the café and opened the door, she stepped in and just stood there for a minute. All eyes went to her as the door rang its little bell. It was a small, closed world filled with the chatter and bustle of people having breakfast or a morning coffee break. The few booths were taken and so were almost all the tables.

They sized her up. Small town, everybody knew everybody except the tourists. Did they think she was one?

All the tables were taken. Vaguely, she thought she remembered that there was another restaurant on the opposite end of town, out past the grocery store.

Clea made a move to turn but someone called, "Oh, don't go." A woman seated with two others at a round table in the middle of the room pushed back her chair and got up. She had amazing curly dark hair and a mischievous smile.

"Come and sit with us," she said, coming to get Clea. "We desperately need a fresh opinion for this argument, and you look worldly and wise. And hungry."

Something inside Clea relaxed. She could use a woman friend. Or maybe even more than one.

"I'm Sharyn Foster," she said, "and I own the gift shop next door."

She went on with the introductions as Clea sat down in the empty captain's chair. "This is Tally Davis, from the bakery across the street. Tally moved out here from Kansas to keep us all supplied with artisanal breads…"

Tally looked like a farm girl from Kansas, blond and blue-eyed, with a sturdy build and a welcoming smile.

"And last, Heather Rowan. She and her husband run an outfitting business and run a cattle ranch south of town."

They all looked at Clea while Sharyn said, "Now tell us who you are and what you're doing here in Pine Lodge after tourist season. Is it true that you're a supermodel hiding out from the press?"

Clea's look of astonishment made them all laugh. "Not quite," she said. "I'm Clea Mathison from Texas."

It felt even more freeing to say that and know she didn't have to hide anymore.

They waited for more information.

"I'm renting a cabin out on the Elkhorn Ranch."

Still waiting. The waitress came and took her order for eggs and toast, and even when she left, they were still waiting.

"I…may get into photography," she said finally, and they realized she didn't want to say any more, so they asked no more questions.

"But what I'm doing right this minute is looking for a companion for an orphan foal," Clea said. "Do you all know of any possibilities?"

That turned the conversation to horses, since they all four rode, and after agreeing that they must get together for a trail ride—ironically enough so Clea could really see some beautiful Montana backcountry—Sharyn glanced up at the television set in the corner, where a morning news show was doing a segment about fashion.

Models were strutting down the runway, showing short leather skirts and fur jackets and marvelous leather bags to die for.

"See?" she said. "Really, Clea, you could be one of them."

"I could never be that skinny," she said. "And I'm way too old and too grungy. Look at me, Sharyn!"

She looked down at herself. Worn Wranglers, two thermal tees layered one on top of the other. Her battered custom Western boots that had cost two thousand dollars—that was in another life—and thrown over the back of her chair, the yellow down-filled ski jacket she'd worn on the horse chase. Thank God she *had* washed it. No bag at all. All her necessities were in the various pockets of her clothing.

Clea Mathison without the most fabulous bag in the room! Unthinkable.

"What's so funny?" Tally asked.

Clea leaned back a little so the waitress could serve her food and gestured toward the screen.

"Yeah," Tally said. "How many women in real life could get one leg into those little skirts?"

That started another topic, which was style versus comfort, and Clea listened with only half an ear.

Real life. This was it. She was living real life now.

She'd had just a glimmer of how life could be real when she'd worked up her nerve and left Brock. She'd learned a little more when he'd contested the divorce and managed to keep Ariel.

She'd caught another glimpse when she'd stolen Ariel back and hauled her up here.

But now Ariel was gone and this was real life with a vengeance. She had changed to meet it. She was changing and would change some more.

She would always love clothes and bags and pretty things, but she didn't care whether she was in step with the trends anymore or simply in her own style. She could wear what she had on for the rest of the winter and be perfectly happy.

She would always want to look good. But now her looks weren't the most important part of her. She had more important things to do than shop and dress herself and groom herself.

Obviously. Her nails were short and plain and she didn't care.

Clea made a mental list of her newly important real-life things while she let the friendly conversation swirl around her and took ravenous bites of the delicious hot eggs that had been scrambled in butter and the thick, homemade wheat toast. When she could get a word in edgewise, she'd ask Tally if it was some of her famous bread.

Number one, the wild baby. Clea could help her grow up to be a confident, useful horse who knew how to live well with people and other horses.

Number two, the winter. She had to survive without Ariel and look for another horse that cost hardly anything to try to buy in the spring. Maybe she could borrow one to keep in the big barn and ride in the indoor arena during the winter.

Perhaps a horse with problems. Another equine life to save. It seemed a shame not to use that arena and stall, since it was part of what she was paying rent for.

Three, she had to decide what to do to make a living.

Four, she had to decide to try to forgive Daddy, which she didn't think she could do. Not yet. That might come in a year or so.

Five, ditto Brock. Or else her heart would be bitter for the rest of her new life.

Six, she had to forget about Jake and store the memories of that one precious night away to pull out when she was old.

Was this how a person went about building a new life? A piece at a time?

The hospitable women all had to get back to work, so when Clea had finished eating, they left together and stood outside in the brilliant fall day for a few minutes, exchanging numbers and making plans to ride.

"Thanks," Clea said, as they parted. "I really enjoyed meeting you all."

"Thank *you,*" Sharyn said. "This is such a small town we're all sick of each other. It's really a treat to get to really talk with somebody new."

They all laughed and waved goodbye. Clea walked up the street toward her truck.

That was another way she'd changed. The old Clea would never have enjoyed that encounter as much as the new Clea had.

She had even been tempted to talk about Ariel, and if they did take that trail ride together, she probably would.

The chilly wind was picking up, sending yellow and red leaves skittering down the sidewalk ahead of her, and she thought of Jake and Ariel. Today definitely was colder than yesterday. There were a few gray clouds above the mountains to the west. Could he catch her before the next storm blew in?

CHAPTER NINETEEN

JAKE TURNED UP the collar of his coat and shifted his position so that the wind would be more to his back. He pulled his hat down against its sharp, cold strength and then put both gloved hands on the binoculars.

He moved the glasses slowly, scanning the valley directly below him. This was approximately the middle of the range Montana Red had stayed in since Jake, Buck and Teddy had known him. It couldn't exactly be called his territory, because many times the ranges of different stallions overlapped. They didn't set boundaries and protect a territory. Instead, they protected a sort of comfort zone around themselves. Another horse band couldn't enter that herd space without causing trouble.

Jake must've been following too close. Many times, the mares sensed danger even before the stallion did. Jake had followed them for four days and then he'd lost them by sleeping until the sun came up. Either they or Montana Red must have sensed his presence and moved the harem before sunrise. He'd had a horrid night of bad dreams when he did sleep and too much thinking when he didn't.

Memories, unwanted ones. Clea's face when he told her he was taking her mare to Texas. Her eyes when she touched the captured mare for the first time, back when she'd innocently expected to keep her.

Doubts about whether what he was doing was right.

He set his jaw so hard his teeth squeaked. He wanted his place and he needed the reward money to secure his freedom. With his place paid for, he could raise and start his own horses and not have to take a job on the side that would take him away from it for hours every day.

This was a dream come true and he wasn't going to look back or second-guess himself. He never had been that kind of man and he wasn't going to start now.

Plus, he *couldn't* quit. He'd taken the job. He'd started it so he had to finish it.

The proudest day of his life was the day when he was nine and determined to ride a rank steer, which he did after getting thrown more times than he could count. That had brought rare praise from his daddy and he could still hear his voice when he called up the memory.

I'm proud of you, son. You've got no quit in you.

He had no quit in him. He would not quit this job, and he would not lose Ariel again.

A slight movement in the corner of his eye caught his attention. He heard the cadence of strong hooves striking the ground, then, out of the brush-spotted tan-and-gray early-morning landscape, he picked out heads and ears, up and pointed, listening. Eyes looking ahead. Nostrils scenting the wind.

One horse, then another and another appeared out of a draw as if by magic.

They had spent the night sheltered in an unseen fold of the earth.

Not Montana Red and his band.

A bay lead horse, a stallion and two other young studs, one paint, one grullo. A bachelor band. Five or six years old, old enough to start needing a harem band of their own.

The last one out was the grullo stallion he and Ted and Buck had noticed before. Jake smiled wryly. Those three looked about like him and the old guys, a bachelor band out in the middle of nowhere. He missed them, but he missed Clea more.

They'd named the grullo Young Gun for his nerve and aggressiveness and tenacity during a fight they watched when he challenged the mean white stallion and lost. Now, only a few months later, he had gone back to his bachelor buddies. Jake would bet money, though, that he hadn't given up on stealing a harem band.

As if to prove his independence, Young Gun peeled off from the others and trotted toward Jake, while they headed away. He moved like he was traveling with a purpose.

What was he thinking? Was he out to cherry-pick a mare from one harem or another? Every bachelor stallion was a stalker looking to steal an established stallion's mares.

Usually spring was the time for that, but hey, loneliness could strike at any time, and fall could be a lonely time of year. Jake could testify to that.

Or maybe Young Gun was feeling frisky in the cold wind and wanting company for the winter. Maybe he'd decided to take a run at getting a whole band of mares for himself.

Whatever he was up to, he looked small and forlorn, friendless while the other two went away together. He looked like a piece of the sky, a piece of the land, a collection of shadows walking along on the ground. His smoky-gray color was the same as that of a wild mouse, what some people would call mouse-colored instead of grullo. It wasn't made by a mixture of colors. Instead, each of the hairs on a grullo's body was smoky or silvery, changeable in the light.

He followed a trail that Jake couldn't see, trotting even faster now toward the hill opposite him, heading east, the same way Jake was facing. He watched as Young Gun moved up the slope and over it, ready to drop out of sight.

The stallion stopped on the hilltop. He threw up his head and looked in all directions, smelling the air and listening. It wasn't Jake he sensed because he was downwind from him.

Young Gun stood frozen. He stared into the distance for a long time.

Trying to decide where he wanted to go. Jake knew how he felt.

For a long time, Jake watched, feeling his nerves gradually work up to high alert. Wild stallions possessed fantastic eyesight, and many times they could detect other horses from over a mile away.

Montana Red! Jake felt the truth of that hunch in his bones but he wouldn't believe it until he saw the old stallion with his own eyes.

Young Gun shook his mane, let out a challenging whinny and took off. When he dropped out of sight over the hill, Jake jumped up and ran for his horse.

CLEA, BUCK AND TEDDY stood leaning on the fence, watching Boss and Jake's little foal at Boss's round rubber feed tub.

"See?" Clea said. "He's a failure as a parent. He's letting Scarlett eat out of his feeder, and she's crowding him, too. He's way too indulgent with her."

"Beats me what's the matter with the old son of a gun," Buck said. "I'm plumb ashamed. He's usually the meanest thing on four legs around here."

"I told you we should use Tricky," Ted said.

Clea spoke fast, before they could start arguing. "When she's grown, behavior like that with other horses'll get her kicked into next week and she'll never understand why."

"You callin' her Scarlett O'Hara?" Teddy asked.

"*Then* she'll learn," Buck said, ignoring Ted. "Me 'n' Teddy listenin' to you about how to raise these orphans proves old men can learn new tricks. Why not old horses, too?"

"Wonder if Jake'll like that name," Teddy said.

Clea shot him an annoyed glance. "Too bad if he doesn't. He should've named her when he first got her."

Teddy raised his eyebrows at her and shook his head sorrowfully. "Don't be too hard on him. Ain't nothin' against you. He's within the law to haul your mare to Texas."

Clea scowled at him, then snapped, "I'm not being hard on him. You'll know it if I am."

She bit her lip and fought down her tangled feelings. She could just strangle Teddy for bringing up the subject. Jake kept coming into her mind all the time, as if he were really present in the room. Or in the truck with her. Or leaning here on the fence.

Like a ghost who was haunting her.

But for a moment, he hadn't been in her thoughts at all until Teddy opened his big mouth. She took a deep breath and tried to put Jake out of her mind.

It wasn't time for him to come back yet. He still had plenty of food, and the old guys had said he could kill a mule deer or elk if he ran out. They'd said she didn't need to worry about him.

But she couldn't help it. "Speaking of Jake. I don't suppose you all have seen any sign of him?"

They shook their heads.

"He'll be in soon. Don't worry about him, Clea," Buck said. "Anyhow, you didn't turn the mare loose. We'll go check on him if he don't show soon."

He gestured toward the little gray colt in the next pen to get them back on task. "And you think the filly'll learn how to behave from this one? He's only about a month older."

"Yes. He's gonna be worried about himself, not her. He won't give in and baby her the way Boss has been doing."

She looked the gray over. "When I picked him up, the guy told me he's from a mare that was a fairly good roping horse. I think you'll get your money back out of him, Buck."

He waved that away. "Forget it. I'll *make* money on him."

"Well," she said, "I asked you to buy him."

He gave her a worried glance. "Quit tryin' to take all the responsibility in the world, girl."

"You gonna name him, too?" Teddy asked.

"Buck paid for him," she said.

"I reckon I'll call him Skipper," Buck said.

"Oughtta be Rhett Butler," Teddy said.

Clea and Buck both turned to look at him.

"Well, ain't you the ro-man-tic one?" Buck said.

Teddy flushed. "Mostly I leave that Cupid stuff to you," he said significantly.

Clea looked from him to Buck. What did he mean by that?

Buck glared back at him.

"Buck?" she said. "Do you have a girlfriend I don't know about?"

"No," he growled, "I've got more sense than that—present company excepted, o' course, Miss Clea. Teddy's the one with the woman-friend."

Buck and Teddy scowled at each other for a minute but they didn't say any more. Then they all turned their attention to the horses again.

Scarlett had eaten all the grain she wanted and was picking at Boss, trying to make him play. He didn't want to play but he didn't kick her away.

"Let's turn Miss Scarlett in with Skipper," Buck said, "and give Boss a chance to eat what's left of his grain and hers, too."

"I'm so glad we found another baby," Clea said, as they all climbed through the fence to open the gate and move the orphan foal. "You were right when you said she could learn the rules when she gets older, Buck, but she would never understand them. She'd always be unhappy and confused."

"What do you mean?"

"I saw it in the first orphan foal I ever raised. The other horses went out of their way to be mean to her whenever she didn't wait her turn or crowded somebody else or broke any other rules, and she'd stand off to the side and try to figure out why."

"How do you know that's what she was thinkin' about?" Teddy asked.

"I could see it in her face. She'd look so puzzled. It was pitiful."

Teddy chuckled. "You ain't a horse whisperer, Clea," he said. "I reckon you're a horse listener instead. No, maybe a horse-face reader is what I'd call you."

He opened the gate. Clea walked in and stopped for a moment. She took a step, and then another toward Scarlett. She was almost within arm's reach when Scarlett backed away. The foal looked at her for a moment, then turned her back on Clea and walked away.

But she didn't kick. Clea smiled with satisfaction. That baby hadn't whirled and kicked out at anybody else since she'd taught her that lesson with the same kind of firmness a mare would've used. Scarlett was a quick learner. And Clea's teaching instincts had been right.

She stood still, then turned her back on the foal in turn.

Buck and Teddy were watching curiously. "She's lookin' at you again," Buck said. "She's interested."

"I'll let her take her time," Clea said. "She's a nosy little thing—she has as much curiosity as a cat."

Sure enough, it wasn't long until Teddy said, "She's headin' your way, all right."

She stood still until she could feel Scarlett's breath on her arm. Slowly, she turned to look at her. The foal looked back.

Clea reached out and stroked her neck. With her other hand, she took hold of the short rope attached to Scarlett's halter.

She began to move, staying close to the foal's shoulder, clucking to her, walking firmly with every expectation Scarlett would come along, and she did.

"Come on, Scarlett-Girl," she murmured, "meet your buddy, Skipper. You two are going to learn a lot with each other."

She led her through the gate and Teddy closed it behind them. Buck went to get Skipper.

"He's fairly well halter broke," Clea said. "But that's all. They haven't messed with him much, and that's good."

"Ever since you give us that lecture, we ain't hardly messed with Scarlett, either," Teddy said. "Jist to get the halter on her is about all. And I brushed her a couple of times."

"That's fine, Ted," she said. "Treating them like puppy dogs is the main thing. They have to know you're not one of them and that people always rank highest and must be obeyed."

Buck caught Skipper's leadrope and walked him to meet Clea and Scarlett. Gradually, they brought the young ones together to touch noses.

They sniffed each other and exchanged licks and butted heads and eyed each other curiously.

"What d'you think?" Buck asked.

"Turn 'em loose, but let's stay in here and watch them for a little while. Skipper hasn't been around other foals, either."

"You're the boss of the babies," he said.

He tied Skipper's leadrope up shorter so he wouldn't step

on it and they turned them loose. The two babies sniffed each other a little more and nuzzled each other, then they seemed to silently communicate a plan. At the same time, they kicked up behind and raced away, staying the same distance apart, not turning until they reached the fence. They came back toward the humans as if to make sure they'd been seen, darting together and then apart, playing all the way.

Suddenly, they stopped still, dropped their heads and began to pick at the grass. Clea couldn't take her eyes off them.

"This is what I want to do," she said.

The idea had fallen into her head from the sky.

She turned to look at Buck and saw that Teddy had joined them. "I want to make my living with horses," she said, more to inform her conscious self than to tell them the news. "I'd rather do this than photography. I know more about it and I'm better at it than I am at taking pictures."

They both looked at her as if *she'd* dropped from the sky.

"I knowed it," Teddy said. "Didn't I tell you? You're a horse reader, Clea. You talk their talk."

"It's the babies I like," she said. "If I could raise them, I could imprint them and halter break them and teach them to lead just a little and make sure they had the right situations to grow in. I could start handling them when they were yearlings and do their groundwork and get them ready to ride. Somebody else could take it from there."

"Jake's the best I ever seen to start one under saddle," Buck said.

Teddy elbowed him. Buck glared back.

"What's that about?" Clea asked.

They just shook their heads and turned to watch the babies, who were snorting and pawing and pretending to work up a fight.

"Little show-offs," Clea said. "Aren't they cute?"

"You sound like the proud mama," Ted said.

Scarlett and Skipper reared up simultaneously, pawing at the air and biting at each other but not connecting.

"See," Clea said, "they're learning to read each other's body language."

"Yes, ma'am."

When it looked as if there wasn't likely to be bloodshed or broken bones anytime soon, Buck motioned toward the house.

"All *right,*" he said. "Let's go to town and take this beautiful horse hauler to lunch, Ted. She said that's all the pay she wants for picking Skipper up for us. Change your boots and comb what little hair you got left on that hard head of yours."

"Humph," Teddy said. "You're the hard-headed one. Don't know a good name for a horse when you hear one. Don't make no sense. You won't let them be Scarlett and Rhett, and you a natural matchmaker, too."

Buck glared at him with a look that told him to be quiet and Clea looked back and forth between them.

"*Are* you a matchmaker, Buck? Is that what Ted meant about Cupid? Who have you gotten together?"

"Nobody," he said gruffly, and shot another warning look at Teddy before they all walked toward the house.

JAKE STAYED back as he followed Young Gun, who was pushing Red and his harem band down into the Beaver Creek drainage, but he wasn't going to stay so far back that he'd lose them. He'd learned that lesson last night. His blood was up now and he felt on top of his game. This was a godsend.

Another good thing about it was that Young Gun had them traveling at a good, brisk pace. Jake came over a hill and saw them strung out ahead of him. He glassed them. The foals were keeping up. They'd learned in the few months since they were born that it was keep up or die.

The little filly he'd saved from the mountain lion wouldn't be that old or that tough, although if Clea had her way the foal would *get* tough. He smiled at the flash of memory, the shock he'd felt when he turned and saw her spanking the baby.

He shook his head at his own ignorance. It'd been a shock because he had stereotyped Clea from the minute he saw her, thinking that she couldn't possibly be competent at anything except maybe spending money.

And also because he himself didn't know as much as he thought he did about horses. He hadn't had a clue as to the best way to raise a lone orphan foal—hadn't even thought about it past feeding her and getting her gentled down enough to handle. Clea was right. He and the old guys would've made a puppy dog out of her if she hadn't come along.

But he didn't want to think about Clea. He did, but he didn't. He couldn't. He had to stay focused. He'd spent enough of his life on this situation. It was time for it to be done so he could put all this energy into starting his own horse ranch. Rain on these wild horses. He'd breed a line of cutting horses and another of all-around ranch horses as good as any that had ever been seen.

Young Gun came off the pace the deeper they went into the valley, letting Montana Red take his mares on down toward the trees. Jake topped a little rise, took out his binoculars again and stopped to scope out the situation.

Red and his bunch were also stopped peacefully grazing in and around a bunch of junipers. They were ignoring Young Gun, who was innocently drinking from the creek on the upper end of the valley and pretending to ignore them, too.

Jake started working around to the west side, trying to get

closer to the harem band without spooking them. Montana Red threw up his head, nostrils wide, but he wasn't looking at Jake. He was sniffing for Young Gun's scent, searching the whole vicinity, looking for what was changing in that moment.

Ariel was mostly interested in eating, but she was throwing up her head and looking at Red between bites. She and the lead mare both seemed to sense something was about to happen.

Jake knew. Young Gun hadn't called a challenge yet, but Jake would bet the reward money that that was coming within minutes.

Montana Red would leave the mares to drive Young Gun away. When he did, Jake needed to be as close to Ariel as he could get.

He touched the colt with his spurs and laid the rein against his neck to send him circling through the dying grass to head in behind the junipers. While he watched what he was doing, he also kept one eye on Ariel and one on Young Gun.

He was moving quiet and slow now, going into stalking mode, drifting toward the lower end of the valley. The mares were all dropping their heads now and cropping at the nutritious, drying grass.

Young Gun let out a bugling challenge that rang against the rocks.

Montana Red left his mares. He trotted out to get a look at Young Gun with his head at an arrogant tilt as if he doubted this could be true. Every line of his body said he couldn't believe any other stallion would have such nerve.

Thank God the wind was right. Jake hit a long, fast trot and got into the screen of trees scattered down the hillside. They thickened at the bottom and that was where the mares were.

He took his loop off the saddle and got it ready, held it down by his side. As he got closer to Ariel's spot, he slowed to a walk and worked his way down, wondering whether he'd be better off on foot. He couldn't chance it. If Ariel pulled back, he couldn't hold her and he was *not* going to lose her again.

Young Gun taunted Red again.

Montana Red roared back an answer in his older, deeper voice, and Jake glimpsed the older stallion put his tail up and start to run. Young Gun would be running to meet him, but Jake couldn't look because had to keep his eyes on Ariel.

He walked his horse toward her. She saw him, but she only dropped her head to graze again. Here she was in the middle of wildness and she was reverting to domesticity. Typical contrary woman.

Jake usually had steel control but at that moment his heart thumped against his ribs as if it would escape. He rode right up to her. Thank goodness she was separated from the other mares by several yards. When they saw him and moved away, she stayed where she was.

"Ariel," he said, soothing her with his tone of voice. "Hey, hey, girl. Stand, Ari. Whoa, girl."

She lifted her head. She let him ride right up beside her and drop his rope over it.

He could not believe it. Or the fact that his hands were shaking.

Great God in heaven. The prospect of fifty thousand dollars could make his *hands* shake?

What did that say about him?

Get the mare and get out. You've got all the way to Texas and back to think. Get this mare the hell out of here and away from Montana Red.

"Come on, princess," he said, as she stuck her nose over to greet his colt as if they were old buddies. "Let's head for the house."

He didn't dare take time to put a halter on her. And he tied the rope to his saddle horn. With a packer's knot.

"This time you're goin' all the way with me, missy," he said. "Time to hit the trail."

He looked at the stallions as he turned to ride back up the hill so he could go around behind them. It'd be like having a seat in an arena with the show down below.

The dueling studs didn't know he was on the planet, and the other mares didn't care, because this was the best grass they'd seen in days. He could stay in the front edge of the trees and ride around the open meadow and watch the fight as he went. The studs were still in the beginning of it—tensely sniffing each other's nostrils and depositing manure piles that then had to be sniffed in turn.

While they sniffed, they were standing nonchalantly side by side, which Jake always thought was funny.

The rage was still there, though. The fireworks just hadn't started yet.

Ariel came along with him like a kitten on a string and he couldn't see any lameness in her cut leg. Clea would be relieved to know that. If she ever let him speak to her again.

If he ever tried to speak to her again.

Why the *hell* did he feel guilty at the thought of her? He didn't owe her a damn thing. She was the one outside the law on this deal, not him. He was only doing what any sane man would do.

"You had enough of the wild life, huh?" he said to the mare, just to change the subject.

But a searing, high-pitched squeal from one of the stallions, and then from the other, drowned him out.

The fight had started. Montana Red went for Young Gun's legs with his teeth flashing and Young Gun reciprocated.

Fighting stallions almost always went mostly for the legs with their bites, trying to sever tendons.

They kept that up for what was probably nearly a minute, then stopped, and they started the cycle all over again. This could go on for an hour or more and he couldn't hang around any longer.

Jake turned face forward and smooched his colt into a long trot. They splashed into the creek and Ariel came right along.

Did she feel she knew him now? What *was* this, a miracle?

As they rode out of the shallow creek and across the gravel that lined the bank, the screaming from the stallions came again, pealing against the mountains. How long a fight would go on depended on the tenacity of the horses. So considering what he knew about both horses involved, this one would be a record setter. He wished he could stay until the end and see who came out the winner.

Usually, in a stud fight, neither horse was killed or even seriously injured. Jake realized he was hoping that would be true in this case. He'd be hard-pressed to pick one over the other. Young Gun and Montana Red both had determination and stubbornness to burn. One had youth and one had experience. It'd be a toss-up.

When Jake topped the hill on the east side of the valley he looked back just in time to see Young Gun turn tail and trot away. The blood running down his silvery neck caught Jake's eye in the sunlight. One leg was bleeding, too, but he wasn't even limping.

Montana Red came after him. Young Gun stopped, turned and charged him with teeth bared. They met, reared, screaming like panthers, and struck fast and hard at each other.

After that, Jake didn't look back any more. He was headed

home and he wasn't stopping until he got there. No sense taking chances the mare might somehow get loose if he staked her out.

Thank God for moonlight. He would ride all night.

CHAPTER TWENTY

CLEA CAME home from checking on the foals and dinner with Buck and Teddy—a delicious dinner, much to her surprise, since it was all cooked in one skillet and consisted of a wild mixture of beef, potatoes, onions, hot peppers, tomatoes, cheddar cheese, sweet peppers, cottage cheese and salsa. Scarlett and Skipper were fine. She'd enjoyed the bantering while she helped the old guys do chores.

She would try to think about all that and get through the rest of the evening until bedtime without obsessing on Jake. Jake and Ariel. Somewhere out there in the wild.

Those two were stubbornly filling her mind when she walked through the door of her cabin to hear the phone ringing. For one insane instant her thought was it might be Jake.

"Hello."

"Just thought you'd like to know I have both your phone numbers."

The sound of Brock's voice hit her like a blow behind the knees.

She leaned back against the kitchen counter.

"You have no idea how much you've cost me, Clea. I had to go through three P.I.'s to find you."

The vitriol of his bitterness was strong enough to peel paint. He sounded so vicious it made her shaky. But he'd already done the worst to her, hadn't he?

"I'll *get* your mare," he said. "If I have to come to Montana myself."

"Because you always get what you want," Clea said, amazed at the calm, hard tone that came out of her mouth. "Don't you, Brock?"

"I also have a printout of Elkhorn Ranch that shows which cabin is yours."

Her arms went weak then. She propped one hand beneath the other elbow to hold the phone to her ear.

"If you're coming after the P.I. money, don't bother," she said sarcastically. "I didn't ask you to spend that on me."

"Ah! But every time you did ask me I bought you whatever you wanted. For *years.* And look at the gratitude you showed me."

She took the phone from her ear and he must've sensed it. Quickly, loudly, he said, "Your daddy."

Her arm froze in midair. "I told him where you are as soon as I found you."

Into her silence, he added, "I knew you'd want him to know."

She hung up.

He didn't call back. He'd just wanted to crow a little. He'd just wanted to rub it in. He didn't actually have possession of Ariel yet and he wanted Clea to know he'd make more attempts if he had to. He hadn't mentioned the wild horses, so he didn't know that Montana Red had beat him to the punch.

Or maybe he did. The sheriff had probably contacted Brock as soon as he hired Jake. Jake had been out chasing Ari for days.

What if Jake failed? Then, would Brock have Clea arrested?

He might. His tone had been vicious.

Would he come out here himself, or send somebody to harass or hurt her? Or would he sue her for the price of the mare if she vanished into the refuge?

Brock had never been violent to her person—he'd never gone past throwing things and breaking things—but he was furious right now. His pride had been hurt. He blamed Clea for that and for all his troubles.

She checked the caller ID, which she should've done before she ever picked up the phone. He'd called from his landline. He was still in Texas.

She was glad she had guns and had learned as much as she had. She still needed to get a dog, though.

The questions, the chill of knowing that Brock knew *exactly* where she was, worry about Jake and Ariel, but most of all, the sound of Brock's crisp, ugly voice in her ear—which made her feel dirty, even after her shower—kept her awake most of the night. She dozed and tossed and turned, and when she wasn't remembering Brock, she was remembering Jake.

When she finally tore her memories away from his smell and his touch and the looks he'd given her and the feel of his hands on her skin, she thought about the last time she'd seen him and how he'd betrayed her. One part of her understood. Really. His need for a place of his own and his hating debt made his decision a given. He'd never have a chance at that much money in one fell swoop again.

But the way he had talked to her and looked at her…and loved her….

It hadn't been love. It *wasn't* love. Real world, Clea. Grow up.

All night long, she rocketed from one emotion to the next with such passion that when dawn finally came, her spirit felt as bruised as her body was from the long horse chase. She was obsessed. She was losing her mind.

She gave up trying to sleep and flipped on the radio. Her old early-morning friend, Farm and Ranch News, was airing an ad for someone to give English riding lessons.

Well, why not? It wouldn't bring much, but it'd be a little bit of money coming in and something to do while she figured out how she could start her own horse business without waiting to be old enough for the trust that her mother left her. It would also give her an entrée into the local horse world.

It would be perfectly fine for her to get out and about in *any* horse world now that Brock knew exactly where she was.

Plus it'd be an excuse to go to town, a reason not to be alone. She would drop by either the gift shop or the bakery, or both. Not to talk to Tally or Sharyn about any of her worries, because it was too early in their acquaintanceship for that, but just to feel she might be connected to a bigger world than the Elkhorn, and Teddy and Buck.

She got up and dressed a little more carefully than usual, since she was going for a job interview. There was no telling how many others she'd be competing with for the position. Surely there weren't *that* many English riders in Pine Lodge looking to teach. But it was still too early. No, wouldn't the bakery be open? It was nearly seven o'clock. The café would be open, too.

When she got to town, the street had plenty of empty parking places and she pulled into one in front of the bakery, which glowed bright and welcoming in the dark, cloudy morning. There were small round tables along the inside of the big windows that bore an arching sign painted in gold script across them both, the words *The Bread Basket* in between waving stalks of wheat.

Tally, who was behind the counter waiting on a customer when Clea went in, greeted her with a big smile and came out to show her around. They made a quick tour of the immaculate kitchen where two people were mixing big vats of bread, and were headed back into the front room when the bell on the door sounded.

"Are there any hot cinnamon rolls?"

"Sharyn," Tally said. "Here for her once-a-week cinnamon roll."

Soon Clea was seated at one of the little tables in the window with Sharyn, each with coffee and a cinnamon roll.

"I get up early to come in while they're hot," Sharyn said, cutting a luscious bite full of icing and lifting it to her lips. "What're you doing out at this ridiculous hour?"

"Does she only make them on Fridays?"

"She makes them every day but once a week is my limit. I don't want to gain so much weight I have to trade for a draft horse."

"They are delicious," Clea mumbled, as she took her first bite. "I can see how this could get to be a problem."

Sharyn looked her over. "Where're you headed at this ungodly hour all the way in from the Elkhorn?"

Clea told her about the ad for a riding instructor, and Sharyn said she knew the owner of the ranch, a woman called Lisa Welch.

"She's a famous predator," Sharyn said. "All the women want to lock up their men when Lisa comes around."

Clea said wryly, "Well, I won't have to worry about that."

"She likes 'em married but they don't have to be. They're all notches on her belt. She's caused two divorces that I know of and then dumped the guys."

Sharyn shook her head sadly. "And both their wives took them back. I couldn't believe it."

Clea thought about Brock. She'd turned a blind eye to his infidelity once. The old Clea just hadn't wanted to see the truth.

The new Clea didn't have that kind of patience—no, she didn't have that kind of need. She could survive just fine without a man if that was the way her life turned out. If she didn't find the right one.

Her heart turned over. Oh, Jake.

Sharyn went on to describe Lisa's facility and its location. Then they talked about horses and the town and what it offered for winter entertainment, which wasn't much, and—in raised voices—about what a fantastic baker Tally was. Smiling, Tally came over to hear all the compliments up close and they all chatted for a minute before the doorbell rang again.

Sharyn said, "Speak of the devil, Clea, there's Lisa now."

Tally gave her a questioning look and Sharyn said, "Lisa's advertising for an English riding instructor. Clea's interested."

Then, fully informed of the latest gossip, Tally went to take Lisa's order.

Sharyn said, "Want to meet her now?"

At Clea's nod, she called, "Lisa, come join us. I want you to meet somebody."

Lisa pulled up another chair, Tally brought her some coffee and a roll, Sharyn introduced them, and Lisa and Clea talked about the job. Lisa couldn't teach all the classes and still run the facility and she didn't jump anyhow, so Clea just might be the answer to her prayers.

They agreed that when they were done here, Clea would follow Lisa out to her place and they'd ride a little and talk about horsemanship philosophies. If they got along, Lisa would get the classes together for Clea, who would give her a percentage of the fees for that and for the use of her arena, which was just on the edge of town. Then they talked about horses and showing until the cinnamon rolls had run out.

Sharyn went to refill their coffee cups because Tally was

busy. Lisa gave Clea a thoroughly assessing look and, in her sultry voice said, "You live out on the Elkhorn, hmm?"

Clea returned the look. "Yes."

"You've met Jake Hawthorne?"

"Right."

"What do you think of him?"

The question let loose a flood of emotions in Clea.

"Do you see a lot of him?" Lisa asked, just as Sharyn returned.

"A lot of whom?" she asked.

"Jake Hawthorne," Lisa said. "He lives on the Elkhorn, too, and…"

"He's…uh, really good, I think," Clea said.

Lisa's smile deepened. Her dark eyes—actually she had bedroom eyes, emphasized by false lashes—bore into Clea's as she said, "You're talking horses, right?"

Heat flooded Clea's throat and face. "Of course."

"He is one hot horseman," Lisa said, still watching Clea. "But he can be pretty damn arrogant with people. I had a colt with him for a while, and every time I'd call to talk about him, Jake was one moody SOB."

Quick anger flashed in Clea.

"You didn't hire him to talk on the phone," she said. "How'd he do with the colt?"

"I don't think he rode him half the time," Lisa drawled. "I think he lied about that."

"Jake's honest," Clea snapped, completely aware that only a few days earlier she'd called him a liar to his face. "And he does what he says he will. Jake wouldn't take your money otherwise."

"It's me I want him to take," Lisa said, taking a sip of her fresh coffee, "I make no bones about that and I'm not giving up."

She smiled. She really did have a sexy smile.

"Didn't mean to get you all bothered, Clea. Just checking on the lay of the land out at the Elkhorn," she said. "I was thinking about taking him another horse to see if he can't do a better job this time."

Clea just looked at her.

"I'd hate to get into your territory," Lisa said slyly, "if you have anything going with him."

Clea set her jaw and stared back at her.

"I just had a flash," she said. "The use of the indoor out at the Elkhorn is included in my rent. It'd be foolish for me to give you a cut of my lesson fees to use your facility. I'll find my own students."

"There aren't that many students around here," Lisa said.

"Mine will fly in," Clea said, suddenly doubly glad that she wasn't hiding from Brock anymore. "I've won a lot of jumping competitions. I know horse people all over the country. I'll get the local ones, too. You said yourself that you don't jump."

"The Elkhorn arena is a lot farther out of town than mine is."

"What're a few more miles when you've already rented a car to drive from the airport at Billings?"

Lisa sighed, set her mug down and stood up. "Well, I'm disappointed," she said, "that we won't be working together after all."

She gave Clea a glintingly mischievous look. A challenge. "See you around."

She walked away. Her walk was as sexy as her smile.

Clea thumped her own mug down onto the table.

Sharyn smiled at her. "No fret, no fear, Clea," she said. "Lisa couldn't carry water for you."

Clea froze. How could she have been so stupid as to defend Jake with such heat? Now Sharyn would think she was interested in Jake, just like Lisa was.

Mentally, she scrambled to recover. "Thanks, Sharyn. I hope I *can* scrape up some students now that I've said I could."

Sharyn nodded. Now she was looking into Clea's eyes with a wise, teasing glint in her own, trying to hide her smile, but a sketch of it was still there.

"I understand," she said. "Perfectly. But anytime you want to talk about it, Clea, I'm a good listener."

She didn't mean teaching little girls to jump horses and she knew Clea knew it. Her tone was kind and sympathetic. She was offering friendship. With confidences. And comfort. And advice.

Clea's tension faded. This woman was probably twenty years older than she, and Clea's guess would be she'd seen a lot of life.

"Thanks," Clea said. "I'll probably take you up on that one of these days."

WHEN CLEA parted from Sharyn and Tally, she climbed into her truck and drove out of town on its only highway, headed in the opposite direction of the Elkhorn. Good. Fine. She didn't care. She needed new landscape to look at while she thought this through.

Dear God, what was the matter with her? She'd had no idea she was going to jump to Jake's defense like that. *Why* should she defend him, considering what he was doing to her this very minute?

And she'd been even more unprepared for the burning shaft of jealousy that had slashed across her heart at the thought of Lisa making a play for him and succeeding. So she hadn't been quick enough to hide those feelings and now Sharyn—*and* Lisa—both thought Clea was in love with Jake.

It couldn't be true. She'd slept with him one time but that meant nothing, even though he'd confided in her and she'd felt close to him at the time. She couldn't love him. She didn't even know him.

Yes, she did. Somehow, at the deepest level, she knew him.

But you have no claim on Jake. Jake's not out there risking his life trying to save your mare to bring her back to you, Miss Queen of Denial. He doesn't care about you.

You don't care about him, either. You admire him because he's selfless enough to be a rescuer, that's all. He saved the baby filly from the mountain lion and he's saving Ariel from breaking her neck running off a cliff or freezing to death this winter. You're grateful for that. You respect him. That's all.

She saw a sign that she was headed toward Billings and didn't even think about turning around. Good. It had looked like a fairly big town when she went through it with Ariel during the great escape from Texas. Right now, a fairly big town would be a terrific distraction. It'd burn up some gasoline to get there, but it'd be worth it if it helped her keep her sanity. When winter came and she was snowed in for weeks at a time, she'd have plenty of time on the Elkhorn, so she should get out while she could.

Her whole encounter with Lisa played through her head again. Very deliberately, she shut it and Jake out of her mind and latched onto her own remark about using the Elkhorn's arena to give lessons. She would make it happen. It'd help her get her money's worth out of her rent, it'd put her with enough other people that she wouldn't go crazy this winter, and it'd give her experience and more connections into the horse world.

Why not?

Making a living. *That's* what she had to think about.

In Billings, she would check out the feedstores and the tack shops and put notices on the bulletin boards that those places usually had. She'd also find a coffee shop with wireless and get on her laptop. There were several horse sites where she could put ads.

Plus, now that Brock knew where she was, she could e-mail people everywhere who showed jumpers, people who'd seen her ride and knew she'd won a lot, people who could spread the word. Horsey girls with money flew all over the country for lessons. Maybe some of them could combine lessons from Clea with ski trips in the winter.

You could also e-mail your dad.

Daddy could've called me. Brock told him where I am. If Daddy had cared more about me than about his pride he could've hired a P. I. who would've found me before Brock's third one did.

Daddy was another person she didn't want to think about. How could she ever open up that can of worms again and still function? No. She would not make the first move. She'd always done so, wanting to earn his love. That was something else she was changing about her life.

Her changing life. Her new life. A little chill ran through her. Was Brock going to try to be in her new life? She could still hear the tone of his voice—sharp and bitter as vinegar—pooled in her ear.

Brock wouldn't be a stalker, would he? Surely he wouldn't do violence to her. No or he already would have. Was that true or not?

With an effort, she found her focus again. She was giving up fear. She was sick of fear. She wasn't going to let Brock take any more of her life, even if it was only the time it took to think of him.

All right. She'd start getting her name out there with the lessons, and then put out the word that she'd work with problem jumpers and start new ones. She could teach jumping lessons to horses as well as riders. Someday, like Jake, she'd buy a farm and raise her own to sell.

That was something she and Jake had in common.

Remember, Clea, the main way you're changing is that you're learning to see reality. Forget about Jake, just like you're trying to forget about Ariel. Gone. The two of them are gone.

Because, in reality, even if she and Jake saw each other every day at the Elkhorn, how could she ever, deep down, forget that he'd taken her mare away? She couldn't. Even if she understood why, even if she forgave him, that hurt would always be between them.

She put in a Mozart CD and listened to it all the way to Billings. It calmed her.

When she left the interstate, she drove into a shopping center that was identical to thousands of others in hundreds of other cities all over the country. She wanted something quaint and every inch old-Montana, and she'd find it later but right now she needed something to eat that wasn't sweet—too many cinnamon rolls—and she was impatient to get online.

She'd just had another idea. Why not start a registry online for people who had one mare and usually one foal a year who would like that foal to have a companion in those formative first months? There would be only a small fee. That would be another way to get her name out there, and she could make a difference in the lives of many, many horses and people.

The idea gave her a lift. She might be a lot better at business than she'd ever thought she would be.

As it turned out, in that shopping center there actually was a coffee shop which, was not a same-old chain franchise and yet not a tiny kiosk in the parking lot, either. It even had a Free Wi-Fi sign in the window.

Inside, it wasn't as cozy or tasteful as Tally's place, but it did smell of baking bread. It offered homemade gourmet sandwiches and soups along with the breads and pastries. Clea found a tiny table in a corner by the window and set up shop.

She ordered, opened up her laptop and logged on. Her screen saver came up. It was the photo she'd taken of Jake bringing Scarlett in across his saddle.

His eyes held hers as if he were real. They looked into hers and searched her heart.

Which was impossible because he hadn't even been able to see her through the dark tint on the truck's window.

This truly was a good photo, if she did say so herself.

But she was not going to look at Jake because she was not going to think about Jake.

She logged on. Jake and Scarlett vanished and the news came up.

SHE WAS NOT going to look at the usual chaos in the world, either. She went to several of the horse sites she thought might be good for her to know, but suddenly she couldn't look at them, either. First, she would write out her ads and get them exactly right—clever and concise.

But she closed the notebook and just sat, hearing but not listening to scraps of conversation from the next table, staring out the window at the parking lot, but seeing a place on the refuge instead. Not a significant place, not one with a real memory attached, just an image like a souvenir of the wild that her senses had taken in, a little piece of the mountains she'd seen that had burned itself into her brain so she could carry it with her.

Rolling, sparsely treed land that ran down to a creek. Several horses standing together in the shine of the sun, head to tail, grooming each other and switching away flies. Horses at home in the wilderness, completely comfortable in their brown and roan and sorrel skins against the incredible blue of the sky.

Above them, a hawk diving, flapping his wings and floating in looping circles on the wind.

That picture in her mind seemed more real than this place she was in.

Jake was out there now. At the mercy of the weather and luck and his own skills and strengths. Sleeping on the ground and eating dried food boiled in water over a campfire, while she and all these other soft people were sitting in a warm room ordering roasted-garlic organic-tomato bisque soup with a piece of freshly baked baguette.

He was riding over rough trails and no trails at all for hours on end with his collar turned up and his hat pulled down to keep from freezing in the wind.

She loved the way he looked when he did that—with his black hair falling onto his forehead and his eyes glinting sharp out from under the hat's wide brim. It made him look mysterious and dangerous, which he was, even though he was a saver of baby horses and foolish mares.

And a marvelous lover of women.

That right there made him as dangerous as an outlaw because it was an experience a woman couldn't forget. He was a different breed from all the men in this room. A different breed from any man she'd ever known before in her life.

She'd known that from the start. Even when she reached out to take him in her arms she hadn't intended for him to actually *mean* anything to her.

He was honest to the bone—discounting lies of omission—and if *she* were going to be honest, she had to admit that she was thinking about him all the time. Consciously or not, in the back or the front of her mind, he was there.

It meant she was worried about his safety, that was all.

Which was perfectly normal after he'd come into the cabin soaked to the skin, shaking with cold shock and covered in blood. It meant she wanted—needed—him to be safe. That was all. She would wish that for anyone, including Brock.

But it was more. She needed to know Jake was alive and well and doing what he wanted to do, even if she never heard from him again. For the rest of her new life she would need that.

Even if he did take Ariel back to Brock.

She looked straight at that truth and felt shaken. It didn't make sense.

And she hadn't felt jealousy like she'd felt with Lisa this morning at Tally's bakery since…

Well, probably not ever. Every time she suspected Brock of cheating, she'd been jealous, yes, but they'd been far enough into the marriage by then that there was already a wide distance between them.

She hadn't felt that fierce protectiveness for Brock that she'd felt at the thought of Lisa going after Jake.

Insane.

She shouldn't feel connected to Jake but she did. She hadn't really slept since she and Buck and Teddy went off and left him—not even before Brock's call. When she did doze off, she dreamed about Jake.

What did it mean?

Did it mean she loved him?

WHEN CLEA got back to the ranch, she stopped at her cabin and changed into her barn clothes. She was so exhausted she felt shaky inside. She threw a glance at the rumpled bed, but there was no hope of sleep right now, and probably not tonight, either. Maybe not even the next night.

She might never sleep again. Yes, she *would.*

She'd had too much caffeine. *That* was making her shaky.

All the way back from Billings, the weather news on the radio had said rain tonight, so she'd decided to put the colts in. Yes, they had to get tough and yes, it probably wouldn't hurt them to stay out, but it would be a cold rain and Scarlett, who'd had a bit of a runny nose yesterday, was not as strong as she would've been if her mother had lived. She'd missed some colostrum because of her mother's death and Jake said she was almost dehydrated when he found her.

When she got to Buck and Teddy's, Clea drove straight to the barn. As she passed the house, she saw that Buck's truck wasn't there. They were probably both gone and that was good. She loved them, but at the moment she wasn't in the mood to talk or listen.

The young ones were in their pen, stretched out on their sides in the sun, eyes closed. They'd probably worn themselves out playing all morning.

Clea parked and headed for the barn. The clouds were forming in the west, over the mountains. Over the wild-horse refuge. Jake had better hurry if he didn't want to get wet again.

How long would it take to catch Ariel? It seemed weeks already, instead of only days. If he couldn't catch her, how long would he stay out there trying? Would he start living off the land or would he come in to the ranch for more supplies?

Inside the good-smelling old wooden barn, she chose an empty stall, and began getting it ready for the two little ones. She tried to keep her mind on them while she cleaned it, spread a generous amount of bedding and filled the water bucket.

Then she ran to the house to wash up and get something

to drink. She glanced behind her to the west and saw the clouds lowering and drifting toward the ranch on a stiff breeze growing steadily colder. No sign of movement on the hill.

The sunlight had vanished. Scarlett and Skipper were awake and up and running ahead of the wind, wispy manes and tails like shadows of flags flying against the gray sky.

"Buck? Teddy?" she called at the back door, just in case one of them was home.

No answer. Clea used the bathroom and scrubbed up, then headed for the kitchen. Hot tea would be good. She'd hang out for a little while and let the babies run some more before she put them in.

She was at the sink, filling the kettle, when the storm hit. With an extra-hard gust of wind, the raindrops slapped against the window in a sliding sheet of water that made the pens and the arena and the mountain behind it waver and blur. A couple of minutes later, it let up for a second. Clea looked out again.

At the crest of the hill, just over the top and coming down, she saw Jake clearly, on the colt—leading Ariel at his side. He had his chin tucked and his hat low and she couldn't see his face.

The rain came back full force. The man and two horses vanished as if they'd never been. As if she'd imagined them.

But she hadn't. She turned off the stove and went to find some towels. Then she put on her coat, pulled up the hood, and ran back to the barn. Every nerve in her body was on edge and her hands were shaking when she dumped the towels on a hay bale and went to get the babies. She could get them in before Jake could get down the hill.

Ariel was safe. That's what she had to keep in the front of her mind. Jake was just somebody who happened to be involved in all this Montana Red mischief, too. Somebody who was connected to her only through her horse. Who wasn't hers anymore.

A few minutes later, when he came trudging into the barn leading both horses, she was in the stall with Scarlett and Skipper, using a burlap sack to wipe away the water standing on their thickening fur. They hadn't been out in it long enough for it to soak in.

She gave them one last swipe, opened the door of the stall, and stepped out into the aisle.

"I brought some towels for you," she said. "Here. Let me have Ariel, and I'll rub her down while you dry off."

Jake stopped in his tracks and stared at her. She couldn't look away. For a second, the world was nothing but the sounds of rain on the roof, the blowing of the two tired horses and the water dripping off them and Jake into the dirt.

And Jake's eyes on her. Her heart crashed against her ribs.

He was looking at her as if he couldn't believe she was there. No, actually, he looked at her as if he wished she *weren't* there.

He shook his head. "I got it." He also *sounded* as if he wanted her to go away.

But he looked at her for a second more before he opened a stall and led Ariel in. The colt stood in the aisle, reins trailing, head down, exhausted.

Clea followed him into the stall to look at Ariel. She walked past Jake without saying any more to him, and ran her hand over the mare's wet back to the hip.

"Get away," he said.

"You're whipped," she said. "You ought to let me help."

"I got plenty left," he said, his voice rasping from exhaustion.

"How's that cut on her leg? Do I need to go get the medicine?"

"No."

The word was a growl, a snap, a warning. *Leave me alone.*

He was busy taking his rope off the mare. Now he wouldn't look at Clea at all.

She examined the cut. It was healing fine. Scabbed over.

"What's wrong? Did you have a hard time catching her?"

His only answer was a grunt. He turned, with a flick of raindrops off the brim of his hat, and left the stall.

"Dry yourself off," she said. "The towels are over there on the hay."

"Don't tell me what to do, dammit."

"Well, you don't have to lose it," she said, in an exaggeratedly calm tone. "I'm only trying to help you since you saved my mare from starving or running off a cliff, or maybe dying trying to foal her first baby *if* she lived through the winter. Nobody else could've caught her."

He took off his hat, slung the water from it down the aisle, and slammed it back onto his head. His hair was rumpled, like it had been the morning after they'd made love. His eyes blazed at her again, too, but not with the same message they'd held that night. It seemed months ago.

"I'm *not* losing it."

He said it calmly, even though she could see it took everything he had not to yell.

"I'm only trying to get one fact through your blond head. That is not *your* mare. Carrying on and fussing over her and saying nobody else could've caught her is not going to make me change my mind."

Fury singed her ragged nerves and set the back of her neck on fire.

But her words came out as chunks of ice. "I'm not stupid enough to think that it would."

"I'll take care of her," he said, starting to unbuckle the

cinch on the colt. "Go to the house. Go home. Go wherever you want. I've got the mare."

"Don't tell *me* what to do, dammit," she said, mimicking him.

She left the stall and brushed past him to get to the tack room and more burlap sacks.

He turned to watch her go by and she glimpsed from the corner of her eye that his lips had parted. But he never did say anything.

When she came back by him, he was throwing the saddle over the wall of an empty stall.

She went to Ariel again and started drying her off, rubbing her back, petting on her. Saying goodbye without words.

From the corner of her eye, she saw Jake go back to the colt. He led him into the stall next to Ariel.

"Look," he said, still trying valiantly for a reasonable tone even though it sounded like his teeth were clenched, "I didn't mean to cuss at you. I'm trying to make it easier for you. I don't care if you like me or not. I already know you'll hate me forever for taking her back to Texas."

Clea dropped the sack and turned to him. She, too, had to fight to keep from yelling, but the words came easily—they leapt out of her mouth with no effort at all on her part. "First you say I'm stupid and now you say I'm unreasonable, as if I can't understand that this is a business deal and you need the money. After all we've been through and all we've shared, even after you told me I was brave and you admired me, deep down you haven't changed your opinion of me one bit. All you know is my hair's blond and you still think I'm so spoiled that I can't understand when I don't get my way, and I can't believe I ever thought I loved you!"

He looked up at that.

She slammed her hand over her mouth. They faced each other over the worn planks of the wall, eyes locked.

Oh, God. Jake believed her. It was in his eyes that first second.

He *believed* her.

And he looked completely horrified. Hurt stabbed through her.

His eyes narrowed as if he hated her. "Good try, Clea, but that's not gonna make me change my mind, either."

"I…I've had a gallon of caffeine today. I don't know what I'm saying…I'm a wreck…"

Then his meaning hit her and she gasped like a fish out of water. "Oh! Oh."

Anger shot through her but then, relief. Good. It was better if he thought she was trying to con him than if he believed she loved him. *Wasn't* it?

For her pride? She had little else left.

She shrugged. "Well, it was worth a try."

He held her transfixed with that narrowed, hard gaze, as if he knew for a fact she was lying then.

"I'm sleep deprived," she said. "That's been proven to be as debilitating as two drinks. I haven't really slept since…well, for days."

She could tell by the look in his eyes that he knew exactly since what day. Or more accurately, what night.

"Cowgirl up," he said, turning away. "Neither have I."

CHAPTER TWENTY-ONE

CLEA STAYED AWAY from Buck and Teddy's place. She'd lost count of the days, but it had been more than a week now since she'd last seen the foals or the old guys. She'd talked to the men on the phone, and they'd followed her orders for taking care of the babies, because she just couldn't go over there right now.

She was miserably busy—one minute hating herself for not telling Jake seriously that she loved him, and the next hating herself for even *hinting* to him that she loved him.

What if she never saw him again? What if he had a fatal wreck on the way to Texas?

How could she ever face him again? How could they live on the same ranch and not see each other? They couldn't. She couldn't give lessons without using the big arena, and he'd have to use it every day breaking colts.

That look in his eyes had been the fiercest she'd ever seen. He did *not* love her.

But he'd been lying awake at night. He hadn't slept, either, since they'd parted on the refuge.

Which probably meant nothing except that he'd been worried he might not catch Ariel and would lose his fifty thousand dollars.

Jake cared about her as a person. She really believed that

he'd been trying to make it easier for her to let Ari go. He just didn't *love* her.

To try to counteract her demons, she'd stayed busy sending and answering e-mails and placing ads for students—she had three, so far.

She'd cleaned out her barn and installed her leased mare, a good jumper Heather heard about whose owner had gone to college. Her parents just wanted a safe place where the mare would be taken care of all winter, so the lease was blessedly cheap. When Clea completely got hold of herself and went back over to Buck and Teddy's, she'd take the mare called Emma, to her winter stall over there.

Or she'd wait until the weather got bad enough to demand that. Emma had been a lot of company to her already.

This winter she wanted to work with the foals, too—only a little, not enough to spoil them—and watch them together to learn their personalities. She could learn to be around Jake and keep her feelings for him closed off in a memory room she would not dare to enter. She could do that.

It'd be good for her. What didn't kill her would make her stronger.

She was staying on the Elkhorn no matter what.

THE WIND came up stronger and stronger as the sun went down. The cold that rode in on it needled into her neck beneath the collar of her Carhartt coat and numbed the tip of her nose, but Clea stayed on the deck. She was sick of being closed in—house or vehicle.

More importantly, she was determined not to let the wind blow the fire out on her little grill with the meat only half-cooked. This was her first lesson on marinades and sauces from Isidore's Internet Cooking School. She'd driven all the way back to Billings to get fresh oregano, soy sauce and specially aged steaks. She was starving.

All those were valid reasons to chance pneumonia, weren't they?

Besides, freezing her fingers kept her from thinking about anything else.

Clea turned the steaks, stirred the reserved marinade and then brushed it onto the meat. Then she took the tools and bowl back into the kitchen and walked to the rail to watch the sunset.

Which was the real reason she was out here enduring the cold wind.

She wanted that feeling again, that sunset feeling she'd had once that said she belonged here. She wanted it to help her find her way to the next big step in her new life. Clea still knew that her true heart was here. She just hadn't quite found it yet.

It's gone with Jake. And that can't be right.

The sun was sliding down faster now, but it was strong enough to streak the sky with an orangey red so bright it reflected from the snow on the mountains. It was nearly the same color as Montana Red.

The growl of a motor and the rattle of a rig sounded out on the road. But instead of fading as it passed on by, it began coming closer, sounding louder. It was in her yard, coming up her driveway.

Clea didn't want to miss the always-fleeting moment when the bright sky faded and gave way to the dark, so she didn't turn to look. Buck and Teddy, no doubt. She'd been wondering when they were going to come by to check on her. They hadn't even seen Emma yet. Most likely they'd have two different opinions about her.

She swung around just as Jake's truck and trailer rolled past the corner of the house. *Jake?*

But it was. The security light was already on. It showed her Jake's personal rig. The battered truck and the plain three-horse trailer.

He stopped. Set the brake. Opened the door. Got out.

Strode around the front of the truck, running his hand through his hair. It caught the light and gleamed blacker than the night. Her fingers remembered exactly how the strands of it felt.

Suddenly hot in the cocoon of her coat, she whirled on the heel of her boot and pounded down the steps, instinctively hurrying to head him off, wanting to *run* him off. She did *not* want to deal with him right now.

When she told herself that she would never be able to look at Jake without thinking of Ariel, she had been telling the truth. She also couldn't look at him without going weak in the knees. She would work really hard to correct that.

He had no right to be here, dammit. Just when she was trying so hard to get her new life in order.

They met.

"Now *you're* the one at the wrong house," she said, surprised at the sound of what *had* to be her voice. It was weird and sarcastic and cold as the wind. "What are you doing here, Jake? Did you come to tell me about your Texas trip?"

He stood there watching her face. His own showed no feeling at all.

"You want your mare here or over at the arena in a heated stall?"

She understood the words. But their meaning escaped her.

"Why do you care? How'd you know I leased her? I haven't even told Buck and Teddy."

"What are you *talking* about?"

"The mare in this barn. She's fine."

"I'm talking about the one in this trailer. *Your* mare."

"Ariel?"

"Yes."

It took her a second, then she ran toward the back of the rig.

She was struggling with the latch when Jake walked up behind her and said, "Let me."

Clea got out of the way. She didn't know what to say. She didn't know what to think, because one part of her mind kept screaming this couldn't be true, while the rest of it knew that Jake wouldn't do this to her if it weren't.

When she watched the door swing open and Jake step up into the trailer, she believed it.

She moved back so she could see better. Jake swung the divider and Ariel's unmistakable butt moved out from behind it. He backed the mare out. When she had all four feet on the ground, he led her to Clea and handed her the lead.

"She's yours," he said.

She took a grip on the rope and stepped up to rub Ari's neck, to feel her warm reality. She felt the mare under her hand, but she couldn't stop looking at Jake.

""What happened? Did my daddy buy her from Brock? Was he there?"

"I never saw your daddy."

You sound like you're ten. Even after all these years and Daddy taking Brock's side, after Daddy let you vanish and didn't try to find you, you never give up hoping that he loves you.

She let herself really look at Jake. Something in his eyes wiped everything else away.

"You changed your mind? Jake! You drove thousands of

miles all the way to Texas and *then* you changed your mind? *Why?*"

"That's about the size of it," he said flatly. He was exhausted. "Come on. Let's put her up and then we'll talk about it."

Jake went ahead of her to open the gate, then walked beside her to the barn. She could feel exactly where he was as surely as if he were touching her. She tried to look at her horse while she fought the wish that he would.

"I'm surprised she can still walk," Clea said, "after riding all the way down there and back in just a few days."

"I laid over at a buddy's place in Western Nebraska last night so she got a little rest. I hated to stop but I knew she had to move around some, and I was about to go to sleep at the wheel."

"If you came all the way from Nebraska today, you must've had a short night."

"Got up at three this mornin'," he said.

Clea was stroking Ariel's neck as she led her into the barn. "But, Jake, I'll have to let her go again. You said it. Brock'll just hire somebody else to come get her now that you changed your mind."

"I've got the papers and a signed transfer form."

Clea stopped and stared at him. He took the lead from her hand and led Ariel into a stall, took the halter off and handed it to Clea as he came out and went to fill the water bucket.

"Brock *always* drives a hard bargain," she said. "And he was thoroughly pissed when he called me the other day. Jake. How did you do it?"

She turned to watch him, to *demand* with her eyes that he talk to her.

"That's not a bad-looking mare," he said, looking Emma over as he passed her stall.

The mares were nickering to each other from across the aisle.

"I leased her," Clea said. "I know Brock. This is some kind of a trick. Or else it's a miracle."

"Hey," he said. "How about pullin' your share, here? I'm not talkin' until the work's done."

Clea went to the tack room and started dragging bags of wood shavings down the aisle. "I just need to stop being scared to be happy," she said. "But I just went through all that agony to give her up and I *can't* do it again."

"Trust me," Jake said.

"I do," she said, and surprised herself as much as him, judging by the assessing look he threw at her.

Once Jake had the water bucket hung on the wall again, he helped her empty three bags of shavings and kick them into a fairly even layer over the stall.

"Kiss Ari good-night," he said, "and let's go. I smell meat cooking."

"Oh, I forgot," she cried. "Steaks on the grill. Come on."

She latched the stall securely, then as they left, she did the same to the barn door. "If Montana Red comes around here tonight, no matter how close of friends you and he have become, I'm getting out my shotgun."

"I've just made a long haul," he said. "I'm not strong enough to deal with you and a loaded gun. You won't need it anyhow. I left Red on the other side of Tilson Ridge, fighting for his life."

"What?"

"Fire!"

She drove the pin home in the latch and whirled to see Jake already running. The cooker sat on the deck shooting out flames. Clea ran, too.

"Tongs on the kitchen cabinet," she yelled. "And platter. Save the meat!"

She raced up the steps as he came out of the house with

the plate and tongs and a glass of water. Clea held the plate while Jake reached through the flames and got the steaks, then he dumped water on the fire.

"The lucky thing is, I sort of like charred meat," she said, looking at exactly that on the plate in her hands.

"That's something we have in common," he said, closing the lid of the cooker on the dying coals. "I love it. Especially if it's the only kind around."

Her little kitchen was abnormally bright and cozy and warm. And full. Jake filled it with his big body and his air of command, and his secret.

He filled the kitchen with himself. Just himself.

Her heart went out of her body. He was so handsome, so strong, so sexy, so…solid and sure.

But he was nervous, too. Somehow she could sense it underneath his confident control.

She took a deep breath to calm herself inside. She smelled the rest of her supper.

"The potato!"

She grabbed a hot pad, ran to the oven and pulled out a potato that had gone way too soft under its crackly skin. When she turned, Jake was staring at the blackened steaks on the white platter.

"Who's the other steak for? Am I interrupting something?"

The strange note in his voice sounded almost like jealousy.

She stood still, searching his face.

"A new recipe," she said, dropping the potato on the cabinet. "Cold steak salad."

"Some other time," he said, opening cabinet doors at random and taking out plates. "I'm eating this one while it's hot."

"Anybody who can get Ariel's papers from Brock can have my steak, too."

He stopped what he was doing to look at his hands. "I need to wash up. Your bathroom's upstairs?"

"Right. Help yourself."

The whole time he was gone, and she was trying to think straight enough to wash her own horsey hands at the sink and set the table, she thought about keeping Ariel. And about keeping Jake.

Could that ever be possible? She did love him. She'd known that beyond any doubt the instant she ran down the steps of the deck to tell him to go away.

Finally, they were settled at the tiny table by the windows. Outside the panes, the night stretched dark and endless. Clea looked at Jake.

"All right," she said, taking a bite of her chilled green salad, which she'd divided into two bowls, "Jake. Spill it."

He cut into his steak. "I bought her."

She stared at him, eyes wide. "*How?* You were *doing* it for the money."

He shrugged. "Yeah. I found out for sure that just isn't me."

He ate a bite of steak while he put butter on his half of the potato.

"Tell me every detail of what happened between you and Brock, or I'm taking that plate away from you right now."

He glanced up at her and grinned. A sheepish, happy, somehow proud grin.

"I couldn't do it," he said. "I realized that around Ogallala. So I thought about what to do the rest of the way, and about how if Brock didn't get the mare, you'd get to see the inside of a cell. When I got to Texas, I took the reward check and then offered it back to him with some added."

She tried to lay her fork down but it fell with a clatter against the plate.

"Knowing Brock, that *some* was a lot. Where'd you get it?"

He took a bite of potato while he searched her face. "That's a pretty personal question."

"You've just done a pretty personal thing for me. I have a right to know why."

"Which do you want first? Why or where?"

He *was* tense. More so than when she'd first noticed. Now he actually looked scared.

"Dear God." Clea breathed the words as a prayer. "You didn't rob a bank or something, did you?"

He laughed. "*You're* the outlaw, remember?"

She grinned. "Right. But…"

"I had my savings wired to his account."

Clea stood up so fast she knocked her chair over.

"No! You didn't! Jake! You need your money for your place."

Then the panic faded. He loved her, or he wouldn't have sacrificed his dream. In two years, she would pay him back…

But hey. She wasn't hiding anymore. Daddy and Brock both knew where she was. And there was that property in Fort Worth that Daddy put in her name long ago….

She picked her chair up and sat down.

"You gave up your place. You destroyed your dream. For me. *Why?*"

He leaned back in his chair and looked at her.

"Because I love you."

She felt the roller coaster rise and fall inside her.

"I don't think so. I'll never forget the panicked look on your face over there in your barn when I barely mentioned the word."

"Well, hell," he said. "You can't hold that against me. A woman says that to any man, he'll panic. That's a word a man has to do something about. Has to say something back to her. Has to make a decision. Has to figure out what he wants."

Clea shook her head. "Jake..."

"Even if he reaches down deep and decides he wants to say it back to her, a man still has to start diggin' for his trust, rememberin' the women he's lost in the past, wonderin' if he could go through that again if she left him."

She took a deep breath and let herself listen. Let herself realize exactly what he was saying. Let herself hear the truth of it.

She really did know him better than she thought she did.

She let herself look at exactly what he'd sacrificed for her. The magnitude of it.

"A woman has the same doubts," she said. "And the same kind of hurts from the past. I think, for both sexes, loving each other and making it last is sort of like riding out into the rough country knowing that you can't have any quit in you, and setting your head that you will not come back until you catch the wild horse you went after."

The look in his green eyes made her lips tremble.

But his eyes held a twinkle. "What are we talking here? Maybe ninety-nine men and women out of a hundred?"

She felt her smile grow as wide as the one taking over his face.

"Exactly," she said. "But my suggestion is we forget about all the others and concentrate on the one of each we've got right here."

They both stood up and the chairs fell.

"I want you to marry me, Clea," he said, as they met and he took her into his arms. "But you're accustomed to the best of everything and I don't have a damn thing to offer you except one spoiled-rotten, cantankerous, pig-headed hunter-jumper mare."

Tears stung her eyes. She wrapped her arms around his back and clung to him, tilting her head to look up into his precious face.

"That black mare," she drawled, "who, ninety-nine chances

out of a hundred, is bred to a wild stallion with the very same kind of obnoxious disposition?"

A chuckle rumbled deep in his chest. "The very same."

Then he sobered. He held her gaze with one that went through her like a blade.

"I just remembered I already gave that mare away," he said softly. "All I've got to give you, Clea, is my heart."

She returned his solemn look.

"Then I'll still have the best of everything," she said.

He picked her up and headed for the stairs.

EPILOGUE

JAKE TOOK off his hat and wiped sweat from his forehead on his way up the steps to the corner porch of the new log house. He couldn't take his eyes off the summer grass, high and thick, that covered the small meadow between the house and the lake.

Green so bright it sparkled in the sunlight and shone back from the blue surface of the water, water so clear that the mares and foals drinking it played with their own reflections. He still could hardly believe they were here to stay.

Clea appeared behind the screened door, trying to open it with her elbow because she carried a full tray above her very pregnant belly.

"The whole place looks so..."

"Lush," Clea said, letting him take the tray. "It looks so lush and full and rich and wonderful, it borders on heaven, right here in the Garnet Range. Jake! Can you believe we've been together nearly *three* years?"

He put the tray on the table between the wooden chairs and rolled his eyes at her. "Is *that* all? Some days it seems like thirty."

Laughing, she pretended to hit at him, but he caught her arm and pulled her close for a quick kiss.

"Here," he said, "let me help you get down into that chair, ma'am."

"The real challenge will be getting me *out* of it."

"Better idea," he said, drawing her into his arms. "Sit on my lap and it won't take so much out of *me* to heave you up. Otherwise, I might have to go get the tractor."

They settled into one chair and he held her steady while she poured the drinks. "Hmm," he said, giving her a squeeze. "Three years can make a lot of difference. I can barely reach around you now and I used to be able to span your waist with my hands…"

"Jake Hawthorne," she warned, holding a full glass over his head.

"All right, I'll be good," he said.

She turned to hand him his drink. Her fingers lay warm against his on the cold glass and now he couldn't take his eyes off *her.*

She put one arm around his neck and tousled his hair.

"It's kind of nice to be alone," she said. "But in another way, I can't wait for Buck and Teddy to build their cabin here."

Both of them glanced toward the spot in the trees where that second home would go. It was a good distance away, up on the side hill that protected their house from the north.

"That'll probably be as soon as this baby comes," Jake said. "I never saw two old coots so crazy excited about a baby in all my life."

"I don't know. They're calling it their retirement cabin, and you know they'll never admit they're old enough to retire."

Clea took a swig of lemonade while she looked at the horses and the view of the lake that neither of them ever got tired of.

"Speaking of foolish old men," he said quietly. "Have you decided yet whether or not to call your dad back?"

She leaned back into him as if to make sure he was still there.

Finally, she whispered. "Yeah. I will. It wouldn't be right to keep his grandbaby from him. But why does he want this? He didn't love me…"

"He thought he did," Jake said, keeping his voice low and calm. This was a sore subject that could bring tears, but she needed to forgive her dad. "He thought he was teaching you a lesson by not chasing you when you disappeared. I believed him when he said it. He was sincere."

"You two are getting to be quite the phone buddies," she said wistfully.

"Don't be jealous," he said softly, rubbing his chin in her hair, caressing the top of her head. "He may like me and he may fall in love with the baby if you let him come up here, but that's only because we belong to you."

She was quiet for a minute, and he thought she was going to cry, but she said thoughtfully, looking out across the meadow as if talking to herself, "You are, without doubt, not only the sexiest man I've ever known but the wisest and the kindest one, too."

"Haven't I tried to tell you that since day one?"

She slapped his hand playfully, then laid her smaller one over it and pressed it tighter against the bulge of her belly.

"You've never lacked confidence," she said wryly.

Then she twisted in his lap to look straight at him.

"Are you ever scared all this is going to vanish in a heartbeat, darlin'? You were the one afraid to try to settle down, but it seems like now I'm the one hoping all this happiness is truly real."

Tears stung the back of his eyes. "No worries. Give it up. I'm not goin' anywhere."

She raised one perfect eyebrow.

"No, you most certainly are not. Believe it. Your rovin' loner days are through, cowboy. Gone. Done."

He brushed a kiss across her sweet lips and then set his glass down so he could hold her tight against his chest and bury his face in her hair.

"We're together," she said, and her voice broke. "And even if, God forbid, we had to leave this place, the three of us are a family forever. I don't need any more than that."

Now she was about to cry. It was only the hormones, but every time, he worked at cheering her up anyhow.

"Hey, this is a little late to tell me you're not sure," he said, teasing her. "You waited until I put all my money into the foundation mare of our broodmare band here at soon-to-be-famous Garnet Range Performance Horses."

"You mean the cantankerous, pig-headed, tall, black mare with the scruffy red half-wild daughter who's already trying to become boss mare?"

"That's the one. The mother of the incorrigible sorrel filly with the sunny disposition of a rattlesnake," he said and was rewarded with that low chuckle of hers that he loved. "Think about it. If Ariel can produce a colt like that every year, we can sell them all to Chase and Elle for the rodeo business and we'll be rich folks."

She sniffed and looked up into his face.

"You realize," she said, "that means we'd have to get Montana Red in here as our foundation stud."

"Right," he said briskly. "So if you'll get off my lap now, I'll saddle up and go after him."

Clea wound her arms around his neck and whispered into his ear. Exactly the words he wanted to hear.

"You're not goin' anywhere, Mr. Hawthorne, except into this house with me."